Guilt-Edged Seduction

Robert Merrick

For John Tsui, the late Barry Bowerman, Garry Farnell and Peter Marshall & Andrew Smee

He said it out loud, though there was no-one there to hear him; there rarely was anyone at that time, before Michael, but that was fine because he was quite used to talking to himself. 'I've finally realised!' he cried and he almost shouted 'Eureka' too, but he stopped himself in time. Everything had become clear in a nanosecond, hence his exuberance: his decades of procrastination, indolence and apathy, the wasted years of passively admiring and envying and watching others succeed while he sat and waited, the perpetual excuse – 'I'm a journalist really, not a novelist.' The years had passed by with nothing done and here he was now and still nothing done, but at last he knew why: as his book was a chronicle of his disintegrating life, he had had to wait until his life had completely fallen apart – in character, mind and more recently, body – before he could write about it. It was that simple. 'Of course, that's it!' he shouted again and he was euphoric.

This was his final epiphany. After so many false ones, this one offered hope and encouragement, it dispelled the despair; no more would he feel that complete abandonment was the most appealing and sensible option, no more think that it would never be finished, that he simply wasn't up to it, that he should never have started it in the first place, no more, *Who do I think I'm kidding?* Granted, it wasn't an epiphany of any significance in the great weft and warp but it *was* of some pith and moment in the pathetic and worthless existence of a murderer.

****

He would finish stirring his soup but something stops him. It's the voice. Again. It has plagued him for nearly half a century and it speaks now, as he stirs his soup, getting it ready for lunch and he has to run for cover once more and take stock and remember just who he is and what he once did; it had never and would never let him forget. 'If only,' it says – of all the times!

'If only,' it whispers and there's another slam in his gut and he creases up, cold sudor oozes from his brow, the tremors start and he smashes the wooden spoon into the saucepan and thick globules of soup fly out and spatter the kitchen tiles; he slumps against the cooker, grips it with both hands, his head falls on his chest and he gets ready to howl. It's always the same. He lifts his head and watches the globules form teardrops and start to trickle imperceptibly down the smooth tiled wall and he looks down again at the cooker's digital counter, sure to see his jinx number 11 showing somewhere in the display, but it's not there, how odd. He needs to sit down until the voice goes away and leaves him in peace and he can breathe again. *Think erotic thoughts to get rid of it, think of somebody who once made you feel good and let you pretend that the bad had never happened like Larry, Jack, or the straight boys you seduced – that one in the south of France, what was his name?* He reaches the swivel chair and lowers himself onto it and there is respite there.

****

So, it had spoken again and he'd heard it, the little voice in his head which said 'if only', reminding him once more that although it was payback time, there was no time left to pay back, not just the money but everything, everything that he'd taken and begged and stolen from life and from the people in his life, reminding him that restitution and atonement was impossible. 'Some people do a terrible thing in life and regret it,' he told the voice. 'They turn their regret into atonement and the atonement is either successful and they're redeemed, or it isn't and they're not; others spend the rest of their lives *trying* to atone and failing miserably and utterly.

2

I'm one of the latter. An unredeemed unshriven murderer. I killed and it's killing me and it's a fucking long time about it.'

Very soon after his fall it was – a fall hardly on the scale of Lucifer's but a disgrace all the same, all those years ago – that the voice first came to him and it had stayed with him ever since, despite all his efforts to be deaf to it, run from it, hide from it and there it was again, come to harass him, niggle him, as he stood at the cooker stirring the soup he was having for lunch that day (butternut squash and ginger). This was how it came, not when he was deep in reminiscence, not when he was fretting about the possibility of another stroke, or pondering the manner of his death (something he did often), not when he was floundering in one of his frequent bouts of melancholy; no, it could irrupt in his head when he was unpreoccupied and unaware, as now when the only preoccupation was his soup. 'If you hadn't done it, if you hadn't done that, if only you'd done that instead of that, if that hadn't happened,' it said. Always the same words, the same pernicious tone, relentless; if only. Why would this interloper not leave him alone? He knew who it was of course, it was Muvvie, it couldn't be anyone else. Muvvie, who brought on these manias, who prompted him incessantly with the inerrant truth: that if he hadn't done what he'd done in the first place, then all the bad that followed would… well, there would have been no bad, nothing so bad, so it could be said that his action *had* invited her and that she wasn't an interloper at all.

At first, as I said, Muvvie's voice was a mere nuisance, but its pernicious insistence – for which Roly never dared to blame her – had grown over the years in tandem, he supposed, with the accretion of his evil, until it had become

3

the remorseless and monotonous menace it now was; hardly an hour passing by without its making its presence known. Worse than pestering creditors it was, worse than a toothache that nagged and Roly stayed slumped against the cooker. There would never be any more love (had there ever been?); he should stop thinking that he deserved anybody or anything good in life, ever again.

He'd learned to counter attack over the years and harangue and he did so now, aloud: 'You never stopped me at the time did you?' And it was true, it had never been there when he needed to be restrained, had never put out a hand to tell him, 'Best you don't do that dear Roly, you'll regret it.' No, it came only after the event to gloat: 'Well, you did it and you'll live with it for the rest of your life and probably beyond. You have only yourself to blame.' *Only myself to blame.* What a splendid epitaph that would be; not long to wait now.

Besides the voice, there was another, equally insidious, assailant: pictures. They flashed into his brain, bat-black and seen through a fuzzy gauze, yet so vivid, blanking out everything else in his waking world and stopping him dead; pictures of lies and theft, bringing on the melancholy, or was it his melancholy that brought *them* on, he could never be sure? He picked up the wooden spoon and stirred the soup again, aware that he'd been hurled one step further along the road to insanity and perdition.

Grotesque pictures they were, of Muvvie and the carnage he brought to her house, detailed for ever in his Journal. Muvvie was more than pictures, she was a presence. She and her kingdom – Harworthy was the house, which she domineered but so benignly – it was always with him, had never left him. He couldn't see her face any more, but he saw her stiff bloated body clearly, marooned each day all day long in her high chair in the drawing room, her body trapped in a prison of arthritis and he heard her feeble quavering voice. Muvvie and Harworthy and the evil day. He could see her daughters, particularly Elspeth, who was on the lookout for someone suitable to move into Harworthy as a companion for her mother and who introduced Roly into the house. And Muvvie warmed to him instantly, called him 'charming' and he moved in. Ned the grandson, came to stay for a few weeks (was he checking on him?) and they got on well – they went out together, they baked bread together on Saturday mornings; and there was Sam, Ned's brother, soon to be Nemesis: he thought that, of all Muvvie's brood, Sam was the least loved in her eyes. Three daughters, two husbands, two grandsons, Muvvie's dynasty, he met them all. And there he was, the council house boy living with landed people, one of the family, a separate family because he couldn't possibly ever have taken his parents there, to meet Muvvie and her clan and show them how he was now living, nor could he ever have disclosed to Muvvie where he'd come from, what he was, not ever, he would die of shame, so he lied again, just as he did when he first left Trenton and went to London. 'Why do they all call you Muvvie?' he asked her one day. 'The girls were tiny,' she told him, 'and they couldn't say "mother" properly,' and she giggled in her second childhood way.

He saw Smollet, the gardener and his wife who did the cooking, (Muvvie lived on scrambled eggs) and the huge garden with the tailored lawns, the immaculate flower beds in full bloom, the great black and green ash and elm trees that ringed the house, the lines of vegetables and fruit, the rundown potholed tennis court and Muvvie's field next door, where Fudge the pony roamed. Roly had only ever ridden a horse once before, but he saddled Fudge and rode her awkwardly on summer evenings past the open french windows, to convince himself and Muvvie that he was to the manor born. He played the piano which Muvvie bought him, in the summer room, while she listened from her chair and hummed along to the Noel Coward songs he pummelled out for her and he drove the Fiat she also bought him, over to Neston, to buy the homemade ice cream, locally renowned, which she loved and oh, the silly things they talked about on afternoons when they were alone – 'People who say "pardon",' she giggled and 'Bye now' and 'The Smollets call us gentry,' and she giggled again and 'What did you have before you came here, Roly? Did you have rooms where you were?' Rooms! How quaint, how correct! It was luxury a life of everything beyond young Roly's dreams – 'You've fallen on your feet,' his friends told him as he showed them the opulence and how easily he'd slithered into it; he needed little convincing of it, this was his destiny, he belonged here and it wouldn't have ended so wretchedly if he hadn't broken the rules, forcing Muvvie to confront him that afternoon in her pathetically ineffectual way, forcing him to admit everything. 'I was sure my money had been going down,' Muvvie said. 'Is someone blackmailing you?' Then they clung to each other in tears and she said, 'I forgive you Roly.' She forgave him and that should have been the end of it. But Sam came to stay, the executioner with his swift axe, merciless and final and what happened next happened without warning. Sam said nothing, had Muvvie told him? There was no confrontation with him, but when Roly came home the next time and sat with Muvvie again, Sam came in and said there was someone to see him in the summer room and Roly thought, 'Oh god, some boy has turned up' and found not a boy waiting for him but two unfamiliar men and one of them spoke and what he said paralysed him and the world stopped dead and he was handcuffed and led away, away from the magic castle.

He'd never intentionally revealed this lamentable slice of his past to anyone, the only way anyone found out about him and Muvvie was by finding him out because he never confessed… never to Jack and certainly never to his even more beloved successor, Larry. His relationships with Larry and Jack and indeed all his liaisons after his Fall – be they romantic entanglements, attempted relationships, friendships, even one night stands – had to be less than frank for them to have even the slightest chance; the 'no secrets' pledge was never an option for him after Harworthy and Muvvie. To contemplate the alternative, to tell all, maybe even show them the Journal and so expose his terribleness, was unconscionable.

****

Harworthy was the end of the future, the realisation that life was no longer spread out before him but lay ruined behind him. If only. If only he could have diagnosed his psychosis and, admitting he was indurate in denial, sought help before the situation became irreversible. Or, if psychosis was a lame excuse, then swap arrogance for humility and acknowledge that he was innately evil. But he was never a humble creature and, anyway, whence help? Where was help for something one couldn't help doing, that couldn't be helped? There were those who maintained that there was no destiny, only choices – if that was the case, then poor creatures like himself who were clearly unable to *make* choices, why, they were damned! Quentin Crisp was right: everything that happens to us is our fault, he said, but that wasn't our fault. Where was there help to fight something whose source and means of sustenance was unknowable?

7

Where help to fight that something, wicked or superhuman or whatever it was, the numinon inside him, which had captured him at birth, destroyed his sinless will and replaced it with its own? Like Macbeth, hands imbrued, Roly after Harworthy was too far gone in blood to go back, but he didn't know then that he still had further to go, until his flaws, peccadilloes and sins accrued to make up the dismal sum of parts that he now was and leave him floundering for ever in an alcoholic, mendacious, thieving, homosexual quicksand; it was the beginning of the *malheur* from which there would never be respite, which was to tarnish his every action and thought and which could never be wiped. Condign punishment indeed.

If only.

If only he'd not been born what he was and not matured into what he became; if only his little voice had spoken to him that day in his infants' school – yes he could still recall it, that was it, where it *began* – to stop him telling that first fib, the one about his father owning a car. 'It's not your dad's car, anyway.' Alison Clark's sharp, shrill pierced the low hubbub of the classroom, as she tried to expose his subterfuge while the other children looked on with accusatory consternation. 'Your dad shares it with Mr Davies! My mum told me.' That his congenital mendacity may have had its roots in his fascination with real cars and the Dinky toys he'd collected and coveted in boyhood gave him consternation. Alison, however, hadn't got it quite right. His father didn't share his car with Mr Davies or anyone, because his father didn't jointly or singly own a car at all. Ever. At the time it was just a childish brag, just as the names of famed steam locomotives underlined in his spotters' manual to show off to schoolfriends and the trips to Australia and China with his diplomat father and the lie to his best friend of the moment,

Robert Scobie, that his parents owned the council house he lived in and that they owned a new-fangled stereo, were later brags. 'Struth, I started so young!' he would declare years later. He was too young to know what that infantile fibbing presaged, only in retrospect did he see the acorn which grew into the gnarled and festering oak which was to cast its towering shadow over him for the rest of his life. It would need a team of psychologists to determine what nurtured the acorn: did he feel inferiority, vanity, deprivation even then? He certainly couldn't provide an answer but what he did know was that what were harmless boasts and guileless fantasies in other children were for him antecedents of the bigger later 'if onlys'; if only his friend hadn't left his silver Dunhill cigarette lighter lying unattended on the table in the restaurant in Knightsbridge where they all had lunch that day... if only Chris hadn't been in the habit of leaving his wallet full of money trustingly in his bedside drawer... if only those innocent honest people hadn't entrusted him with the money for the bank (and he desperate for that day's whisky) or if he'd declined to handle it... if only alcoholism hadn't crept up on him over the decades and swamped him... if only he hadn't borrowed money by hook and crook and, when he earned the good salaries he did, had repaid the many friends, pub landlords, banks and credit companies who'd lent it to him instead of squandering it in whisky and the search for boys... if only that excess of alcohol hadn't caused the stroke which left him half crippled... if only there had been no Muvvie and the heinous deed. Muvvie and her Luvvie; the bad Luvvie went to Muvvie and she was good to him so he killed her.

If only.

Afterwards, he had to retreat, go home to parents perturbed at his unscheduled return, though resentfully happy to see him and there was food and a fire for him and the bed was made up – sheets and blankets then – ready for a return or as though he'd never gone. And he walked in the door and greeted them, 'Here I am and this is my life' he announced and concealed his ignominy. It had to be concealed, disguised with bluff and, 'Oh well, it was not for me, I had to get out, I shall go back to London where I belong, I never should have left' and his father said, 'Quite right, son, you should never have gone there and mixed with that sort of people, they were no good for you… better off out of it' and he didn't defend the 'sort of people' and didn't undeceive his father's fatherly, favourably-biased misconception.

But ever after, Roly would look back at Harworthy and see that, if he'd possessed one, he would have got into a barrel and started the long scraping of the bottom of it, for that's what his life was from then, the bottom of a barrel. And after the Harworthy too, long after, across the vast expanse of muddied water that lay between, had come Michael, bedizened in his discrete baseball cap, whom he'd first seen very soon after moving to his present flat in the village. If only Michael hadn't been the kind of boy who *would* catch his eye! That cap was a beacon, he'd seen no other like it sported in the neighbourhood; in a window-pane beige check and he, who had no great liking for them, considering their ubiquity monotonous, even he thought it had a touch of style. It was paradoxical that he, a boy-watcher to the marrow, should have noticed the cap before the wearer, but that was only for a moment. The cap wasn't so distracting as to prevent his eyes searching and quickly focusing on the cynosure under it. He was in a group, his gang he supposed: about half a dozen or so boys who gambolled, nymphs and shepherds, on the patch of grass and the tarmaced parking area immediately outside his livingroom window; it was their playground, their football pitch and their street corner and it was plain by their movements, their reactions, how they bent their admiring bodies towards him, how they followed him, how they made way for him, how they fawned on him, that the boy with the cap was their bellwether. Their little world of play swirled around him, his presence was magnet to their subconscious love. He was never without that cap. And what joy, that first gander; it was just like when you saw a figure in a cap in the distance and you knew it was highly likely that the figure was a youth and you hoped it was a beautiful youth and, yes, he came near and your expectation was rewarded. So it was with him. Then the chain of events, the causality which that discrete cap and that boy set in motion, the 'if only' again: if only it hadn't been *that cap*, *that boy* and if only *that boy* hadn't played there for him to see, then all that ensued wouldn't have. If none of it had happened, or if some of it at least hadn't happened… but it had and he had no piety or wit to lure any of it back to cancel and no tears to wash it away. It begged the question and the question befogged the mind: what was this coming together of events, this hex of coincidence and synchronisation, who conjured it and how? And that led him to wonder: could the adoration of an exquisite boy bring him redemption? He'd warned Michael at the very start, but the warning had gone unheeded, it proved futile, wasted on one so young. 'Michael, you are life-full, I beg you to stay away from me,' he implored and he told him how crippled in body and spirit he was: 'I will corrupt you,' he warned. 'Stay away and do one thing above all else, do everything you can to make sure you don't die with guilt and regret in your soul. Guilt and regret eat you, they destroy your very fibres, they kill you but leave you alive to rot. When your hour comes, when you see the archangel coming to meet you, to take you, you must be able to welcome him and say to him, "I have no guilt and I have nothing to regret".'

So much was unfinished, so much lacking, so much wrong and adoration wasn't the resolution, in fact it brought ambivalence, because on the one hand he was continuing the quest for the perfection that he believed would ensure his happiness and on the other he bore the experience which taught him he could never be happy, never satisfied with his lot; he could never reassure himself that everything was in order and in its place and the inventory was complete, because if he did feel even a moment's contentment, it would be only a matter of time before he'd reach for his self-destruct button and obliterate it, somehow he would, he always had. Behind him lay a putrefying wasteland of petty crime and dishonesty, of broken promises, money borrowed and never repaid, friends betrayed - their charity callously dismissed — bills and rents unpaid; a despicable dishonourable history with no hope of reparation and it clamoured to him relentlessly that he'd made one mux of his life after another, all through his life and that the only success he'd ever achieved was in wantonness and degeneracy. No, if Michael was the agent, even the angel, of redemption, he had come too late.

****

The days pass, they fly, past his window and past his life, fleeting; he doesn't live in days, in life any more, he lives in yesterdays, in what used to be and what might have been, in if only; suddenly it's Friday and he can't remember last Friday, or living through Sunday or Tuesday or Wenneday and he watches the flying days through his sad window, by sorry sunlight or by the light of a mournful moon that looks water-borne, as though you see it reflected in a pond rather than hanging in the sky. 'A living death and no sex,' he thinks aloud, 'what a turn-on!' And his thoughts turn once more and inexorably to *The Go-Between* (It showed on the television the other night, is that what prompted them this time?) and its success and he cusses the man who wrote it, much as he does all successful writers. He recites its first line to himself regularly: 'The past is a foreign country'. And then he reminds himself: 'Besides being a degenerate, I'm a literary charlatan,' he says through his sad window and he smiles.

For yes, my dears, Roly the writer, or rather Roly the journalist who'd always wanted to be a writer, one day decided to write a novel. But he hadn't reckoned with *The Go-Between* and L P Hartley and his damnable first line nor, later, with Michael, who'd hurricanoed into his world and together with Mr-bloody-L P-fucking-Hartley had contrived to demoralise and discourage him to the point where he doubted he'd ever had any creativity in his soul at all, that he'd only deluded himself all along. L P Hartley had beaten him to it, it was as simple as that, he had *got there first* (and he'd lost count of how many times that had happened to him); his opening line was just the opening line Roly wanted, because his book, like *The Go-Between,* was about the past. Could he not use the line anyway? When it came to plagiarism, after all, he'd started early and was well-practised, as he'd noted in his Journal all those years ago:

When Senor Alvarez handed me back my Spanish essay in college today he asked me if I'd ever thought I might one day write for a living? 'You have the imagination for it,' he said. Thank God he's obviously never read Huysman's *A Rebours,* which is where I lifted the story from!

so he saw no reason why he shouldn't perpetrate the same deception for this, his Great Work.

Someone once said that copying from another writer was called theft, but copying from a lot of writers was research, so he could purloin Hartley... and Shakespeare too – something that authors had done for four centuries, the Bard was a literary reference library for Heaven's sake and himself the most illustrious and one of the most prodigious of borrowers! – and all the novelists he most admired, Dickens, Hardy, Murdoch, Weldon, Woolf, and go plundering along his *soi disant* creative road. To hell with it: he'd never be regarded as a great writer, he'd have to settle for being honoured as that great 'researcher', a renowned epigone; so bereft was he that he'd no choice but to continue to ape the authors he'd read, watch television dramas and films and listen to plays on the radio with a pen and paper to hand, jotting down the good lines and bon mots from the scripts and appropriating them. The book would end up being an anthology of words written by everyone else except him, a pilchard dressed up as a lobster, but if it sold did it matter? He had no shame. 'Literary charlatans, like degenerates, have no shame,' he'd said.

So he'd persevered and managed a few thousand words:

His beautiful face, eyes and body arrived right on my doorstep out of the grey and cold of an autumn morning. Beautiful he was and semi-literate. It was coffee time and I went into the kitchen to make it and then the doorbell chimed. Why was a doorbell so often a harsh untimely intrusion rather than a heartwarming sound? Same with the telephone. I went to answer it and found myself staring at a young man whose beauty scorched my eyeballs and sent my breathing into stasis. His rich ebony skin, his bottomless black eyes... the way his dark blue baseball cap overhung his brow to give him a hint of voluptuous menace... and his figure framed, an Orson long before he met Michael, but the boy came on the wind of the storm and soaked and shattered him midstream. Hartley at the boarding pier and Michael midstream, a daunting combination which made nailing jelly to a wall suddenly a far more inviting proposition than writing a novel. He called Michael the most beautiful boy in the world, (how many boys had he called that?), on the day they first touched and Michael had accused and surmised. 'I bet you've said that to a million lads' and he replied, 'Most definitely and it was true of most of them and I meant it each time. That's the joy of infatuation, you see. Infatuation is inexhaustible, it goes on forever and doesn't wither with a change of personnel. Oh, and I mean it now, with you. And not only because you're my last, I assure you. I won't die the best author in the world but I will die with the best boy in the world.' He *had* said the very same words, to nameless boys, but in particular and sincerely to his boyfriends: to Jack, who was a year younger and in whose lavish oriental grace he lay for two contented years; and to his enduring lover Larry, also a year younger, whose almost hypnotic feline beauty and scatty intelligence gave him those years of sexual exhilaration, spiced with the alcohol, poppers, hash, cocaine and uppers they shared. Both men were his gods, different gods but gods; he drank deeply of Jack's nectar and gorged on Larry's ambrosia and he was... as happy as Muvvie allowed. Those two lovers and those forgotten and nameless others had been at their appointed hour the most beautiful boys in the world, but now Michael was to be The Most Beautiful Boy in The World and it was surely not reprehensible to replicate an adaptable and versatile truth with various people on different occasions.

15

At first he tried to make little of the detrimental impact of Michael upon his literary career and tried to convince himself that pornography was the problem because his novel was not pornographic. Most definitely not. Graphic, yes. Homoerotic, yes. But not pornographic. And he was, or had been, a pornographer, churning out short stories with consummate ease back in the day for the likes of *Him* and *Zipper* and *Qboy* or *Blueboy* or whatever hell the skinflick magazine was called. He'd had no trouble with L P-fucking-Hartley and his first line then! But for his book, he'd resolved not to demean himself, his book was above the pornographic, he would not stoop and he had been meticulous, indeed, in his avoidance of the conventional tetragrams and timeworn vulgarities:

> *'May I penetrate you?' he asked and he said yes'* and *'He applied the lubricant, pushed the boy's legs back over his shoulders and slid his erect member into the waiting sphincter'*,

he'd written. Much harder than mere pornography, yes, no-one could deny it. He found himself pleading, as he struggled, to whatever guardian spirit may have been listening: 'Don't let this work be one more failed venture that's first considered worthless but is later snapped up by others, don't allow someone to plagiarise *me,* for that would be the final, the cruellest, the most unbearable yet probably the most just of ironic cuts; this is the first and only book I'll ever write and I'm not concerned about dying either praised or condemned, but about dying unrecognised' and he could see – if his manuscript ever grew into the flesh and bones of book – how it would lie unknown, only to be discovered in the distant future by some inquisitive antiquarian sifting his way through the ruins of time.

But before all that, there he had been, at the cooker, stirring soup, agonising yet again over how he could breach Hartley's and Michael's blockade, convinced that if he did, his book would write itself, because its time had come. At the cooker with the grief, the disgrace and with the delusion – that one day he'd be a published author living in a Queen Anne rectory in deepest rural Sussex, a silken-gowned antiquarian, a man of letters, retired from affairs, in his elm-panelled first editions-lined library with a log fire, with cabinetmaker furniture and Wilton carpets, a globe and orrery and priceless prints, drinking claret, vintage port and Manzanilla from Waterford crystal, dining off Wedgwood china using Sheffield master cutlery, playing host to social worthies, intellectuals, literati, glitterati, even some illuminati, aristocracy, perhaps royalty and with a magnificently square-jawed, square-pectoralled young man in tight briefs displaying a permanent torus and tending to his every whim with wicked smiles. 'It will never be,' he had to tell himself and he was mortified at the bleakness.

****

And so, my dears, we have reached the point where Roly was fully aware that the end of the wayworn cul-de-sac down which he'd been walking for years lay now only a short way away; the span of his future was rapidly diminishing and at the bottom of that cul-de-sac hopelessness hung like a great black baldaquin ready to engulf him. It was the time when he could no longer get away with promising to 'do something', or offer the excuse that he hadn't yet reached his full potential; the days of procrastination were over, summer's lease had expired. He was an old man who lived in a retrospective landscape of dangling threads, frayed and haywire and defacing the whole tapestry; threads, shreds and patches he saw, the world of a 'Nearly Man' full of loose

17

ends. 'An old man,' he said and he no longer said it in that frivolous way people have of dismissing their advanced years saying, 'Age is just a number' or, 'You are as old as you feel' and similar inanities. He had to take his age seriously now because a flaw he'd been reluctant to acknowledge in youth had become chronic in age: his inability to admit ignorance. 'I am too old for ignorance,' he said, 'I should know everything worth knowing by now.' He'd always been of the opinion that to be ignorant of something was a failing, a mark of foolishness and he'd rather have drunk hemlock than be taken for a fool. Back in the day, an encounter with anyone who knew something he didn't, or worse, dared to correct or contradict him, would fan the flames of his indignation; he never said, 'I didn't know that', because he wouldn't give way and the only superior intellects he could admire were dead ones and if ever he was exposed, he'd wriggle out of the corner he'd forced himself into with obfuscation or smart evasion or even lies. (Now, there was at least the cowardly refuge, the pretext of an old and tattered memory: 'Yes, I knew that but I'd forgotten it.'). New knowledge and experiences which had once been a source of relish were now anathema and it was too late to resume what had been left off: playing the piano, for instance, which had begun in childhood and was abandoned in his teens for various reasons and so never mastered and the foreign languages that he'd learned at school but foresook when he dropped out of university without a degree (which he often lied about) and shorthand (his journalists' training course ended in disarray without a certificate and he would have to conceal that deficiency throughout his professional life). His only skill would be bluff; he had an insatiable curiosity to acquire knowledge but lacked the application to learn, delighting instead in pulling most of the wool over many of the people's eyes for a good deal of the time. He was a dilettante, a true amateur. Who wanted to be an expert?

For 'What have I achieved?' he asks and looks over his shoulder and sees the trail behind him, the trail of the Nearly Man: who once nearly had a play produced on the West End stage... who *nearly* managed to sell his idea for the new medium of video before anyone else, as far as he knew, had been aware of the potential... who *nearly* travelled the world, but had to settle for jumping impetuously on a plane one day and going to work in Hong Kong for a mere few months... who *nearly* secured the chief subeditor's post but lost out to his rival and had to settle for deputy... who *nearly* bought a London house but was gazumped three times and never managed to raise the deposit for a mortgage anyway... who *nearly* learned to swim as an adult, having failed to as a child... who joined a gym with the crazy notion of building a shaped and muscled body so that he could be admired as he admired others, but went twice and never again... who made a half-hearted attempt to resume the martial arts he'd taken up as a teenager, but went to only three classes... who took up dozens of fads and crazes with alacrity and dropped them as suddenly when the exhilaration of novelty wore off and apathy took over... who never read *Remembrance of Things Past* or Plato or Montaigne or Thomas Paine... who never saw Verdi's *Othello* except on television... who had, as it happened, driven through Paris in a sports car with the warm wind in his hair, but who'd never sailed in a liner to Italy to see the Renaissance in the flesh. 'I nearly read Rousseau's *Social Contract* at school,' he reflected. 'Got to about page 50 and gave up and so, naturally, I was an expert. It's time I read *The Rights of Man,* it really is.'

The world was full of his 'Nearlyness'. And now he was nearly a novelist, but L P-fucking-Hartley and Michael stood in his way and they served only to emphasise that his lacunae and missed opportunities, the things he had *not done,* not *learned,* were the sure signs that in the end he was nothing more than a cursory and perfunctory gleaner, a sciolist who really didn't know anything at all. And over that shoulder he also sees his fathomless desire for young men and alcohol – sometimes, but not nearly as often as he'd wished, he'd got into their knickers and often and far more often than he wished, he'd drunk enough to float the Titanic – and that was about all, the great unravelling of threads, the loose ends that pointed inexorably nowhere except to the almighty fuck-up that life now was.

****

His soup was ready at last. He reached into a cupboard for a packet of crisps – he ate the baked variety, he was mindful of his cholesterol levels – and even this menial action gave him a jolt; roast ham-flavoured they were and Barbara, the landlady of one the pubs he drank in when he lived in Wales, was renowned for her homemade honey-roasted ham and he owed her 300 pounds, still owed it after 15 years, his bar tab for whisky, left unpaid because he went up to London to go to his part-time job one day as usual and never went back. Ham-flavoured crisps, Barbara's ham: he was being destroyed by word association. He poured the soup into a bowl and took it with a bread roll, a raisin Nutrigrain bar and a mug of decaff to the computer room. He ate breakfast and lunch at his desk, but never supper; he was punctilious about the main meal of the day and always laid the dining-table and carried his meal to it and sat and dined in solitary formality, for he was Roly Hunter, gastronome, epicure, foodie, that's what he was or at least that is how he liked to think of himself; almost as passionate about food as he was about young men, the social, aesthetical, moral, historical and mechanical ethos of cooking and eating all fascinated him and, back in the day, was one of his greatest pleasures. He was a true devotee, with his quality cookware and the arcane ingredients he sought out: samphire, seabeet, calalloo, cisco and those once rare and now universal items restored to favour: yams, celeriac, mutton, oxtails, langoustines, sea bream, goat, wild boar, rabbit, venison, and he always utilised his small but precious herb collection to the full. He read cookbooks for pleasure as well as for ideas, he had his own extensive recipe collection and his culinary heroes – Delia Smith, Rick Stein, Mark Hicks – and he watched television cookery avidly. Nowadays, creating a dish and eating it alone wasn't a pleasurable experience, but there he had no choice, yet cooking was still therapeutic, at least when he was sober and he ate well, as he had and would today; his breakfasts were seasonal, always porridge in the winter and shredded wheat in the warmer months and the morning having been a very warm one in a very warm late May, he'd tucked into a bowl of the latter. He ate both, not with the customary milk, but with his own confection of stoned prunes and raisins and with vanilla yoghurt stirred in on serving. He pepared batches of the prunes and raisins first by simmering them in water with powdered ginger, ground allspice and a squeeze of lemon juice and stored them for daily consumption. Lunch was soup or a salad or wholemeal rolls filled with mixes of his own invention. And as for his 'formal' nightly suppers: despite the stroke affecting his sureness, making the toting of pans, the measuring out of ingredients, the stirring, whisking, straining and ladling arduous, he persevered and created as honest a dish as he could because he wouldn't compromise. Only when he succumbed to recurring blasts of alcoholism and suffered the increasingly deleterious effects on his enthusiasm and physical capability, only then did he find himself ringing for the Chinese or Indian takeaways and the pizzas to be delivered (why did he never get pretty delivery boys?). But in sobriety, homemade and fresh were his bastion, the only takeaway indulgence would be occasional fish and chips. If he wanted a curry or a Chinese dish, he made it. If he wanted soup, he made it: carrot and tarragon, herb, potato and lovage, tomato and basil, pea and ham, borshcht. His pasta was bought but what dishes he made with it were his own, as was the tuna and pasta baked in a sauce of onions, garlic, tomatoes and fresh basil planned for that night.

I said 'carried his meal'; to give you a full picture of Roly, my dears, I must tell you that to carry anything, he needed his waitress trolley – yes, indoors, he was a trolley-dolly! The stroke that incapacitated him five years ago was a peripheral neuropathy which, though painless, left him unable to balance and walk without support and to carry anything remotely bulky, such as a plate of food, was out of the question, so he used a trolley to walk with and to carry things on about the flat and so to be precise, he trundled rather than carried his lunch to his desk and as he trundled he gave a grateful thought, as he always did, to the occupational therapist who'd provided him with this ad hoc aid, because without it he'd be helpless and static.

He usually played mahjong or Sudoku over lunch, or Bookworm or even dominoes. Today it was Sudoku and when he finished that and the soup, he'd continue with his Journal; nothing had happened that day worthy of recording, but he'd recently started making entries in his Journal again – the Journal he once assiduously kept – for the very good reason that he now had Michael to write about, not to mention that, apart from writing a novel ha ha, it kept his hands and his brain occupied in typing; stroke victim he may be, but he wasn't yet prevented from adhering to the Protestant work ethic that was ingrained in him from birth, regardless of whether it earned him money or not.

Before he could concentrate on writing however, there was the homeworker, due today. The helpers from the agency were invariably women and pleasant and obliging though they were, he wished the agency would surprise him and send a square-jawed, square-chested, steel-buttocked hunk to dust and polish in a pinafore and thong for once. He'd spent a lifetime pining for a hunk, a genuine 42-inch chested 30-inch waisted one with acres of pectoral muscle, wanted just once to hold one naked, hold great handfuls of him, an armful of prime beefcake flesh that would submit to him. But it was dowdy mousy-haired Claire who let herself in again, talking of her rebellious children and saying thank god this was her last day before having a week off. She Dysoned the carpets, polished the furniture, mopped kitchen and bathroom, changed the duvet, he paid her and she left. He never attempted to work while his homeworkers flitted around him. Like any writer, he needed absolute privacy but he had no garden shed or attic to retreat to and he wasn't one of those who could shut himself off if anyone else was in the flat. When a homeworker was there, he had to small chat with her, or rather listen to hers, because he didn't want to seem aloof and untouchable, the grand old writer locked away with his muse, disturb him at your peril. He was no Pirandello, who had to contend with a lunatic wife hammering at his study door all day long as he created those ingenious mind-game plays of his and he marvelled at how the poor man managed to write a full sentence let alone theatrical masterpieces; he couldn't write a word with the distracting presence of a cleaning woman, even a sane one.

****

In a bedroom in a house that lay about 100 yards across the small housing association estate behind the flat he'd recently moved into, but not in his view, two young school chums, Michael Hollis and Danny Hodgkins, best mates, sat together giggling and guffawing and nudging and pinching and pushing and pulling each other in the way high-jinxed boys will when they are taking part in some proscribed pastime for which they know their parents would punish them and their contemporaries mock them mercilessly if they were discovered; as if that weren't already doubly daring and enlivening, the contents they were glued to on the computer screen that particular afternoon made the adventure triply so. For they'd discovered a gay website. Neither of them knew why they'd logged into it, it was of no sexual interest to them; they'd neither of them given much thought to whether or not they were sympathetic or homophobic, queers were a laughable and harmless oddity provided they didn't touch nor were touched by them (such as was the case with the old man, Poofter Pete they called him, who lived alone in Bluebell Cottage up by the Swan pub) and what they were doing was just a lark. They entered one chatroom after another and their howls of hilarity were unconfined, a juvenile cacophony; they weren't so much disgusted as more shocked than they'd care to admit to each other, at the typed sexually explicit conversations of the men in the rooms spidering across the screen; they looked at lists of profiles and photo galleries and screeched at buttocks and penises, testicles and nipples and howled at bodies frozen in their various poses: straightforward, alluring, esoteric, from the sensual to algolagnia, tranvestism and transgenderism, the panoply of the gay internet was laid literally bare before their callow eyes. After some time, it was Michael who suggested they search for local names and faces among the profiles and go particularly into the Trenton room to see if anyone they might know was lurking there, the anononymity of 'handle' names, false names, fake pictures or no pictures at all and the other ways in which people disguised or hid their identities in such places, notwithstanding. And Michael it was who spotted the old man, as old as his grandad, whom he and his gang had seen a few weeks before moving into the flat in the row in the High Street. But he said not a word and registered no reaction when Danny didn't notice or comment. Their caper was brought to an end when they heard Michael's mother come home from her part time job at the village off-licence and shout to her son from the bottom of the stairs. Like two frightened rabbits, they scurried and scrabbled, switching off the computer, tidying what mess they could find, suppressing their hilarity into sniggers and gathering themselves to walk, as much like two innocent votive altar boys emerging solemnly from the church vestibule as possible, downstairs. 'What you two bin up to, somethin' no good as usual?' Yvette asked, affably enough, when the boys walked into the kitchen. 'Just chillin' Mrs 'Ollis,' Danny answered for them. 'Danny bought his new Tekken round,' Michael added, to back up his co-conspirator. 'We're goin' down the field. Did ya get me any pop?' he asked, opening the fridge door and taking out two cans. 'Tarra,' he cried and flung the distinctive checked beige baseball cap, the bellwether, which he'd pulled off the peg behind his bedroom door, onto his head. 'Tarra missus,' Danny chimed as he followed him and Yvette watched her son trot out of the house and across the communal patch of grass with his friend.

Yvette Kelly, née Hollis, 34 years old, was a slender, quite tall woman with a cheerful pretty face framed in a mass of black hair that hung in long tresses to her shoulders. Michael had inherited her hair together with her complexion and lips. She wore a calf length diaphonous white summer smock covered with tiny purple flowers, trimmed with lace on the sleeves and hem and at the neck, which swirled in billows around her form. She hardly ever wore trousers and there were mules on her feet. She watched her son walk away, absently fingering the thick gold necklace she was wearing and touching one of her large green glass butterfly earrings and then turning the sapphire signet ring around on her middle finger. She was a woman fond of her showy rather vulgar jewellery, regretting deeply that she never had the money to buy any of the real thing, for she had taste. What little money she earned from family benefits and her job, she lavished on the son and younger daughter she adored, indulging every whim of theirs she could manage to scrape the money together to pay for. 'I'd walk through fire for me children,' was her proud boast and she'd emphasise it with tales of how she sometimes found herself walking home from work and going to the shop with the dilemma of what to do with the few coppers left in her purse on a particular day – buy a loaf of bread for the children's tea or a packet of cigarettes for herself and saying the loaf always won. She'd brought up her children single handedly after the gambling and violence-addicted man she'd married so young had finally stopped hitting her and commandeering her money when he disappeared with a young woman from Lyme never to be heard of again. She could dismiss her short and unhappy marriage, not think about it at all, could bury any bitterness and regret and convert the negativity and destruction of those emotions into positive love and compassionate care for her cherished offspring. Yvette Hollis was a woman strong of purpose, a woman with no delusions, certainly no delusions about her son, whose adorable retreating figure she followed through the kitchen window as she wondered again how gay he was becoming, for with a mother's instinct, she suspected that gay was what he was. She also intuited that he didn't know it, for she knew he was seeing a lot of that girl from the other side of the village and knew he was handsome enough to attract the attention of a number of neighbourhood girls, all of whom seemed to swarm to his side at different times and all of whom he was known to encourage and flirt with. She'd noticed that she'd disturbed him and Danny just now and seen how they'd come downstairs with the forced nonchalance that drew attention to rather than masked whatever misdemeanours they'd been perpetrating, probably on the computer, but she was also confident that he'd not been 'experimenting' or 'exploring' in any sexual way with Danny, certainly not seriously, because she also had the mother's gut feeling that, if she were right and Michael was about to emerge homosexual, a contemporary wouldn't be his choice of first, or indeed any later, partner. She didn't know how she knew that, but suspected strongly that things would happen that way because of Michael's need for a father. His being gay would solve the problem, because he'd choose, as a natural matter of course, to go only with an older man, she was convinced of the truth of it and therefore convinced that she'd not missed by a breath coming upon Michael having sex with his schoolfriend. It didn't occur to her to oppose or discourage in any way her son's homosexuality, if her instinct were true; she was too young to concern herself with any thoughts of dynasty, the carrying on of a name and line. Her only concern, in a life of many concerns, was the happiness of her children and the quality of their future lives. And that was why, she told herself, she wouldn't give a straw if one or even both of them turned out to be gay and she turned on the kitchen tap and started to wash the dishes left from the morning.

Michael and Danny meanwhile had walked and cantered to the field where Danny suddenly asked, 'Would you ever take it up the arse?' and Michael stopped dead in his tracks, turned penetratingly accusatory black eyes full on his friend and told him with quiet vehemence to 'Fuck off', which put an abrupt end to any further mention of the subject, something they'd shared but which was taboo, something however that didn't prevent a conflict of sensations that his first exposure to explicit images of homosexual culture had set teeming in his head. They reached their gang friends who were kicking a football about and they joined in the game but instead of the football, Michael saw flickering and invasive pictures of naked flesh, male flesh and saw those typwritten lines of lurid conversation in the chatroom. And in his room that night, in the hush and dark of solitude, knowing it was forbidden, he sat at his computer again and clicked and browsed and watched, not participating, oh certainly not, but mesmerised once more by the rolling words and more than once he clicked and read and stared at the profile and photo of the man he'd seen who lived around the corner and he was baffled and bewildered, as though he were staring at an optical illusion which made no sense to his eye and brain, but was intriguing nonetheless. Before he closed down for the night, a wild and crazy notion seized him and he turned to the site's 'Help' section and read the instructions on how to carry out the task he intended to perform. He went back to the profile of the man and he clicked on the appropriate screen icon. Too late, he'd done it, too late for regret or second thoughts; if not panic, then at least a disorienting giddiness overwhelmed him, sickening and elating in turns and he shut down his computer and jumped out of his chair as if both were on fire and he stood and ripped off his clothes and threw himself into his bed and lay rigid, sweating slightly and breathing heavily, horrified and excited and disturbed and aware of something ineluctable his afternoon and nocturnal dalliances had produced and he closed his eyes and caressed the part of himself that was inexplicably aroused and felt becalmed.

****

He decided, while eating his soup and waiting for Claire to finish cleaning, that it was time to look at his manuscript again, on what impulse after so long he couldn't imagine. Maybe Michael was an adjuvant, a Muse after all and not the distraction, the barrier he'd at first considered him to be and as he clicked and summoned the file and looked at the words, he laughed to himself with gruesome wryness as he saw the first line that he'd eventually decided upon. 'The past is a *dangerous* country', was what he'd typed and when he had he asked, 'How's that?' with the flourish of a triumphant arm; he could get away with the line, he was sure, because it was only half a cheat and he'd prinked himself by imagining the critics' reviews, an imagining he'd hoped would prove to be vatic: 'Roland Hunter has paid cunning tribute to one of the old masters with his clever opening tributary paraphrase', they would say.

Some sudden movement in the carpark outside his window caught the corner of his eye. He turned from the screen and watched four workmen getting out of their van, humping ladders on their shoulders. One of them was a tall young, fair crop-haired youth, ('You're a yoof,' he said softly) with his

29

torso bare and looking very fine indeed from 10 yards away; a little tattoo just discernible on his chest and as his tight denim-clad buttocks disappeared into a garden Roly raised a smile at the reminiscence of the window-cleaning lad in Kensington 30 years before, who suffered from vertigo and had to light up a joint before he could tackle any windows above the first floor of the block of flats where he and Larry lived and whom he used to tease mercilessly through the window while he was on his ladder: 'That juicy packet of yours is at eye level again, Darren,' he'd yell, as Darren stretched and wiped.

Roland Hunter. He'd said the name, or Muvvie had said it, oh dear oh damn. He'd never got used to it: whenever he thought it, said it or wrote it, he felt a kick in the head, because it wasn't his own name of course and he'd borne it with a perverse sense of guilt all these years. Why so? The disaster of Muvvie and Nemesis Sam was probably the reason, plus remembering how his father had somehow contrived to link his name change with his downfall. Sam, not content with seeing Roly disgraced, had tried to kick him when he was down, had found his Auntie Vera's phone number (Roly's parents weren't yet on the phone) and rang her to reveal all and poor Auntie Vera had taken a bus ride to Roly's refuge, the council house, to relate the conversation and so the secret was out; his father came home from work, there was a ghastly scene and Roly grabbed his car key and headed for the door intending to flee the council house (not for the first time in his life). His father managed to restrain him and he was persuaded to go, with his mother, there and then to find a solicitor and the solicitor wrote to Sam and Sam wrote back, pointing out in suitable language what an unmitigated bastard Roly was, that Hunter wasn't even his real name and that what he'd done to his grandmother and his family was reprehensible and unforgiveable.

He sat at his computer, fighting of this remembrance which Muvvie was drilling into in his mind.

Roly's father, with his opinion that his son had become involved with 'the wrong people' and been led astray, now couldn't resist lacing his paternal defence with a dig over his change of name. 'If you had to go and change your name, you could at least have added Hunter to Wanger instead of getting rid of the one you were born with altogether,' he observed plaintively at the tea table. His mother had been more quiescent, probably because she was inwardly proud that it was her maiden name Roly had chosen, her beloved father's name and his grandfather's, though she never said as much. His identity had become a farrago and the mismash surrounding it was traceable back to Neville Ladderbanks. Neville, the first real queer he knew (Raymond Quipp at school didn't count, as he, like himself, didn't consider himself a queer but a boy worshipper) and one daring night he told Neville he wanted to have sex with a boy and asked him to find him one. Neville wasn't the one who did eventually find him a boy, someone else did, but he was the one who plunged him into the identity morass, which was to drag him down through confusion and disarray for the rest of his life. Before he knew it, he'd been laden with a disguise which became so multi-layered it rendered him unable at times to know who he really was, led to the habit of inventing new characters for himself and made him question how many lives he could live, how many realities inhabit. Embarrassments and predicaments were to dog him, efforts to liken himself with other prestigious name-changers before him – the royal family for instance – were no help: that two boys who were christened David and Albert ended up on the throne as Edward and George, or that the first emperor of Rome had about three different sets of names before he became Augustus, or that the great Elton John's name was manufactured and that even his musical god, Mozart, had taken it into his head one day that his middle name was to be Amadeus, was neither a boost to confidence nor a comfort; he was never to find peace being someone else.

Thus, his name change, identity crisis, call it what you will, together with his sexual frustration, had a common denominator in and were inextricably linked with Neville Ladderbanks and that daring night arrived, the night when he felt so desperate that he cast all care of consequence aside and Neville, titillated by being so unexpectedly accosted by a young man in a sexual predicament, asked him a vital question with prurient curiosity (Neville's manner, whether inquiring after your health or asking you the time, was always confidential and whispered and bordered on the conspiratorial). 'Have you ever kissed a boy?' he wanted to know first of all and the question echoed loud in Roly's ear to this day. He closed his book file and brought up the one labelled 'Journal' and found the entry he'd written not long after that meeting.

The dark alley with its single lamp which Neville led me into gave our talk a conspiratorial feel, there was danger in the air. With his oleaginous manner and the subject we were dealing with, well it was like we were plotting treason. He grabbed my arm to turn me and stop me walking any further and I started to tremble, afraid that I had aroused his predatory instinct. Although he was relaxing against the stone wall and I was standing free, I felt I was

pinioned, so leeringly close was his face. We were right under the lamp, one of the new tin ones it was and we were both dimly highlighted by its peroxide glow, like a pair of Harry Limes in the long shadows of a Vienna night. We were in the alley which led to the footbridge over the old loopline and the way to my home on the council estate.
They were not far from Katie Beans field.

I was afraid Neville was about to 'surge', an expression I was not familiar with yet but would often hear used when I became an habitué of the Trenton gay circle. Trenton queers used it to indicate their intention of making an advance to someone who they thought might 'play' or was rumoured to. 'If someone is available, dear, TBH, To Be Had,' Neville was to explain to me one night in the Trenton gay pub, 'as opposed to naff, Not Available For Fucking, then you surge on him before he gets away.' In the deserted alley, Neville asked the question about kissing softly, as though someone might overhear it, and seductively enough to make me fear that answering him truthfully in the negative would give him the impression that I wanted him to demonstrate what it was like. I lived quite near to Neville who, though 10 years older than I, was still with his parents in a smart house overlooking the park. People in the town, including my mother, called him 'funny' because he was suspected of and reviled as being the town queer. He was also a brilliant pianist and had appeared once on *Opportunity Knocks*, was crazy about trains and had a fantastic model layout in his attic and was a rabid misogynist who doted on his mother. Our lives had touched only slightly, but I had long wanted to get the opportunity to get closer to him, not to have sex with him, perish the thought, but to use him as my ticket into the gay arena which I fervently hoped he was a member of. If Neville was really what everybody said, then he could help me. Neville was an outsider like me, because of both his, as yet, alleged sexual and his cultured leanings.

There was the confrontation with his mother in the garden of the council house one summer evening a few months later; gossip had reached her and had aroused her disapproval and prejudice and the fear that her son was being corrupted: 'You've been seeing that Neville Ladderbanks haven't you?' she asked with the familiar pouting black face of distaste. 'He's one of the few people in this town I can have an intellectual conversation with,' was his retort and his defence of his hoped-for saviour, but it only made her scowl the more.

I felt, now that I had at last buttonholed him, albeit in the confinement of that silent and dimly lit alley, that I was on the verge of something momentous. But there was still doubt. I had no evidence, I was not 100 percent sure that Neville was indeed queer. I had only the town gossip to go on but then I was also aware of something about Neville which other people had not appeared to notice, or certainly had not mentioned, and it was something which appeared to tip the balance in favour of my guesswork and had emboldened me to make this approach: Neville walked with a mince. Not only that, he walked with a mince and he talked with a mince and his hair, though worn fashionably long, perched oddly on top of his slender figure and somehow added to his effeminacy. But was that enough? 'Surely,' the young logic of my mind persisted, 'he must be queer?' But before I could establish whether he was or not, before the alley, I had caught the last bus home from Hanbridge and there he was, at the back of the top deck, sitting with and apparently playing around with, certainly giggling with, one of the most beautiful blond young men I had ever seen and I decided to risk all and seize the moment, it could be the only chance I would have. When the bus reached Turnhurst, we stood at the head of the stairs ready to go down and I swooped. 'Hello, Neville.' 'Oh, hello!' Neville squeaked and I did not know whether he feigned the surprise or, more probably, avoided acknowledging me for the reason he did with almost everyone: the possibility of receiving some mental or even physical abuse, not that he would cower from either. Or perhaps he was genuinely surprised to hear a greeting that was not hostile? 'Had a good night?' I asked. 'Yes. Have you?' 'No I haven't', I replied sulkily, then I asked nonchalantly, 'Who was that you were with, by the way?', making sure he knew I had seen the shenanigans with the blond boy. 'Oh dear, why ever not?' said Neville. 'Who, that boy? That was Tony, oh yes. So what's the matter? Aren't you getting any rumpy-pumpy, hmmm?' 'Neville, I haven't so much as touched a girl... or a boy for that matter.' There, I had blurted it out and Neville let out a salacious 'Ooooooooh'. 'Come on,' he said, 'I think we'd better walk along Park Road for a bit, hadn't we? You must tell me more. Mmm, yes.' This prologue, which I took to be a positive indicator and the mental juggling over Neville's sexuality, combined finally to allow me to commit myself and 'No,' was my eventual answer to Neville's furtive enquiry about kissing a boy when we reached the alley and I went on to give Neville the sorry and sordid tale of that Saturday night and the vomiting Martin Willis. Neville shrieked theatrically in falsetto; it was a mannerism I was to become very familiar with. 'I see. Mmm, yes,' he said. 'But you want to, don't you? I mean, you want trade, don't you, dear?' I had a notion what 'trade' was and cried out, 'Christ, yes I do!' in desperation. 'Well, dear, we'll have to do something about that won't we? Mmm? Yes.' I now steeled myself in an effort to stop the shaking and to figure out what I was going to do if he did try to kiss me, but to my relief he discerned my anxiety and said, 'Don't worry, dear, your mother's not going to surge. Now, what are you doing – ooh, erm, let me see, Thursday night?'

But two weeks later nothing had happened. Where was this glamorous gay world? Why had the new, forbidden oyster not opened up and yielded its nacre? Where were the free love and the orgies everyone went to every night? Where was a boyfriend? If not a boyfriend, then what about someone who I could just have sex with? Proper sex, I mean, now that the classroom gropes were gone forever? Yes, Neville had done what he said he would and taken me 'on town'. People were 'on town' rather than 'out'. 'Out' was not a word in currency yet and it would not apply anyway because only a few lucky or brave people were what could possibly be called 'out' in a town like Trenton in those medieval days. 'On town' was the catchword, more akin to the debutant meaning of coming out than to any open declaration or reference to closets. Out of the closet did not really pertain in Trenton. You could be gay in the gay bars behind closed gay doors among other gay people, but not anywhere else. The new law had done nothing yet to rid places like Trenton of the infamy and the fear and a flourish of closet doors being flung wide was as yet a consummation devoutly to be wished.

'Stay with your mother, dear,' Neville had urged, as we stood on that first night out at the door of the iniquitous and notorious Gazelle pub, outside which Quipp and I had spent time, not daring to go in, but watching the patrons come in and out in an attempt to find out what a real queer looked like. Neville adopted his conspiratorial manner again. 'Be very careful what you say, dear. There are some evil people in here. Evil. Don't tell anyone anything. Oh Christ, here comes fat Sid. She's got the biggest mouth on town.' Neville thought for a moment, then proclaimed suddenly, 'Right, your name is ...' he gabbled and mumbled... 'Pete. You're Pete from now on, dear. That's your name on town and in here. Never tell anybody your real name or say where you live,' he admonished.

I wondered, but did not ask, why a false name was necessary. People were calling Neville, Neville, so what was wrong with my own real name? And, 'Why did you call him she?' I asked, when we were inside and I was sipping my first gay half pint of Ind Coope bitter at the bar. 'What?' 'That fat chap. Sid? You called him she.' 'Oh, her! Because she's a terrible old queen, dear. Like most of them in here, oooooh yes,' Neville replied with contempt and a meretricious curl of his lip. What struck me as most odd about my first gay pub as I looked around was how ordinary it was: its tawdry décor, its lack of any all-male Bacchanalian debauchery, The Supremes singing *The Happening* on the jukebox and two very large, rotund people, mine hosts Abel and Mabel, floundering behind the bar like two cribbed and confined walruses; there were no men holding hands or kissing, they were just talking and drinking, there was no cavorting, no wild behaviour, no naked flesh to be seen, there was absolutely nothing that could possibly offend your grandmother, it was like any pub in any town, filled with men, but workingclass boozers in workingclass towns are always filled with men, nobody chatted me up or tried to molest me, I went to the toilet on my own, urinated on my own and came back on my own, nobody followed me, watched me, touched or talked to me, nobody did anything, nothing happened, it had not exactly been a swinging night, not a happening.

'This town and its people are scum, dear, oh yes. Now, Manchester, that's the place, mmm. You must come to Manch with me, dear. I go every Friday. We'll go on the train. Mother loves the train ride to Manch, mmm yes,' Neville said on the bus home.

A plague on this city!

In bed that night, despite my disappointment, I nevertheless felt a tingle of privilege; I had now gained admission to a closed society and before

Quipp too! I had lots to tell him now that I was a member of the wicked society.

But I also feared that what I had spent hours and days in front of the mirror trying to convince myself was not so – that I was not attractive to gay men – was in fact the truth. It was the hair! Nights of sleeping with it wet, or stuck down with cellotape, or plastered with Brylcreem or the new Trugel, produced the same infuriating result: in the morning my fringe had *not* curved from left to right over my forehead as I wanted, but had stubbornly returned to its natural fall of right to left. 'It's the wrong way! Why oh why can't I have straight hair?' I cried. There were hours of fighting to create a centre parting, but soaking it, shampooing it, leaving it wet, blowdrying it or putting my mother's curlers in it all proved futile. Why could my hair not do as it was told, like the perfectly groomed hair on the heads of the popstars on the pin-up posters on my bedroom wall? To be honest, it was not just the hair was it? My ears were too big, my eyes were too close together and my lips were horribly thin. No gay boy was ever going to want to have sex with me.

Why were so many of the men I saw that night so effeminate, I wondered as I drifted off to sleep; was it *de rigueur*?

Indeed, the whole issue of his physiology was to grow from early fixation to late obsession when he reached the point where nothing could be rectified; he could, for instance, now no longer regulate his weight, the small paunch he'd carried on him from childhood and which he'd never been able to be rid of had become a huge and ungainly mass – seeing his flesh wobble about while he showered and sitting bloated with the waistband of trousers squeezing painfully into him made him nauseous. He'd ballooned once before – the calories of alcohol were to blame then – but Larry never mentioned it, never found it repugnant, it never stopped them making love. Nevertheless, he managed to go teetotal for a while and that and the adoption of the F-Plan diet regime saw him lose over a stone. Now the culprit was lack of exercise through lack of mobility. How far he used to walk! He walked everywhere: the totting up of miles was a joy, seeing all London on foot, climbing the hills of the Peak District, the Lake District and Wales, roaming through Hong Kong, evening walks on long summer evenings or bracing ones in winter through Katie Beans field and on along the grassed-over loopline to escape the funereal atmosphere of the council house and his parents, walking, walking, he loved it. But he should care, there was nobody to impress now: those agonising hours of staring at his miserable reflected image, willing it to make him trim and athletic like Robert Scobie or handsome like... like almost everyone else he could think of, despising his pigeon chest, his thick wrists and contrasting meagre arms, his ungainly rack of shoulders, the miniscule button of a nose inherited from his father, his pinched mouth, the eyes like pinpoints set in a moon of a face, the elongated chin, the endless list of deformities – all the despising was no longer necessary and he was reconciled to what he was – *look at me, in the final stages of mortality* – overweight, five-foot-9, with receding hair, flaking skin, very few teeth and legs that could no long carry him and he often asked himself, 'What are the wages of sin?' and answered, 'A murky twilight of late-flowering lust and depressing and humiliating physical collapse.' *Is it true that if you hate yourself you can't love anyone?*

What truly bothered him about Neville's *ipse dixit* about his pseudonym, more than the confusion it caused him, was that, being at the time a putative queer with Wildean expectations and florid dreams, he couldn't forgive Neville's lack of invention; he deserved a more intriguing pseudonym than the workmanlike 'Pete' and it was his surname he hated and longed to change, not his perfectly acceptable forename. Wanger was his original surname – did one call it a birth name these days? – and he was given the name Roland by crestfallen parents; they had hoped for a girl, whom they would have named Christine so they told him. He was Roland, then later in the gay ambience of Trenton he became Pete for a time and then he was Roland again... then Roland Wanger-Hunter... then he dropped the Wanger altogether and was Roland Hunter... then Roly in places and at times and Roland at others. Putting it down in the Journal later made him recall a childhood game he had when, instead of going out to play in the street with the other children (his mother took him to see the doctor about it, so worried was she), he stayed indoors writing stories, creating a world where he was a private detective, like Sexton Blake in his comic and he invented a name for himself – he even remembered it, Rushton Spencer it was – and he decided that was who he was going to be when he grew up and it was wonderful. So was it ordained, this relabelling? Some kind of cosmic conspiracy? That first was a child's fantasy, Neville's was foisted on him, the others were voluntary acts. Did it mean anything?

He moved away from the world of Neville and the Gazelle and went to be a student in London and there were no evil provincial queens and no need for disguise and he could dispense with Pete and revert to Roland. But then he had to go and change his surname didn't he? And this was not to protect his identity, but simply because he hated, had always hated, the one he'd been born with and just as soon as he was free from any parental restraints, he acted and changed it by deed poll to Wanger-Hunter. But even this was botched because shortly afterwards he had second thoughts and had to repreat the deed poll process when he amended himself to plain Hunter.

Scrolling on and reading random passages he came to:

> I'm being throttled, ligatures of literary trickery are choking me, I'm being buried under a pile of devices and conceits. Why the hell do I try to be so damned clever, I never learn do I? My cleverness, what cleverness? My cleverness is, always has been, a sham and here comes the black shroud of melancholy again and I'm smothered as well as throttled.

and felt immediately that such writer's angst – writer? angst? – needed alleviating, so he went to his CD carousel and as he'd just read 'sham', pulled out the piece of sham music he was so fond of, to match the mood: *España,* the orchestral piece with a supposed Spanish flavour written by a Frenchman. It was sunshine music and it always warmed him. He pulled out his Bobby Darin CD to play after it; *Artificial Flowers* was either too serious for its own good or it was merely camp, either way it made him laugh. Then he remembered another piece he'd discovered only recently and had played and played, never sickening of it, so he changed his mind and picked out *Danzón for Orchestra No 2* by the Mexican Márquez, which was quite delightfully mesmerizing, its beguiling Veracruzian rhythms making him clap his hands and dance about in his chair like an over-excited baby and making him somehow... happy, without feeling guilty. If he'd had alcohol in the house, he may well have sat and got gently blotto to the sound of Chopin, which would take him as near as it was possible to get to Nibbana, the deathless plain where one was free from all defilement. When his mind was attuned like this, when accidie was upon him, he'd often play the game of picking the five greatest pieces of music ever written, an impossible task, his choices changed by the minute!

Never mind music, what of literature, what of his novel? What was to become of the hero he'd created, who seduces a straight young man, a chance journeyman, a magnificent black buck called Denzel, who lies with him after the act in anabiotic haze:

'The past is a dangerous country', he said
(he'd written)

'and as for the present, the present is just a microsecond of awareness and we are just two binary dots in it. It's gone in the time it takes to know it's there; there's no security in the present. So where is there to go?' (And here came the conceit), *'And of course the past is a foreign country too, like the man wrote and no matter how hard we try and how wise it is not to, we can't help going there. We can't avoid it or ignore it, we have to live in it over and over again and suffer and if we do turn our back on it will only creep up and bite us on the backside.'*

He couldn't decide, not when he wrote it at the time and not now, was it clever prose or was it convoluted rubbish? Worse: writing fiction and his Journal entries simultaneously confounded, no positively unhinged him; the theme of the one was derived from the subject matter of the other and it was the devil to know sometimes which was which. He'd used extracts from the Journal, but it had been a mistake to think he could write a work of fiction based on his personal history. That was where every would-be author mistakenly started wasn't it? Only to find that no-one would publish it. He would fare better concentrating on newspaper and magazine features, but he couldn't think of anything to write about. Oh calamity!

****

The summer holidays, 30 years ago: he was between school and university and was about to start a year – a gap year they called it now – as a student teacher; many a day and long he lay with his dog in Katie Beans field, which was reached by the path that led from behind the council house down to the loopline near the stream and the pool. He committed the memory of that summer to paper, perhaps five years afterwards and it wasn't a painful thing to do because he was living the warm and cosy life with Jack by then and he could look back at teenage torment and smile. Exhuming it now, though, wasn't therapeutic; the passage of years hadn't depleted or diminished the vividness of the memory but enhanced it rather and Katie Beans now figured as the augur of the more dreadful future that was waiting to ambush him. He read and without effort was pulled back into space and time and the resonances of that summer were loud and what had lain locked away in a dusty cranny emerged to swamp his consciousness; he heard the mournful song, the soundtrack of his happy and unhappy youth and the nostalgia was viscid and The Mamas and Papas sang,

Monday, Monday, so good to me,
Monday, Monday, it was all
I hoped it would be
on his transistor radio again:

I'd finished my A-level exams, the academic moil was over and I lay otiose in Katie Beans field every

44

day with nothing to do but wait for my results. Time on my hands, an extreme tyrant sun, the searing air – everything was somehow sapped and lifeless; it was like lying under a pair of those massive velvet curtains, the ones it takes all your strength to draw together across a window. I never wore shorts, except for playing tennis in the park with Robert and Will and the others and I considered being shirtless in public, except on the beach, *infra dig*. Goodlooking boys walking around half-naked in the streets in the hot weather were all very well, but it was kind of uncouth too. So I lay there fully clothed and sweltering, with the dandelion puffballs drifting by on the imperceptible breeze and the wasps whirring with muted menace above my head like tiny helicopters. Every so often, I would close my eyes and stretch out a languid hand to touch Stephen, he of the mahogany skin and Martin, whose hair was the colour of a haystack, my two special boys from two years below me at Trenton High School, leched over through six or seven terms and I relished breaking the law of the land and disrupting the public repose by stroking their silky thighs and kissing their sherbert-and-saliva lips. *Sacrificing myself on the altar of their unbridled passion.* So real was the yearning so lost in daydreams was I one day that I sat bolt upright and sent my mocking laughter out over the grassy bank when I realised it wasn't a boy but my dog, lying panting beside me, that I was stroking. No, Martin and Stephen were not there; yes, I was alone, alone on that wretched hillock by the loopline, behind the marlpit by the brickworks and any sacrifice, any kissing and stroking of Martin or Stephen or any boys were mere velleities. When their delectable figures appeared in my mind's eye and brought on my adolescent erection, which was about every half hour, I ached and not only phallically. *What's it like to kiss a boy?*

In the near distance, the mechanical diggers rattled and clanged incessantly while the workmen bellowed to each other and it was all such a gross intrusion on his idyll. My boys, together with the copy of *A Rebours* I was reading, did their best to protect me from it, but an erotic shield wasn't enough and I had to admit that I was, after all, lying pained and bewildered in Katie Beans field, bombarded by noise and dust, overlooking an old railway loopline in Trenton and not in the asphodel fields of Arcadia. *Just look at me: 16 years old, lying next to a marlpit of unreachable dreams and a brickworks of frustration!*

The discovery so early that the world has nothing so glorious to offer as a boy in the full bloom of adolescence was the thing that made my schooldays so happy and so maddening. Their faces, their hair, their shapes and curves and angles. All that boyness: enticing me, fascinating me. I watched their bottoms swinging along the corridors and in the playground, their shorts-clad thighs on the sports field and I so wanted to touch them. In particular, I wanted to touch Martin Willis's because Martin had by far the peachiest bum in the school. I was not discreet, I proclaimed my boy love as much as I could. My predilections soon attracted the attention of my fellow schoolchums, making them raise their eyebrows and earning me a reputation, but I didn't care. What I did care about was that I had taste: the boys I called my favourites and whom I gently domineered in my capacity of prefect in an attempt to gain their acquiescence, were the juiciest in the place. I was living dangerously: reputation turned to notoriety and it wasn't long before my school peers decided that they had a queer in their midst. While I sported no green carnation nor displayed any stereotypical effeminacy, my unconcealed favouritism towards these pretty creatures was reed upon in various ways. But it never provoked any confrontation or hostility; I considered my schoolmates too purblind and insipid for controversy of that kind. I was never bullied or physically attacked; there were innuendoes and scandalmongering behind my back and, on the one occasion when the libellous "Wanger wears lipstick and goes to the Gazelle" was chalked on the blackboard in the prefects' room, it was more lampoon than indictment, the authors laughing it off rather than believing it.

That first school trip to Spain: I contrived to share a bunk bed with one boy and on the coach to Switzerland the following Easter I coerced Stephen Steadley to sit next to me all the way from Ostend to Lucerne and play the game of groping his privates every hour on the hour. But the night I invited Martin Willis to come and listen to records when my parents were out, when I fancied that all my endeavours were about to come to fruition, was a seduction disaster. I put my arm around his shoulders, told him I loved him and asked if I could kiss him – sweet syllables which scared the hell out of him. He said he felt sick, poor beleaguered boy and he jumped up, bolted to the back door and threw up in the yard.

Malcolm, the son of my father's friend, was a year older than I and this focus of my teenage infatuation on an older boy was unwonted but bore no less intensity. I stayed for besotted weekends at Malcolm's, (though I can't now remember sharing a bed with him). What I do remember vividly is that he had a wonderful smell about him. It drove me crazy. Was it perfume? On a boy? Surely not. A certain soap? I didn't find out, but I somehow managed to get one of his pullovers to wear and I made off with it and hid at the bottom of my bedroom drawer and spent the next few weeks surreptitiously sniffing it – which I now suppose gave me a sexual thrill – until it faded.

Cousin Paul: the shiniest star, the Sirius among in the firmament of boys. Paul lived with his widowed mother in Kent and my Auntie Vera took me to stay there one summer holiday. Oh Paul, you hero: athlete, footballer, swimmer, cricketer and all round handsome juvenile beefcake, everything I aspired to be, but couldn't and I worshipped him and envied him until it hurt. The only recompense that assuaged the agony of having to desire my cousin from a distance, was that Paul liked nothing better than to come to my bed in the mornings, jump between the sheets and find out if I had the one thing he himself didn't have yet – a morning erection. Of course I did and Paul found it amusing and fascinating and grabbed hold of it. Bliss. A handful of boys, at least one heavy crush and probably a few more adolescent fumblings I couldn't remember, that, alas, was the extent of my homoerotic life so far. So what was I supposed to do? Ignore, pretend I didn't find boys attractive, resist looking at them? Why were boys invented, if not to gratify me? I wrestled with these questions in bed at masturbation time, the time when I had the space to reflect on the sexual shadows, the sinfully tingling dark waters I was now treading. How did I intuitively know it was considered amiss to find boys sexually attractive? Why do young people anyway automatically hide their incipient sexual impulses and gay young people doubly so and feel disapprobation is inevitable? God should not have made boys desirable. Society's condemnation of boy's love for boy was mighty hypocritical, it was also intrusive and sanctimonious. My teenage mind thought a moral code which tolerated war, famine, political corruption, exploitation of the poor and pollution was hopelessly inane, that killing a thousand people a year with motor cars was accepted, but that falling in love with Ganymede was deemed perverted – what a topsy-turvey planet.

Once again, I renewed become my daily pledge: to make a career of my adoration of male beauty and to be noble and fine in its pursuit. I'd already dedicated myself to Oscar Wilde's credo (I read him all and early), like some enthused oblate: that life should be lived entirely for pleasure and combining both those pursuits was my recipe for success. Pleasure was boys, boys pleasure. I was going to be a boy-worshipping cybarite and if society had any objections, it was too bad and society would have a rebel on its hands, a rebel with a cause. Never, never was I going to 'admit' to being queer, as though I were owning up to a crime. (There would be other crimes for that.) *People don't have to 'admit' to being normal, do they?* Never was living a gay life going to be 'flaunting it' as the newspapers like to put it. I would never 'defend' myself because I would have nothing to defend.

Then, when the afternoon thrills and delusions were over and it was time for tea, there was the sulky walk home and the petulant kicking at the stones and clumps of grass which rolled away and carried my dreams with them. *Boys! How I love boys!* My eyes glazed over with the despair of being the only virgin in the world; I felt resentment that everybody else but me was having sex and my face contorted at the possibility that I'd never lie with a naked boy. I could feel my brain about to burst open at any minute. I wanted to holler to the workmen, but they wouldn't hear me over their raucous machines and wouldn't understand if they did and what could they do? Nobody could help. 'I'm a virgin,' I said aloud to no-one, relieved that there was no-one to hear my shameful admission, 'and that is not fashionable any more.' I must do something. I must speak to Neville Ladderbanks...

The tableau as it were deliquesced and he returned to the present and wresting a long 'Aaah' from deep within, he sank back fatigued in a heap of sighs and sardonic laughter, the laughter coming from the little joke he told himself: that boy wasn't standing on the burning deck, he was lying in the burning grass, ha ha. Stretched out in that field, that real field, as a boy, a real boy; memory, the scorching heat and smothering ennui made the two or three weeks an eternity; they should have been halcyon nonetheless, just like Michael's, but he remembers only being deluged by an existential sense, a nullity, knowing he would never have what he wanted and he remembers the whisper, when something told him that he wasn't just different from the rest, but different from the different rest and that his destiny lay in a freakish and defragmented life.

****

He closed down the Journal and the novel; more health worries stole upon him unawares. The problem with his gums, he supposed, had grown concurrently with the years that went by without his going near a dentist, years spent blithely assuming that his dental health was in good order. He managed to find a NHS dentist (they were a rare breed then) and round the corner in Bleakridge too, who advised him to see a specialist, but he declined the invitation because he couldn't possibly afford private fees (how he hated having to say it) and he left the surgery with the resigned acceptance that his mouth was going the way as the rest of his body. His seborrhoea was a decades-long ailment he'd come to tolerate with indifference, like his alcoholism and he was blasé about the daily snowfalls of dry scalp flakes from his head. He used prescription scalp lotions and antiseptic and coconut shampoos but their efficacy, like his erections, was variable. His alcoholism, his stroke, his tinnitus, his gums, his seborrhoea, now his penile dysfunction – more broken threads.

****

When he'd finished a full day's editing the manuscript, he dared to think he could finish the book, then find an agent, who would then find a publisher and then... But no, who was

51

he fooling? Of a sudden, it was no use, sexual fantasy and reality, longings and self-delusion, fact and fiction, he could never make a distinction between them and was ever liberal with the truth both in life and in his writing and he was baffled.

What is truth and what is fable,
Where is youth and who is Abel?

He had to think again yet again. He'd have to dispense with that prelapsarian hero in Katie Beans field, that boy who hadn't yet been tainted, nor had tainted others and dispense too with the indispensable straight Denzel, kill them both off. He needed new hooks; his Great Idea of a protagonist lying postcoitally with the heterosexual Denzel and recounting the story of his life to the boy, Casanova-like, was nothing short of trite. In other words, telling *his* story through a character's lips and to a steaming naked youth at that, no, it was a preposterous and unreadable scenario and plot.

And what a tortuous and labyrinthine *modus operandi* that was: writing a book about writing a book! Why had he attempted this literary device? Why not tell it simply? Why? Because it was all part of hiding, there had to be the frills and furbelows and the smokescreen of fiction, if not for dramatic effect, then at least to stave off public exposure, so that people wouldn't know it was he, wouldn't know his disgrace.

****

The high sun glared down into the computer room, the blue panel of sky where it hung was strafed with only a few cirrus wisps; it was an afternoon that reminded him of the one when he saw the baseball-capped boy topless, the same boy he'd spotted only days after he moved into his new flat, the same boy who stopped his breath and scalded his eyes.

His new flat. It wasn't *his*, it was a housing association property in the 'village', the urban village of Jamage, which lay a whisker's breadth north of Trenton in the neighbouring borough of Lyme. As a boy, brought up in Turnhurst, the most northerly of Trenton's six towns a mile away, he and his playmates knew nothing of Jamage apart from its name, it was a mystery place, you never went, you knew nobody who lived there, up on top of the hill, beyond the vast expanse of Bradhill Wood on the escarpment, somewhere over the main London to Mancester railway line, the Trent and Mersey canal and the high road on the very top, the bus went there but no-one got on it. That was all anyone ever knew of Jamage, there, down in Turnhurst. And it was, until residential sprawl extended around it, a village indeed but now only a villagey core remained: the Co-op and post office, Chinese and kebab takeaways, four pubs, off licence, church, surgery, school, village hall, two farmyards and funeral parlour were all in a walking distance of each other, but that cluster was surrounded by roads, avenues and crescents of red brick semi and detached houses and bungalows and a few blocks of flats, some patioed and dormer-windowed and drivewayed in nouveau riche aspiration, with their gardens front and back and pocket handkerchief lawns and satellite dishes and trappings of monotonous mediocre, boxed urban, late 20th century living. A few of the original village properties, a couple of terraced rows and a handful of pre-Second World War houses showed, with their outer walls held upright by iron clamps and rods, that parts of Jamage stood on coal seams, now long unworked and were still under the threat of the subsidence which had been a hazard all over this northern part of the county since the need for mining began.

The boy in the check baseball cap, that champagne and chateaubriand boy (he'd called someone that before), who smiled all the time with the smile of impeccable youth, was a product and native of the modern, expanded Jamage village. To see him was maddening, walking sometimes with a girl, engrossed by her and never looking in at him while he was sitting or hobbling around, despite his livingroom bay window being easily large enough to give anyone outside an ample view inside, never once catching him looking at him; their eyes hadn't met, he walked by indifferently, for all Roly knew the boy was completely unaware of his existence. Seeing him out there and oblivious, he wished for that power you sometimes have when you watch a person who isn't looking at you and that person intuits that you are looking at him and turns round to meet your gaze, as though you made him do it. It was a common enough phenomenon and could occur both when you want it and when not and can produce either pleasant or unpleasant results, but in this case Roly couldn't invoke it, sadly his boy magnet no longer appeared to work. 'Turandot,' he thought aloud, when he passed by. '*Nella tua fredda stanza.* He's like Turandot, unapproachable and unapproaching in his beauty.' Yet so captivating in his entirety.

The discrete cap was always on his head and he noticed something else, a thick dark gilt and black collar strung tightly about his neck; it gave him the look of a dauphin, or at least a dandy. The face under the cap became a familiar sight in a short time; it was pretty, the features were soft but for the line of the jaw, which was particularly stern in one so young and heralded future rugged handsomeness. There was the merest show of black hair beneath the rim of the cap which gave Roly relief – at least the boy had some and wasn't cropped nearly bald as per the current hideous fashion. Broad shoulders sat above his princely torso, he didn't slouch, his gait was rather majestic in fact; Roly never saw him expectorate (a more than usual widespread practice hereabouts – every time he caught a glimpse of a local teenager walking by, it seemed he would spit as if on cue; it was like watching footballers) and he never saw a cigarette in his mouth or a mobile phone to his ear. His form, the cap and the choker all made up his conspicuousness whereas his clothes, though clean and fresh, conformed as was expected to the monotonous adolescent code – teeshirt, tracksuit bottoms and trainers; every boy of 15, which is what Roly estimated he must be, dressed the same, wore them everywhere.

Then came the topless show, the wait wasn't long, the weather was in his favour – oh joy! and praise be for sunshine and heat and shirtless boys. He drove out to go shopping and suddenly there he was ahead of him, running across the roundabout at the end of the road, the sun on him, the signature cap on his head and nothing on his upper body save for the choker. There was just time to take him in, an ectomorph in his pomp he was, svelt and yes, what a bonus, what a surprise – there they were, the incipient pectorals! Hanging in succulent relief above the flat of his abdomen, a contour of shadow under them, a Line of Beauty... was he a swimmer or perhaps a novice weightlifter? He felt the pang of yearning for a fetish he'd long nursed, how he envied them and those who sported them, how many times he'd ached to cup a handful of solid chest muscle, an attribute none of his many bedfellows had possessed. He felt dizzy and drunk; he tried to stem his yearning with the sobering thought that no doubt the image, as with all images, wouldn't bear out reality: the boy probably swore like a footballer, drank cider by the litre bottle, smoked like a steam engine and snorted crystal meth or whatever it was and most asssuredly had regular sex with that girl but, hey-ho, as the man said, we all have our illusions and all he asked was that he be allowed to pursue them. And then he had to return his concentration to the road ahead and leave the boy to run where he would.

A boy's will is the wind's will,

And the thoughts of youth are long, long thoughts.

He returned home with images of a body he'd never touch drilling and cramming his brain and that frustration soon induced thoughts of his pet hate – his penury – and he pondered it yet again and that in turn started him off, hectoring and raging against the injustice of it. He was floundering in the loathsome mire of poverty, but why should poverty make him unhappy? 'When you're down, the worst thing anyone can tell you to try to help is that there's always someone worse off than you,' a friend once told him. How true! *He had no shoes to wear and that made him miserable and then he saw a man who had no feet and he was thankful* – what rubbish! So revenge was called for and the only way to get that, now that venting his wrath on a willing young arse was out of the question, was to do something defiant with money, to be reckless as he'd not been for so long. He reached for a credit card, picked up the phone and, *nolen volens* and to hell with deprivation, he ordered something he'd wanted for a long time and was damned well going to get – a handmade mechanical regulator from a clockmaker's website. He'd spotted one a while ago, a German model, in a walnut case, with a dial of Roman numerals and a Westminster chime, rather elegantly simple, no Tompion admittedly, but he'd pretend it was a piece worthy of the attention of *Antiques Roadshow* experts and one which would grace the wall of any country house. It would certainly grace his flat.

This misery was compounded when he couldn't find any work, when his tireless search for editing and proofreading commissions and his half-cocked attempts at writing for profit produced no dividends. Didn't they know he was once a Fleet Street sub-editor? *Let there be work, give me some work and I will do good with the money I earn.* This was proof that the universe hadn't been running as it should, not for five years, the last time he'd had regular work. Other people should be poor, not he, not this late, not now when he should be living off the fruits of toil, off accumulated profit, when he should have the means to live the life he was destined to live and not be forced to suffer in this continued morbid state of underbred pride. When he was really down, feeling truly hard-done by, as he'd now talked himself into being, he would turn to a deprived upbringing by impoverished parents for support, but when he remembered his collection of beloved Dinky toys, his train set, his smart bicycle, a playroom of his own no less!... remembered daddy bringing home an unlimited supply of stationery for him, how he loved his paper and pens!... remembered fields, parks, Bradhill Wood and the glorious Peak District on his doorstep, remembered the enviable grammar school education and the free university education after it, remembered the holidays in Blackpool and Bournemouth and Kent to meet cousin Paul and schooltrips in the Lakes and Middlesex and Spain and Switzerland and remembered the Mini Minor they bought him – when he remembered and reflected on all that, he had to acknowledge that relatively little had been denied him and so there was no support for a theory of deprivation at all and that only frustrated and confused him the more and made him ask again why he wasn't now living in that Queen Anne rectory he yearned for – why not was a mystery. There was none of that, the Roly Hunter demesne was a housing association flat in urban Trenton and yes, he had squandered much, but he wasn't alone in that; there were countless profligates before him he could think of who had contrived to live in elegance and luxury, so why not he? And if that was not to be, why wasn't he a man who could learn to be happy living on little? But he couldn't, he scorned the Franciscan credo which claimed that the less we have materially, the more we have spiritually and the Buddhist one too, which would have it that the way to be happy was to not want anything. The worst thing about the poor was their poor aspirations; he preferred the view that aesthetic standards could only be maintained by buying fine things even if it meant wantonness; it wasn't a preoccupation with the material things he couldn't and didn't have that fed his melancholic anger so much as what he *could* have had (the crystal, the Sheffield cutlery, the Wedgwood and a piano again... he added to the list all the time). The notion of a life of self-denial had been anathema to him from the start, without his knowing it; his oxygen was excess, he must 'fling roses, roses riotously with the throng'. But how had he ever been able to attain even a paltry taste of such hedonism? – only now, in these final brooding days, did he know the answer and the answer had been by beggary and theft. His taste for extravagance could, he supposed, be traced back to when he was a student when, away from the economic apron strings of home for the first time in his life, he had a degree of autonomy over his spending. But he combined indulgence with prodigality from the outset and that was his undoing; he remembered receiving the cheque for his first term grant and spending almost all of it in a men's boutique on Ealing Broadway in the space of an hour. He knew he was spending nearly all he had, but he wasn't frightened, he had to have that leather jacket, those trousers, the shirts.

Later, in times of plenty, his enjoyment of paying the price of quality, paying over the odds as it were in an effort to achieve individuality, continued, because where he could he would go for the bespoke, the custom-made rather than the mass-produced, what were mystifyingly called 'designer' goods and which were naturally the more expensive. Now he was a poor man, but aesthetic tastes neither waxed nor waned with the vicissitudes of income. He refused to allow the financial strictures he would undoubtedly suffer as a consequence of the purchase of a wall clock to blight his relish; money wasn't, must never be, the metewand of the price of beauty. He had to concede, however, that this instance of indulgence was in part a consolation for his disability, as well as an exercise in the tasting of unadulterated pleasure. Oh dear, this Schopenhaurean philosophy was a seedling bed, black flowers flourished in it and he'd better stop cultivating it. Besides, he now decided, the curse of being penniless was so acute and chronic, it evoked an indifference, a kind of *nonsenselessness* where the presence or absence of money was irrelevant to whether or not and how he continued his everyday existence.

At that moment, Jason appeared to him – where on earth did *he* come from? A meagre consoling memory of a triumph this, a straw to be clutched and he thought once more how everything connects: Michael, virgins, straight boys, straight but not sure, straight until shown different, straight but negotiable, Murdoch and Harry, ham-flavoured crisps and – when gay life was gayer than it was now – Jason on the Riviera that summer. Everything connects... but then breaks... breaks into loose ends. He was unable to resist going to his Journal again.

...hard to think that this time two weeks ago I was in the middle of a wild romp in an hotel room in Cap d'Agde with a groovy straight boy from Essex. A cornucopia: two weeks of sunshine, excellent food, fine wine, beach boys and... two days of taking a straight cherry, a sensational and memorable seduction. I must write down every detail of it here now while it's fresh in my mind – not that I think I shall ever forget it or him. His name was Jason and it started in the early morning at Gatwick Airport... with the two young men coming up to him and Harry and asking what checking in was. They were on their first trip abroad and their first ever flight and Roly pointed to where they had to go and as his eyes followed the blond one's pert receding bottom, Harry nudged him in the ribs: 'Hands off Joyce, butch jail bait'. To Harry's surprise and Roly's delight, when they boarded their plane, the boys called out to them; they were travelling to the same place. Two days later, they were sitting under the canopy in a quayside brasserie with their pre-lunch aperitifs when they heard 'Hiya!' and looked up to see both boys standing over them and without hesitation Roly invited them to join their table and they sat and swopped proper introductions. They were brothers, Jason, the fetching blond one and Wayne, also blond but less fetching and they worked together in Braintree as warehouse packers. Roly's eyes were firmly on Jason's laden white shorts and the scanty teeshirt through which his nipples poked in relief. He was model-in-a-glossy-magazine cute with a fulsome head of hair and Roly was relieved to see that he hadn't yet succumbed to the new teenage fad for tattoos although he had nodded to it with his gold earring. His effervescent Essex twang was sexy. 'Red alert, Martha,' was Roly's aside to Harry, 'about midnight tonight.' 'Not a chance Joyce,' Harry whispered back. 'Straight if ever I saw it.' 'Jeremiah,' he hissed back and continued to feast on Jason, sprawled in his chair, legs apart showing off the wares between them and pushing his shoulders out when he spoke. 'Imagine that young, supple body going taut and trying to resist when his rectum feels the piston push of my rigid cock inside it,' Roly whispered to Harry behind his paper, making him splutter into his beer. 'You merciless queen,' he rasped. They wanted to know if Roly and Harry had 'scored' yet and when Roly pointed out that hunting for girls wasn't their thing and affirmed, 'Yes, I'm gay' and added, 'Oh and so is Harry here' and sat back with a smug smile that challenged any possible forthcoming hostile comment, Harry, whose seduction technique didn't include shock tactics, prickled. 'Far out,' Jason said. 'As long as we don't shove it down your throat, eh?' Roly smirked. 'Live and let live and all that,' Wayne said. 'That's very kind of you,' Roly replied, with light irony. Wayne ventured gingerly, 'Are you two - you know?' 'Know what?' Could the boy bring himself to say the words? 'You know – together?' 'We're footloose,' Harry chimed in. 'Dunno if you can help,' Jason began and the two brothers came to the real reason they'd stopped to talk: the nightclub they went into on their first night ripped them off 10 pounds' entrance fee and a pound a time for a beer and they'd brought only 50 pounds a piece with them for a two-week package holiday, so just two days into their holiday, they were broke. Jason quickly pointed out that he had money in his Braintree bank account and wanted to know how could he get at it. Roly saw his chance and jumped in; he immediately offered to take the boy to a Credit Lyonnais bank. 'Don't worry, dear,' he said aside to Harry. 'I'll bring him back.' 'In how many ravaged pieces I wonder?' Harry whispered back. On the way, Jason asked, 'How long you been a left footer then?' 'It dawned on me when I looked at Martin Willis's arse at school and I fell in love with it and with him. But it dawned on God before he got up one morning, I suppose, and he gave his genetic engineers instructions about me while I was still incubating.' 'There sure is some cracking crumpet here.' Jason's head swivelled from side to side and front and back as dozens of female bodies in their various skimpy swim suits passed by. 'And some of the girls are quite tasty too, are they?' 'Funny guy,' he laughed. They went into the first bank they found and Roly, fooling himself that his A-level French was still *courant*, explained the problem to the young clerk behind the counter and understood hardly a word of the torrented reply, but heard sufficient to gather that the bank could do nothing to help. They slinked away but outside, Roly had a brainwave and he would swear to his last day that he had not the least thought of repayment in kind. He told Jason to wait and went back inside where he cashed a cheque of his own for two hundred pounds. Outside again, to Jason's utter consternation, he pressed the francs into his hand making him promise on his grandmother's name that he'd send him or bring him the money when they were back home. 'Why you doing this?' The boy's relief and gratitude were unconfined. 'Tell me where you work and I'll come round personally with the bread,' he said. Roly dismissed the consequences with his bank manager – yet another of his wantonly cashed cheques adding to his already overdrawn overdraft if the boy didn't keep his promise – and they went back to Harry and Wayne, who was as effusive in his gratitude as Jason, while Harry was flabbergasted that Roly may have laid himself open to a con trick, but saved that remonstrance until they were in private when Roly was to dismiss it with a carefree, 'If that happens, dear, it will be just deserts' and a smile. They prepared to go for lunch and Roly told the brothers to look them up in their hotel if they had any more difficulties and gave them their room numbers. 'You can ask for Hunter or Manifold.' He couldn't resist a taunting pay-off, 'If you're brave enough,' and he and Harry left them, wondering if the pair would spend the rest of the holiday avoiding them.

So he was pleasantly surprised, later that afternoon, as he was taking an alcohol and heat-induced siesta and reading a porn novel, when there was a knock on his door and, at his call, Jason walked in. 'Well hello, darling boy,' he put the book down on the bed careful to leave its cover with the picture of two naked boys in a clinch on view. 'Hiya,' Jason said, still in his shorts and teeshirt, very appealing and he sat in a whicker chair, legs spreadeagled and Roly beamed at him as mischievously as he could. *If he doesn't close his legs...* Jason caught sight of the book and picked it up. 'Porn eh? You been having a Barclays?' 'A what?' 'The porn, a Barclays Bank, wank.' 'Oh, that's a new one. Yes, well, I... I was about to but you've rudely interrupted me. Would you oblige me?' 'Geddout,' he snarled with a smile and threw the book down. 'How d'you get off on that?' 'Shall I show you?' 'You're a weirdo.' He was laughing. 'So what can I do for you?' 'Where's your mate?' 'Sleeping lunch off, I think. Is he the one you've come to see?' 'What are you, then, the giver or the taker?' 'That's a very personal question,' Roly said, pretending to be outraged. 'Would you like to find out?' 'I thought you were a nice bloke.' 'I am, but probably not the way you think of as nice.' He looked at Roly quizzically. 'You fancy me, right?' he asked. 'Too right I do, you stunner.' 'And your friend?' 'Oh, he has good taste too, but I don't think you quite meet his – no offence.' 'But I'm not – you know – gay.' 'Well quelle surprise mon cher! Labels are so convenient aren't they?' The sardonic tone went unheeded. 'If you see a beautiful woman and you find out that woman is a dyke, does it mean she immediately stops being beautiful? Yes, you're straight but that doesn't stop you being pleasing to a gay man's eye. Are you with me? If a gay man fancies you, it doesn't mean that you've suddenly become unattractive to women or turned into a nancy boy. Your masculinity remains safe.' He told him to pour them both a drink. 'Whisky no ice please.' 'Yes, you're an attractive boy,' he said, taking the glass from him, 'and yes I think I could show you a thing or two... your being straight adds to the challenge, straight is a big turn-on for us gays, you know, we like to think we can show them what real sex is, especially when they sit with their legs open like yours are now.' Jason looked down at himself and didn't close his legs. 'Yeah, but if a straight guy does it, he has to be an iron all along and don't know it, right?' 'Labels again... are they straight, are they a bit gay, are they bi? Sometimes I wonder if there's any difference and you have no idea how many of them can be persuaded.' Neither did he, but it was a fine thing to fantasise about. 'Geddout,' Jason said, unbelieving. Then, after a slurp of his drink: 'So you never been straight, never been with a woman?' 'Let's get one thing straight, I never have been. I can't even think straight. I 'go' with my own sex. I never found a woman with the right equipment, you see, it was always the problem.' 'Why do you keep saying boys?' 'Oh, don't worry, boys means young men in my book, not schoolkids in short trousers, I assure you. It's just that boy is a sexier word. Any road up,' he said in mockney to mock, 'as it doesn't look like I'm not going to get into your temptingly tight shorts, it's time I moved. I shall have a shower, get some dinner and spend the evening swooning at the boys of the town and you are going to get very drunk trying to 'score',

no doubt. If you don't have any luck and you'd like to find out
what a proper rogering feels like, Harry and I will be back
about midnight.' And he dismissed him with a leering smile
and a friendly pat on his bottom. He could get away with it,
he was unlikely to run into him again until he was back in
London and if at all then, should he turn out to be a wrong
'un over his money, which was always a possibility. Over
dinner with Harry, Roly with more wine-fuelled courage,
flirted with their waiter and the waiter flirted back and told
them his name was Jean; odours of cooking and Balmain
cologne wafted from him. 'So you think he'd give it a twirl?'
Harry asked. 'Who? Oh Jason? Yes dear, packers from
Essex are lucky for me, doncha know.' 'You say that with – '
'– Alcoholic rodomontade.' 'It could screw him up.' 'A
felicitous phrase Harriet! I'd love to think I could... screw
him... up.' He grinned gloatingly. 'I think he's a boy curiosity
could quite easily get the better of,' he added confidingly.
'With some low lights, whisky and a following wind.' They
summoned Jean to bring the bill, Roly asked to borrow his
pen and as he counted out his francs, he scribbled their
names and hotel room on the back of the bill and wished him
'bonne nuit' with a knowing wink.

It was one o'clock when the knock came but it wasn't Jean.
Roly opened the door to find Jason hanging on to the jamb.
'Quite, but not hopelessly, drunk I see,' he smiled. 'Ah well
it's a normal state for a boy who's failed to find c-, or in your
case pussy,' he said. 'Haven't you got a shag yourself, then?'
came the slurred question back. 'Ha-ha.' 'Can I have a
drink?' He staggered in and fell on the bed. 'Christ, couldn't
even score a dog tonight,' he groused. 'Not fair.' He fell
morosely quiet and Roly thought he'd passed out but he
suddenly raised his head. 'About what you said...' 'And what
did I say?' 'Well...about...y'know.' He took a breath. 'D'you

still want to do me?' 'You ought to know better. I would never say I "want to do you". Kindly don't cocktease. Have your drink and go or crash out on that other bed.' 'Not in yours? Ain't that the deal?' 'I didn't know we'd struck a deal.' 'Well I'm randy.' He gulped his drink and thought for a while. 'You're not a bad-looking geezer, ya know.' 'Heavens to Betsy, you *must* be pissed.' 'Look at it this way: I couldn't find myself a bird so I've settled for you, ain't I?' 'That's the nicest thing anyone's ever said to me.' 'I know what I'm saying, don't you worry.' Did he? Roly dared to think that he really wasn't joking all that much, but then he told himself he was too drunk and, oh my, Harworthy and Pat and Gerry came flooding back. It was time to find out; Jason would either punch him in the face or run off, he didn't care and he sprang up and went to him and grabbed his head and planted a kiss smack on his mouth and Jason pulled away and stared in disbelief. Then he made Roly stare equally incredulously: 'Hey that wasn't so bad,' he said, smiling impishly, 'but you need a shave.' Roly composed himself and looked him over as though sizing him up for a suit. 'Look at you, a prime fillet, a chateaubriand, fabulously good-looking, bedroom eyes, fine body, great from behind and with pezazz at the front, so what ails you, alone and palely loitering?' 'Poet are you?' With his face right up to his, Roly whispered, 'Don't be afraid of liking it. I've already forgiven you for having green eyes. I'm praying you haven't got a hairy chest. Please tell me you haven't got a hairy chest.' 'What's it like, anyway?' 'What's what like?' 'Having sex with another man?' 'O-ooh, just as good as having it with the man before him usually.' 'Just thought… my bloody brother.' 'Ah, yes, there's always something isn't there? A girl, or a brother. Where is he?' 'Don't know, lost him in the crowd. But if I'm not back, he'll – ' 'He'll what? Come looking for you?' 'I don't

66

think I'll be much good at it, you know... in bed, I mean... with a man.' 'That's all right, you can turn over and we'll go to sleep, back to back, like spoons.' 'You'll have to show me what to do, that's if you still want it.' 'Oh, Jason, you're very sweet, but I wish you'd stop teasing, you're giving me one helluva penile ache.' Jason opened his legs and stroked his crotch, looking like a touting tart, giving Roly a drunken glad eye. 'That's a very big come-on,' he admonished. 'Have a care.' He thought, hey-ho to the wind with prudence and I'll see how far this sodden creature can go and pulled the teeshirt over his head, yanked him to his feet, undid the belt on his slacks, zipped them down and peeled them off his legs as Jason supported himself on his shoulders. Stripped to his briefs, he stood looking down at him, his arms hanging loosely at his side and Roly let out a guttural 'Haaaaaa, lovely in tight Stripes, an enticing and mysterious parcel of genital delights. You look like a whoring barbary pirate.' 'You gay boys give the best beejays don't you?' he asked. 'Where did you hear that one?' 'You going to or not?' 'Not if you demand it like that I won't,' he said, leaning over to switch off the lamp. 'In the sack, I'm the team leader' and with that Jason felt for the first time in his young life the weight of a man on top of him, kissing him while Roly thought of previous first-time boys and how history repeats and laughed and asked himself, why do straight boys do this? 'Come to my arms, my beamish boy,' he said, pulling his only slightly recalcitrant body tightly to him, 'callooh callay. You'll be fine, don't fight it, think of Samantha Fox or Linda Lusardi.' 'I feel like a woman,' he cried. 'That you most certainly are not,' Roly told him before he kissed him again and positioned himself ready to enter Babylon.

'Here, get me more whisky, boy,' Roly said half an hour later, 'and whatever you want and then, if you're staying the night as you say, I think we'll do something you can tell your grandchildren about.' 'Oh yeah?' They had more to drink, then more, which they carried out naked to the verandah, inhibition thrown to the French night breeze and, as Roly was 'bending your sweet little Essex tush over this balcony rail and swiving you from here to Morocco,' he heard what he was sure were sounds of passionate coupling from close by and looked around and when he focused, he could make out, in the black corner of the next balcony, a pair of bare buttocks, thrusting up and down between a pair of raised legs on a lilo to the accompaniment of much grunting. The buttocks, he assumed, were Harry's. Who the legs belonged

to, he had no idea. 'Harry?' he called. 'Are those your bouncing prats?' 'In the back way you might say,' Harry's voice replied, 'if you don't mind.' 'And whose are the hoisted legs may I ask?' 'Waiter.' Roly roared with laughter. 'Vive la meme chose!' 'Oh mais oui and laissez-faire and crêpes suzettes!' Harry shouted back. The live porn show renewed Roly's ardour and he turned back to Jason's bent body and, not caring if they were on view to anyone who might choose to look, rammed into his al fresco buttocks in a frenzied transport of passion. 'Cast your seed upon French soil, straight boy, and there'll be another corner of a foreign field that's forever England!' he bellowed.

During the remainder of the holiday, the two twosomes saw each other about the town and shared a beer in a bar together, when Jason showed an edginess that said he hadn't told his brother about his adventures and that he was fearful of either Roly or Harry making a faux pas, but they both respected his needs and kept quiet. Then, one day, they were gone and Harry and Roly sat soaking themselves with whisky and reminiscence on whichever balcony it was, as an engorged, orange balloon of a sun sank slowly through grey-and-gold tinged belts of cirrostratus into a calm sea. The warmth of the evening caressed them and cicadas sang clickety-click in French. Roly's blurred vision slid from sea to sun,

'Ensanguining the skies, how heavily it dies, into the west away;
Past touch and sight and sound, not further to be found
How hopeless underground
Falls the remorseless day', he chanted absently.

Harry was philosophical and sozzled. 'That was your second virgin, dear. At least that I know to and it's me you have to thank for both of them. Well, not really. I meant I must be some sort of vestal talisman for you.' 'Actually, I think he was the fourth. Adam and Bangkok were the unawakened gay ones. This one... what do you think? Did it for the hell of it? He certainly threw himself in with gusto. I think the poor sod felt he was the chosen one, for a while. You know. The target of adulation.' 'He's probably never been so idolised before and the fact that the adulation was coming from a man made no difference. He felt wanted and that softened any antagonism he may have nurtured beforehand.' 'Are you a psychologist?' 'Viennese school. 1894.' 'His emotions seemed sincere. The sex could have been the action of a drunken, slightly reckless straight boy agreeing to it because his dick got the better of him one night, because it was a wild, unthinkable dare to set himself. Quite clearly, it wasn't the money. He'd had that before the sex. But he wanted seconds, that's what amazed me.' 'And thirds, if you're to be believed.' 'From proclaiming his hetero – his heteroseckshality 24 hours before...' 'Hetroflexibul.' 'What was that?' 'Het-ero-flex-ible, he ain't hetroseckshul, he's hetroflexibul.' Harry was giggling helplessly. 'Geddit? I just invented that, I'm such a clever bijou little Berkeley Hunt ya know.' Roly was laughing and spluttering also now. 'Well,' finally managing words. 'He definitely crossed the Rubicon didn't he? Discovered something in himself he didn't know about. 'Til he met me. Extraordinary.' 'He discovered that he liked it up him, is the simple explanation, Joyce. I wish I could pick up boys like you, old chum.' 'Boys like me?' 'I mean I wish I could pick up boys like you pick up boys, you frigging pedant!' 'Whadyoomean? You had the waiter boy. He was peachy. Very nice little chunky compact economy size number as I remember, with eyes like crystal and very deep sockets. And I didn't "pick up". I see-DUCED him. Just like I ar – seduced Pat the docker and Gerry the art student. In that order and only a week apart. Don't remember whether I did arse Pat, though, come to think of it, or Gerry for that matter. I was legless at the time. I don't want to make false claims. Oh, I don't know. I'm pretty sure I penetrated Gerry, if only momentarily and he certainly –' 'Joyce, enough!' Harry yelled. 'Pat was a drunken fluke and a giggle, Gerry was a fluke and a mistake. Jason was a – he was the full serendipity, can someone be a serendipity?' 'Flukes and serendipity are very common occurrences, Roly, my dear old petal. That's not to disp – dips –arage them (Harry was likewise). The thing about Jason is, was, his arse wanted dick and what d'ya know? There you were, right on cue. It's all quite simple, old flowerpot. It's so simple that it's unfathom-abubble. Aristotle, three hundred and 85 BC.' His flourishing hand forgot it was holding a full glass of gin and tonic and he drenched himself. 'Oh, testicles,' he simpered. Roly ignored his discomfort. 'It scares me.' 'What does?' he asked, absently, lying down and helping himself to more gin. 'Sexual success. I feel there's some catastrophe on the way, because I don't deserve it and have to pay for it afterwards. I must have broken hearts and cheated, but I don't feel any qualms along the way, not a single one. Every pretty young man, my cock goes zing. I'm a sex schemer, amorous and sly. I'm constantly boy-hungry and I can't help it but you know what?' 'What, lover boy?' 'I'm promiscuous for the wrong reason. It's astonishing.' 'Really.' 'Yes. It's as though I try the goods on approval and haven't found any I like enough to keep. Yes, that's it. Novelty is too new for me. The instant appeal, too strong to fight, too easy to discard, the instant appeal lost its instancy. What was it Marlowe wrote? Well, it wasn't true. That moment when your breath is taken away, all-consuming but ephemeral. No, constancy, continued loyalty to the object of adoration requires a stamina I don't possess. I can't handle the ontology of familiarisation.' He was quiet for a spell. 'Then again, I'd love to have a lover.' 'I know your problem.' 'Do you?' 'Yes. I haven't told you this before but I can now. I can tell, in the pure, unabashed honesty of being pissed out of my skull and in the total candour of drink-addled friendship that –' 'What?' 'What?' 'What are you going to tell me?' 'What am I going to tell you?' 'Yes.' 'I don't know what I'm going to tell you. Tell me what I'm going to tell you then I'll tell you what it is.' 'That I don't have a sufficiently high opinion of myself to believe that when a boy starts to pledge some kind of devotion to me, as Adam did and one or two others, by the way … that's what you're going to tell me. I don't believe they know or mean what they say they're feeling. Jack was the big exception and I threw that away, like I throw everything away. I have one mother of a self-destruct button, Harry.' 'What have you thrown away, dear?' 'Everything!' 'In other words, you're a worthless shit.' 'I'm a worthless shit and don't say "No you're not".' 'I won't say "No you're not" but I will say "Have another enormous glass of whisky, pal".' 'I think I've got one.' 'Have another enormous glass of whisky then.' 'I do care, though, Harry, visage de mon coeur. Scruples.' 'Scruples? Zat the new board game?' Zit any good?' 'Scruples. I have scruples. It's just that I don't seem to apply them. I do have a heart!' 'Ssh. They'll hear you in the next room.' 'We're in the next room.' 'Are we?' 'You know, whenever I'm copulating –' ''S a very big word.' 'What is?' 'What you just said.' 'When I am, there's always a moment... when I feel him here and that's the truth.' 'What is truth and what is fable, who is Ruth and where is Mabel?' 'I love sex, you know.' 'I know. Sex is a thing we use for love, we humans don't have anything else, I'm afraid.' 'Sex is my occupation, my preoccupation and my hobby.' 'I've got hiccups.' 'Love, on the other hand. Now that's something completely different.' 'And now for something completely different.' Harry was giggling helplessly. 'But it doesn't happen.' 'What doesn't?' 'I remember a conversation with Murdoch along these very lines a while ago... When I made the poignant observation that, as a lover of Chopin, I always hoped that one day, one boy, just one, would play on my heartstrings and I would hear the maestro's music. But I am still to hear it.' 'Well bloody well tell him to play bloody louder. What are you going to do, if anything, about, about... thingummy. The brother of Wayne?' 'See him again, of course, I hope. But he did call a rather abrupt halt to things. Amicably though, I had to say.' 'Have you turned him into a full blown shirt-lifter stroke arse-bandit, d'you think? Or is he a biseckshooalist now?' 'Mmm. Yes, I suppose he is. Doesn't look like one does he? He's too tall.' They giggled more and spluttered into their drinks. 'He's found a new sort of sex. Biseckshulls scare me, you know. They have too many hang-ups. I know they can't help it, but biseckshulls are very selfish. By their nature. If they can't have one, they want the other. Or they want both. Doesn't leave anything for us, does it?' 'Don't be uncharitable, you'll catch a cold. But I think I agree with you.' 'Down with all bisikools. Have you noticed? The married ones, or the ones with girlfriends, are very happy to reveal that they go with women to their boyfriends but are shit scared as hell to tell their girls that they go with men. "Oo-oh, she'd kill me if she found out." That's bicycles for you. Are you bitter, like me, dear boy?' 'I fell for a boy once – I was crazy about him – and when he ditched me, I went to see him to try and talk to him and you know what he said? He said he didn't think a sex had been invented for him yet. And, oh yes! My beautiful Michael Condom, Condon. I'll never forget the day I rang him.' 'Why did you ring Martin Condom?' 'Because I hadn't seen him for ages, you twerp.' 'And you wanted his bottom?' 'Of course I did! And his lips and his soft, silky body... I wanted his everything...' 'What happened?' 'Some female answered the phone, that's what. I get insanely jealous when a female answers a gay boy's phone. It's like trespassers on your property. Jason will get married and have children, but he's found out that he likes sex with men, too.' 'That's a non sequitur.' 'He said, he said, "No, I don't walk down the street now looking at men. I like sex with *you*." He meant me. He said, "Shit, I dunno how you did it, but you somehow turned me on. I don't understand it."' 'What? You don't understand it or he doesn't understand it?' 'Then his problems really begin. Is he going to find a woman who understands his need for anal intercourse? That would be the ideal, but it's unlikely. So he will have to live two lives: one furtively deceiving those he loves and is responsbile for, and the other secreting his homoerotic desires and lurking in closets and corners and hiding behind the respectable semi-detached family unit. And it will all be my doing.' 'You have a very bleak view of his future. It's like a Munch landscape. Ugh!' 'He will of course have all the men he wants queuing up for his pretty little love bubble, that's the tragedy. He literally won't know which way to turn. I think I may have... hurt him.' 'I shan't console you with any reassurance to the contrary.' 'Well, if not me, somebody would quite possibly. It might be my curse, you know, to get there first... pretty boy like that.' 'Yes, they're not safe with you around dear, that's for sure,' Harry sniffed. 'And what's it matter? Screwed up or the best of all in the best of all possible worlds. Sometimes, I think the two are synonymous.' 'I hope he can look back on me as just a holiday romance, I've always wanted to be a holiday romance.' 'You sound wistful and I feel sick.'

I've been back home for four days and Jason's promised cheque has arrived together with his phone call. 'Thank you for the cheque,' I said. 'Man of your word.' He sounded sincere in his expression of gratitude again, we said nothing about the sex; I have no idea what he thinks of it now and of me and that, I know, is the the last I shall see of him.

****

While the old man reads about his long-gone sex life, the young boy seeks his future one. 'When we gonna do it then?' he asks. 'Dunno what ya mean,' the young girl answers. 'Don't be a numpty,' he sighs, exasperated. 'When am I gonna get me shag?' 'I'm not a slut, ya know.' 'Didn't say you were did I? Anyway, you done it 'aven't ya?' 'Maybe I 'ave, I'm not tellin' ya. Why, 'aven't you then?' ''Course I 'ave.' 'Oh yeah, who with, Donna?' 'Cum on, let's go round to yours, there's nobody in is there? That K's made me dead 'orny.'

The first speaker is the boy in the check baseball cap, leaning with his back against a brick wall across the carpark from Roly's window and the second the girl he is holding with

74

both arms about her waist; they are in the still clear and frank light of an early Saturday evening and Roly is watching them, dismayed. What a blow this is, his fears (not entirely unexpected, he must admit) are confirmed: the boy is cavorting with the girl, not merely walking as before and now there is no doubt that he is heterosexual. There has been more than the usual amount of noise around the place all day, it must have been something to do with the World Cup. People have thronged in the streets, raucous, seen and unseen, party cacophony blares out from some houses at the back, the pub is much noisier than usual. This isn't what upsets him: he saw the cap again and the boy and the boy walking hand in hand with the girl. They were in a group and all disappeared up the passage by the nursery and after a short while, he and she came back alone and they stopped by the wall. Roly cranes his neck, the boy now lifts the girl off the ground while he kisses her. He puts her down and then, horrors, his hand darts quite brutally to latch on to her crotch and he keeps it there and she, slattern, she doesn't so much as flinch! They carry on talking and Roly can't remember seeing such blatant flaunting; so this is modern public adolescent courtship. *O tempora, o mores.* It's barely a minute, but to Roly they seem frozen for agonising hours. Then, suddenly, the girl breaks from the squalid embrace and runs off. It takes a second for the boy to realise what has happened and react. He turns and runs after her and as he turns Roly is presented with a final torment, for there, in full show even from the distance, is the distinct outline of his erection pushing out against his shorts and Roly is decidedly chagrined. Fine, the boy is straight and he couldn't do anything about it if he weren't. Would he have felt any better if he'd seen the boy bussing a *boy* and grabbing a *boy's* crotch? No. He doesn't want him to kiss anyone; he wants to kiss him himself.

****

He comes to one of many stops. 'For torture it is,' he says aloud. 'Am I, after all, writing my memoirs, my autobiography, the badly-written history of a charlatan and loser?' Heaven forfend, not even he could fool himself that anyone, in or out of his right mind, would want to buy such a work. 'Torture,' he says again: thumbscrews, racks, Iron Maidens, dripping taps and electrodes couldn't compare with a writer's wrestling and any Torquemada, Stalin, Pol Pot or Mao would have had far less bother and could have coerced or eliminated far many more enemies and gained far more sadistic pleasure if only they'd decreed that their victims be forced to write a book. Writing was both disease and catharsis, his means of purging and scourging himself; he could expose his cupboard skeletons only behind the screen of writing. And there was the vainglorious hope of money, of yanking himself out of poverty by the pen. J K Rowling had lived on state benefits, so did he; she'd won phenomenal success by writing bestsellers, so would he.

It had been 30 years in the thinking and his risible and ironic excuse was that he'd always been too busy with journalism, too busy writing to write. And there were the other distractions: chasing boys and drinking alcohol to be precise. Time was when he would avoid as far as possible doing anything or going anywhere that didn't include those two pursuits. He knew that it had no claim to being a clever or even literary work. No memorable words or phrases would leap from his keypad; no reader would find himself eager to turn pages to see what happened next. There would be no searing eloquence or startling originality; any hint of literary competence he may have once had had been stultified by

76

that aforementioned career of writing news stories and sub-editing. There could be no favourable comparisons with any writers of renown; if some readers did perchance find themselves saying, as a compliment, 'Ah that reminds me of ...', they will have been hoodwinked and his prose will have passed the test or, if it was an accusation of copycattery, that would be entirely justified. He was a hack not a novelist, a recorder of facts not fiction and that was his intention, to record things and if in doing so, he happened to borrow from his betters, so be it. Publish and be sued, said he.

There wouldn't be even the tiniest possibility of a book at all without his Journal; it was the only memory he had now. He'd started it when his life was relatively unblemished, primordial but for the few commonplace peccadilloes of puberty and adolescence. The accumulation of those peccadilloes into the evil deeds of manhood perhaps should have put an end to it, but no, he carried on in the knowledge that its contents were privy to his mind alone. He'd made his very first entry – he remembered it distinctly to this day – on a heartbreaking night, a night when a boy let him down. Clive was his name and he befriended him, desired him and finally invited him to his digs one evening for the big seduction, when his landlady and the two fellow students he shared with were away. But Clive failed to show and he picked up a pen and some foolscap paper and recorded his very first tearful entry. He thinks he had some whisky to drink to assist the self-pitying flow.

So the Journal was born and he kept it industriously, writing near-daily entries, or twice and thrice weekly at least and there was never an intent of publication or financial gain, never the notion that he was recording history, however parochial and it certainly never occurred to him that it could be the blueprint for a novel. No, it was an automatic, almost unconscious process, perhaps merely writing practice and its purpose, if purpose there was, had never been revealed until now, when in old age it had assumed the role of an aide-memoire and one full of bitterness and regret at that; there was no dotage of wallowing in fond nostalgia for him, it was more like his *Krapp's Last Tape,* something to be despised and thrown across the room in a fit of loathing, a wallow in black. Now, he'd come to use it more and more as a concordance, a means of finding the events his memory had misplaced or, in some cases, obliterated. Even so, as a log of the contemporaneous, as history, he couldn't help distrusting its reliability. That false companion, memory! He was an old man with a poor one and, like Mark Twain, he could remember everything that never happened very clearly and where memory failed, invention sufficed. He would look back at an account of a particular occurrence, which he'd written about often on the same day or at least very soon afterwards, only to be horrified to find that what he'd written was completely at odds with what he *remembered* had happened. His recall had been ambushed from the start, even before his brain damage: memory rarely played back what it had taped, or what he thought it taped; memory wasn't a record, it was an impression, it distorted and changed times, places and events, it altered the shape of rooms and changed the colours of everything. Deceiving and deluding at best, at worst it was a downright liar. It was what he liked to think he was thinking at the time, but who knew? And who cared? He didn't know if he'd told the truth as it happened, let alone remember if it ever did. This was not intentional lying on his part. What was more, he'd come to hate writing about himself and although his Journal was about him, he didn't much care to remember the kind of person he had grown up to be. That person was someone he didn't want to know, he didn't like him, but right now, given his age and the friability of a condition which could obliterate him at any minute, it was no small exigency to ask himself, 'Who the hell am I?'; a question which needed an increasingly urgent answer as each day passed and brought his death nearer. And it was meagre comfort, probably a false notion, in the periods of sombre and oppressive melancholia, that his evil in retrospect was far worse than it had been in actuality; using the Journal as fuel for a novel, with the lamina of fiction too thin to preserve his anonymity – was he prepared to do this? If he was, then Michael had to be told first, before he told the world; Michael would be the channel through which he'd resurrect and expose and publish his shame. He'd tell Michael and only Michael (how infatuated with him he was), in a forlorn unbosoming, in the belief that the boy was his final chance to put things right, that he was finally past the point where he wished to hide his sins any longer and that he, Michael, was the one and only person in the world he could honour and burden with a full confession. Which, on reflection, was ludicrous; he was too morally weak, 'the backbone of a lugworm,' he told himself. He knew, deep down, that if he used the nescient Michael for this purpose, the boy would be completely befuddled. It was a futile hope. He couldn't tell him or anyone the truth and that was his eternal cross. He didn't fool himself, when he really thought it out, that he could achieve some kind of purgation without any cost to himself, that Michael would accept him, all warts, and carry on with him regardless. No, confession would bring destruction. He'd closeted his skeletons out of sight of Jack and Larry, if he hadn't he'd have lost them and he had no reason to suppose that he was other than condemned to do the same with Michael.

79

On second thoughts, using the Journal would at least preclude the stressful necessity of searching for inspiration to invent storylines like novelists did; he'd let both the tricks of memory and his own proclivity for lying do that for him.

****

It took him hours to regain composure after what happened, days to realise what was happening. He'd trundled himself and his trolley into the kitchen to make a mug of coffee. First of all, he had to pass through one of those moments of senility, they happened more and more, perhaps you may know them: losing or misplacing things... trying to remember if you've done what you meant to do and trying to remember if you remembered... forgetting whether you brushed your teeth half an hour ago... turning a light off when you leave a room then having to go back to check if you left the light on... switching off the cooker when you finish cooking, sitting down to your meal and getting up again to see if you remembered to switch off the cooker. He reached for the kettle, but instead of going to it, his hand went to the bread bin and while his brain told him that bread has nothing to do with making coffee, it wasn't quick enough to stop the hand and so he lifted the lid of the bin and, only then realising the error, pulled it down again. He then depressed the kettle switch. Straightaway, his eye was pulled to the digital clock on the microwave oven and he knew before he saw that the display would be showing 10.11. Eleven; it had been like this for years now and he damned all digital clocks, they were operated by sprites and trolls and caught him out every time, viced him in their paranoia-inducing grip. It had started some time ago with his noticing mere harmless coincidences, synchronicity, but coincidences had turned to blight. It was now more sinister, skullduggery of the worst kind, everytime he caught sight of digital clocks the number on it was 11 or

80

combinations of 11 and this behaviour baffled and perturbed him: it happened with the microwave – before it went ping!, if he dared to look how much time was left it was always 11 seconds, or before the oven timer went bleep! bleep! bleep!, there were always 11 minutes to go. The computer clock, his radio alarm, every time he glanced at them they showed 11-something or something-11. The 11 was bad enough; sometimes he caught the clock or timer at 11 minutes and 11 seconds and that made him rabid. Eleven and 11.11, they were plaguing him and why, if he knew beforehand what the clock would show, was he drawn to look at it? He was being stalked by clocks; at first it was a quirky amusement, then it was coincidental, then a constantly recurring and spooky thing; why was it? Eleven. When he'd brought home his new hi-fi system and unwrapped it, the first thing he noticed was the model number of the tuner – it was SP11. He plays Bookworm on his computer and it scores by levels: he plays for a while and looks at his score and – what do you know? – he's on level 11! He watches quiz shows on the television, *Mastermind* and *The Weakest Link,* for example, where a clock in the corner of the screen counts down the contestants' times and although his brain warns him not to look at the display, his eyes are compelled to turn to it and sure as salt the time the contestant has left will be 11 seconds or 1.11 or his score will be 11. And this could happen two or three times in one programme. There are those who say that once you are obsessed by a number, you'll look for it wherever you can find it. He scowled and hissed 'wormwood and gall' at the kettle, he was going mad as well as senile. As it boiled, he looked through the window and what he saw sent freezing electricity through him. On the lawn, not six feet away, a figure was bending over the terracotta pots of herbs he kept there, its pert keister stretching the blue tracksuit bottoms it was wrapped in sticking up and pointing at him invitingly. The firgure straightened and turned to look in through the window. On his head was a check baseball cap. He saw Roly and smiled and Roly thought wildly that it was the menacing smile of the juvenile urban terrorist, not *Death in Venice* but Death with Menace. It took but a moment. The boy looked away and walked off without looking back, frightened off or indifferent wasn't to be known. As far as Roly could tell, he hadn't touched or damaged the herbs, it was a horticultural stopover, intriguing, a little worrying. He thought about it, couldn't come to any conclusions, carried on making his coffee and, dazed, trundled back to his computer.

The muse had been with him from early that day as he worked on the radio monologue he was hoping to send to the BBC, words had flowed but after the kettle, the number 11, the boy in the baseball cap and the smile, fecundity withered, words were barren. There was more disarray with the knock that now came at the front door. It startled him, as all knocks, bangs, crashes, even the telephone did these days: everything was louder than it used to be, it was hyperacusis, associated, he'd been told, with the tinnitus that already afflicted him. He was anyway always apprehensive when unscheduled knocks came and he grabbed his walking stick and hobbled nervously to the door. He opened it on its chain and what he saw made him gape. 'Hiya mate,' piped a cheery voice, a boy's treble. It was check baseball cap! Here on his doorstep! Talking to him! He was smiling broadly and Roly was struck dumb, he couldn't move, couldn't react, he was pinioned, this was a thunderbolt, he smelt the scent of a boy and he smelt danger. He thought madly, the boy called him 'mate', a form of address he despised, *but that doesn't matter, not here, I forgive him his familiarity.* 'Yer flowers need waterin', they're gonna die,' the boy said, pointing at the herb pots. 'Can't ya get out to do 'em?' *Eye-yuh mate, gerrout* – solid Trenton dialect indurated with the tones and inflections peculiar to it, a foreign language to many but not to Roly, though always a distanced one and while he spoke in it he performed a little on-the-spot dance or jig to some music only he could hear, shaking his lower arms loosely and shuffling his weight from one leg to the other. His smile broadened even more, it gave him an impish look, it also showed well-kept dentition and Roly finally stammered hello and pointed out in a daze that they were herbs not flowers. 'And I'm not your mate,' he added. 'Oh. Whatever,' the boy replied, dismissive of the remonstrance. 'I'll water 'em for ya if you've got a can. *If yuh've gorra can.* 'I haven't got a can, I use a –' '– 'Ang about, I'll go get ours if you want. Shan't be a mo.' And before Roly knew it he'd turned on Mercury heels and was gone, leaving him poleaxed.

He didn't know how long he'd be or if he'd return at all and when he regained his composure his impression was that he'd fallen for a yobbish prank of some kind, a wind-up, probably homophobic, so he closed the door. He'd been within touching distance! He headed as fast as he could back to his computer, his mind swarming, to capture the happening in print and, as he hobbled, he compiled an ad hoc mental prosopography of the boy, the previously seen-through-the-window check-capped wonder boy who had magically 'made himself flesh'. What had just occurred would have to go in the Journal, no question; it was earth-shattering. No sooner had he reached his chair than he caught the flicker of a dark shadow across the frosted pane of the bathroom window at the front of the flat and then heard knock knock again – he'd come back – and he scurried back to the door cursing and, without thinking this time, unhooked the security chain and flung the door wide. 'Can ya fill it mate?' The boy was holding a watering can out to him. 'S'okay, put the chain back on if ya want. You gorra be safe an' you can pass it me through the window yeah?' *Winder,* to rhyme with cinder. This consideration for his security made Roly wary of being lulled into a false sense of it. 'Who are you?' he demanded. 'And why this sudden interest in my herb garden?' 'Michael 'Ollis. S'okay mate, I've seen ya before. I live round in Ashfield, number 23. It's just... I thought... if they died that's all.' 'It would be a tragedy. Come in Michael Hollis, with an aitch yes? And fill up your can yourself. And please do stop calling me mate, my name is Roly.' 'Whatever,' he breezed and stepped inside. He ushered Michael Hollis by him and followed him down the hall, his eyes glued to the nubile motion of his buttocks. 'Through there, turn right.' Michael Hollis filled his can and went back out and Roly watched him through the window, ogling his taut young limbs and sinews and wondering if serendipity had thrown a rare thing in his path, a street arab with a kind streak. 'You enjoy gardening do you?' he asked when he'd finished and come back in. 'Oh yeah,' Michael enthused. 'That's what I'm gonna do. At college next year.' Liar, Roly thought. 'I'm afraid I can't pay you, I –' '– For waterin' flowers? Don't be daft,' Michael scoffed, quick as light. 'And anythin' you want just shout us,' he said. 'I do loads for 'em round 'ere, Mrs Lucas, old Bill and the rest. It's me that puts your wheelies out on a Tuesday before school. Didn't know that was me did ya?' 'Well, no and that's very kind of you, very community spirited, I –' '– And it's not an ASBO, if that's what yer thinkin',' he smirked. 'I wasn't.' 'I'm pukka, 'onest. Ask anybody. I just like 'elpin' mate, er oh, er Roly.' They stood rather transfixed, eyeing one another while

Roly thought, 'The boy at play and walking in the street past my window, the very same boy, here in my kitchen!' 'How old are you Michael?' 'Fifteen.' He felt something leap and dive at the sound of the number, a proscribed one. It was what he'd expected and his fears were confirmed. He'd lusted over this boy from afar and done so fully aware that the lust could only be transcendental, that transforming it into the physical and real could only ever be a lunatic dream.

He was no paedophile, an ephebophile yes, a 'boyaholic' who had always revelled and always would in the adoration of male adolescence, never wishing to abuse it and certainly not rape it – no, no paedophile. He had in his time been able to indulge his taste, but no more – now it was all quixotic. The percentages were against him anyway, percentages which decreed that a boy picked out at random on the street or indeed knocking on your door, was more likely to be straight than gay and further decreed that if that boy on the street or at your door were gay, his interest in you would be non-existent, non-existent if you weren't 51 years of age, infinitely less than non-existent if, like Roly, you were.

This insurmountable stacking of odds, however, couldn't deter one so dedicated to the cause of beauty as he and he went on to reflect how, from 10 yards away through his window this Michael had been eyecatching, but now that he was inches away, he was mesmerising. His face was too fresh and clean with a soft warm sheen to have 'character', it was the colour of caramel and had nothing to maculate it, no adolescent acne or boils, no wrinkles of age or wear, only tiny pinpoints of sprouting stubble on the chin and a faint furry shadow on the upper lip. Roly congratulated himself at having lost none of his discernment and told himself how privileged he was, for here of his own volition and in his kitchen was the sum of all the youth a lover of youth such as he could hope for and what a miracle it was that a boy as fresh as the new day was made of stardust billions of years old; for the moment, he was the stuff of many boys and the only boy ever. Roly scrutinised the eyes, they were jet black and shiny and seemed to radiate from an infinite space; they sat deep under slightly arced eyebrows set wide above high cheekbones, his nose was short and concave, thin at the brow and spreading quite markedly to slightly snub nostrils, his mouth was wide with long luxurious lips, the upper shaped into a pair of sweeping classical crescents, the lower a lush cushion and both, like the curves of the pectorals he had previously seen, were Lines of Beauty. A jawline (which he'd also previously noted) that was chiselled die-straight and a prominent chin might have made his overall physiognomy forbidding, were it not for a redeeming deep dimple in that chin which gave him the look of a cheeky and embraceable scallywag, especially when he smiled. His aspect could shift from eager to tranquil, from the mischievous sprite to the farouche teenager with ease and there was also an occasional glint to be caught when his head bowed demurely and his body adopted a certain stance which hinted waggishly, 'Yes, I am desirable and I know you want me and that you dream of me.' While he was absorbing all this, the boy lifted his cap to readjust it on his head and lush straight black hair, pleasingly more than Roly expected, was revealed, groomed and gelled and reaching to his ears with fine straight fronds of it fingering their way down his brow; it was the sleek elegance of Xerxes. On the day he saw his blooming bare torso, he'd spotted no disfiguring body decoration (he had ambiguous opinions about tattoos) and he could also see now that he wore no earring. Perhaps they were finally becoming passé. He continued to look into his eyes, which sparkled with the kind of hope and optimism which only youth possesses, but which for a fleeting moment flicked shame into Roly's fibre and sent a cold shiver through him. 'Awright now?' Michael asked breezily, startling him from his trance. 'Wha? – oh – yes, yes. Thank you very much.' 'See ya'round then.' And before Roly knew it, he had turned on Mercury heels again and with the minimum of ceremony headed out the door. 'Thank you, er, thank you... Michael,' he called after him. 'I'll shut yer door. Give ya a knock next time and wash yer car for ya, okay?' he shouted back and Roly heard the door bang and saw him wave as he ran past his window.

And then he tottered, the hurricane had hit, lifted him off the ground and hurled him back down. He went straight back to his keypad to write down what had just happened while it was fresh and to convince himself that it had happened. He would have to capture the 'jizz' of him, use all his journalist's lapidary skills to depict him, give him life and a voice and he racked his brain to remember what few words he'd heard and how the boy spoke them, rapidly and with sloppy grammar, the sad symptoms of limited intellect he feared. Yes, he was hoi polloi; Roly's wont was to notice such things straightaway, in fact he'd known it before hearing him at all, having seen his body language when he was at play and 'sized him up': no aitches, the elisions, collisions and apocopes, the genuine Trenton patois article. This was no time to be picky and pedantic, the boy was sublime and to hell with dialect and slang, but it was essential to record his speech in order to capture that 'jizz' and there lay the problem: the slang and twang of the Trenton tongue, it defied transcription. Even Arnold Bennett had to tone down his characters' speech so as not to alienate the greater audience outside his provincial bailiwick. Roly, as a native, understood the patois of course but he knew it was uninterpretable. His readers, if readers there were to be, would be bored with translations and explanations everywhere in parenthesis, so in recording the boy's words, he knew he'd have to dilute and purify him lingually just as Bennett had to do, while attempting to retain the authentic flavour. Slang was bad enough, a layer of modern day teenspeak on top was worse, Trenton teenspeak was a 'whole lot worser'. But having a Michael speak any other way would be a travesty. He pressed on with the entry and sweated blood and the 30-years-old memory of the stunning blond on the train came to him – Mother Mary and all the orphans, what the hell was he thinking of, was he hoping for a repeat of a flirtation of 30 years ago? Thirty years on and look at him, prissy, lascivious and cretinous, pretending he still had a libido and fondly deluding himself – he was even to say to Michael one day, 'Forgive me, I have been fond' – that a boy of 15 could have any interest at all in him other than doing what he'd just done, help with odd jobs. And yet here he was contemplating charming an adolescent angel and rolling the dice of seduction, should he call again, which he doubted. *Oh, don't be mortified*, he told himself, *that you still have the glad eye for a pretty youth, that you can still slaver, but understand that the power of your desire doesn't match the power of your attraction any more (did it ever?) and isn't strong enough to overcome your innate fear of rejection (and there is now much more to reject); you are way out of practice old man, had it, lost it and done for.* 'I am withered on the vine, dear boy,' he shouted at his monitor screen. 'Don't look to me for any more virility. I had little enough when I was fit and now I have none at all. I must just admire you and have done.' The boy on the train was pushing 50 himself now and was somewhere, elsewhere, long out of Roly's time; this boy Michael was not his metempsychosis, nor had time turned back, but still the memories were ignited. There was the day, five years ago this one, when he made a fool of himself on Newcastle station; his excuse, that he was tipsy at the time and was more desperate then and in a better position to try to do something about it than he was now, did nothing to prevent a hot and cold shiver of embarrassment coursing through him. He had sat alone at a table outside the platform bar, drinking cider, having just been required to leave yet another job and, because of a bounced cheque, to leave yet another property. Alone again, in a city he hardly knew, without a job and broke. Again, again, again. The boy sat down at his table and he engaged him and he seemed willing enough and after half an hour of friendly cider-assisted conversation, he got up to leave and Roly said 'Pity. and he said, 'Why?' and Roly said, 'I thought you'd like to come home and get naked for me' and there was no hostility, just a pitying Geordie smile and an 'Aw, I didn't think you were like that' and with that he went.

Oh the stimulus of them, the boys, the scrapes and near scrapes, the forwardness, the outrageous behaviour, the tingle of danger. This boy, this Michael, like the Geordie, had come right up to him so to speak, but where he had been gauche and drunk and bold with the former, sensing success, this boy was merely too young and too late. Naturally, he was flattened with infatuation, but treatment at arm's length was called for. Infatuation had had a long run, from the beginning at Trenton High with Martin and Stephen, through cousin Paul and Malcolm and ... and yes, by the Furies, of course, Raymond Quipp. Hadn't it all started, not with Neville Ladderbanks, but with Raymond Quipp?

No, Quipp wasn't one of his boys. Quipp was the one with whom he shared his Big Secret in school that afternoon, that life-enhancing afternoon, in an English lesson, the afternoon when two pubescent gay minds collided and why the syzygy took place at that moment, with that schoolfriend, who in fact was no friend at all, he had never been able to figure. They had never mixed, they had never even sat together in class before, but there they were, placed next to each other like strangers on a train. Roland was surreptitiously carving some words into the desktop with the point of his biro and Quipp glanced over to see what he was writing. Roland looked up at him. 'It's all right,' he whispered. 'It's my alter ego. I've got an alter ego.' The words he'd carved read: 'I love Harris 4D.' Coming out hadn't been invented yet, closets were American cupboards and he had only the vaguest idea what an alter ego was, he was showing off because he was in the middle of a fad for psychotherapy and had been taking Freud's, Adler's and Jung's books out of the library. (Was that dabbling the beginning of his sciolism, he wondered?) So he thought he would blind Quipp with science and when he explained, *sotto voce,* that he was in love with a boy named Harris from form 4D and Quipp *sotto voce*-d back to him, 'I've got one as well', the world of Roland and Quipp was created.

Quipp, gangly, unattractive, painfully shy Quipp, with his long sallow face behind huge wire-rimmed glasses. He was awkward and uncoordinated and his conversation, or rather his means of communication, was abstruse and often barely audible, coming as it did from under his breath and in fragmented sentences. He would address, not only me, but nearly everyone with 'Oi' rather than their name. That's if he bothered to address at all, usually he grabbed your clothing ferociously as a way of gaining attention. He was by no means my schoolfriend of choice, which made finding myself placed next to him in a class and opening up to him there and then all the more extraordinary; fate, I suppose, or a serendipitous collision of like spirits and in that very first whispered exchange we discovered to our mutual astonishment that we were the only two boys among the 600 or so at Trenton High School who shared a unique and awesome predilection. Boys! For a reason I have never been able to fathom, I brazenly pointed out to a fellow pupil I had hardly spoken to in the four years we had been sharing the same space that I was crazy about a boy and knew his name.

I took the first opportunity to point out the adorable creature in the playground and Quipp approved of my choice and after that we would watch young Harris everywhere – in the playground, in the corridors - and I even managed to call something inane to him once as he passed us. I somehow found out where he lived and used to cycle by his house in the hope of seeing him. I'd be called a stalker now. The big moment came on the day of the inter-house cross country race. Harris was a competitor too and there he was in the changing rooms and I felt the ineffable buzz at seeing him strip off. I left one memento of my time at Trenton School behind me; I had scratched 'I love Harris 4D' into every desktop that I sat at in that school, but whether Harris ever saw one of my inscriptions... I never saw any acknowledgement, any 'Fuck off you poof' or 'You wanna kiss me then?' Nothing.

From that day, Quipp and I were welded into conspiracy and became the founders of the school gay brotherhood with a membership of two. And like the Brontes and Robert Louis Stevenson and countless other childhood imaginations before us, we created our own world in which to live – a forbidden world, one of which everyone around us would disapprove and seek to destroy, because it was wrong and immoral and wicked and exciting. We quickly established rules, signs, symbols, trysts, we catalogued our heroes and idols and spent all the time we could together exchanging erotic fantasies, which were greatly assisted by Quipp's skill at sketching the male nude form for us to slaver over: a talent which provided us both with much needed stimulation and drove us wild. I see him now, curled up in his chair with his legs tucked under him, sketchpad and a stick of charcoal in his blackened fingers, his tongue in his cheek in concentration, turning out our favourite pop stars and Trenton High School boys. Naked. He also reproduced Aubrey Beardsley creations, which I encouraged as part of our homage to the decadents of history.

We founded our own clique: CHAPS we called ourselves proudly, The Company of Hopelessly Adoring Pederasts. I would go to Quipp's house and I remember how nervous he was, ushering me into the front room before I could say anything more than hello to his mother. We talked endlessly about Harris and other boys, about Oscar Wilde and explored all the homoerotic relevancies we could unearth or invent and we shared countless editions of the only soft porn that was available to us: pop magazine pin-ups. It was all so delightfully daring and rebellious: Quipp sketching away, ever fearful that mother would barge in at any moment; listening to *Beyond the Fringe, Pieces of Eight and The Goons* LPs; talking of H P Lovecraft and vampires and anything occult; and about seeing *If...,* which we went to see because we'd heard it was about a boys' school and had naked boys in it. And we had *Round the Horne*. This was more than a juvenile fad; Kenneth Williams was an idée fixe and one which would very soon lead me to my first gay showbiz party, at the home of another of the show's stars in Regent's Park. That made Quipp green, but how I got into trouble, later, with the owners of a gay drinking club in Pimlico where Kenneth Williams used to go, Quipp would never know. *Round the Horne* was our private territory and by worshipping it we established our identity – it was the muzak in our own gay bar. We revelled obtusely in its innuendoes, pretending to understand the world of camp and parlari and though some things were too outré even for us queers, we knew the code was in there somewhere and spent hours trying to crack it. We knew it was naughty and outrageous and laughed in the pretence of knowing what we were laughing at, because it nonplussed our parents and so added to our mystique and our notion that we were members of a clique. Fantabulosa duckie.

Among those 600 boys at Trenton High were Martin and Stephen, the later phantasms of Katie Beans field and so many pretty boys for us to enjoy ogling each day, all of them with generous helpings of beauty which not one of them, alas, showed any inclination to share. 'If only they'd unzip their trousers and oblige with their favours,' I'd sigh. 'Yeah, if only,' Quipp sighed back. Dreaming the impossible dream had been a continuous frustrating excitement but the boys had begun to fade from the canvas when Quipp and I met for our last rendezvous at the Concourse coffee lounge in Trenton town centre, where we met on Saturday mornings to talk in whispered innuendoes about boys and sex, using as much parlare as we'd gleaned, while we drank frothy coffee at the very low tables. Varder the dolly eek on 'im over there. Bona lallies. Chaste frustrated schooldays finally ended and virginity's lease was running short. The Gazelle and serious men who were serious about sex were, geographically and emotionally, round the corner. 'My bedroom treasures are my sine qua non,' I announced to him. 'Ooooh, get you and your Latin O-level, duckie,' Quipp scoffed. He was always scoffing at my pretentiousness, perceiving I was pretentious long before I did. I was alluding, among other things, to the copy of *A Rebours* I had discovered. 'I've nearly finished it, by the way, then you can borrow it. You've got to read it, it's fab and groovy and very wicked. I want it back though. I need it for my full membership of the pantheon,' I told him. And I went on. About aspiring to that pantheon of aestheticism and hedonism, where I would be alongside the dilettantes and homosexual voluptuaries I worshipped. And on. About my lust for the knowledge one shouldn't know, for the heavy scents and flavours of a life which is not on any college syllabus. Only then would I be able to be at one with the titans of depravity and sample the lechery which dares not speak its name; only then would I rank alongside Wilde and Gilles de Rais, Coward and Kenneth Williams, Elagabulus and Caligula. (And John Betjeman too, though he wasn't queer, but his poetry was wonderful and his television programmes were unmissable and he had camp friends such as Harold Acton, so he counted and what's more he was living and I was determined to meet him one day.) I couldn't wait to fly away to where I could lie in porphyry with my own Bosies and Robbies 'and live the life and die the death of Oscar.' I was mapping dangerous and wonderful terrain, which neither my parents nor most of the people around me knew anything of and, more important, didn't know that I knew. And the thought of it thrilled me to bits. Hee hee. 'Ooh, get you,' Quipp said, 'you big fairy,' no doubt thinking to himself how easily I set myself up. 'You definitely going for Ealing Poly then?' he asked. 'I can't wait,' said I. 'That's where I belong – with the gay and debauched elite of London.'

From then on, I, Roland Wanger, decided that all I wanted was to devote myself to exotic things, to the erotic, the arcane and everything that was beautiful; that is why I was reading *A Rebours,* Oscar Wilde, *Salammbo,* Firbank and Genet now, to cram in as much gorgeous depravity as I could. 'I'm voracious and in years to come I won't know if all this aesthetic nonsense has poisoned my mind or improved it but, quite honestly, duckie, as long as I've got beautiful boys all around me, I won't much care and London is full of beautiful boys, n'est-ce pas?' 'And clap, duckie,' Quipp quipped. I'd made a modest start on my journey already; I'd become a closet aesthete, a Regency fop but one without the bravado. I drank Earl Grey tea with lemon, wore a deerstalker hat and a Norfolk jacket, a corduroy waistcoat and my grandad's fob watch and I went for solitary walks in the park, smoking aromatic Dutch-blend tobacco furtively in my six pipes, which I'd taken up in favour of cigarettes because, excepting Dunhill or Passing Clouds, I considered cigarettes as fit only for plebs. It was the closest I could get to opium. Drinking absinthe must come next, but I hadn't yet worked out how I could get to do that. I had a subscription to *Country Life* magazine, which seemed a most apposite accompaniment to these affectations and which nurtured my love of Georgian and Regency architecture. Fostering my dedication to ogling and fawning over the boys at school at every opportunity, I regarded as an essential to my aesthetic education.   'Is that paperboy still giving you palpitations, by the way?' Quipp asked, spooning around the foam on his coffee and I feigned a swoon. 'Aaaah, him! You swine.' Quipp hit an extremely sensitive area of my libido with the question about the devastingly sexy paperboy, my current craze, whose daily round took him past the council house window. I would sneak furtive glances at this lad whenever he came by, I was a curtain twitcher, and I peeked at him and wondered if the boy sensed me watching, foaming at the mouth behind those net curtains, watching him strut his pert and tightly jeaned bottom from door to door, with his bag hanging from his shoulder and banging against his divine thigh. He brought me what was surely the only copy of *The Times* to be delivered to a council house – possibly any house – in the whole of Trenton and I inwardly serenaded his beauty each day and thanked him for the aesthetic and sexual workout he gave me. Too agonising to think of, so I changed the subject. 'The Youth Hostel trip in the Lake District was aesthetic, not sexual,' I said. I and my Spanish teacher – whose favourite I was and whom I was allowed to call Ernest *ex cathedra* – paired off on a jaunt to the extraordinarily atmospheric country estate of Hutton-in-the-Forest, where we were taken on a tour by Lady Hutton herself. It was just the sort of adventure that indemnified my taking the radiant way, but it also rankled with my conviction that there had been some appalling cosmic mistake over my birth. 'It's reinforced my view that I was born into the hopelessly wrong century and the wrong class,' I told him. 'I really can't bear to think of myself as a peasant.' The visit to Hutton was my chance to write to John Betjeman, who happened to appear on a chat show just about then. It seemed so right: Betjeman was my property and nobody I knew could quote his poems. I was absolutely overjoyed when the great man replied, calling me 'Mr', congratulating me on my Hutton expedition and mentioning the revolutionary use of primary colours in Trenton's building schemes. What a genius, telling you more than you know yourself about your own city in a few lines! Quipp was unimpressed, as he was by any interest outside our mutual ones and called me a big nancy. 'Yes, Ealing Poly it is. So off you go to boring Leicester and bore yourself stupid with your boring physics,' I said, pompously. 'You have no right. You have sold your artistic soul to the devil of science. Aroint thee, witch!.' 'You won't want to see this then?' And he produced one of his blue folders and didn't have to say what was in it, as I already knew – his latest drawing, one of our choice schoolboys or pop singers, in naked fantasy. Quipp's concept of the erect penis was awe-inspiring. 'Who is it this time? Let's have a varder,' I said, excitedly grabbing for the folder. 'Not here, ya twit. Go in the bog.' When I came back from the gents, Quipp asked, as though it had just occured to him, 'What the hell are we going to have to look at now from nine o'clock to 4 every weekday?' And with that we were forced to tacitly acknowledge that our days of hidden leching were at an end. I was now waiting to start a year of student teaching at a school up the road, (but it was a junior school, so there would be no boys to drool over there) and Quipp was preparing for Leicester University next month.

As part of our search for a university we had contrived to go to London together for a day for interviews and later met up to linger in the Kings Road, which was at the centre of the universe and a total gas.

Yes, there I was on a Wednesday afternoon, in the Kings Road, Chelsea, an 18-year-old boy from a council house in Trenton standing and staring surrounded by all the Bohemian posh! And it felt so… right! How did I do it, how did I get there, how did it happen?

I wrote again to my 'old friend', the Poet Laureate, to tell him I'd be in London for a day and to ask if we could go to Cloth Fair and meet him.' Unfortunately, his secretary wrote back to say that Mr Betjeman was very sorry that he would not be at home on that date. London was not the magnet for Quipp yet and would not pull him there for another four years. He really was going for the best university he could get into whereas I chose Ealing Poly, turning down the headmaster's offer to try for Oxbridge, ostensibly because it had a pioneering language laboratory, but really because I knew it was 'within spitting distance of all the debauchery and feasting panthers that I shall possibly want.'

As though Oxford and Cambridge weren't – that was yet another wrong turn on the road of your life!)

When I look back on that impulsive decision in the headmaster's study, the day I found out that I'd achieved three decent A-level grades, I have to say that that was the pivotal moment, the moment when the insidious malevolent gene which was born when I was, matured and took hold of my fate. 'You're an idiot for turning London down, a fool for believing you choose a university for its academic record and a traitor for doing physics,' was my admonishment to Quipp. Neither of us dared mention 'end of an era' that morning in the Concourse coffee lounge, but a melancholia began to hang in the air between us. Our mutually exclusive partnership, more collaboration than friendship, was vanishing, and we knew it. We had enjoyed and endured the privilege and the isolation of being the only two queers in the school, so we thought, of being weird and different together and of being two complete opposites both with a shared sexual interest, but it was coming to an end.

A few years later, I found that Quipp's gaucheness had not waned nor his social skills waxed, when I came upon him unexpectedly one night in the Coleherne in London. 'Hello Quippy!' I hailed over a few heads. Would he have talked to me if I hadn't? What different people we had become, changed with nothing private and sacred between us any more. Holding his glass to his chest in his long straggly fingers, he was in the company of a young man he introduced in an almost deprecatory whisper and I said a perfunctory hello and without any further explanation forthcoming, I was left to surmise at the nature of anything more than a friendship between them, until Quipp volunteered, 'We've got a flat round the corner' as the only allusion to cohabitation. I wondered later if Quipp was shy or embarrassed at being so discovered. I noticed that he and his friend were wearing the Coleherne dress code of leather jackets, narrow leather chokers round their necks and certain amounts of silver chain work dangling from pockets. *So my schoolfriend is now a leather queen?* The bond of our shared and exclusive schoolboy gayness had diluted into a public one; we were now stilted with each other and neither of us regretted it. As the encounter dragged on, I was torn between making an effort to chat and making an excuse to leave, particularly as the pair littered their talk with petty sarcasms, giving me the impression that they were regarding me as a sort of figure of fun. But perhaps that was paranoia about the inadequate image I already had of myself at not yet quite measuring up to let alone finding the glamour of the gay scene I had specifically come to London to be part of. I also hadn't yet learned not to take myself seriously. Perhaps I never would.

'Why's he talk so posh, who does he think he is?' Quipp's 'friend' would ask of Roly later. 'Always was piss elegant. Posh when he was in Trenton,' was how Quipp would explain him. 'Not really a Coleherne queen is he?' 'The jacket and flares you mean?' Quipp would observe with his customary curled lip.

I called on them one Saturday morning on my way home from a very, for me, kinky night in the Kings Road. A number had picked me up outside the Coleherne but when we got to his place and started the business, every time I tried to kiss him he said, 'No, later,' then he put clips on my nipples and started tugging them! 'He was kinky,' I said and they sniggered. 'What are you laughing at?' I asked indignantly, wondering why I wasn't impressing them with the details of this sexual novelty. Quipp and friend exchanged smirks. 'Oh, nothing,' said Quipp. 'Your use of that quaint outdated word, that's all.' He was after all a leather queen by then and spoke with authority and knew the latest terminology while making fun of mine. He was still curling that lip at my pretensions and aspirations and was, I supposed, pointing out that I was not as 'swinging London' as I liked to think and that causes me chagrin to this day.

****

He was trying to make sense of the startling and yes, the stimulating, *interruptus peuris* of the previous week and he was still tossed and jostled in the wake of it. Hurricane Michael had staunched progress with the radio script and as for any more writing about the fabulous heterosexual Denzel... No, his little life of trying to create little art was at a temporary standstill. Michael had brought an end to creativity, except the creativity needed to conjure ways of stirring his loins. No, he was listless and lifeless in the eye of the storm.

The heat wave continued, even Finns and Alaskans were roasting according to the world weather report, while in Trenton and Lyme, the naked torsos of 'yoof' (and those of the older and fatter denizens too) were everywhere to be seen. The workingclass male had no compunction at baring its collective chest in public, no sense of occasion. He of all people should complain about a strutting naked chest! But the vestige of a sense of old-fashioned propriety clashed with lust whenever he saw shirtless young men ambling through the supermarket or in cafes and pubs, even – on the occasion when his neighbour asked him to give her a lift there – in the foyer of the magistrates' court – or in any other place where dress should, he felt, be *comme il faut*. The last time he witnessed an example of a like opinion was when gentleman Greg, head barman of the Rising Sun in Marylebone High Street, politely and firmy told two navvies that they were welcome to a drink if they would kindly put their shirts on and when they said they didn't have their shirts with them, asked them if they would be so good as to take their drinks outside. That was 15 years since.

Workingclass tattoos and number one haircuts; he very rarely saw what he considered a tasteful tattoo, most were acquired by youths who were plastered and the result was plastered bodies, desecrated, crude and as for number one haircuts – so many dishy young men looked like suspects from *Crimewatch.* Shorn hair had been around too long, but there was comfort in the thought of cyclical things and he was confident that tracksuit bottoms and baseball caps (*the* baseball cap excepted) would soon be out and the return of heads of plentiful hair along with skintight jeans and trousers was imminent.

****

Michael came to water the pot herbs again, Roly asked him if he'd help to put his newly-arrived clock up on the wall and he said he'd borrow a power drill and rawlplugs from his grandfather at the weekend and fix it. Roly was rather less stupified, a little more at ease this time and he delayed the boy for a chat and even tried a flirt. 'Do you were that cap in bed? Every time I see you –' 'This? 'Ow cool is it eh?' he swaggered, pulling it off and flourishing it. '– you're wearing it.' 'It's me street marker and pukka Burberry and not a fake neether. I got it last Christmas.' 'I'm all in favour of "if you've got it flaunt it", but you wear your hair long and –' '– I don't like short 'air.' '– baseball caps and long hair don't really go together. It's a pity to hide it. I have a liking for –' '– I wash it,' he exclaimed, taking umbrage at the implication that he didn't. '– longish well groomed hair on a boy and I'm sure you wear yours very well. If only it were on show.' This aposiopesis was no fault of Roly's: Michael had an infuriating habit of finishing other people's sentences for them and to answer or comment on something only yet half voiced. *I must go steady with the compliments,* he reminded himself, *they might unsettle the boy.* 'Who do you have at home?' he inquired, to end the flirting. 'What are your parents like, do you get on?' 'There's me mum and me clingon.' 'Your… clingon… what, pray is a –?' 'Me little sister. Clingon, she

103

clings on right?' 'And what about dad?' 'I 'aven't got a dad.' 'Oh. I see. Sorry.' 'I'm not. 'E went didn't 'e? Ages ago.' 'You mean – ?' 'We don't talk about 'im.' 'Oh, right, I don't mean to –' ''E ran off with 'is slapper when we were kids an' we 'aven't 'eard from 'im since.' 'Oh, right.' He shrugged. 'They're still tryin' to find 'im, that child agency lot. Mum could do with 'is money.' 'A bit of a bummer that,' Roly proffered as sympathetically as he could. 'He was a.' He spoke quietly and his body drooped and the unfinished insinuation brought silence. 'He gave you a bad time did he?' Roly asked gently. 'More me mum than me,' he answered, numbly. 'Spent all their money on gamblin', then 'e beat 'er up when she didn't 'ave no more to give 'im.' Pained furrows appeared on his brow as he gave this potted history and Roly thought better of correcting his double negative. 'Bloody hell,' was all he could think to say. 'He's a twat. That's why I changed me name.' The jolt that buffeted Roly at the words was excruciating. 'You changed your name,' he gasped in disbelief, half to himself. 'Well me mum did, well not changed, I'm just Michael now, I was Warren Michael Buckley when I was born and now I'm just Michael and mum changed 'er name back to 'er – what's it called? – maiden name. So she's Yvette 'Ollis and so am I, I mean I'm Michael 'Ollis, same as me grandad. When me dad went off, mum said she didn't want... anything of 'im left around, so she dropped the Warren 'cos that was 'is name. I was named after 'im.' 'You changed your name,' Roly muttered again. 'Yeah, sort of.'

He felt nauseous and dizzy, his head was whirlygigging; this was an unimagineable déjà vu, as if by proxy, a bitter coincidence, an acid irony which he could hardly assimilate. 'Bloody hell,' he said again and, 'You couldn't make it up,' under his breath. Then, 'God's ballocks' and he wanted to stop this boy, stop him from going any further along a track he had himself trod with such a disastrous outcome. He looked at him hard and was filled with dread for him and made a wish that he would never be touched by grief. 'I shall have to call you Angelo,' he said, the first nonsensical endearment he could think of and he said it as raillery to brighten the sombre mood that had eclipsed the boy. 'Angelo?' Michael asked, perplexed. 'What? Oh, yes. Michelangelo. Have you never heard of Michelangelo?' Roly was totally distracted. 'Oh right, wasn't 'e an old painter or somethin'?' 'David. He made David,' Roly mumbled, staring into the distance. 'Although the later Bernini is far superior, a different interpretation anyway, fluent not static like Michelangelo's, the body caught in motion on the turn, in the act of throwing, the furrowed brow, the granite look... But as far as I can remember, Bernini wasn't called Michael, so Angelo you will have to be and Michelangelo's David you will remain...' He jolted himself to and gave the boy a rueful smile. 'Don't regret anything,' he said to him. 'What?' He said nothing and continued to smile at him. Michael then jumped out of his own bewilderment, seemed to jump out of his body as well as his thoughts and announced sharply, 'Right, I'm goin',' and lifting the watering can, said, 'I'll put this in yer shed yeah for next time. S'okay, it's a spare.' He turned to go, but stopped himself midway, as if a thought had struck him and then he spoke and the oh so tiresome question, the almost inevitable bane of a question, the one he always suspected was a trap designed to expose his fraud, the one that so perplexed Trenton people, came from his lips: 'You're not from round 'ere are ya, you're kinda posh, are you from London or somethin'?' and Roly inwardly groaned at the prospect of having to face yet another catechism.

I have just emerged from a very narrow escape and returned home, bloodied but not bowed and this I must write before I turn in. Rosalind from the office invited me to her place in Kilburn for dinner tonight. It was just the two of us and everything went swimmingly – she cooked a mean lasagne which my bottle of Barolo complemented nicely and we had a few good laughs. But. She has never mentioned her flatmate and said flatmate, Carol, came home just as I was leaving and I stayed on out of courtesy to meet her and then came the horror – not only has Rosalind never mentioned this girl but she certainly has never mentioned where she was from. Bloody Trenton! And can you believe – can I believe – no I can't – she comes from Pittsbank!!! Round the effing corner from me on the Dorkins estate! Jesus! I nearly died. I could hardly deny being a Trenton man could I? I've already idiotically told Rosalind where I was born so I spent the 10 minutes that I stayed for squirming in embarrasment and doing my best to water down my long 'a's and being at pains to stress – even though the girl showed no sign of ever knowing me, nor did I recognise her – that my family home was in Furlough Road and I hope to God she bought it and I was convincing enough. And then I made my getaway, disguising my shock with as much calm and composure as I could. Christ, what a scrape! I'm still shaking and gasping for breath. I think – I hope – I got away with it.

Roly's audible groan of exasperation was drawn out and deep. Ever since he'd first boarded a train for London at the age of 19, speaking properly but with a provincial Trenton accent and returned with the long 'a's' of the Home Counties (having learned on the way that dinner was lunch and tea was supper, a serviette was a napkin and that you didn't hold your knife like a pencil when you eat), the curiosity the people of his hometown displayed and the probing questions they asked about the way he spoke too often seemed obsessional to him and made him feel cornered, turning what was a source of pride down south into one of paranoia in Trenton, making him self-conscious about what he regarded as his self-improvement, making him think that they thought he was a charlatan. He couldn't explain why he 'talked nicely' without tying himself up in an embarrassing knot of prevarication and elaboration. He was forced to admit to himself in time that it was all due to his being ashamed of his roots and his conviction that he was born at the wrong time in the wrong place, but he'd doctored the flat vowels of his workingclass, council house upbringing (yet even on the estate he'd been berated as posh and 'stuck-up') and he felt uneasy ever after with the dichotomy he'd created. Now and often, in conversation with his fellow natives, he would check himself, tone down, avoid certain words likely to make him sound too refined and superior to them or sometimes he simply kept his mouth shut altogether. He would tell, if pushed, that he'd had to adopt a BBC accent in order to get on in his radio career (which, even as far back as the 70s was no longer the case), or that he'd been born and raised in Kent and he even resorted on occasion to claiming that his accent was the result of a (minor) public school education. Why he could never dismiss the question by simply saying he hated the Trenton voice – as he'd hated his name – and had changed it because that was his right was a mystery to him and one he couldn't solve. He couldn't make light of it in the way that Alan Bennett did – he called it the 'terminal illness of the vowels' suffered by everyone north of Trent who shifts southward – or joke that he was born in Trenton because that was where his mother was at the time rather than being in Chesham or Chichester or Cheltenham (but by god, how he wished that she *had* been in one of those places). He chided himself, called himself pathetic, people changed their accents all the time (as some did their names): a flat-vowelled grocer's daughter from Lincolnshire modified hers and became our first woman prime minister, why couldn't he emulate her?

So, already raised dialect-free, the boy up the road who talked 'nice', he was an object of despite for some of his contemporaries because of it and he went on to refine himself further. In the days and months after quitting Trenton (thinking it was for good), he could never recall there being an epiphany morning when he woke up vowing that he would now speak, or realise he was now speaking, in a middle class Home Counties voice. If it was snobbery, he swore it was subliminal not wilful because, as he was often to observe, if it weren't so then the transition wouldn't have been so effortless. He was of the opinion that the English befuddled those three entities, dialect, accent and class and confused them and he thought he didn't, but in fact they confounded him as much as they did society (and probably contributed to his downfall) and prevented him from admitting to himself that he had social aspirations which were born of an unremitting sense of inadequacy. Only latterly did he concede that, when he went south, it was to see the seeds of the middle-class customs, culture and accent that had been already sown in working-class Trenton soil, seeds he was unable to and refused to acknowlege as seeds of snobbery, bear fruit. But no, he was not to go over all that now, not with Michael; he wasn't going to expound on that 'terminal illness'. He only acknowledged the boy's question and that grudgingly. 'No, I was born in Bursley,' he confessed, 'and I'll tell you the story of my posh accent some other time,' and with that he guided him gently towards the door and out and called him inwardly a yokel but a very stunning one.

****

It was some days later that Michael called round, true to his word, with the tools for hanging the clock. 'I told ya I would,' he responded, to Roly's look of near disbelief. *He's so fresh, so alive, he chirps, like a happy parrot.* He directed him to where exactly he wanted the clock to hang and watched him drill the hole, hoist the clock and manoeuvre it into place – 'Up a bit more and to the right, that's it. Prima!' – and his eyes oozed cupidity at the sight of his stretching and undulating juicy little keisters. *How I've have missed him over these past days.* Emboldened by the flirting on his last visit, 'That's an admirable erection,' he smirked, when the clock was mounted and Michael turned to him, coyly agrin and Roly stood admiring it and he felt, he really did feel, deep satisfaction: here was something of substance, something tasteful, made by craftsmen and he had bought it. He took the big gilt key, wound the time, strike and chime, set the hands, swung the glittering gold pendulum, listened to the soothing tick tock and waited. The quarter hour struck and he felt another frisson. 'Man,' said Michael, wide-eyed, ''ow ya gonna hear the telly with that goin' all night?' 'On the contrary,' he smiled, 'how am I going to hear the clock with the telly on?' But he pointed to the tiny switch next to the dial which muted the chime. He was as delighted with Michael's handiwork as he was with his purchase and he reached for his wallet on the trolley, took out a five-pound note and held it out to him. 'What's that for?' 'Honest coin for honest work.'

109

'Don't be daft,' he protested. 'Take it please.' 'I told you,' Michael insisted, 'I don't want payin' for 'elpin' you.' 'I'll be upset and offended if you don't.' He took the boy's hand and pressed the note into it and Michael closed his hand around it. 'Thanks but there's… I mean ya don't need…' His words drifted off and they stood facing each other, speechless for a moment, until inspiration suddenly galvanised Roly, a ruse that gave him a rush of foolish glee: he'd been shopping, he lied and had forgotten the one thing he needed for supper and would he mind, could he spare the time to go with him in the car to the supermarket and run in for a baking potato? 'No probs.' Michael was happy to oblige and to Roly's relief didn't have the presence of mind to suggest that he might run along to the village store instead or to the farm shop round the corner from where he could have fetched potatoes in minutes. In the car, Roly asked with sarcastic levity: 'You do know what a baking potato is I suppose?' 'Durbrain,' Michael answered, with a more mordant voice. 'Like it's one o' them spuds with skin on that you put in the microwave and pile loadsa butter an' cheese on and eat yeah I do know!' 'Jamie Oliver speaks,' Roly mocked in return and he started the car and set off, tingling with unexpected anticipation. The mile long drive with a delicious boy in his passenger seat was reminiscent of his 'Katie Beans summer', when he 'kidnapped' Alan Ward and Doug on a few afternoons and whisked them down the country lanes of the Peak District in the Mini Minor. He let them drive when they were out of the city and while their hands were occupied with steering he would fondle their private parts. Doug, blond strapping Doug, quite wanted it; Alan accepted it out of gratitude. This time though, the country lane led to Turnhurst, the nearest town and the most northerly of the Trenton six towns and to Asda but this time there was no fondling. It was a long-remembered road from his childhood, through what remained now left of Bradhill Wood, crossing over the canal at Chatterley, the entrance to Harecastle tunnel hidden away beneath the trees down in the corner there, squashed in below the small gatehouse. Sadly, the mysterious and awesome Harecastle railway tunnel on the other side was long unused and its own gaping maw grown over. On the left was Black Pool, now landscaped and a popular cruising area, but where he walked his dog as a boy and where, later, the psycopathic monster held the young heiress prisoner in a dank underground drain, the cord that would finally strangle her tied around her neck to keep her in precarious place on the ledge from which she eventually fell and strangled to death. He knew the tale well because he read out the story of the police hunt for her in his first newsreading job on the new commercial radio station. And there the reminiscence abrupty stopped; it was a memory and a pain too far for other reasons. For Michael, Black Pool bore no hint of 1950s childhood adventures or a grisly murder of the 1970s although, to Roly's astonishment, he was well aware of its present status: 'That's where the queers go doggin' ya know,' he said, pointing to it as they passed and Roly's mouth dropped: 'Well slap my thighs and call me old-fashioned,' he said, glancing at him. 'How does a wet-eared straight boy like you know that?' 'It is, didn't ya know? Ya can see all their cars lined up and they're all sittin' there lookin' at each other. Then they all go off for a shag in the trees. It's a right laugh.' 'Yes, it's a gas.' 'It's a gas?' 'That's cool to you.' They reached home and Roly thanked him for the clock again and Michael collected his tools and sped away.

****

Three days went by, Roly didn't see him. He didn't know if he'd been to water the herbs without his knowledge, he didn't see him at play out the back or walking by at the front either and he hadn't knocked or rung the bell, he'd said nothing about going AWOL. Where was he?

Yet a different homeworker came, yet another woman and he made sly grumbling noises as she foraged in the broom cupboard. Her manicured and garishly painted fingernails made her look rather too glamorous for housework and he was reluctant to tell her what to do for fear of being sued if they broke. But she fared adequately, whistling while she worked, a dwarf in drag and she brought back all the provisions he'd put on the shopping list with nothing superfluous, nothing wrongly bought and nothing of her own choice subsitituted for what hadn't been available of his.

****

Finally. Michael came to call to explain his absence, blaming it on 'fuckin' revision'. 'I sent ya texts, but ya never answered.' 'Oh poo-poo to texts, I don't read them and I don't text back. I never use my mobile, dear boy, I only carry it when I'm out on my own in the event of being stranded and need to ring the emergency wallahs.' Michael said he'd been more or less confined to his bedroom on his mother's orders for a week. 'Playing on your computer, I suppose?' This he denied, confessing that his mother had been obliged to sign up to the Family Education programme at his school, which meant she was responsible for ensuring her son completed the quota of work required out of school hours to prevent his having to attend Saturday and even holiday classes to catch up. 'I just thought I'd better call round and see if you needed anythin,' he said. 'That's very kind of you, but I don't thanks.' 'Okay, cool.' He didn't break into his Mercury spin and flight. Instead, he followed Roly into the kitchen. 'I'm just preparing my supper,' Roly said. 'Want some?' Michael didn't answer but Roly heard him titter, turned and saw his face set in a risus sardonicus. 'What's funny?' 'Supper,' Michael said, still grinning. 'All right, dinner then.' 'Dinner,' he said, mocking now. 'Six o'clock and you call it dinner.' 'So you call it tea.' 'It *is* tea, ya dork. Dinner's what we 'ave at school at 12 o'clock intit?' *Intit* for *isn't it* and much older than the fashionable *innit.* 'I don't go to school and –' '– Numpty,' he scoffed, 'that's why it's called dinner hour. And we 'ave dinner ladies.' '– at 12 o'clock or thereabouts one has lunch.' 'One has,' he echoed, laughing quite raucously now, but not maliciously. Roly pointed a chopping knife at him. 'You are a rapscallion.' 'Thanks very much.' 'Breakfast, lunch and dinner if it's formal, supper if not. That's the rota, dear boy.' 'You're just a posh git, in ours we 'ave breakfast, dinner and tea.' Roly turned back to slicing the chicken breast on the chopping board. 'What you makin' anyway chef?' 'Mango chicken stir-fry and rice.' 'Stir-fry? Chinese? You make yer own stir-fry?' 'It is and I do.' 'Wow, respect.' 'No need to be impressed, there's nothing to it. Stir-frying is one of the quickest and simplest ways to cook. A few minutes in the wok and you have a meal, a utensil of genius is the wok. D'you like Chinese?' 'Yeah. Takeaway's not bad 'ere and me mum gets Morrisons stuff. That's ace.' 'Hmm, chop suey and chips I dare say.' Michael didn't rise to that. 'You do all yer own cookin' then? I mean all yourself, you never 'ave no microwave stuff?' 'Please the pigs!' Roly shrieked, 'never if I can help it!' 'When I'm completely incapable… and probably not then, I'd rather starve. Why on earth people prefer to eat packaged food stuffed with chemicals, salt and additives at twice the cost of fresh ingredients to their pockets and everlasting detriment to their health… Yes, I cook everything myself. There's no-one else to do it and besides, I love cooking. I've always cooked. Of course, it's much nicer if you

113

have someone to cook for and to share the whole experience with, but...' he held his hands up and shrugged. He put down the knife and leant on the chopping board. 'Jack cooked for me a lot,' he said, wistfully. 'He was good. Funny though,' he added. 'What is?' 'What? Oh. Nothing. I've just remembered again that Jack, Chinese Jack and good cook, never had a wok. And it wasn't he that taught me to cook Chinese either.' 'Who did then?' 'Nobody. Well... I did get one of the great Kenneth Lo's books from the library one day and I bought a wok on a whim and decided to have a go. Hmm,' he smiled to himself. 'Sweet and sour something, I think it was and probably chow mein or whatever, just for Larry and me one evening. I finished up with enough for eight, there was a tableful, dishes everywhere, a banquet!' 'You're a clever sod, ain't ya?' 'Not for me to say, I love doing it and love trying to get it right.' He picked up the knife and sliced again. 'So have you caught up with the revision?' ''Spose,' he replied with a shrug of indifference. 'I 'ate bein' a wonk.' He sat himself down on the swivel chair by the freezer and fell silent and shortly, the silence began to rise like a miasma, then it hung between them; it palled as it endured and as if to emphasise it, a black cumulonimbus, big as a country, heaved itself across the sun, the world outside darkened and the kitchen was plunged into shadow. Roly looked out and up at it crouched ominously above them. Rain began to pour, it was followed by a flash and a roll of thunder and he sniffed curiosity in the suddenly dank air and turned back round and saw Michael twitching, working himself up to say something, ask a question and, to deflect any of his unworldly teenage inquisitiveness, made an inane observation. 'Those are smart,' he said, nodding at his tracksuit bottoms. 'You may be an urchin but you're no ragamuffin. Are they new?' 'No,' he said, curtly, as though interrupted. 'I've 'ad 'em ages.' 'I haven't noticed them before.' Michael shrugged again. Another silence fell on them, but this time it was brief, touching them for a moment then vanishing like a phantom when the boy blurted, "Aven't you ever been married?'

Ah, the silence was a precursor, a rehearsal and it was the abruptness of the question, rather than the non sequitur, that took him by surprise and he froze, the knife he'd picked up hovering over the still whole mango he was steadying and was about to slice. The question was bound to come some time, but he hadn't expected it so soon and had prepared no suitable public relations statement to keep him sweet. Then, on second thoughts, he recognised that Michael's directness, like his outspoken allusion to gay cruising at Black Pool, being quite out of context and synch, were jejune and disarming enough not to seem prying. 'I mean... you're on yer own 'ere yeah, so are you divorced or what?' Roly could forbear because the boy was so beautiful. 'I thought you'd have noticed that by now. On my own and alone yes,' he said. 'I have sequestered myself away from the world,' he added, grandiloquently. 'Yeah, whatever that is,' Michael said. 'I s'pose you're too old now for...' *See what I mean about disarming?* 'Move yourself, my boy, I need to sit down. My legs have enough with only a little standing. Come into the livingroom.' He led the way, Michael followed and they sat at the dining table. 'What do you mean, too old? Too old for what?' Roly asked when he had settled. 'Except you could always get a girl round I s'pose.' 'A girl round? What –? Are you talking sex here, Michael marauder?' He didn't answer, but his dimple flexed and his impish grin crept over his crescent lips. 'By girl do you mean prostitute?' 'Escort purleese,' Michael cried in mock outrage. *Oh don't worry lad, I browse the escort sites regularly, but not for girls of course*

 No, he decided that despite the boy's streetwise candour, he was too young, too Trenton and too much of a neophyte to hear what he wanted and felt he ought to tell him. 'So you never bin married then?' he persisted. 'No, I'm not married and never have been and no I don't have escorts to visit.' 'Haaaa,' Michael yelled. 'Smokin'!' With the ejaculation, he became suddenly animated, jumping up and punching the air with a 'Yay!' while Roly frowned at him. 'What have I said?' he asked, bewildered. 'Oh nuthin', I've won me bet that's all.' 'Bet? What bet?' 'Nuthin',' he guffawd in admonishment and 'Mind yer own business,' he bellowed. 'Michael.' Roly said the name in a disapproving tone. 'Danny 'Odge owes me a fiver that's all. Yay!' and he rubbed his hands in gleeful triumph. 'A wager eh? On me. I'm intrigued. If you've won a bet with your friend about me, I want to know what it is.' 'Chill, it doesn't matter.' 'I won't chill till you spill,' he rejoindered playfully. 'This Danny said I used prostitutes did he? And why would Danny Odge be prepared to bet five quid on that?' 'Danny 'Odgkins, we call 'im 'Odge,' Michael corrected. 'So how does Daniel Hodgkins come to lose his stake? I told you I don't use... escort girls... so he'll believe you will he? And pay up?' Michael sat down again and looked at the floor between his legs. Roly thought he heard him mutter 'not girls'. 'What did you say?' 'Nuthin'.' Comprehension was instantaneous. 'Oh I get it.' 'Get what?' 'Oh I get it all right. Never mind. I get it.' 'No you don't.' 'Oh but I do.' 'Go on then.' 'No.' 'See.'

There was no more thunder or lightning, but when Roly looked out he saw three or four new mountainous stormclouds slowly amassing, white on black like snow on slag heaps, dramatic and minatory. It had dawned on him what Michael and his friend may have bet on: whether he was gay and if he used rent boys, but he was damned if he was going to either deny or confirm. He turned his gaze back to the top of the boy's bowed head and when he raised it, he gave him what he hoped was a supercilious look, one which said, 'I am indifferent so stop there'. To his relief, the boy had clammed and maybe it was the fear of overstepping which made him turn his gaze away and focus on the door. After a beat, he at last did his Mercury with a 'Right, I'm not 'ere' and got to his feet again and with a tuneful 'Catch ya laters', he went out and scurried down the hall. Roly heard the door close, sat back half amused and thought, 'Fine, Michael has decided that I'm a homosexual and has had a childish wager on it with his cronies.' He rumbled himself and his trolley back to the kitchen to carry on with supper and then he became perturbed: was a homophobic campaign about to start in his new home? He wouldn't let the notion disturb him. He prepared his stir-fry and rice and served himself an uplifting and mouthwatering meal. As he ate to the accompaniment of Mozart's *Jupiter Symphony* on the hi- fi, the cumulonimbus sat sprawled and swollen outside the window, obdurate, until it emptied the water it was silently discharging on Staffordshire and he said 'Sod it' to himself audibly.

****

The doorbell rang just after noon, noon on a Sunday, when he was listening to *Just a Minute* (if it had been earlier and *The Archers,* he would have ignored it or have answered it and been very annoyed indeed, that would have been sacrilege). Patagonian Lamb, from a receipt he'd copied from the BBC cookery website, was ready to go in the oven. He went to the door, expecting bothersome evangelists from the Church of the Adventists or something similar, but when

117

he opened it, there stood Michael, or rather there he jigged, in a light blue teeshirt and dark pants, Chinos or some such, not trackies for once and *no checked cap;* his hair was free and Xerxes shiny again and looked delectable, he wanted to run fingers through it. 'Michael of the morning!' Roly cried. 'My chanticleer. What news does he bring?' Michael jumped back. 'You okay?' 'Ah,' he bellowed and ushered him into the livingroom. 'You've come to tell me about the bet.' Though he had the advantage of youth, fitness, strength, health and height over him, Roly fancied he shied away a little. 'What ya mean?' 'I think you know what I mean,' he said, speaking as though he was about to address an annual general meeting. 'Sit down please,' he instructed and the boy did. 'I've cottoned on to why you connected with me –' '– It's not what you think.' Roly would have none of the aposiopesis this time. 'Please have the goodness to let me finish,' he ordered. 'You and your so-called *mates* have marked me down. You've conspired and you've been coming round, or they sent you round, to find out if I'm a faggot, to take the – forgive the pun – Michael. Your allusion to cruising at Black Pool was made to see how I'd react and you've had a bet on me and so, what's next? Bricks through the window, dog turds through the letterbox, shouting at me in the street, daubing my car with "Queermobile" or "Faggot tractor"?' Michael gaped. 'Hey, chill, okay? It's not like that,' he said and his tone was conciliatory. Roly had no idea whether he appeared relieved to the boy, but he thought he at least managed to show he wasn't intimidated. He perceived a boy for whom there wasn't much sacred and said to him with as much dignified acerbity as he could muster, 'The tortoise of your guesswork has outrun the hare of logical deduction this time. Congratulations, you've worked out I'm gay and now you and your cronies know it and you can have your laugh and I hope you're going to leave me in peace.' 'I said chill, okay? It's cool, 'onest.' 'What is cool about it, pray?' He asked with sarcastic emphasis on the 'cool' and through gritted teeth. 'What I mean is nobody's gonna hassle ya, we're not like that, we're not tossers.' His defence was strident, he sounded like a quisling discovered. 'There's one down the road, anyway,' he said more quietly. 'Phil. Faggot Phil. We've never mithered 'im. Dya know 'im?' 'Should I?' 'Well 'e's a g-boy like you.' 'Boy I'm not.' 'Well, ya know.' 'Not every gay man knows every other gay man in the world, darling.' Did he call him darling? He called everybody dear boy, or darling, but he said it this time with contempt. 'E's lived 'ere for yonks. 'E's 'armless, 'e's never tried to, ya know. 'E's a right laff but he isn't 'alf a minger. I don't think 'e ever gets any, ya know, like –' 'Any what? Cock? A shag?' His barnstorming might cower him more and Michael did stretch his eyes in surprise for an instant. 'That's as maybe and, as you can see, I'm harmless too. Not that I've ever been a danger, a *danger* to boys, even when I was a boy myself.' He tempered the aggressive tone and sat back. 'I wish I could believe,' he went on calmly, 'that the age of liberal enlightenment and tolerance towards gay brothers and sisters has at last penetrated this far, even as far as the invincibly bigoted workingclass community of Trenton – I sound like Neville Ladderbanks – but I can't. So if you want me to believe you, you'll have to prove it. In the meantime, I don't think it's too much to ask that you all leave me in peace and you don't force me into the position of having to call the police every day.' 'Like we'd do that,' Michael retorted, indignant at the suggestion. 'We were only messin' ya know. It's nothin', 'onest. All it is right, Danny said you weren't...' Big breath. 'Gay, cos you don't nancy around and you don't 'ave any queers callin' –' 'It's not easy to nancy around with a trolley and a walking stick,' he scowled. Michael was shamed into awkward laughter. 'I didn't mean... I mean, ya don't look, ya know... gay.' He illustrated the word by holding out an arm and bending his wrist. 'Oh take me, earth and cherish me,' Roly cried in theatrical exasperation, 'belief can still be beggared in the twenty-first century, even in Trenton! Don't be a granny grunt all your life, for pity's sake,' he patronised. 'Get modern, boy, there are enough *heterosexual* limp wrists and lisps to go round.' He passed that one over or hadn't understood him. 'Anyway, it was like, I told 'im I'd talked to ya an' like, I said you wanna bet an' we bet a fiver an'...' He finished sheepishly, 'I said I'd ask ya.' They both went quiet as Roly considered whether to believe him. 'You didn't ask, you assumed.' 'You always been... then?' he asked, seeking confirmation of the assumption. Roly wondered why he baulked at the word, perhaps the boy didn't want to be pejorative? 'Oh yes, always a hundred and ten percent queer,' he told him proudly. 'So now you know I'm the new old queen on the block and what I know is that you're a fifteen-year-old boy alone with him in his flat and that's not good for the image is it? Yours or mine.' 'Doesn't bother me,' he answered, brushing aside reservations. 'I had hopes for you and me. I liked you, despite your boorishness. I thought we might become friends,' Roly said and brusquely, so as not to display sentimentality, or worse, affection. 'We are friends!' he protested and when Roly didn't react, 'Least I – I mean, I like you as well. You're clever and everythin',' he added. 'You're a laff and you're not an old suit.' 'And I've taken a shine to you, Michael. You have goodness in you, but there are dangers when a single old man and a young boy –' '– We 'aven't done anythin', he protested again. 'I mean, you 'aven't tried anythin' on with me, 'ave you?' 'Stop that wretched habit of speaking across me will you? I meant to say, when society sees an old man and a young boy who are patently not father and son, together, it can think the worst and act accordingly. Correction, it can't think at all and do the worst.' Michael either didn't understand the point or passed over it anyway to cut to the chase. 'Can you still do it tho' with yer... ya know?' He emphasised his curiosity by pointing at Roly's legs, realised he was being tactless again and tried to recover ground. 'Hey,' he gasped. 'I bet you go in them chatrooms right, the gay ones.' He thought the notion amusing, tried to lift the gravitas, giggled. 'Phwoar, dirty old perv,' he smirked. 'I am shocked,' said Roly, feigning a high moral stance, 'that an innocent and highly underaged young pup like you knows about gay chatrooms –' '– Lots of 'em talk about it on MySpace.' '– and gay chatrooms. Cruising, dogging, taking bets on the local queer, whatever next? What's the world coming to? The world is always coming to something, whatever age people live in, but it never gets there. Nothing is sacred and the world is going to sod. What do you do, go into chat and hurl obscenities –?' '– You got a webcam?' Now he was nearing the bone and Roly wasn't to be drawn into talking about his scopophilia. 'If you must know, I don't look for and don't enjoy casual or mechanical sex and certainly not cybersex and never have, although I've been there,' he stated clearly and then attempted an epigram to himself, 'I used to believe that a one-night stand could be for ever.' 'So you don't wanna meet nobody then.' 'Anybody. It would be pleasant to have someone like-minded, I suppose. I crave company, a companion sometimes.' Was that true? 'I'm not a complete misanthropist. Yet. And I'm certainly not a misandrist –' 'Wot's a mizz, mizz wot?' '– but I like being alone too, alone not lonely that is.' He gave a long sigh. 'As for sex, well, as the lady said, "after the hurly-burly of the chaise longue"...' he broke off and gave Michael a patronising look which said *you wouldn't know Mrs Patrick Campbell would you?* 'Why on earth are we having this conversation?' he blustered. Then he heard himself saying, 'I've had my partners, two of them' and immediately couldn't quite believe he'd said it. 'When you were young an' fit yeah?' He asked sympathetically. 'Ha,' he mocked loudly. 'Is that fit as in healthy or your teenage definition of fit as in Jodie Marsh the fit babe or Tom Welling the fit man?' He looked out of the window and addressed the car park. 'I was young, yes. I was twenty-five and Jack was, what was he, two years younger? I was twenty-nine when I met Larry and he was a year younger. So I'm not exclusively a chicken farmer or a cherry boy picker, you see.' He threw that in for good measure, turning back to fix him in the eye as he said it. 'That must 'ave been yonks ago! 'Aven't you 'ad nobody since then?' 'Anybody.' The word animated him as much as the double negative. 'Haven't I had anybody?' *Had*? You don't *have* people, dear boy.' *Yes they do, yes you did, you hypocrite.* He mellowed his tone. 'Larry and I were together for twenty years,' he said softly. 'Now I'm an old invalid and all my years are yester and love and lovers and casual sex and the whole damned shemozzle... it's dead and gone. They don't have a place in my life any more. Besides, why are you interested? I find it morbid. You're a teenager and you're supposed to think that anyone over the age of twenty-five who has sex is a pervert and that anyone over thirty who has it should be put down or at least arrested.' *And you shouldn't be talking like this to a fifteen-year-old boy.* 'Oh you sad minger.' 'Such insolence!' 'I don't think like that. I reckon it's good to have somebody intit, no matter how old you are? A partner I mean.' Roly couldn't really answer. He heard what he thought was the warm concern in his voice and felt he couldn't discourage such youthful hope. 'Yes, it's good, even when you don't deserve it, it's good. Is that what *you* want, a partner?' He didn't wait for an answer. 'I'm a special case now. If I could combine a partner with a carer... Oh I can't explain, how can you explain? It was inconceivable to me. If you're like I was at your age, here in your pomp, you can't possibly imagine saying in forty years' time that you have lost interest in sex. How can people live without sex, you think? When they're old, yes and you think poor buggers, why don't they commit suicide? And when you're fifteen, old never happens. It's like – oyvay, how blind is youth – like those friends of your parents, men who never married and women who didn't want children, spinsters and bachelors. They weren't real men and women, they had something missing, spooky people. Do you think you can be a whole person without sex? We, I, couldn't understand celibacy –' '– That means goin' without sex yeah?' 'Unimagineable isn't it? People who don't do sex are so weird aren't they? Or too old. Aren't I right?' he smiled. 'But I understand it now, oh yes, even though I'm forced to accept it because my appetite has been taken away. And d'you know, I don't resent that and that I don't resent it amazes me every day. Still, it's all here in my head... and that can be where the best sex takes place.' When Michael asked, after a longish thoughtful pause, 'Hey, can I ask you somethin'?' Roly asked, 'What?' 'Don't go sick.' 'So don't make me.' 'D'you... ya know... d'you like... d'ya fancy me?' He didn't ask it in a confrontational way, but with a kind of childlike apprehension and, once again, with the disarming naivety which Roly was fast recognising as his major trait. He would have asked his opinion on a new pair of trainers as blithely. But Roly was wary, still wary of a dark motive. *I don't know this boy, what he is.* 'Oh-oh, I see the game,' he said and wagged his finger. 'There's no game,' Michael insisted, but

Roly mistrusted. 'The game is that you get me to tell you that I fan – I hate that word – that I think you're goodlooking, then you go and tell your *mates* "the old faggot fancies me" and they all go "Eeew" and pretend to vomit and you all fall about and have a wingding at my expense. I can hear them: "That old queen, the disabled one, he tried to grope Michael".' Michael derided: 'Naaah, as if. If I told that lot you fancy me they'd all call *me* a queer!' Roly couldn't help firing off another 'Ha!' at such stoical ignorance. 'Oh my dear Michael,' he sighed, 'you've voiced, how can I put this? You've voiced a universal preconception, a misconception, you've put your finger on one of life's truths. The great unwashed out there think if a homosexual likes you, then you must be gay yourself. Geddit?' 'No way am I a g-boy,' Michael boomed, 'I told ya.' 'I know that, you morsel! But d'you see? You have to be defensive even with me. No way what? No way you're gay or no way that's how people think?' 'You're doin' me 'ead in now. I'm not a poof.' 'I'm not saying you are. I'm talking about popular thinking, I'm talking about what people think. Not how things are, but how people think they are.' 'Whatever,' he sulked, still not fully grasping the point. 'Anyway, I don't tell 'em fuck all about me and...' 'There's still time to moderate your slatternly execrations, Michael. Why don't you try "naff all" for a refreshing change? Or, better still – banjax. Yes, banjax all, banjaxing hell, banjax off, that's quite poetic, if a little clumsy.' 'What you say?' 'What don't you give a naff or a banjax about my boy?' 'Oh, well, ya know... about... I don't care what they think. When I'm not with 'em I mean. I mean, I've got me own space innit? They don't know.' Roly thought he was about to disclose bedroom fantasies for his ears only, but then thought that was being rather too wishful. 'But they must know you're here,' he said instead. 'This is practically a village after all. There's not much room for doing things on the QT, I would have thought.' 'None o' their business,' Michael said defiantly, defensively again, continuing his sulk. 'What's QT?'

Pace the boy, Roly raised a hand. 'Fine, fine, you do your own thing and you're your own man, boy. That's good, good for you, no problem.' The boy went deathly quiet, he stared ahead of him but his prying eyes looked at nothing; it was as if he were pondering some intractable mystery. Roly watched him and waited, then the boy spoke or rather mumbled. 'It's wrong though intit?' 'What is?' 'Ya know. Two men.' Now he focused his eyes. 'Doin' it.' 'Wrong? What is wrong? Who or what says it's wrong?' 'Well...' He was hesitant, reluctant, unsure now, fumbling. 'The Bible,' he proffered. 'Yeah, the Bible,' he said with more surety. 'I mean... 'ow it says you gay lot shouldn't do it an' you'll all go to 'ell and all that.' The handful of weeds – ignorance and myth (*They never die*, he thought) – picked at random and mistaken for flowers of knowledge, induced a deep groan then a mildly surprised 'Ooh' and then his arms drooped lifeless to his sides. 'The Bible,' he said, with full contempt. 'That collection of fairy stories. Well, my good boy, what is it that the Bible says, huh?' 'I dunno do I? It says men doin' it is wrong.' 'Six!' he shouted. 'You'll find six can't do's and don't do's in the sodding Bible if you choose to look. Six warnings for gay men and how many does it have for "you straight lot" hmm? Come on!' 'I dunno, he said again, defending the onslaught. 'Three hundred and sixty-two no less, scholars have counted them. The Bible contains three hundred and sixty-two admonishments for heterosexuals. Of course, I don't suppose that means that God doesn't love you, just that you need more supervision I'd say. 'Besides, if God was against us, why does he give us all the advantages of being gay?'

'Advantages? Woddyamean?' He stretched his eyes. 'Oh they're legion, my dear. You really couldn't give a damn about who Paris Hilton is sleeping with for instance, you can call anyone "darling", you understand the vital importance of good lighting, you can ask your girl friends to tell you everything you want to know about their boyfriends and they'll tell you – *everything*. You can have pictures of naked men you don't know in your home and you can have naked men you don't know in your home.' He beamed at him supercilioulsy but how much of the irony Michael took in wasn't clear, he merely rippled his face into a soft grimace and let out an insouciant 'Hmph'. 'Why is it that people are more comfortable seeing two men holding guns than holding hands?' Michael gave no answer and Roly saw that he was now exhausted by sophistry as the change of the direction of his desultory mind showed. 'You've never told me what's with the stick and trolley any'ow. What 'appened to you?' 'I did tell you but you weren't listening. I had a mild stroke, two. I lost my ability to balance and I need the trolley to carry things and a stick or a friendly arm to walk with.' 'Aww, I can carry stuff for ya.' A touch of sympathy in his voice now, how sarcastic was it? 'So can't you work now?' 'Oh I can most definitely work, unfortunately nobody wants me to work for them.' He shot him a wry smile. 'I love working, I love getting paid for working. No matter, I don't have any work and I have all the time in the world not to do any and as a result, I'm so downwardly mobile I've fallen off the bottom, gone from a Ginki to a Ninki in no time.' 'What's a ginky and an inky?' 'Good Income And No Kids to No Income And No Kids.' 'Oh. You on income support then?' 'Yes, as nobody will pay me to work for them, the government has to. It has to repay the money I paid to it when I did work. That's how I live, survive. All expenses paid.' 'You worked before though yeah? I bet you were somethin' 'igh up, right, in a suit?' 'Oh yes, I was high up head chef and cleaner at my pub in Kensington don't ya know, burgers cooked to order; barman before that from the Albion in Hanbridge to the White Hart, Llandovery and hostelries, dives and taverns in between, let's see, messenger boy at British Gas in Holborn, posting fliers through letterboxes in SW1, working behind a bar with my boyfriend in Coventry. Oh yes, I've had a full and rewarding working life. But mostly I've been a fulltime waste of time.' 'Behave, ya muppet,' Michael giggled. Roly hadn't intended to amuse him. 'Barman and cleaner,' he mocked. 'You must 'ave 'ad proper jobs.' 'No, never a proper job. I am, I *was,* a journalist. It's a profession.' 'What, like a reporter?' 'Yes.' 'You worked for the Signal then?' 'Oh please the pigs!' He breathed exasperation again. 'The Signal. Save us from the Signal. Why the natives of Trenton see Trenton's own evening paper as the pinnacle of a journalist's career, I will never know. If you don't write for the Signal, you're not a real journalist. Has Trenton still not yet heard of *The Guardian?* I have in my time been a little further afield. The *TVTimes, Independent, the Mirror*, London and... and yes, there, that place... and Tyneside and Hong Kong. And not only papers. I've done radio too. Radio 4 and commercial stations. I even worked for Trent Radio here for a spell.' 'Trent Radio? You never.' 'Please don't be impressed,' Roly yawned. 'I worked for Trent Radio, ain't that an eye-roller?' 'Did you 'ave yer own show?' 'I was a journalist, not a DJ. DJs have shows, journalists don't.' Radio, to the masses, means music, Roly thought. It detracted from the prestige of your being in broadcasting if you didn't play music. 'Huh, what little there was of prestige,' he murmured out loud. If you weren't a DJ with your name on your own show, you didn't count. 'I used to report the news and read it. And please don't ask me if

I've interviewed any famous sons of Trenton like Robbie Williams –' '– Hey yeah, 'e's the man. 'Ave you met 'im?' '– because they'll be names you've never heard of. Robbie Williams? As it happens, I know his aunt and I met his mother once. I saw him in a show when he was fourteen and gave him a rave review. I think my words at the time were, "If that boy isn't a huge star in five years, I will drink water from the Trent and Mersey canal." His mother came up to me in a pub after that and shook my hand. He also happened to do a week's work experience at Trent, then he was spotted for Take That and it was all starting for him and then I'd see him getting out of a Rolls Royce outside his house or hear him shout to me in the street to tell me he'd just got back from Korea or somewhere.' 'Is 'e gay then? No, 'e can't be. 'E shagged Nicole Kidman didn't 'e?' 'I don't know if he's gay,' Roly stormed. 'And there you go with popular assumption again. You must try not to assume, Michael. Please don't label people whom gay people know or have been associated with as gay themselves. Not all of a gay man's friends are gay you know. I never thought he was or wasn't. It wasn't and isn't a matter of interest to me. I can't say I know him intimately, I never penetrated his inner circle I'm afraid.' 'Bet you fancied 'im though.' 'And the other thing is not to assume that a gay man "fancies" every other man. Really, I have to start from first base with you don't I? No I didn't fancy him and I repeat, "fancy" is not a word that sits comfortably in my lexicon. I don't fancy people, I find them attractive. As for work, darling, I now try to work at home. I write. I'm a writer… I'm writing… a…' He was not going to explain what a factional novel was. 'A book.' 'Cool. What's it called?' 'No, I must be honest with you. I thought being a journalist was being an apprentice for a novelist. But I was wrong. I'm not writing a book, I'm fooling myself into thinking

I am. Whoever whispered in my ear the word 'talent' as I lay mewling in the crib was an arrant liar. But that doesn't matter. We seem to have moved away from talking about what does matter and what matters is, that in view of what you've done with your friend Hodgkins, I don't think it's a very good idea for you to come here any more.' This serious and sinister volution of mood seemed genuinely to shock. 'Why?' What 'ave I done?' 'Perhaps you're telling the truth, perhaps you and your friends don't wish me any harm –' '– They don't, we don't.' '– but you have to see it my way.' He did his best to simplify. 'I'm an old poofter, you're a handsome young boy calling on me. There'll be scuttlebutt, gossip, my Michael, my angelo, my Michelangelo. People, your pals, will... popular assumption says... people jump to conclusions and –' 'If there's any goss, they can go f–' 'you might get a reputation. People can be hurtful. You might get a name for something you're not. You may be branded.' 'Like I said, I don't give tho'. I'm comin' round 'ere to 'elp you out. So you're an old poofter? Like I care.' He had conviction, Roly had to credit him with that much and it made him waver. He turned quite endearingly penitent: 'I'm sorry about the crazy bet,' he said, 'but ya don't 'ave to kick me out for it. There won't be no more messin'.' In the lull, Roly studied him. He was now looking down at the carpet and one of his feet was tracing a slow circle across the pile. 'Bugger off Mr Titchmarsh and thank you for your help,' he said and Michael's head jerked up and he looked surprised and puzzled. 'Titchmarsh?' 'I thought you'd know who he is. He presents gardening programmes on the telly box.' 'Oh. Yeah,' came the mumble. He didn't know at all. He held Roly's gaze, looking plaintive: 'I *will* help you out if you want, I mean with jobs and stuff. And I'll carry on waterin' the herbs and I'm sorry I thought they were flowers, in the first place I mean.' He was aspirating deliberately – to impress? The first aitch Roly had heard him pronounce in the first grammatically sound sentence he had spoken to him so far made him dare to look closer at him while trying to smile and appear harmless; those deep eyes of his, eyes that could reflect one's secrets and penetrate and expose all one's thoughts were not at all disquieting, they were empathetic. He took in his face anew and amended his previous appraisal: it was smoother than he'd realised, like a polished tabletop, the rose mouth more voluptuous and his straight nose which widened and turned a little snub at the end, cutified him. 'Just be careful Michael,' he said in an effort to sound concerned for his wellbeing, which in effect he was. 'Come and water the blithering herbs and carry... stuff... for me, but be vigilant.' Michael beamed brightly now. 'Yeah,' he cried, like a winner of something. 'We mates then?' 'We're mates as long as you don't call me mate,' Roly smiled back. The tension dispersed, nevertheless he wanted him out of the way so that he could work and also give himself time to reflect on the inevitable perils of this blossoming unorthodox liaison of theirs. But he didn't want the boy to take a dismissal amiss, so he detained him by suggesting that if he wanted to be useful right now he could vacuum his car. He was quick to comply and when he'd finished, he made a coffee and sat with him drinking a can of Fanta, staring at the wall ahead of him. After a while, Roly saw his lips move ready for speech, he intuited instantly that the inevitable question was coming. He didn't know how, but even before Michael asked it he knew his fifteen-year-old naivety was either going to ask, 'When did you first..?' or, 'When did you know you were..?' but in the end, 'Before, like... didn't ya want no pussy?' came out and gave him a jolt and he was thrown back 36 years to that night, when Neville

Ladderbanks asked, 'So you've never kissed a boy then?' Which he proceeded to tell Michael all about.

'And in answer to your coarsely couched question, no, I never wanted sex with a girl,' he said when he finished. 'So you 'ate women then.' 'No I don't hate women. Some of my best women are friends.' Michael grimaced. 'Doncha mean some of your best friends –?' 'Yes, yes.' It was true, he wasn't a feminophobe. 'I can recognise a beautiful woman. Paris Hilton is beautiful, don't you agree? It's simply that I've never been sexually attracted to them. I found myself on a bed with a girl one day when I was about your age, we were messing around in a friend's house…' 'And?' 'And nothing. I suddenly realised she didn't have what a boy has so I rolled off her. QED.' 'You don't know what yer missin'.' 'On the contrary, I do know and I don't miss it. And I can say the same for you, so yah boo sucks.'

Michael, probably bored with tales of antediluvian gay life and probably not wanting to hang around to be further exposed over his horticultural fib about herbs or not wanting his offer of help to 'carry stuff' to be spurned, shot out of his chair, turned tail with his sign off line of 'See ya' more abruptly than before and darted out of the room. Roly tried to stay him. 'I have helpers you know,' he called after him by way of explanation. 'Careworkers. I'm not sure I have much for you to do.' 'S'okay, I'll still give you a knock anyway if you want,' he called back from the hall and then with 'I'll shut the door', he was gone. Roly went to lock it and when he went back to the computer room, Michael was at the window. He'd run round to the back of the building and now stood on the grass where he nymphed and shepherded with his pals and he smiled and gave a wave and Roly felt strangely and reluctantly reassured. Michael turned and ran; Roly sat and started to write up the episode. But writing about it did nothing to quell his doubts about the boy's integrity and intentions and those of his crowd. Thinking badly of him after their encounters so far had been so amicable and after his explanation of the bet plausible, was vigilant but unkind. He was still scared by the possibility, despite the boy's protestations, of that ridicule in the streets, those bricks through the windows, that excrement through the letter box. He was alone, sick, mostly helpless and gay and when Michael reported back to his chums about his visit and the revelations, if those chums did turn into marauders after all, he would be at their mercy. Whatever transpired from here, he must walk on eggshells with this forward boy, must still regard him, however reluctantly, as a potential juvenile danger. In other words, he couldn't yet fully trust him.

He finished this journal entry – or was it a part of his novel now? – and then he smiled at the prospect of the invented and imagined masturbatory figure of Denzel being replaced by the extant one of Michael. *Oh what am I like?* He so far dared not even so much as entertain the notion that Michael's inquistiveness had been fishing, that he'd been dipping his toes in the coming-out waters. His boy's waters were murky and churning, as most boys' waters were, that was all. He'd met someone who intrigued him and had gained access to information which excited his curiosity. Roly sat and reflected on his own 'coming out', for which both he and his parents were totally unprepared; more of a finding out than a 'coming out' it was.

That afternoon when I got home, my father was standing at the top of the stairs, brandishing my precious black diary. Cold outrage struck me as I ealised what he'd been reading. 'You've been going to that bloody Gazelle, haven't you?' he demanded, his face flushed with anger and Saturday lunchtime beer. 'You've no business reading that!' I screamed and turned on my heels, fleeing from the council house, from my father's anger and my mother's bewilderment to the Mini Minor they had recently bought for me. My father was out of the front door and charging down the garden steps behind me. I managed to start the car and drive off before I could be reached and stopped. 'I'm running away,' I told myself as I drove to Bakewell, where Alan Ward worked. 'I've run away,' I told him, across his fruit and veg stall, and he laughed. Later, I made a phone call to the cricket club where my parents always went on a Saturday night (their son had run away from home and they went out for the night!) and they fetched my father. 'Come home son,' was all he said and his manner had mellowed since the rage of the afternoon, and I was soon back to embarrassment and recriminations and exhortations to forget 'this boyish phase' as soon as possible.

****

Michael his foundling, his faun.

If he was, as he said, 'pukka' and if his offer of help was sincere, he had left Roly with no address but for the name of his road, not that that was of any use to him and it may not be where he lived at all. Nor had he given him a phone number. But wait. He'd said he sent texts, so didn't that mean his number would have stored itself in his mobile? How could he find it, oh how did these things work? If the discovery of his sexuality was Michael's sole purpose for making contact with him, to settle a childish wager, then he'd achieved his aim and he doubted he'd ever call again. He'd

133

been told by the friendly woman neighbour when he moved in, that the wheelie bins were taken care of by the elderly gentleman in the end flat of the block. The boy hadn't known his herbs were herbs, yet he said he liked gardening and was going to study it and his concern about the wretched things had seemed real. This fear, loathing and scepticism came on him when it dawned that Michael had had chance to look around the flat. He would have seen there was nothing worth taking, so why this street lad, this scallywag, scally stayed was a puzzle.

There was so much conflicting surmise.

****

The horror looms and he sees how it ends: the decayed and squalid old man and the sparkling adolescent, the ephebus of dreams. Tantalus, the old man, thirsts but the water, the untouchable youth, recedes and stays out of reach and his mind is cast into the sleazy pit of the demi-monde, where the sounds, smells and tastes of corruption and criminality fester and where he spent too much of his life, in an affront to his sensibilities; all the thieves, whores, murderers, swindlers and drug pedlars of the world are here and it's where his corrupt soul belongs. The rose-remembered days, the champagne on balmy-evening honeysuckle-scented balconies, (He loved champagne; he used to say he'd drink champagne all day long, every day, if he could afford it, but he couldn't afford it, so he chose whisky and drank that, if not all day long, as near as dammit and certainly every day and his ratiocination was that it was more sensible to spend all his money buying more of the something he couldn't afford (whisky) rather than less (champagne), the romps with sunshine boys in sunshine meadows, beautiful people doing beautiful things; he sees how all this is gone forever, he sees a tiny dirty life in his rented flat approaching fast, the dirty old

134

queer who lives alone and reeks of piss – 'Stay away from there, all children!' – the neighbourhood pervert who has young lads calling, stretching the folly of his youth to make it the shame of his old age. What would he do? Perhaps have a touch or even a grope behind closed curtains and give them a couple of quid, sordid and seamy and despicable and degrading both himself and them. To be an old gay man in a young gay world, to be an old crippled gay man in that world, to be an older crippled criminal gay man: ye gods, put up the shutters and lock the hermitage! He is resolute: Michael Hollis with an aitch had better not bring his cornucopia of temptations anywhere near him again.

****

'Naah, I told ya, she's binned. Ya know what she said right? She said I told 'Odge she was a slapper but I didn't though. I said, I said to Jezzer, that's me other mate yeah? I said if she's gonna 'ang around at the Swan snoggin' and playin' around with lads… all I said was, like, if she carries on like that, right, people'll think she's a slapper. So 'e goes back to 'er and 'e's like I called 'er one but I didn't and…' Michael's disquisition on the problems of teenage love spouted forth without an intake of breath after he rang Roly's doorbell and was in response to Roly's inquiry about his girlfriend. Yes, my dears, his last resolve immediately deliquesced when Michael called to ask if he needed 'anythin' from the Co-op' and he was in his presence again. Roly hadn't seen him for a week (he hadn't been to water his herbs again to his knowledge) and although he'd seen him from his livingroom on the grass outside with his friends in the meantime and walking past in the street and caught sight of him two days before when he drove out, not once had Michael looked in at him, waved, or acknowledged that he was there. He was relieved and grateful that, after that day, the day of

135

revelations, it appeared that he'd reported nothing to incite his mates to the hostility he had feared; there had been no boys pressing their noses intimidatingly up against his window as there were at his previous flat, there had been no bricks, no knocking on the door and running off, no dog poo, nothing. Michael and they had simply ignored him. Now Michael called on the Co-op pretext, out of the blue when Roly was in the middle of not writing anything and said there was nothing he wanted but Michael said he was going to get himself a can and at that he suggested he might like to come back and drink it with him. 'If you've nothing else on.' What he had on was a top with horizontal blue and white stripes and knee length shorts that were the year's warm weather teen wear (and had been for some time, he thought). He ran out and Roly went to check on what was cooking – a Moroccan aubergine casserole: aubergine, passata, sweet chilli, mint and yoghurt. He wished it could remind him of sultry Moroccan boys in Tangier, but it could not, because he'd never been there to sample their delights. 'It's like a motherfuckin' oven in 'ere,' Michael said as he breezed back in, free and easy with an expletive again. *Motherfucking*: the time had come to speak out again, this time forcefully. 'Michael, I'm no prude, I'm not offended but please, try not to be so barbarian when you swear.' Socrates remonstrating with his Alcibiades and Alcibiades made a whimpering noise. 'Adjust to the occasion and the company and do it with panache, avoid the ill-mannered delivery, the curled lip.' *Because, in your case, the curl defaces your crescents.* 'There's a way of cussing with grace and a certain amount of splendour. Really, boys like you know nothing of *bon ton*. Fucking this and that every time, it doesn't do, it's so tiresome, it shows a lamentable lack of vocabulary, despite what the pundits say. I must get you a thesaurus. Besides, the enduring power of the four letter expletive has waned, its ability to shock has been diluted by overuse and the people who overuse it are themselves boring.' *And when handsome boys like you swear in that acidulous tone they become ugly.* 'But the most important thing is that when *you* swear in that manner you become ugly and that is unforgiveable.' Either his objurgation fell on deaf ears, or Michael didn't have the remotest idea what he was talking about, because he looked bleak and blank and said nothing. Roly assumed that he assumed that he was simply saying he didn't like his swearing. He ended the hiatus. 'I've just noticed,' he said and he had. 'What?' 'Where's your celebrated cap?' Michael touched his hair as if to check whether or not he was wearing it. 'You told me you didn't like it,' he said. 'I said no such thing,' he corrected him. 'I said some people who wear a baseball cap and let their hair grow so that it sticks out below it often look... (he was about to say unsexy) silly. And I said, if I remember, that you have splendid hair and it would be even more splendid if it were a bit longer.' 'Whatever. I'm lettin' it grow now anyway.' *For me?* Without any by your leave he then whipped his teeshirt over his head and threw it over the back of the chair and Roly felt a frisson. He flopped down into the chair, can of Fanta in hand, legs inelegantly apart, unwittingly attracting Roly's leering attention. 'This isn't the beach, dear boy,' he said, pointing at the naked midriff. 'Whassup?' Michael cried, looking down at his navel as if Roly had seen something amiss. 'Heeeey, chill out,' he said, looking up. 'I give y'a flash of me gorgeous body for nuthin' and your complainin'.' He beamed his sardonic grin. 'Oh you're so generous, but I've already seen your body.' 'Yeah, 'course you 'ave,' he sneered, 'in yer dreams.' Roly told him where and when, 'Ha ha so there,' but didn't mention his admiration of the aborning pecs. 'Well I bet that was a kick for ya,' Michael trilled impudently and beamed widely and tauntingly. 'And stop lookin' up my legs you dirty pedo.' Roly saw this as an attempt to be the all-knowing grown-up and he grinned back. 'Well, I must say... I had to get used to "You can look but don't touch" from boys in gay discos very early on,' he said, 'because every boy I wanted never wanted me, but coming from a straight boy in my home who knows that I'm a harmless old poofter who has only told him what a goodlooking heartbreaker he is –' '– No you 'aven't.' 'Alackaday,' he sighed theatrically. 'I thought I had. If you don't want me to look, cross your legs and don't spurn the compliments of your admirers, by the way. You may be grateful for them one day.' Michael looked him in the eye for long seconds, then smiled and said, 'S'okay, you can look,' softly, coyly. 'That's more like it. You don't have to flaunt, but at least be proud of what nature has done for you.' 'Somethin' smells nice.' 'It doesn't smell, it scents and it's my lunch, dinner, supper.' Roly emphasised the names and smiled at him superciliously. 'Now who's bein' sarky? What yer makin'?' Roly told him but didn't mention Morrocan boys. 'So what do those *mates* of yours think of you calling on the dirty pedo again?' he asked him quickly. 'They must know, you must have told them. Is that what they're calling me now by the way?' 'Fuck 'em – ooh, I mean...what did ya tell me?' 'Banjax.' 'Banjax 'em.' Roly couldn' resist a smile. 'I'm sad you haven't been to water my herbs again. We've had no rain.' 'Oh, purleese, you pez,' Michael yelled. 'Who d'ya think's bin gettin' the can outta yer shed and fillin' it under Bill's tap and waterin' em for you? Twice this week. And you 'aven't noticed. Thanks for nuthin'.' 'Well, how was I to know?' he cried with remorse. 'And what is pez?' 'Peasant. An' so you should be sorry. I told you I'd do things didn't I?' He went into a sulky silence, then broke it with, 'What d'you

138

do with 'erbs anyway? They're just sittin' there.' 'I cook with them. When I can make an effort to go out and cut some that is.' 'Cook what?' 'There's fresh mint in the dish you can scent now, for example.' 'Oh.' 'I make herb soup and it's gorgeous. My dear old friend in Kensington, Dolly Braithwaite, bless her cottons, who's no longer with us, used to serve it to us at Sunday lunches in the summer after gin and tonics in the Scarsdale. He never –. 'He? You said "she". '– Never did get round to giving me the recipe, the bugger and it later occurred to me he didn't have one. I think he bought it ready-made at Harrods – he could be devious that way. "Come to lunch tomorrow, Roly,' he barked one Saturday, I remember and he went off up Ken High Street to do his shopping and came storming back into the pub in high dudgeon shouting, "There is no borage to be found in Barkers", just to show off. Remind me to save you a portion next time I make it. I *do* make it, I got a recipe from Delia in the end. Dolly's real name was Alfred Braywood, by the way.' Talk of camp nicknames seemed to pass over Michael. 'Not only am I a very good cook, I'll have you know, I'm quite good in bed too.' 'Whoo-hoo, get you,' Michael scoffed. 'And I s'pose you've got a big knob as well,' he guffawed, quite gravelling his throat. 'If you like good food and if you're a good child, I may invite you to lunch or supper one day, so brush up your table manners. I doubt you've ever sat at a table and eaten a meal have you –?' '– We do at me gramma's – ' '– Except at MacDonalds.' 'And you're not picky about food are you? Lacanophobic or turophobic, or anything like that?' The filling of time with idle chat, be it with familiars or strangers, was never Roly's forte, but Michael's boy racer mind and his fast tongue and his sitting half naked, pulled them through. School wasn't 'cool,' he said when Roly asked him about it, but, unusual to hear, Roly thought, his mother and sister

139

were. He didn't like cricket or football, but the earlier guess was right, he was mad keen on swimming and swam for his school and was hoping for a place in the county team. Otherwise, he was archetypally bored, with 'nothing to do in Trenton, 'cause it's a 'dump.' 'Everywhere is a dump to teenagers,' Roly said. At one point the boy leaned forward to examine the CDs on the carousel rack and it came as no surprise to hear him disparage his treasured collection.' 'Ow many you got? There's just about one I'd play outta that lot, it's all that classical crap.' *Oh, grant this boy some finesse in his criticisms and some diluting of his philistine soul.* 'Not even Van Morrison or Morrissey? Your philistine opinions are not welcome, get out of my house. I suppose you are all Eminem and Project 8,' he said, with contempt. 'Naah,' Michael snarled. 'Rap is square daddy. Drum n' bass. Yay!' he cried in triumph and threw up his arms and clenched his fists and Roly clutched his brow. 'Not the ubiquitous jungle throb,' he moaned. 'I knew there was something.' 'Doncha like it? It's wicked.' 'Like it? It's arse gravy of the worst kind, a total dish of stool water the lot of it. Incessant rhythmic non-melodic manure.' It was clear they wouldn't be sharing music, not yet. *Socrates has much to teach.* He found himself returning to the subject he'd previously mentally proscribed and to the evening he would rather forget. 'She's not my girlfriend,' Michael said when he mentioned the evening in question and went on to his breathless explanation. 'But I saw you with her. Your hand was glued to her front bum.' 'Yeah, well I was flyin' innit.' 'Flying? Flying on what, cider?' 'That and.' He wasn't going to expound. 'Michael,' Roly urged quietly, 'and what?' He looked sheepish. 'I took somethin'. We were messin' around.' 'Oh I see. Was it E?' 'No.' 'Oh, what then? Crystral meth or is there a new thing now?' 'It's not new. K.' 'Ah yes. That wasn't around when I dabbled.' 'What's dabbled, you did pills?' 'Don't be so surprised. I was where you are now too, you know, when life was full of daft things and I was drunk. Not quite so young as you, but you haven't invented reckless. What does K do?' 'Buzzes you up, man. Bit like strong poppers.' Poppers he was surprised at. 'I suppose I shouldn't be surprised. We got our dopamine from lemonade and Smith's crisps. When your lot get good grades you go and get drunk and you lose your innocence with mind-altering substances. Ou sont les neiges d'antan? Don't try and answer that.' Why? Why was he, who was so venal himself, so judgemental? 'Do you use it often?' 'No, that was the first time.' 'Did you like it?' 'I dunno. It kinda makes you droopy and you don't know what you're doin' really.' 'Did you know what you were doing with your girlfriend?' He paused. 'Roly man, the honest truth is I don't remember anythin' about it.' 'Oh I see.' 'She ran off and you ran after her. That's when I saw your –' '– Oh yeah, she did. Saw my what?' 'It's not always prudent to lose control. Be careful next time.' 'There won't be a next time. I told ya, she's binned but yer right, I don't like it when I don't know what I'm doin'. You can land in trouble and. I s'pose you think I'm bad doncha?' 'No, no, I don't think anything. I've done it myself so I can't judge you. I can think you're making a mistake, but there's not much I can do to stop you making it is there?' 'What did you do?' 'Oh, a little weed, a little coke, some amphetamines and a lot and I mean a lot of the worst of them all.' 'H?' 'Alcohol, booze, grog, tincture, what you will. Whisky mainly, usquebaugh, the water of life, or in my case the water of screaming and slow death, destruction in a bottle.' After a pause, a tease, 'If I'm honest, you and your K gave me a buzz as well, if a little pang too.' 'How come?' 'I saw the cider and K didn't give you brewer's droop.' 'What you talkin' about?' He told him about the public display in his shorts and a deep red flush spread up from the boy's chest to swamp his face and he wriggled and spluttered. 'Yeah, though, no!' and then he murmured softly, 'Anyway, that was before I' and then he changed his mind and said firmly, 'Don't diss me an' my, my... what d'ya call it? my.' 'I'd call it a healthy phallic response,' Roly said smugly, 'and nothing less than I'd expect from a testosterone-charged young buck. Or a you a dude? Positively priapic it was, made me come over all queer. Not much shocks me, Michael, but there you were and there she was and, I don't know, it was just the way you made it look as though it was the most natural thing in the world to stand with your hand clamped to a girl's groin on a street corner.' 'Like you said, she ran off and like you never did anythin' stupid. Like I said, I was flyin'. It was just messin' and so you saw me with a stiffy, so what? I don't give,' he protested. 'Well you should give,' Roly aped, 'and comport yourself with dignity, even when your hormones are jostling.' He thought it best to forego any further critique of teenage behaviour; the presence of youth may have rejuvenated him for a while, but it hadn't removed the rage he felt over its anomie from time to time. 'An' I'm not bothered,' Michael concluded, 'she can go and... f... *banjax* 'erself. She was well butter anyway, dunno wot I saw in 'er.' He sipped his Fanta. 'Butter?' He explained the play on words. 'Nice tits butter face,' he said, deadpan. 'I might hit on Leanne Brookes, I know she's well 'ot for me. She'll let me give 'er one. Only trouble is Danny's bin there first.' He paused and looked thoughtful. 'Girls are mank, I think I'll be a faggot.' Whether this last was self-mockery or mockery of him Roly couldn't calculate. He refrained from encouraging him in any such thought anyhow, thinking his indifference over his girl may have been feigned, that a more painful chord than he was willing to let him hear had been struck, because he rapidly finished the last of his can, grabbed his teeshirt and jumped out of his chair on a pretext of having to rush home to catch his favourite TV programme. 'It's on in a bit. I'm off,' he said, customarily curtly. 'Oh yes, so it is. Stay and watch it here if you like.' 'You don't watch it do ya?' He asked, pulling on the shirt, 'It's kids' stuff.' He reached the open door and draped himself round it, swinging his leg sinuously over the handle and resting it there, bent. 'My kids' stuff was travelling in the Tardis, before you were thought of.' 'Before I was a twitch in me dad's bollocks yer mean.' 'Coarse child,' he chided. 'What was in that Fanta?' 'Ohsorreeevulgar,' he intoned, lah-de-dah. 'On your velocipede, young man. Skeedaddle.' He made to shoo him off. 'You don't 'alf speak long words with yer posh voice. You're a brainiac innit. I like it though,' he said as he undraped himself from the door. 'Turns me on, ha-ha' and with that and with 'Laters', he was gone again, leaving Roly wondering if how much he felt he'd embarrassed himself. He decided on trout steamed in the bamboo steamer with lemon slices and sprouting broccoli for supper that night.

****

Michael scampered out of school and skipped his way to tell Roly he'd mentioned to his mother that he'd worked for Radio Trent and that she'd never heard of him. 'She asked me if you read the news out under yer own name.' Needless to say, he was baffled by the outburst of sour laughter with which Roly greeted this. 'My own name, what's my name and what's in a name?' he asked when he'd quietened. 'Oh lordy, dear Michael, don't mind me.'

I walked into the editor's office one afternoon and told him I was going to change my name by deedpoll. My colleagues had greeted this plan with

143

hilarity when I announced it to them, but Harold France took the news affably. He was a mild-mannered, almost timid man was Harold, who walked like Groucho Marx. He was fair-minded and everyone liked him. 'That's your personal decision,' he said. 'May I ask why?' I didn't say that I had, in fact, already signed a Change of Name Deed and the deed, as it were, was done. 'Just that I don't like the one I've got so I'm taking my mother's maiden name,' I said. 'Fair enough,' said Harold. 'So what do we know you as in future?' 'It's Hunter,' I said. And Harold scribbled it down.

'Yeah, well, there's nothing wrong with that is there? I told ya before, I changed mine innit? There's loads o' celebs change their names. 'Oo's that old guy me mum likes? Elton John. That's not 'is real name ya know.' Roly told him how his changing of name had nothing to do with promoting any celebrity he may have once thought he had claim to, far from it and then, on a sudden compulsion, he started telling him the whole botched history of his identity: how he went to his first gay bar in London, the Imperial Hotel at Richmond and was accepted into the group of regulars, characters and good people all, who congregated in the top corner and how he was introduced to Geoffrey the barrister – 'who was a much older man, the kindest of men, who never laid a finger on me, never asked for anything in return for his lusting after me. He shared my taste for oriental boys, did Geoffrey,' he said and he smiled. 'He used to say, "They veneer the aged, y'know, m'dear' – and how Geoffrey drew up the Change of Name Deed and signed it with a fountain pen and tied it with the pukka pink ribbon. He explained why he'd first decided to add a name to his existing one, rather than change anything and become double-barrelled. 'It wasn't entirely pretentious, it was more as a sop to my family (which did I hate more, them or their name?), so as not to turn my back on my heritage, such as it is, entirely – a qualm about dropping my family name altogether it was, so rather than obliterate it I added the name Hunter to it.' Being double-barrelled, he confessed, appealed to him and so with a flourish of snobbish vanity he became Roland Wanger-Hunter. 'But only for a few weeks. I went back to Geoffrey with a change of heart for yet another changed name. I really could make a dog's dinner of things even then, couldn't I? Geoffrey never asked me my reasons and I didn't volunteer any. I was too flummoxed and I was relieved and grateful.'

He stopped there, realising he'd unloaded this tranche of mottled biography on Michael unwittingly; well, he was the only audience he had, his bafflement over his identity had no interest for his chatroom chums or his homeworkers. The unloading was his way of demagnetizing the lodestone, to record the whole contentious and farcical hoedown and have it in black and white for all time, to stop it hammering against his brain and perhaps he was thinking that, by telling Michael about those two episodes some – he doesn't quite know – *significance* would show itself to him, or at least the strands of his legion selves would be tied and he could finally decide who he was and is in front of someone. He guessed that telling the story must also have been encouraged by the recurring rankle: what was Michael's motive for befriending him? Perhaps this was unkind, perhaps his befriending *was* altruistic, but still it rankled, the direct and elliptical probing, which may or may not have been his awkward way of familiarising himself with him, of forging a friendship, of eliciting his affection and making it 'pukka'. But when Roly finished telling him about deed polls, he still asked himself what it was this enchanting urchin wanted. Not urchin, that was too pejorative a word for a boy who, so far, had shown no inclination to do him harm and on the contrary had behaved, in his rough-hewn way, with decorum. But that first lie about the herbs, it stuck in his craw and he knew more than most about lies and they frightened him. He had now been in his flat alone with him twice and had shown no inclination to any physical or verbal abuse, neither was anything missing as far as he could see and he'd shown himself to be precociously openminded. Perhaps I'm paranoid, he thought and this weird and wonderful friendship is progressing as normally as... well, as normally as these things do progress.

Michael goes home and after a supper of corned beef hash and baked beans, a banana and coffee, TV, a crossword and his drinking chocolate nightcap, Roly (*Me, drinking chocolate for a nightcap!*) finally goes to his bed on a fiercely humid night, with his quandaries, their resolution not assisted by the struggle he has with the heat and damp. He never should have invested in a duvet, he knew it was a mistake when he bought it. He was always a sheets and blankets man, duvets made him sweat in the summer and didn't prevent him freezing in winter and the persuasion of his social worker, who had gone with him on his flat furbishing shopping trips, was the only reason he had one. 'They're much more hygienic, you know and there's less washing.' Jesus, it was hot and wet tonight! and he threw the thing off and lay there without moving to allow what fresh air there was to waft around his body. Combatting the heat led him to forget his fear of potential intruders: he opened his bedroom window wide to the elements and to danger. It was nights like this, lying uncovered in damp heat, that reminded him of Thailand and smooth ebony boys…

The boy managed to say his name was Prasong and that was the extent of their verbal communication, they mated in sign language...

... and when he came over to me by the swimmingpool, his smile was all I needed. He was an Alfa Romeo of a boy, sleek and shiny, nought to sexy in a flash. A prostitute was standing next to him, pestering him and shouting at me. 'He is boy. He don't got this,' she yelled and dug her tit out of her dress and juggled it around. I gave her a only a gentle shove but she slipped and went arse over that tit and her other one into the water and I whisked Prasong away. Of course, I was unable to understand, while I was splicing his buns, that he was losing his cherry. Sign language doesn't accommodate that contingency in its vocabulary. Not that it mattered to either of us: I would have rogered the little beauty anyway, pristine or not and Prasong was getting what he set out to get that night – his cherry picked by a European. The next day he went off to wherever it was and made a date, with the help of the English-speaking hotel barmaid, to come back that night. When he appeared, he was with a boy called A. The who, what and why of this boy being there were beyond my ken. I knew only, through the barmaid, that Prasong had brought his friend as a present for me. I supposed that Prasong supposed that, after the previous night, I was the man to bring his friends to. It was futile to question the sexual shenanigans of the Orient, I told myself. They are enchantingly perplexing and while I was lustily cornholing the newcomer in my room an hour later, Prasong waited his turn in the garden below. *My God, they're queueing up for me!* The boy in the Bangkok police cell; now that's what I call serendipity. I had taken my previous night's pickup to lunch and said goodbye to him outside the restaurant. When I got to my hire car, I saw a piece of paper pinned under the windscreenwiper. I assumed it was a parking ticket and I got someone to direct me to a police station before I was arrested and left to rot in the 'Bangkok Hilton'. The police station consisted of a small, white room with one window and a desk. To the side was an open space framed with metal bars. While the young woman police officer counted my 500 baht and filled in a form, I looked over at the 'cell'. About a dozen people were squashed on to the one wooden bench, others squatted on the floor and my eye was immediately caught by the gorgeous boy making gestures to me. He looked about 16 and wore a dark blue teeshirt and jeans the orange colour of the Buddhist monks' robes. He was miming holding a bowl in his hand and scooping invisible food from it to his mouth with an expression of supplication.

I asked the policewoman if he was hungry. 'Ob course,' she said. I asked what he was in there for. 'He is bery bad young man. He sits outside big hotel, begs from bisitors.' And she shouted something abusive at the boy. I asked how long he'd be in prison. 'He got no money to pay to get out,' she said. So I asked her if I could buy some rice or something for him, as he looked so hungry. 'You pay for rice? Pay his fine. Bowl of rice more expensive.' So I took out my wallet again, not thinking for a moment I might be buying the boy's body – this was simply some on-the-spot philanthropy – and paid the fine and whether it was indeed for a bowl of rice, a beggar's fine or police pocket money, or all three, I didn't know or care, but the officer took my money, unlocked the cell door and ushered the boy out - and a girl at the same time. 'His sister go too,' she said, smiling brightly. The two youngsters both bowed and wouldn't stop bowing until the officer shooed them out with some stern words. I took my receipt and my leave of the Thai police system for the last time, I hoped. Outside, the boy and his sister were standing on the pavement in animated conversation, the girl seemingly giving her brother what for in a shrill tirade. She knew some English. 'Thank you, thank you kind man. You want me now?' she asked. 'We go your hotel?' I waved her away as though she were leprous, said no thank you and told them to go home and stay out of trouble.' The girl persisted and, to my amazement, pushed the boy forward and said, 'You want my brother?' The boy flashed a captivating smile and I felt my legs buckle. 'Has he known a man before?' I asked her, imperiously. Like that mattered to them! The girl answered me with that brand of oriental logic which brooks no dispute, 'No, my brother likes girl. He go with you now.' And half an hour later, his beatific smile was transformed into a rictus of sweet agony as he repaid me for his rescue, spreadeagling his lissom body and swinging his legs high as I bifurcated his firm and tender prats as wide as I could on the bed in my room at the Dusit Thani Hotel.

His reminiscence of the adventitious conquest was cut off when he heard the noise, a muffled sound, a kind of rustling. This was odd because his bedroom window was open and there was still no hint of a wind in the humid night. And it was deathly one o'clock quiet. He dared to look sideways at the thin angled blinds covering the window. He could just make out, by the light which beamed weakly into the room from the streetlamp over on the other side of the carpark area, the silhouette of a figure. Somebody was at his window. Fright took hold, then panic. The violent end at the hand of some intruder he had so often hardly dared contemplate became a possibility. He froze, not knowing whether to cry out or try to creep unheard out of bed and make for the phone. He lay there, stiff, sweating, helpless and terrified for what seemed like hours. He thought of a daring ploy, it was all he could think of. He shouted, 'Sarah! When you come to bed, bring me a glass of water would you?' He doubted this would fool the lurking shadow but he was desperate. Thank the gods he was wrong, for as soon as he'd spoken, the shadow flitted across the blinds and vanished and he heard the stifled sound of running footsteps on grass fade into the distance. His would-be attacker had fled. He had no time to be relieved. His bladder had instantly filled and, though bursting, he struggled out of bed, grabbed his trolley for support and shuffled, as urgently as he could, round the foot of the bed and to the window, reaching for the handle and yanking it shut with all the force he could manage. He had no thought of poking his head out to try to spot a figure lest it got hit by a baseball bat. His urine dribbled into his briefs as he stood breathless and quaking, leaning on the sill, feeling ludicrous. He realised his tinnitus was ringing more loudly and intrusively than usual and he made the futile, instinctive move of covering his ears with his hands, which he hadn't had to do for a long time. He hadn't known terror like this since the night in the council house a few years before, when he woke to find the enormous black beast sitting on the bed, a wild dog it was or something hideously like. That hallucination could be put down to drink, but this fright wasn't illusory, he was sober and had been for two years. Eventually, his breathing rhythm returned, the trembling stopped and he manoeuvred himself back round the bed to reach for his baby wipes. He rubbed himself down as best he could and got back on the bed and tried thinking of sex or life as a successful author, or what he would have for lunch, anything to clear his head of the terror he had just gone through and of this dire existence, this life of real and imagined fears in which he was trapped.

He now had the horrors. He couldn't get back to sleep, the fear that the stalker was lingering or would return wouldn't allow it, so he got out of bed and went, still traumatised, into the computer room. He sat at the desk and looked up at the blue-grey blanket of a high summer dawn sky, then he quickly pulled the blinds to shut it out. The avian chorus was just beginning, one or two pairs of housemartins had set up home, as far he could tell, in the roof above him and he guessed it was them. He turned the computer on and fetched up his Journal file; he should try writing an entry to stabilise himself but he didn't have the first idea what he was going to say. His brain was a cataract, he could hear the thoughts cascading into it, but not ones of Muvvie, she didn't bother him that morning, his fear had shoved guilt aside. The last time he had the horrors was when he watched the film *Pulp Fiction* only a few nights before. That is, he tried to watch it, but he got the horrors. This happened more frequently nowadays; his melancholia turned jet black.

Violent films didn't help, they did nothing to help him escape the unwanted and ever-present awareness of his solitary existence. How vulnerable being alone made him feel now, foreboding was constant. And he had become squeamish. He couldn't watch the scenes where people were pointing guns at each other and had to look away before the bangs and the blood. He had a vision of a gunman coming here, to the flat, crazed and braindead after sniffing cocaine or nandrilone. His window was the one the man happened to choose to come to. He pointed his Kalashnikov rifle and riddled the room with his bullets and blood spattered the walls.

Some night later, he had a dream of dead people and of an actor friend he used to have called Esmond. He had fallen over in the road under the railway bridge near the council estate that used to carry the loopline that ran past Katie Beans field. (He often fell over in his dreams, or floundered chest-high in water, was often rendered helpless in some such way.) Esmond helped him to his feet and took him round the corner to a house where the dead people, people he had known, were – Maddie and Danny among them – and Maddie explained that they weren't dead but were hiding and she made him promise not to tell anyone, then he opened his bedroom blinds, saw his reflection in the window and felt straightaway a stab of sheer horror and he was engulfed by a sensation of something liquid, as though the horror were real blood. He was becoming more aware and more terrified by the minute that he was probably destined to meet a violent end.

As he stared at his computer screen, the cataract thundered and the carousel span and suddenly Robert Middlemas jumped out. Why Robert Middlemas, why that particular horror, what had he got to do with anything? 'Now I know madness,' he said to himself and started to type what he could remember typing over 30 years before. Nineteen seventy-two it must have been and he knew the opening sentence off pat. 'All bisexuals are perplexed and selfish', it went. It was written with bile, brimstone and no treacle, Robert Middlemas had crushed him, made him cry, all bisexuals took advantage of gay men and made them cry eventually. 'And all queers who've had sex with women are not genuine card-carrying poofters'. What bigotry he flourished and took pride in then.

He'd read a profile recently, a young man on one of the gay websites; he'd copied and pasted it into his notes, so fascinated and intrigued by it had he been:

> Ideally bi-curious, that's the way I am and you must accept that. I'm str8... and yeah I AM STR8... I've spent a long time thinking about this and it's something I want to try but I don't think I should put myself at risk, so you must be genuine and sincere and very discreet. If you're not, then please don't waste your time or mine.

He wondered what brain wrenching processes had the young man been going through. The wording indicated that he'd spent time carefully considering his situation and attitudes and had come to a decision to turn words and thought into action that was not at all reckless, but Roly speculated on the outcome. Would he regret the experience or surprise himself by enjoying it and, if he did, would he bitterly regret having wasted time, would his life be ruined and remorseful after he had tasted gay sex, would he become a queer basher, or would he find that he was, after all, gay or at least bisexual? The permutations were manifold. He himself had had to suffer no such mental conflict, his adolescent rites of passage had been relatively straightforward and his sexuality had been destined and indefeasible from the start, no doubt or shillyshallying about it. He hated having been intransigent in this, refusing to accept that others' paths of exploration and revelation could be strewn with confusion and sometimes fear, he'd had no time for ditherers and he now accepted that his hatred of Robert Middlemas and his ilk had been irrational and ingenuous, born of nescience, intolerance and the failure to understand. This hatred was equalled by and linked to the loathing of himself, his past and the home town which, almost as soon as he left it, he realised had been a prison, of that he was sure. But which had spawned which he couldn't answer; he only knew that everything connects.

In one of the 'eras' of his boyhood, his architectural one, he had foraged in the local library and had discovered Pevsner's guides to Britain. The man was an august authority but that had not prevented his falling into the 'Arnold Bennet trap'. Arnold Bennet, Trenton's most illustrious son and successful novelist immortalised the city but, for unknown reasons, always wrote of the 'Five Towns' ignoring the fact that Trenton was made up of six distinct towns and was properly called 'The Six Towns' or 'The Potteries', its world-celebrated ceramics being its claim to fame. Pevsner called it 'an insignificant city' and 'an urban tragedy' 'The national seat of an industry and what is it?,' he asked. 'Five or to be correct, six mean towns hopelessy interconnected by factories and streets of slummy cottages and with no real centre, not even an attempt at one'.

This city, 'insignificant' Pevsner called it, lies sprawled over hills that are black-remembered from my childhood, black with industrial grime and now cosmeticised by forestry and municipal facelifts. The hills and the cols between them are crammed with a new generation of tawdry shacks, sheds, warehouses and depots of manufacture; the great conglomerates of pottery, coal and steel have disappeared, built on with estates of new houses which look like identical slices from a single building block. There are still drab leftovers of old fashioned honest manufacture to be found: some small potteries survive, at least one tall chimney spends its days belching white smoke, though I don't quite know why, there are small higgledy-piggledy corrugated factories with mysterious signs reading R & H Filters Ltd and Douglas Turbines and Blurton Oxides, wood and brick merchants seem prosperous and there are still coal and coke bunkers in the railway sidings. Here and there are remnant rows of back-to-backs, a few elegant Victorian and Edwardian villas and terraces lord it over parks and there are high streets of empty and decaying shops which contrast with the thriving enclaves of designer retail parks. There are schools, a hospital, people and traffic and there's still the place that once was Katie Beans field and the brickworks, now an area of landscaped special natural interest or something. This city burgeoned and prospered and grew grotesque thanks to the products it manufactured from the mass of marl and the coal seams it sat on; it has made the transition to the cleaner modernity of 'service' commerce and today, as I write, it pulsates and bustles and shimmers, a commercial anthill under heaven's June eye, which looks down with too much fire through a murky swirling haze. Try as I might, I can't rid my mind's eye of the city that's memorialised and has remained static in the mind of Roland Wanger, who was born and brought up here and has despised it always, who still sees the air thick with the disgorged smog of bottle kilns, the skeletal pithead wheelshafts rotating in silhouette against leaden skies and still sees, down in Chatterley Valley, the tall chimneys of the iron foundries belching out hellfire, their flames turning the night sky molten red and their poisonous vapours drifting up to smother the starlight and make this dirty little corner of the universe even more confining. I can't be rid of this image: for me, the city will always be the inescapably filthy, smoke-ridden Five Towns of Arnold Bennet – though in fact there are six and, in fact, the people who live in them still wear his 'grim smile'. You can tell that in Trenton I'm misanthropic; I resent the place because having left it and disowned it in my nonage, I've been compelled to return on several occasions over the years and now I'm stuck here for ever. It's still all so shabby. I see its mass of people and don't like them very much: there are too many of them, they get in the way, they throw litter, spit in the streets and wear dreary clothes – all faded denims and scrappy jackets and flimsy summer frocks on bulbous thighs – and they have gross tattoos on their arms and cheap jewellery round their necks and in their ears. I look down on this humanity with a sour hauteur, I can't summon any feelings of warmth; I question why I despise my home town and feel such antipathy towards its people and think how hard it is to feel at one with someone and something you look down on. How much this is due to my own inverted snobbery and pride and how much of it I subconsciously acquired from Neville Ladderbanks, I will never know. I hear Neville's bitchy asides in the Gazelle and see him standing at the front window of his house watching the people going into the church opposite: 'Look at them!' he shouts through the glass. 'There they are, Nelllie Pemberton and Dorothy Brookes in their hats looking so righteous. Fucking hypocrites!' I've never been as vehement and vociferous as Neville but sometimes I don't feel I'm of the same species as the people of Trenton at all.

Perhaps I should not be so cranky. I have now, after all, moved from the shabby city centre recently to this flat on the semi-rural outskirts, where I'm surrounded by high fields of cattle and sheep, with the village hall opposite and the village shop yards away. I was welcomed by my new neighbours, straight couples, one old man and one elderly woman, good people who invited me to call on them any time I needed anything. Life here is not so unpleasant. True, I'm still among the savage tribes of Trenton: the plebs who drop their litter and expectorate, the tattooed young women pushing their babies while smoking, the occasional loud drunken weekend shouting in the street, the quiet sometimes disturbed by passing oiks in their souped-up Clios with their windows wound down and their drum n' bass blaring to heaven. But life here is not so unpleasant. It would of course be more pleasant if the one neighbour I've spotted, the young man who lives in the end terraced house bang opposite my kitchen window, would pay me the same courtesy. Maybe he's too engrossed with the young woman he lives with, bah. I've been watching him at work on the patio he's constructing in his backyard, which I have a view of, in only his shorts. He's fair-haired and in his mid-20s I'd say and he's one of *that* type of young men; you know the type – robust, strapping, before they're gone to fat or seed, with torsoes that aren't overly muscular or necessarily gym-trained, but which fill their teeshirts leaving no slack drooping folds and with firm buttocks which their jeans and tracksuits stick to. Mr Peachy I call him over the road, because he is not that tall and is quite compact; his chest sports quite prominent nipples I can see clearly from here, agony to watch. 'Go on, look this way, look at me. See me watching you, why don't you.' I wonder if he's one of those lusty lads who live in domestic and sexual contentment with their girlfriends, their football, their lads' nights out and their Volkswagen Polos who have to sneak off from time to time to satisfy their need to be fellated by and, often, fellate a man and, more common than we expect, be anally penetrated. Yes, life here is not so unpleasant. Or is it, with all the dark thoughts and memories that beset and pester me?

A visitor who happened along the ridge beside the city and went up the stretch of straight road and turned into the semi-rural side street, past the bungalows and stopped at the small terrace and went into his flat and then into the small lemon yellow room, would come upon him at his computer keypad, inhaling the regrets and sorrows which are accumulating once more in his memory to form a vast and melancholic thunder cloud around him. His visitor might find him either distracting himself in the gay chatroom, talking to internet chums, flirting with young men and 'perving' their profiles, or sending emails to apply for jobs and reading the replies telling him his application hasn't been successful this time, or writing features and sending them to editors and receiving their rejections, or worse, receiving nothing at all, or playing mahjong or word puzzles, or doing research in various websites, or, oh yes, reading his Journal. That was what he was doing now, making use of his insomia by reading of Robert Middlemas, the drama student with bewitching dark eyes and succulent black hair who broke his spirit and did more than anyone to fuel his sour grapes opinion of bisexuality. It could be pointed out that he could never come to terms with gay men shaking women, because he never then and still now had never been sexually attracted to females, in fact, it was true to say that he had an almost primordial fear of the vagina and the mammaries and from the moment he realised he was queer, he determined that the doorway to female sexuality was staunchly barricaded. That black and white fixation of his: it blighted him and polluted all his perceptions, even affecting the adoration of his gay idols – he couldn't even now forgive his beloved Oscar Wilde for having been married and as for his Renaissance man idol, Stephen Fry and the idol of camp, Julian Clary, both admitting to having penetrated a woman… well, it wasn't the real McCoy was it? Not pukka, not kosher, not pure-simon. They were traitors to the cause and in the case of Stephen Fry it was double treason, because like him, Fry had once been a thief and it offered no solace to his own wretchedness to worship a flawed hero who had betrayed him by having been to bed with a woman.

He reads of the day he took his unretractable foreskin to hospital to have it cut off so that he could at last have active intercourse and reads of celebrating his inaugural act of buggery with the boy in Bristol who took him back to his bedsit and opened his legs for him willingly. 'Can I fuck you?' he heard himself whispering, for the first time in his life, in the dark 30 years ago, 'Yes,' came the reply. He did it! And he reads about Larry; Friday the 13th it was, in the Princess Victoria in Kensington, dear Tiplow's turn to entertain the gang to lunch. He walked into the pub and immediately saw a ravishing young man talking to David, one of the actors in the gang. They had once worked together; David introduced them and he and Larry shook hands and Larry asked, with that quirk he had, a jerky giggle then a brilliant open smile and a coy tilt of his head: 'Oh, are you in the business too?' Reading how, when Tiplow turned up, he pulled him to one side and asked him if he had room for David's gorgeous friend for lunch. 'I was just thinking the same thing,' Tiplow said, so Larry was invited and he accepted. At closing time, the others trooped off to Tiplow's place in Earl's Terrace while it was his turn to go over to the off-licence to buy the wine. On the way to the Terrace, a dollop of pigeon shit landed on his jacket and when he got toTiplow's he asked him for a cloth but David, in his finest booming Shakespearean voice, bellowed, 'No! Roly you must *not* wipe that off. It's Friday the thirteenth and you've been shat on by a pigeon and this is the luckiest day of your life' and some four hours later, he was in bed with Larry and was thanking David heartily. The day he met his love, his wonderful singing day.

Only connect, E M Forster said, he believed if people would only connect, all would be well. Roly saw 'Only connect' one

160

day, somewhere, he couldn't remember where or when and he wondered how he could connect Chris the barrister, the Dunhill lighter, Muvvie, Stephen Fry, Robert, John, Larry, thieves and victims, bisexuals, gays; wondered how to connect all those dangling broken bedraggled threads. Everything connects.

The blue-grey summer dawn had now coloured into a deeper blue morning spattered with cumulous cushions and he could draw wide the blinds. This was nature's crass trope, he thought, its way of showing how it could appease the near narcotically mental gloom that was festering inside him. It was going to be a brilliant day, but the sun touched heavily on his eyes, eyes which he thought must be, but couldn't look into the mirror to confirm, bloodshot. He fetched his breakfast and a mug of coffee and took it back to his desk to eat while he read on.

Robert... and, yes him, another Michael, Michael Condon, the pretty chorus boy he pounced on when he was producing his radio documentary about the Society. He was willing enough to be pounced on but he was another bisexual catastrophe. He heard someone say – was it on the telly box the other day? – that bisexuality was the nightmare the gay world lived with and he wished *he* had thought of that. As you see, he kept a roster of corpses, that is to say boys and men who are dead in the sense that they constitute the detritus of his sexual history, you understand, my dears: liaisons which evanesced, usually in misery, were ended on one side or the other with a brutal final blow. Memories of them travel the years and pay house calls from time to time and bring those overwhelming thunderclouds of gloom with them. When that happens – and it happens more and more often now – he realises he has lived this long simply to allow time for the amount of regret he was destined to suffer to accumulate. (Oh yes, he sulks for England, my dears).

Now there was the second Michael, his satyr, faun, faunlet Michael Hollis: he didn't dare contemplate what source of regret Michael was destined to become should their lives entwine. Entwined lives? Did he just think that? What delusions did he have about their lives *entwining*? He and a 15-year-old boy? Preposterous. The dichotomy was unadjustable: on one side, the beautiful and blessed young Michael and on the other, the remorseful and remorselessly melancholic, damned and *old* Roland Hunter. Roly was neither beautiful nor blessed. He didn't have, never had, Michael's lean swimming-toned body; he turned no heads, he attracted few admirers ('twas always thus). The days when this bothered him, days of teeth-gnashing and nights of wailing, were long gone. He was far from being an unfulfilled virgin and now, the enforced celibacy he was enduring didn't irk him. He amazed himself that he had become one of those whom he previously regarded as hopeless inadequates, one who, truly, didn't need sex. Who would have thought it? One minute you think you can't live, can't function properly, without sex and the next you realise it's not the life-sustaining force you were for so long deluded into believing it to be. Perversely though, he sometimes felt irked not to be irked and he did sometimes get a twinge of the arrow of unrequited passion, the barb of sexual jealousy, the dagger of frustration, (he had to admit he was upset at seeing Michael grab that girl's crotch), but in spite of it he was a contented have-not and what was even more amazing was that he wasn't at all amazed.

No, celibacy wasn't the problem. Looking back and scrabbling around in the rubble of his years and seeing himself, that other him, progress from back-to-back and council house mediocrity, through the spectrum of self-improvement, through the sham and inadequacy and the failure which had been outrageously out of proportion to the fulfillment of the not unreasonable amount of ambition that he once had. He would have to speak to Michael, before friendship took hold, about the meaning of flying ducks on livingroom walls and Rolf Harris and his Auntie Vera and striving to better himself but failing and instead going through life pretending to be someone he was not. Though he wasn't at all sure Michael's infant brain would comprehend any of it.

Sunbeams were teeming through the window by now, bringing a brilliant sadness with them and it was a summer day in bloom, the frightening night completely banished. And a sunshine boy (swarthy complexion and black hair didn't clash with or disperse Michael's radiance) had walked into his world but brought no radiance with him. If he thought that after Michael the world would be all roses and rainbows, he was deluded. A fleeting thing, a bagatelle like him wouldn't redeeem him. He no longer had the power, Michael wasn't one of his straight protégé conquests and if he weren't straight, he was too young and would always be too young; he constituted, in short, an impossibility. He was radiant,yes, but brought no radiance to Roly's soul. The boy wasn't an illusion, he was only too real, but whatever Roly hoped was an illusion. Hope itself, the act of hoping, was illusory. Somerset Maugham it was who said that sometimes the only thing we have to hang on to is our illusions and, like him, the only thing he asked was to be allowed to pursue them. It was also doubly hypothetical because there was the little matter, regarding taking the boy to bed and ravishing him, of his erectile dysfunction; he had lost the rapacity which was necessary for seduction and carnal tuition. The boy gave him an erection in his head, that was all.

His flat lay at such a kilter that the late morning and afternoon beams streamed through the window and hung in refracted squares on the walls and floor. He looked out and saw the cotton cumulus clouds skit across the sky and looked at the grass where Michael played, at the carpark and cars, at the nursery where he saw young mothers (and the odd delectable father) deposit their toddlers every day and at the backs of the houses opposite and the tops of trees (the big ash tree was still not in leaf, was it dying?).

He had one of the longings that overwhelmed him from time to time, when the black dog came to sit with him, his very own gytrash, how often depended on the degree of his melancholy. This time, it was the longing to simply go for a walk so that he could feel the sun on his face and back and breath open air like he once could, but he had to remind himself that was now impossible. Such yearnings were sometimes strong enough to make him believe he wasn't disabled at all, to think it was a trick, that all he had to do was to snap out of the bad dream and do the oh so simple thing of walking on legs. He would at least like to open the window, but didn't dare, not after his terrifying night episode.

He logged into a chatroom for some light relief and found a few Breakfast Club members in the Over 50 room, including Woofle from Birmingham, Beau in Nottingham and sthcroydon in, yes, South Croydon. Sth set him a poser. Last night he watched the *Kenneth Williams Night* that BBC Three was showing and he remembered Roly once telling the room about meeting Williams in that drinking club in Pimlico. 'What was the name of the place? he asked him. Well, he would wouldn't he and Roly was buggered if he could remember it. While he was in chat and on a whim, he thought he would pander to vanity and have a look to see if any interesting young men had looked at his profile recently, something he hadn't done for a while. There was a motley of interested parties on the View Tracks page, but the one that grabbed his particular attention was 'Curiouslad', with a posted age of 16 and a lapidary and tantalising tagline next to the thumbnail which read: 'Virgin needs older teacher,' but alas there was no photo to click on and perv over so he pursued it no further. Such restraint.

****

Fatigue eventually caught up with him and he managed to go to bed and sleep for a couple of hours. He dreamt about the Queen; those who claimed to know these things said it was quite common for people who aren't the Queen to dream about her or about being her. Did the Duke of Edinburgh or Prince Charles dream about her and did she dream about being herself? He emerged from the nap to a letter sat on the hall mat. It was from the Jobcentre, or the Department of Murk and Tensions as he lampooned it and he opened it to find that they had suspended his benefit and that he would owe a week's rent. It was his punishment for being honest and declaring that he did four days' work subediting for a locally produced magazine two months before and he smiled awry to himself at the synchronicity of such news arriving after such a night. He'd earned 175 pounds for the work, he would lose 90 pounds of benefit and would have to pay 60 pounds rent. He wiped and dressed and ate his shredded wheat summer breakfast, brushed his teeth and went back to the computer to write to his MP (whom he'd interviewed several times in his journalist's capacity, but expected no favours from) to complain about the punitive effects and futility of trying to escape from the state benefit trap by doing occasional work. He pointed out that he had cashed in his

165

life insurance to pay for his house move, had a thousand pounds in his ISA account which was the sum total of his wealth and added that with the prospect of work and a decent salary diminishing by the day, the future looked nothing but bleaker and bleaker.

He printed, signed and addressed the letter and put it down for his homeworker to post and thought of food. He'd been unjustly and severely penalised for being honest and he would wreak revenge by buying himself an extravagance. He grabbed his walking stick and car key, stuck his deerstalker on his head and went out to the car. He drove round to the farm shop and bought a bunch of the season's first asparagus for one pound 95. 'Never eat it after Ascot, dear,' some upperclass dowager somewhere, he couldn't remember who, had warned him once and he smiled because Ascot was still three weeks away so he was breaching no society etiquette. He also spotted a pack of rabbit loins and legs in the freezer cabinet and bought those to keep for a casserole at some later date. Back home in the kitchen, he snapped off the woody ends of eight of the asparagus spears and steamed them for four minutes. He didn't unfortunately have any Parma ham but made do with two slices of Wiltshire smoked. He wrapped those around two bundles of 4 spears, drizzled them with oil and baked them in the oven for 5 minutes until the ham was crisp. He drizzled more oil and some balsamic vinegar over them and seasoned them with salt and black pepper. He picked out a Kellog's Nutrigrain bar, poured himself a glass of cranberry juice and carried the lot on his trolley back to his desk, where he tucked in and began to feel his temper subside. When he finished he thought about supper: there were chicken breasts and portions of Jamie Oliver curry sauce in the freezer and the curry leaves he'd bought a week ago were still usable, so he would make his version of boiled spiced chicken, serve it to himself with rice and mango chutney and eat it in – hardly splendid – isolation and he would *enjoy* it.

****

It was a week since the night of the stalker-cum-burglar and there had been no repeat visit, for which he felt much relief. He finished his lunch of chilled cucumber and watercress soup and logged into chat to look at who, if anyone, had looked in on him. Curiouslad had once again 'visited' and left his calling card and Roly fancied again that he was the culprit, that he had taken a quantum leap across cyberspace to his bedroom window to spook him that night. This time, despite there still being no photo with the thumbnail, his willpower snapped and he brought up the profile. It proved a fruitless exercise; the profile was decidedly bereft of personal information and told him nothing except that he was, or said he was, a 16-year-old virgin from London. Willpower returned; his rule was no photo, no response, so he passed on doing anything further. He sipped his coffee and toked on his cigarette and out of nowhere Dr Johnson's aphorism sprung to mind: 'If you are idle, be not alone; if you are alone, be not idle.' He could do nothing about alone and, in the absence of any afflatus for writing, do little but occupy himself skimming around AOL and chat. AOL's top news story that day – did they have a news editor? – was that someone called Nushka, who apparently won the previous year's Big Brother competition on TV, 'lands top TV job'. He was invited to click on some photographs of children to try to identify which celebrities they'd grown up to be and to read about stars and their cars. When, he wondered, would they invite him to click on the 'hot pics' taken in the womb and identify the celebrity foetus in the 'Stars Before They Were Born' section? Not for the first time, he cringed at the rum

167

and valueless world of cyber headlines, where everything was 'hot' and 'top' and 'new' and 'great'. 'How celebs beat the flab – 10 hot workout tips', 'This summer's hottest fashion tips', but of '100 children dying each day in top Zimbabwe famine' or the latest 'hot' news from the Asian tsunami there was no mention, for that would spoil the fun of cyberworld. One task he'd set himself and which he carried out diligently each day was to visit the 'Hunger Site' website in order to send a daily bowl of food where it was needed at no cost to himself. He was no campaigner but he sported the 'Feed the World' white armband and let organisations send protest emails to world leaders on his behalf. Not conscience money, but conscience sympathy at least, a widow's mite by proxy, he couldn't afford to send charitable donations any more and that, for some reason – how the mind rambles! – led him once more to dredge through the slurry that was his past and think of how he was slowly rotting, led him with his head down through dark snow-muffled streets where no other people walked and where the cold spectres of black cars skidded and slid in slow motion as they made their way to unknown destinations and on he walked, on to the End of the World Party where they were celebrating his aloneness, the first time he'd been alone as well as lonely. For he was without so much as a flatmate now and what friends he'd had were either dispersed or dead. Geography, his gypsy meanderings, now disability and other more impalpable and sinister reasons, meant that his opportunity for comity was pared down to nothing. While he'd accustomed himself to periods of his own company, continual aloneness made him vulnerable, sometimes downright frightened. The creakings and bangings of the house, especially at night, loud traffic in the road outside, fierce gusts of wind, all seemed exaggerated and all were designed to further crush the spirit.

That was here, now; before the now there had been his father's death and what a timely death it was; it had come just after he'd been booted out of his radio job in Newcastle-upon-Tyne. After the funeral, when he asked his mother if she wanted him to return home permanently to be with her, she said yes and he breathed freely for a moment, not because he had the chance of demonstrating filial devotion in her hour of need, oh no, but rather because it would enable his return from self-exile and poverty and so he returned – yet again – to the council house and about the same time, Larry rang him from Coventry to say he'd met a Scottish postman and was living with him in his house. Job, partner and his own flat all gone, but the whisky stayed faithful and he spent more time with it than ever before. Then he began to have difficulty balancing and walking and suddenly and unknowingly he'd had a stroke and that was the end of the comfort and refuge of alcohol. 'More alcohol will destroy you,' the neurosurgeon said, when he handed him the results of the brain scan and though it took him a while to decide whether or not he was bothered about destruction, for his mother's sake, whose life he was making a hell, he decided to board the wagon. Which brought him to the place and time where his boat may have been sinking, but he was far too miserable and unready and uncourageous to think about throwing himself overboard just yet and anyway, when that day did come, perhaps by some fluke there would be a human lifebuoy to grasp hold of to prevent his drowning. That was the salvation he craved.

After leaving the council house and his mother for the last time ever and before Michael, visits by earnest and embarrassingly caring social workers with their 'scattergun' approach to his problems and by agency homeworkers who mostly couldn't care less were his only regular human contact in the desolate desert he was stranded in apart, that is, from the phone calls from mother, banal, inane and silence-laden chats they were about nothing at all and apart from occasional calls to and from from his oldest friends, Perry and Alistair, formerly his neighbours in Kensington and now living in some apparent splendour in rural Suffolk. But it became enervating to speak with them, each conversation added more and more to the numbing sense of regret which they felt but dared not give voice to, that they were now sad scions of a once glorious, sun-kissed society which was long gone and which was only a remnant of their exclusive brand of nostalgia. 'Nostalgia,' he said to Perry on one of these occasions, 'that's the fond yearning for some wonderful times that never took place isn't it and why are they always 20 years ago?' and Perry laughed. Their reminiscences were the mutually realised sense of being catapulted towards the oblivion that had too soon snatched their friends from them.

A telephone mother, social workers, homeworkers, displaced friends – they were the only meagre oases left in the desolate sands... and then had come chatrooms – his parish pumps, his community centres, his firesides. On his very first visit to a chatroom, Caffmos it was, when he was wary, timid and disorientated, when he didn't know what and when to click or where to type anything or how to speak to anyone, he thought his browser had misdirected him: people with the handles of 'ChrisofHarrow', 'Surreygeezer' and 'Ariesworcester', people more sedately, more restrainedly named than the likes of the blatant or the innuendoed 'Throatful' or 'Second-coming' or 'Pussyboyslut' on other sites, were discussing pound shops, Awayday railtickets and ironing, anything but the talk of man-on-man sex he'd expected. At one point, one of them dashed out of the room 'screeching' that it had started raining and he had to 'get me washing in quick'. These were among the names that greeted him and made him feel welcome and he could soon lay claim to some interesting and likeable internet friends, especially those who dropped in early of a morning, like himself and with whom he could chat before the serious cruising-for-sex-business of the day began. This was the Breakfast Club and the other people looking, quite naturally, for a life partner or a one-off squeeze or a blowjob, must have thought they were nuts, with their talk of minutiae. As much as he knew of these 'friends', they seemed to be retired, or of a status where they didn't have to work for money, or who had jobs that gave them the flexibility to be able to spend hours in a chatroom almost every day. Someone always seemed to be flying to Buenos Aires for six months, or emigrating to Umbria, or going to his second home in Miami for Christmas; whatever these men were doing they were doing more and better than he; they were men of a substance much greater than his own.

The novelty of spending all day every day browsing (or, in the argot of the room, 'perving') was enduring, stoked by the new names and profiles of the thousands of young men for whom older men like him were the sexual focus appearing every day. He became addicted, spending each day and often well into the small hours loitering, chatting, 'perving', reluctant to leave the screen for a moment for fear of missing someone or something. Hours wasted when he should have been touting for proofreading and writing commissions, but Caffmos and then Gaydar became a prop and though he'd never previously had the slightest interest in ersatz cyber sex, yet as a mental panacea for his increasing concern over penile dysfunction, unsatisfying though it was and pathetic as it made him feel, it was a solace. For his sexual activity had become entirely cerebral, he'd always had scopophilic inclinations and now they were all he had. He wasn't looking for potential partners, not doing any wooing; he initiated private conversations and responded to the rare requests for one if the someone had a face to show and not, as was sadly so often the case, just a picture of an erect penis on a torso cut off at the neck; not that he had any pudeur, the sight of a firm pair of buttocks or pectorals could be inspiring, but he couldn't summon much enthusiasm for disembodied parts. No, he needed to see the face that went with them and needed the boy or young man to have a sufficient amount of intellect for a coherent, affectionate or suggestive conversation, to prove there was something appealing between the ears as well as the legs. He was happy to slaver over some cute, preferably physically well-defined, sexually rampant young man and talk as filthily as all getout to him or, he might be harbouring fantastical thoughts of romance and be polite and restrained, it all depended on mood and occasion, he prided himself on his sense of occasion. Whichever it was, he would be flirtatious, sometimes taunting and unkind, sometimes non-commital, other times lying through his teeth by offering devotion and a lifetime of romance. But in honest moods, he knew he was tired of the hunt; he'd become blasé, cynical and the sexual merry-go-round filled him with ennui. He suffered from 'sex in the head', he always had, but unlike in his able-bodied freedom days he had no alternative, no means to physically search for one. His libido had him believe it was still active enough to make him the great seducer, but the truth was that desire held dominion over prowess, the cumulative effects of alcohol and nicotine and the brain damage caused by his strokes had made sure of that. Sometimes his excitement overwhelmed him, enthusiasm would become calenture and he'd forget that he'd had at least two young men ask for an encounter and he'd invited them and calamitous non-performance was the outcome. But in more well-tempered moods he no longer felt he was under any pressure, there was no urgency to have sex, a great weight had been lifted and he could forget what it was like to wish to be desired and carrry on instead indulging his scopophilia unfettered.

The face; he was a sap for a handsome face, of that there was no doubt. He had always looked first to the face; a face had to be appealing (and young of course) in order for his bells to ring. Following closely on that was the novelty factor; he was a slave to novelty and it took him quite a while to ask himself how much he was a slave to the novelty of a face rather than to the quality of the beauty of it. Whatever the answer was, he knew he was an ideologue, highly susceptible to superficial impact and capable of devoting many an hour searching for the answer to the riddle: what made one face attractive and another repellent? If that required critical assessment, of course, then he was lost, because he possessed absolutely no critical faculty whatsovever. 'I just like it,' or 'I just don't', was his stock response whenever he was asked why he liked a piece of music or a book or a painting, he couldn't explain why and it was the same with a face and he had one conviction that he held dear: no-one was ugly, ugly was not in his vocabulary or his thinking; his credo was that everyone was good-looking in degrees.

The face; he'd heard or read somewhere the intriguing theory: that each individual on the planet was separated by just six degrees; how much more intriguing then to imagine each face on the planet could be separated by a mere thousandth of a millimetre of tissue, or tiniest fraction of an angle of eyes, cheekbone, jaw, chin, hairline. It was

173

breathtaking: six billion faces with 99.9 per cent of indentical DNA, leaving only point one of a percent to render each face unique; the endless supply of faces was either a monumental fluke or a miracle. Or was it endless? Weren't the variations in physiognomy finite, didn't one see a face and in time forget it and see it again as new, see it and not realise that one had seen it before? The statistical permutations were fascinating: out of, for argument's sake, 30 faces one saw in the street or in a bar, some would be 'passable', some would rate as acceptable, some would invite being made love to and some would most definitely not – and there would be one, just one, on the right day, in the right light, which would be mouth-slaveringly, eye-poppingly, heart-stoppingly, spine-tinglingly, hair-raisingly, sweat-pouringly, crotch-dampingly gorgeous. Perfection, however, wasn't an absolute, it was manifold in its attributes and legion in its instances and the assessment of a face as either attractive and flawless or unattractive and imperfect was contingent upon subliminal impulses that beat at a particular moment and on one's mood, on what one was doing, where one was, what the weather was like, what one had eaten or drunk, the state of one's health. In the end, he decided that attraction was labile, a fickle thing – what was acceptable yesterday may not be today, it was no reliable barometer. So if one thought a particular face perfect, one would be speaking the truth, for in the instant, it was and there was the added help of the imagination and its ability to lie and persuade and convince, to elaborate and embellish, enabling one to see what wasn't there but what one wanted to see there.

Not everyone attached the same amount of devotion, fixation, esteem to the face as he did, however. Indeed, he'd encountered downright hostility from a few young men he'd tried to pay court to. 'Well if you're so shallow that you'll only chat if I show you my face, you can fuck off,' they said. Shallow! 'How could the appreciation of a face be shallow?' he implored. People were secretive and feared being recognised, they were hiding from girlfriends and wives or from friends who didn't know about their sexuality, but he found that excuse for guarding anonymity pathetically illogical.

They appeared from time to time, they provided the occasional and welcome thrill, they came and went, those young men, who knew where? They were curious, or bemused, or reckless, or they'd lost all reason for a moment, who knew? You may speak to them and then, more than likely, they would never be seen again. Did they appear on a whim, did they log in and immediately regret it, did what seemed like a good idea become something spooky, who knew? The young man who appeared on this occasion would probably turn out to belong in one or the other of these categories, he was sure. The name – 'Straightmuscle' – screamed at him: 'Open wide that "queer eye for a straight guy" you're so proud of,' it called and he simply couldn't ignore it. He clicked on it and a touchstone was revealed. The pseudonym was apposite, his profile showed a handsome young man with a bare and wonderfully sculpted torso – oh the pecs! – and better yet, he was within a cockstride over the county boundary in nextdoor Cheshire. He clicked his name again to engage him in private chat and, as if his physical attributes weren't enough heavenly provender, his open and cheerful response and his insistence on emphasising in nearly every other sentence just how heterosexual he was drove Roly wild and his heart, already pounding and his brow soaked, fair lurched from his chest when he saw him type: 'Do you drive?' 'Yes,' he typed back. 'So why don't I get rid of the gf for the day and you drive over now and have your way with me?' This was torture by Sod's Law at it callous worst and he all but burst into tears: what he wouldn't have done in his able-bodied days, the cruel injustice of there having been no internet five years ago. 'All is vanity,' he murmured to himself; it was futile, there was nothing to be done and he curtailed his euphoria and the conversation with a regretful curse and said goodbye and drooped in his chair and wondered if he really would have upped and hied off right there and then to the encounter of a lifetime had he been able to? Ah, how he liked to think he would have and then he thought, therein lay the nature of that strange singularity, fantasy, which was seductive and destructive in equal parts; and he thought, not for the first time, that fantasy was pure concept and chimera, its only reality was possibility and anyone who saw it as a passepartout to eternal happiness would always be thwarted. Fantasy must keep thirst unslaked, must feed on yearning and remain with the stars, unreachable. Be careful what you wish for, they said... Amen to that and abandon all hope, he thought: 'Physical attraction doesn't matter. Stunning young men are stunning only for the blink of an eye and it really is a waste of time and energy pursuing a beauty which is so ephemeral. Why, even the latest football darling, sexy blond Paul Smith, has started to go off! Or his novelty has. Yes, that's the trouble, you look at a beautiful face long enough and it ceases to be beautiful, or at least you cease to find it beautiful any more but then again, come to think of it, Jack's never did, nor Larry's.' He gave up with an 'Oh, what the hell... as sage Montaigne so sagely said: "Que sais je?" I can't for the life of me figure out if it's beauty that fades or my evaluation of it.'

176

****

He awoke next day with thoughts of oily fish, but not before a journey through the realm of hypnopompic thought first:

My sexual orientation is horizontal, usually… socionics is a theory of personality and interpersonal interaction based on Jung and Freud and somebody else's theory of something, I can't remember his name but he believed that each personality type has a distinct purpose in society… I must test the theory of socionics on Michael… deism, what is deism?... the answer to a question on University Challenge last night was the 11th day of the 11th month in the year 1111 but I'm buggered if I can remember what the question was… 'He needed an instruction book to tie his shoelaces' – where did I hear that? I must remember it for a putdown in chat… homosexuality is God's way of ensuring that the truly gifted are not responsible for the overcrowding of the planet… closets are for clothes… if you're gay you can tell a girl you love her bathing suit and mean her bathing suit… you can get away with saying 'fabulous'… 'Ladies and gentlemen, I stand before you, to be beside you, to say a few words before I speak. As next Monday is Good Friday I have arranged for an open-air meeting to be held in the vestry to decide on what colour to whitewash the chapel'… The words were groovy, dig it, windy, in, swingin', with it, hip, hep, square when I was young, I never said cool or pants or minging… hair is Tony Blair or Lionel Blair in rhyming slang, or just say Tony or Lionel and piles is Farmer Giles or just farmers, rub-a-dub is a pub and Conan Doyle is a boil, 'I got a Conan'… CRAFT is the acronym for 'Can't Remember a Fucking Thing' which I read in The Oldie of all places… Why can't I remember lines of poetry, or song lyrics, or quote Shakespeare? I must put 'on the qui vive' and 'tosh' in the book somewhere… 'He was a blackguard, not quite the sort

177

Yes, he craved Omega-3 oil and would put tuna, salmon, herring, sardines or mackerel on the shopping list for the homeworker to buy later – mackerel yes, that night he would stuff and bake a mackerel. He clambered out of bed and wrapped himself in his dressing-gown (he refused to call it a robe); it was late May and he was still wearing it over his house clothes, though he was warm enough to do without a morning blast of central heating by now. He made a mug of instant decaff and trundled into the computer room, smoked three cigarettes while he did his duty on the Hunger Site and played a few games of mahjong with Radio 3 music in the background. The news junkie in him had given up listening to Radio 4's *Today* programme because it had gone the way of much broadcasting, descending from an informative and incisive news programme into a two-way 'interactive' show, infected by listeners' emails, read out every few minutes. It was listener participation gone berserk. He missed his early morning fix of news, he couldn't afford to buy the *Guardian* every day so settled for the five-minute Radio 3 bulletins and those pathetically frivolous AOL so-called headlines.

Through the window, the day was sunny and looked quite windy; the graceful ash tree as far as he could tell was starting to leaf and the may blossom was waving creamy white handkerchieves in the nursery's garden. It was sunny in bursts through the clouds, the sky being packed with huge piles of grey and white stratocumulus candyfloss sailing serenely north to south, not stopping to be admired over Jamage. He made another coffee, heard the clock strike 10 and remembered Rachmaninov's Third Symphony was featuring in *Classical Collection* today; he couldn't think he'd ever heard it before and wanted to give it his attention. He went to the lavatory, went back to his desk and drew the blinds so as not to cause consternation to the girl in the white cook's hat standing at the window of the nursery or to any mothers delivering tots or to any other passers-by with a view of him wiping his bum with the fragrant baby wipes and pulling his knickers on. Showering or standing at the sink to wash was impossible because if water or soap got into his eyes and forced him to shut them he'd lose balance and fall over; he was still waiting for the social services to install a walk-in shower with a seat, so he had to settle for sitting at his desk to do the necessary meanwhile. He sometimes thought mischeviously that he might try his morning toilet ritual in the kitchen, when young fair haired Mister Peachy was out working on his patio fence one morning, ha ha. He didn't shave, it wasn't a shaving day, the third day. Though he never went out anywhere to show it off, he still sported his designer stubble out of vanity. He made his warm weather breakfast and another coffee and ate and drank, waiting for

Rachmaninov and playing more mahjong. He also browsed the *Bent* and *Puffta* sites he'd recently discovered, admiring the twinks in their Speedos and briefs and out of them.

Michael hadn't shown himself for days; he hadn't rung and there were no texts, probably because he'd expressed his hatred of the things to the boy previously and warned him never to send him one because he wouldn't respond to it. He logged onto chat to look for signs of Curiouslad; thoughts of his admirer must be festering at the back of his brain, because he was now checking his tracks each time before going into chat. Sure enough, the curious one had been there every day; he was making quite a career of laying down his internet spoor. Roly counted up some dozen or so visits by now, but he remained adamant in his policy of not pursuing facially anonymous boys, however much a desideratum a hidden face once revealed may turn out to be.

From there, his day was as nondescript as most. Claire the homeworker turned up and went shopping for him, he spent too many hours playing mahjong and sudoku and too many lingering around chatrooms, in the vain hope of spotting and cornering Curiouslad, mostly perving profiles and swapping camperies with whoever who called in. He made asparagus soup with the remaining spears and left it to chill for lunch, hobbled out to his pot herbs on the front lawn and cut sprigs of rosemary, thyme, sage, tarragon and mint for his mackerel supper, stuffed the beast in the evening and when the time came, ate it with some new potatoes and a rocket and watercress vinaigrette salad. A microwaved apple and blackcurrant crumble, two mugs of decaff, *Agatha Christie's Poirot* and the film, *Monster's Ball,* his nightcap of drinking chocolate and a late night return to the Over 50 room and some perving for an hour later, he was in bed.

****

'Have mercy for I have succumbed,' He muttered to himself after he had done the deed.

Besides the gandering and the raunchy chatting you see, my dears, there was one more pastime he indulged in when the mood took him and it was one which gave him ample scope to exercise his flair for the written word and the seductive turn of phrase and the number of attractive young men he chased with flattering messages and emails – well he lost count. He practised his brazen lechery in the traditional way, no hi-tech exponent he, no electronic shorthand and symbols in his messages and emails, no no, they were *letters*. They were his *billets doux*.

He knew he was bound in the end to do it, to write to Curiouslad. He was given impetus by the fact that, already by 10 o'clock in the morning the boy, whoever he was, had called on him again and left another track and this time with the flame symbol next to the thumbnail to indicate that he thought Roly was 'hot'. He must leave his mark each morning before he goes off to school or college, he thought. Oh, who was he and why was his name never on any of the rooms' lists? It was perplexing, intriguing and exciting and he could hold back no longer. He told himself it was a wind-up and a cocktease if ever he saw one, but he went ahead regardless. He succumbed, clicked 'Send a Message' and began writing.

Hello Curiouslad. It's Saturday and this is Roly at LovetheBoys Cottage. Your name paints a picture of nubility and tight Speedos. I hope I'm right. It's a non-day here, with nothing much to do and nowhere to go. It's 10 o'clock and I'm surfing, listening to Rachmaninov. I came across your tracking of me a few days ago and I eventually fell for your tantalising charms and clicked on

181

your profile, I see that you are a 16-year-old who says he's a virgin. I was mortified that you don't have a photo of yourself on there to remind me what a young virgin looks like. Really, you boys should have a care; the messages you send out send my blood pressure rocketing, my tinnitus clanging and make my 51-year-old carpals crumble. Not to mention the bringing on of the vapours. I can't help myself; I can't let it go without writing to you, just to indulge my fantasies and stimulate myself as I think of swapping messages and e-mails with you and even phone calls and see you, through a mist of romatic lust, coming to stay with me. We'll have music and movies, food and wine and we'll sit together, your head in my lap, while I run my fingers through your hair and squeeze the tumescence between your legs and kiss your ruby mouth. I'll take you to the bedroom, lie back and watch you undress. You are smooth, sensuous and all adolescent; you show your defined pectorals and your flat stomach and look sensational in those Speedos. You'll lie down with me and be nervous that you'll orgasm prematurely. I'll prepare you with osculation, elate you with fellatio, drive you to a frenzy with anilinctus and finally beatify you with pedication: you will look magnificent as I congregate with your pristine cavum pueris and you'll be unable to prevent yourself ejaculating while I'm inside you… Zoweeee! So much for the fantasy. I must say I'm dumbfounded: those who know me know I would rather undergo root canal work without anaesthetic than have my photograph taken, because my face always looks like a squashed gateau left out in a rainstorm, but that doesn't seem to have deterred you from continuing to browse my profile every time you go online. Your enthusiasm must be indomitable. Is there any point in telling you more about myself than you already know from profile? That the gods weren't particularly lavish with physical gifts and that any attractions I may have are spiritual? That my grey eyes are too close together, my nose is too small, my lips are too thin, my skin is craggy and the colour of pastry, my short brown-and-grey hair is too curly, my body is slimmish, with some midriff flab and my chest is lightly hairy? I'm 51 but pass for 72 in the right light and a following wind. I have charm, intelligence and humour but no soul. I'm clean, sometimes bearded when too idle to shave, romantic, melancholic, liberal, agnostic and egotistical. I hate violence and injustice and believe in love and the truth of the imagination. I have a ravenous libido but a diminished prowess, but I do have pleasant memories of enjoying kissing, fellatio, nippleplay, anilinctus and penetrating the atrium. I am a writer, but can't sell any of my work, so I have no income and am very poor. I enjoy music and looking at young men and pornography, I like trees and clouds and herbs and I love cooking. About 5 years ago my decades of excessive alcohol consumption, for which I've been detoxed, rehabbed and therapised, punished my brain with a minor stroke, which has left all my faculties intact, except my powers of balance, so I don't get out without help from a walking frame, a stick and other people. I smoke like a witch. I live in the post-industrial tawdry backwater of Trenton, which is noted for its pottery, bigotry and not a little homophobia and is a place where, if you have any sense of the beauty of life and any sense at all, you do not get off the train to visit when it stops here. Life is a game of solitaire, the wheels have fallen off and enforced celibacy is seriously damaging my health. I am between a rock and a hard place: I need a relationship not a one-off shake, but I know that I can't sustain one. My philanderering, infidelity, lies, unpaid debts, shambolic treatment of other people – don't you agree that, to force someone you are in debt to into having to ask for their money back is conduct of the most despicable kind, that it's unforgiveable? I am guilty of that conduct and forgive myself I never can – my overall irresponsibility, unaccountability, indigence and all-round personal unattractiveness and self-loathing prevents that now, but at least there is the one consolatory advantage of being alone: it means I'me free to pee in the sink and fart in bed. I hope you at least tell me a little about yourself and your virginal state to keep me amused. What are you? Do you like music, do you go clubbing? Are you at school or college and what are you studying? Are you outgoing or quiet, sporty or nerdy, funny or serious? Are you slim, chunky, broad, narrow? Have you got erectile nipples and a bottom like a peach? Do you look brainbustingly gorgeous in tightie whitie briefs or a thong and do you know the capital of Greenland and JK Rowling's middle name? Do you look like Johnny Depp or the boys from Hollyoaks or Home and Away'? I don't mind - just as long as you look like a boy, walk like a boy, talk like a boy and smell like a boy and do all the nice things real boys do, like eat burgers and chewmex at midnight and masturbate at least fourteen times a week. Now my poor erection is getting a headache thinking about you. Whatever will you think of me? I wish you happiness and love and wealth and fine things and hope you find a good man to lose that cherry to. I wish it could be me. I'll see you on the ice!

How about putting up a picture of that virgin face, all the same?

... was the result and he despatched it with a smile and a feeling of satisfaction. Nothing would ever come of it and he didn't particularly want it to but composing some vintage prose had been very satisfying. He'd done it purely for amusement and not for hope of any positive outcome. What use to him was a boy who-knew-where in cyberland other than to have some mildly stimulating erotic fun and perhaps distant exchanges with? Besides, as with so many, he half expected, if he was the unitiated virgin he claimed to be, that he'd be too frightened to reply now that he'd been confronted; perhaps, if it amused him, he would politely acknowledge it and thank him, perhaps even send him a photo, perhaps they would strike up a correspondence... perhaps, perhaps, perhaps. Perhaps not.

****

Days had passed and there was no comeback from Curiouslad; Roly didn't think it meant that his slender expectations were thwarted. He expected nothing, he wasn't waiting for anything and so the matter was completely out of his thoughts. He didn't even care for the moment to check if Curiouslad was still tracking him. This wouldn't be the case had there been a photo with his profile: that would at least have provided him with some masturbatory fodder, a way of keeping the boy in his thoughts, for a while at least and until the next photogenic supernova arrived in the internet firmament and he happened upon him. Although for that, for the time being, he had his creation, albeit abandoned, Denzel. Oh yes, he was still mad crazy wild about Denzel and his phantom presence in his bed at night was sufficient for his meagre libidinous needs. He hadn't yet dared to look for that stimulus in Michael because he feared that doing so, thinking of him erotically, would somehow bring grief. To them both.

185

Any disappointment he may have felt about the lack of response to his billet doux was more than compensated by the triumph he was still relishing over his titillating prose. He was also very pleased with his oily fish creations: the stuffed mackerel, created from Anthony Worrall Thompson's receipt, was excellent and he'd made very satisfactory sardine tomatoes too and had awarded himself first prize again with Delia's herrings with mustard sauce. That night he would ring the changes with meat: the homeworker could fetch some minced lamb and he would make a shepherd's pie or perhaps lamb steak, some yams and green beans and he would do a stir-fry. Tomorrow he would return to Omega-3 with his tuna, tomato and pasta bake. He needed basil. But before that, Michael turned up with a chirruping 'Hiya, yawright?' when Roly opened the door. 'I asked me mum and she says what if I do the work for ya instead of them careworkers, she says if I wanta do it I can if it's okay with you it's okay with 'er an' you can pay me less than you pay them and I'll come round after school and everythin' and weekends an' I can 'oover and I know how to iron stuff and work the washer an' she says give me a trial for a week for free an' see 'ow I do and then say yes or no. Oh yeah, an' she asked me if your okay and I said yes, he's a nice old bloke an' disabled an' everythin' and she said that sounds all right then.' Roly wondered if, when he came knocking, Michael walked from his house to the flat rehearsing the lines he was going to bombard him with as he went, or whether it gushed from his racing mind extempore. Whichever it was, Michael's method was to drown him in verbiage before he could say hello and ask him how he was.

'Come in,' he said, abandoning at a stroke those hasty resolutions he'd made to have him not come too near him, haha and when he'd sat him down and asked him if he was serious, that he wanted to do housework for him on a regular basis and go shopping with him, he said he did. 'Yep'. Roly was highly sceptical; a teenage boy wanting a part-time domestic career was an oddity, although the money was an obvious incentive. 'Can you wash dishes? Dust and polish? And you say you know how to use a vacuum cleaner and an iron do you?' 'Nuthin' to it,' Michael answered brashly. But Roly wanted to dent his over-confidence. 'I must warn you, my compulsion for tidiness can be a pain in the arras both for others and myself. A placemat which doesn't sit squarely to the edge of the table, a picture which hangs ever so slightly out of perpendicular on the wall, CDs jutting out aslant in the rack, they all have me diving to readjust their lie like I'm saving a drowning man. And as for dried rings left by wet mugs and glasses on tables, or smudges on paintwork... it's boring I know but I am a spick and span old queen, my dear and clutter has me reaching for the sal volatile.' 'I wish you'd speak English,' was Michael's deadpan reaction, 'but I think you mean you're cool with me yeah.' 'Hang on, it can mean more than polishing and errands, good boy. What about the times when I'm stuck for something? It's very unlikely, but I might have to ring you at home or when you're out with your friends. Somehow I can't see you coming running at my beck and call.' 'You can 'ave me mobile number. Get 'old of me anywhere.' He wore his beaming rictus smile; he had given some considerable time and thought to this plan and was satisfied with all contingencies. 'And you have to put me and my needs before your good times. When you're out groping your girlfriend, for instance,' He couldn't resist the barb, 'I really can't believe you'd leave her mid-service with her knickers round her ankles and run off to me.' *If he knew how to say I was beyond the pale, he would, but he has no idea what a paling fence is I'm sure.* He was annoyed neverthless and tried to muster inidignity: 'I told you, I chucked 'er. There's no girl in the way.' 'What about, I mean… don't you have your own things to do? Do you paint or play an instrument up in your room or?' The one time-eating interest he knew he didn't have was school, homework and exams and such, so he saw no point in putting that forward as a possible barrier. 'I don't think so Michael,' he said at length. 'What d'ya mean?' Disappointment struck him like an iron girder and his face went black. 'Oh, there's all the hassle,' Roly said, worldwearily. 'I, I don't want you to see me hobbling along with my wheelie frame, to get to and from the car, to follow me in my disabled shopping scooter around Morrisons and Asda and the city centre. I'm embarrassed in public and I wouldn't want to be an albatross around the neck of a free-spirited 15-year-old. You're immortal, Michael, nothing can hold you back, you run wild on your way to ruling the world. Bubbling testosterone and churning hormones are what a boy like you should be dealing with and trips to Alton Towers and spending hours in MySpace and watching DVDs, not tending to an invalid. Waiting around for me, helping me in and out and up and down, watching out to stop me falling, what a drudge for a golden youth! You'll get sick of it in no time.' 'No I won't,' he protested. 'I dunno what you mean by bubbling stuff, but I've been to Alton Towers, I don't do MySpace, I like me downloads and stuff and I like me swimmin' but it's not like that's me whole life.' 'I can't help it,' Roly went on, along his own tangent, 'and it's not just that. It's knowing that I'm now handicapped when I didn't used to be and the handicap is entirely self-inflicted. I didn't drink myself to death but I did drink nearly to a full stop. I try not to feel self-pitying. I know I'm being punished for being bad, you see – mmm,' he moaned doubtfully and stopped himself from pursuing the path of good and evil. 'Michael, looking after a –' '– I told you, it's what I wanna do an' I'm good. Why won't you let me 'elp ya?' 'Why, tell me why? Why do you want to do it?' 'I dunno,' he answered sharply; he felt the question was intrusive. 'I jus' like doin' stuff and… well, there's nothin' else I can do is there? I'm thick me. Nobody –' Roly's loud 'Ha' was boomed out in mockery, to put down the put down of himself. 'To the world you may be one person, but to one person you may be the world,' he told him. Michael fell silent and then, 'And you, you're, well you're cool,' he muttered under his breath. 'Oh, I'm cool am I?' 'Yeah,' he drawled. 'You're like… interestin' to talk to an' that. I like 'earing about the things you've done while I do stuff for ya.' 'I'm not sure. I'll have to speak to your mother about it. I need her opinion and say so. Have you told her about me?' ''Course I 'ave.' *Just what has he told her?* 'And told her you want to help me out?' 'She said it's okay.' 'But you haven't told her I'm gay.' 'She don't care about that.' He said that with gusto. 'You don't know me mum, she's cool. She buys me condoms for me.' *Not for you to have sex with men.* 'You haven't told her.' 'I will if you want.' Roly didn't know if he did want. Michael gave him his home number. 'Tell her I'll call her tonight and I must meet her. But before you go, I've something to tell you. I've had a scare.' As Roly told him about the night adventure with the night stalker, he registered one change in him. For once, Michael didn't interject. He sat and listened, rapt, looking both fascinated and somewhat frightened, which Roly attributed to concern for his safety and wellbeing. When he'd finished, he was astounded and, he had to say, very touched by Michael's first words of response. 'Why the f – why didn't ya ring the rozzers? Why didn't ya ring me?' he asked, in a solicitous voice full of frustration at having missed a chance to be of help, to play the Samaritan. 'It was one in the morning, dear boy,' Roly said. 'You'd have been in deep sleep. Not to mention your mum and sister. No, I couldn't –.' Then an interjection did come; he was too animated to stay quiet for long and he blurted out an outlandish proposal: '– tell ya what. I can bring me sleepin' bag round and stop on the floor in the next room if you want. They won't try and get in with me 'ere.' 'Oh, my guardian angel Michael now,' Roly sighed, feeling hopeless and helpless that a 15-year-old boy should have enough trust in his fitness and strength and fearlessness to consider trying to protect him. 'I don't want to sound ungrateful but your wish to help me out doesn't include bodyguard duties.' But Michael was fired by the idea of, if not an SAS adventure, then a boy scout one. 'I'd do it for ya, no problem.' 'Yes, I'm sure you would. But whoever it was hasn't been back so let's just hope it was a one-off. Probably someone staggeringly drunk who thought it was his own flat or something. I speak from experience.' *Please don't ask me about the night in London when I managed to let myself into the flat next door.* He did not. 'So you gonna ring me mum?' he asked. 'Give me her number.'

****

He called her that night. 'Mrs Hollis? I think you know who I am.' Mrs Hollis – Yvette – sounded friendly and somewhat over-excited and her high-pitched, 'Ooh yes, hello duck' was followed by a torrent of a character reference for Michael, "E's a good lad really, but keep yer eye on 'im and make sure 'e does the work and earns 'is money. I'm always tellin' 'im to stay on the bricks' which, when she stopped, gave Roly to understand where Michael had inherited his own capacity for non-stop babble. 'We'd better get together,' Roly suggested and invited her to call on him when it was convenient. 'Or you can cum round 'ere, sugar, when I'm not at work. Oh, are you awright for getting' round? Or Michael'll

190

'elp you round. There's no steps. Michael,' she shrilled to the distance. 'You'll 'elp Mr – er – Roly what's-his-name round one night won't ya? Yeah, 'course 'e will,' she said, back with him and answering for him, 'it'll be lovely to meet ya, duck. Just tell 'im to bring you round.' Michael took the phone from her and sounded elated: 'Me mum says you're pukka.' 'Does she indeed?' 'She says you got a lovely voice, posh but you sound nice. When d'you want me to fetch you round?' The following evening seemed as good a time as any and he told Michael to come to fetch him 'after your tea and my supper', Michael's home being only a walk of a few corners away but a car journey for him. 'Me mum's cool, you'll get on with 'er,' he told him in the car. They pulled up outside a small plain brown-bricked terrace of six two-storied double-glazed and gardened houses and Michael helped him in. Mum, 'Oh call me Yvette, please', was in a green shirt and ankle length black skirt. She was wearing a goodly selection of Ratner's cheap gold jewellery, earrings, rings, amulets, two delicate necklaces and she wore a permanent smile under long black hair strikingly like her son's. She showed Roly into a clean and tidy livingroom with 'I'm Yvette' and a 'Sorry about the mess' apology which wasn't needed. White walls, two two-seater cream sofas, a deep-piled plush-looking mushroom coloured carpet, a stone fireplace topped with various glass ornaments around an electric fire, a huge television which Roly thought would have sat better in a cinema and a tiled coffee table littered with magazines in the middle of the floor, all shouted typical provincial lounge. A girl of about Michael's age, who Roly assumed was Michael's sister, lay sprawled on one of the sofas with a sketch pad on her knee and a crayon in her hand. She straightened up as Roly walked in with his stick, took the crayon out and said 'Hiya' politely and with a warm smile.

'That's Bryony,' Yvette giggled nervously. 'Sit down, sugar,' she ordered hospitably as she tidied the magazines before perching on the arm of the sofa next to her daughter who she then instructed to go and put the kettle on and asked Roly if he wanted tea or coffee. She expressed the hope that Michael hadn't been pestering him, briefly mentioned the problems of bringing up two children without a husband, told him about her part-time job in the village off-licence, said her children were both good kids really 'considering everythin'' and finally told him if he was sure he wanted Michael to help him, she would make sure in her turn that he didn't let him down. All through it, Roly was content to listen and say little, feeling once more like a fraud, feeling the old inhibitions and self-consciousness about what an ordinary Trenton woman like this would inevitably see as his 'poshness' surfacing and restraining him and putting a distance between him and her. She would, like so many, inevitably think him charming enough, but reserved, aloof, a snob. And also through it, Michael stood slumped against the door jamb, listening to his mother and watching for Roly's reactions and keeping silent for once. ''E won't rip you off, sugar,' she assured Roly at last and Michael whined, 'Mum' disapprovingly. 'Huh, I know what you're like,' she responded, jokingly. 'Tea or coffee?' came the young girl's shouted request from the kitchen at one point. 'Black coffee, sis' Michael put in, ordering Roly's drink for him. 'Milk and sugar?' 'Black coffee, you flake,' Michael shouted back. 'Shurrup.' With an 'ever so nice to meet ya' from Yvette and 'get 'im to bring you round any time when we're in, sugar', Roly took his leave. He wasn't unpleasantly surprised when Yvette took hold of him in a light embrace at the front door and gave him a fleeting peck on the cheek. He turned down Michael's offer to see him home and drove himself back nursing the thought that his and the boy's joint destiny, or at least their short-term future, were sealed.

When he reminded Michael that he was on a week's trial and that the arrangement had been witnessed and thus sanctified by his mother, Michael said, 'Deal, I'll see ya right, dude.' 'My Hyacinthus of the hoover, Wonderboy of the washer and Gannymede of the garden herbs. And ninety pounds is what you get.' 'Oh yeah.' The gratifying sound of wages brought a warm smile to his lips. 'Wicked,' he said. 'And one other thing –' *No, I will* not *ask him to wear a thong.* ' – mobile phones are banned. This is work and you are not to spend the time texting your friends and playing games. You can leave the thing at home, or at least make sure it's switched off while you're here.' 'Cool.' So he worked out his week, he dusted, he washed, he cleaned, all after school and at the weekend. 'You're a proper little Mary Whitehouse aren't you?' Roly teased one day. 'Geddit? White house?' 'Who?' 'Never mind darling.' And he patted Michael's bottom for the first time and Michael didn't flinch. The week passed and there were no disasters, no conflicts; the boy went to his chores with gusto and Roly waited for the novelty to wear off as soon as he gave him his first wage. On pay day, he handed him a bank debit card. 'Now go round to the cash machine and take out ninety pounds and bring the receipt. If you take out any more, if you try to pull a fast one, I will know,' he warned and regretted his circumspection. 'No way I'm gonna rip you off,' Michael asserted. When he returned with the cash and the receipt, he gave both to Roly and Roly handed him his wages and Michael said thank you. 'Now, what do you think? Are you going to continue?' 'Oh yeah,' he said and with enthusiasm. 'The next thing is to see how you cope with shopping. You can count yourself lucky that I've just found a supplier of samphire on the interweb, that's a marsh plant I've known about and wanted to try for a long time which, the word is, is coming into fashion and I want to order some. So I won't be putting you through the embarrassment of having to ask about it in the greengroceries of Trenton and subjecting you to blank stares from girl shop assistants who will never have heard of it and will look at you as though you are speaking Mandarin. But there will be things I need from places where I can't get and I'll be relying on you to get them on your own or help me into the shops. If you pass muster, then I'll cancel my homeworkers, tell the county council, who pay me the money to pay you and you will be my official homeworker. You'd better be up to it,' he said, sternly. 'I'll be your official and I'm up for it,' he said and Roly heard some pride in the voice. Roly's feelings were mixed: how wonderful it was to have a dreamboy homehelp but how niggling that he was putting himself into the hands of an an infant. But he gave due credit, the boy had worked, the place was clean, he was so far a good and faithful servant. Came the day and Roly booked his scooter at the supermarket – 'We'll do the simple task first' – and they set off. The more testing errands to the butcher, the farm shop and the many other specialities that he needed most help to get, he would leave until later. How Michael would cope with ordering a loin of lamb, or dry-cured bacon and pork and garlic sausages from the Bacon Shop, or with asking for a herring to be boned and filleted, or with dropping off and collecting his prescriptions and a dozen other requirements which would crop up remained to be seen. 'What's this stuff?' he'd ask as he followed Roly's scooter around the aisles. 'It's all ecofriendly with me, my boy, nothing toxic if I can help it.' The boy's ignorance and bafflement soon showed when it came to the – to him –

esoteric foodstuffs and household cleaners Roly pointed out he would have to buy ('What d'ya do with that?' he asked about a fennel bulb).

Away from the shopping, he continued to tend the precious herbs, the herbs that were responsible for setting in motion this domesticity and he fed the hanging basket outside the front door and all in all eased himself into a routine which suited both him and Roly, even to the point of Roly's being able to trust him with the key of the door. Roly revelled in issuing lust-laden instructions. ('Put some bircabonate of soda in the bottom of that bin before you put a new bag in it.' 'What for?' 'It kills odours.'). It wasn't quite like hiring the swarthy semi-naked pinafored and thonged hunk he'd often yearned for, but the boy's – albeit clothed – body moving around him while he was at his tasks, ('Soda crystals down the plugholes, please and after that the fridge needs boraxing.'), was an adequate compromise, an aesthetic feast for his jaded eyes and careworn soul.

****

Silverdaddies was a site he'd had little to do with in the two years since someone had told him about it. He'd found its promotional blurb – 'a meeting place for mature men and other men (both daddies and younger), who are interested in keeping their daddy happy and/or sexually satisfied' – enticing enough at first, but then he remembered he rather deplored the concept of the relationship between a younger and an older man being that of father and son and wasn't prepared to take part in the roleplay so many of the site's juicy young patrons demanded nearly every time he clicked on a name for a private chat. Silverdaddies by comparison to other site was raw: explicit sex chat, obscene profiles, men masturbating in public on webcams, sex, sex, sex. He went through the motions of creating a profile and more or less

195

forgot about it, returning to the familiar comfort of the more familarly reticent rooms. When he received emails from the site – mostly people in the USA – he either acknowledged them out of politeness or sent a full reply if the senders met his criteria of physical attraction and there was a photo attached to verify it. He logged on for a desultory flick through its photo galleries and to read profiles from time to time:

Dominant dudes is the name of the game, and gettin in my black bttm is the way to play. I'm a black bttm willing to do almost anything with the right dominant guy. I'm on a serch for a real dad with a aggressive edge, and ALL men are welcome to apply. Thick build is a plus, and any daddy who thinks they can blow my back out is on the right track, and YES THOSE ARE MY PICTURES and YES I AM OF LEGAL AGE (I would think it would be daddies' dream to pump a barely legal bttm boi!) bttm only, can't really travel cause I'm in college, don't 'do drugs, just drink and expect the cum to keep drippin, cause i'm hungry!

23yr old guy into older guys. Am versatile and into most things, U.K. and 55+ prefered, group scenes a bonus! Also looking for a guy 40+ to do a friend of mine.......... but only if I can watch.

Horny, masculine, athletic, toned cute jock I've had my first anal sex experience and I loved it. Now I want to try it more and see if I like it as much as I think I do now. New to the experiences but getting used to it really fast. My first was an older man so thats what I am looking for. Race and size of tool not important,just pleasuring one another is. Still new so I would want you to be gentle at first but once I'm "opened up" you can let it rip for as long as you want. Love the feel of a cock filling my ass now and I want more! Love to surrender my ass for deep fucking by an older man.

But it was many months since he'd had any truck with Silverdaddies, so he was surprised and intrigued when an email arrived one day telling him there was a message waiting for him. He logged into his inbox and surprise quickly turned to incredulity when he saw who'd written to him – none other than Curiouslad. Could this be the same? Had he now traced him here? If it was he, then he really was exploring all avenues and attacking on all flanks. He opened the message. 'Hi' was all it said and he went to the profile. Whereas on the other sites, Curiouslad had held back his personal details, here he was a little more forthcoming. Roly now learned that he was six feet tall and weighed 126 pounds and also that he'd mysteriously moved from London to Staffordshire, no less. What was more, he would like it to be known that:

Ive never been with another man but I so want to be an older mans boy. I feel like a freak because I aint done sex yet. Dont get me wrong Im sure I'll enjoy it but I want my first time to be enjoyable for me as well as for you. I am very open minded but I dont know about it as well. I hope he will be very gentle and that this will be my first time doing this, Im not into pain and I dont want it to hurt, but Im very willing to be trained. If you are interested please email me and I will answer all emails and if you live close by we could meet for real at a local caff or something so we can get to know each other better and who knows what else might happen I suppose people will say theres something wrong with me because its not normal. I dont have a problem getting a hard on and I wank all the time. But am I screwed up?

After reading with ever-widening eyes and berating him, naturally, for his spelling, his wilful neglect of apostrophes, his dreadful punctuation and his lack of syntax, he berated him further for still not showing himself and oh, he wished he would and oh, he wanted him to be attractive and oh, he had to be. His reasoning went so: 1) It was not the same person 2) It was the same person playing a teasing game 3) If it were the same person he will have received his XXX-rated billet doux 4) If it were not the same person all he had to do was cut and paste the billet doux and send it off again this time to this boy (was he a boy?) 5) Forget it for now and wait for a reply, if any.

****

Michael was about his chores and Roly thought, 'He's teenage moody today, he's not his usual bright self.' The boy had answered his inquiries about his mother and about how his exams were progressing with sulky words. Roly let him alone. When he finished, he went into the computer room showing Roly a decidedly distrait face; he looked at him but seemed not to see him, looking beyond him at the car park. 'Can I ask ya somethin'?' came out and he started moving to his silent music, foot to foot, but this this time his dance was a slow waltz. 'May I,' said Roly sharply. 'What?' 'What do you want to ask?' He looked quickly away, as though the question and whatever answer he was expecting was too candid for eye contact. 'Ya know when I asked you if you fancied me before?' Roly went weak. This 'fancying' was fast becoming an idée fixe and he had to nip it. The paranoid fear of being toyed with by the gods came over him again: they've sent me the male equivalent of a siren, a boy Lolita, whatever one of them is called. 'Boil my ballocks and call me Rudolf,' he groaned in a boom. 'Get it in your head will you? You are a very attractive boy and in that sense, if you like, I "fancy" you. Chatsworth House is a very attractive building and I "fancy" that. It excites me, but I don't want to have sex with it. Now, also get it into your head that I'm too old and too homosexual and you are too young and too straight for me to.' He was going to say, 'have any physical designs on you', but that would have been lying, because of course he had designs. 'I'm fifteen,' he said, with sullen firmness. 'And heterosexual and I'm fifty-one and gay.' He found that amusing and a smile twisted his lips and, 'You're older than me mum,' he tittered. 'The way I feel at this very moment I'm older than anybody, too old, as I've thought many times, to have any ancestors. And I know you're fifteen but, leaving your age aside, this, this attraction I have for you is no secret is it? Why are you banging on about it? Yes, I think you're attractive, but my attraction to you is pure metaphysics. Oh what a boy you are,' he growled in exasperation. 'You're making me feel like Svengali. If you think I think there is the slightest minute microscopic molecule of a possibility that.' Did he need to expound? 'You are an exquisite boy. There.' 'I'm fifteen,' he repeated, robotically. Roly stared at him, trying to fathom what thoughts were hidden behind the fathomless eyes. 'Now we come to your tender years –' '– Sixteen next year. February the fifth. Legal.' 'Oh well, muzzeltoff,' he snidely sang.' 'Isn't it a bit late for a deflowering party though?' Michael parried, 'Naah, I got plans,' he sang back and shot him a sly grin. 'For when I'm legal I mean...' He seemed to lose himself in whatever sophistry he was concocting and went quiet again, dropping his head. Then he lifted it and found, Roly supposed, his point. 'Are you, like... are you lonely?' 'If you're asking am I sex starved the answer is no.' 'Yeah, but you must want a – ' He was blithe: 'I have my pictures, they are all I need. Either living pictures, the young men I see on the street, or the websites and DVDs –' '– You got porn DVDs?' he asked with a sort of wary enthusiasm, 'what? Men stuff?' '– but I have far too much thinking to do about how to keep body and soul together these days to be bothered looking for sex.' Michael continued to shuffle, not responding, more or less forcing Roly to say more. 'I don't imagine I'll ever actively pursue sex again, or respond to an advance if I ever get one. I've retired, it's over, past my sell-by date and shelf life. I told you, I've lost my libido. That means I've lost my desires. I like to have someone around to care for me and be here when I need it, that's what my life is now Michael. That's why I'm so glad I've found you, or rather you've found me. Your arrival at least means I don't have to depend on the kindness of strangers any more.' He turned and looked out the window too. 'I'm not Blanche Dubois,' he muttered, but another soupçon of camp was again lost on the boy. He felt a sudden twinge of nostalgia, why couldn't he keep his mouth shut? 'I miss my friends,' he sighed, without thinking. 'I miss them dreadfully, my old friends, the ones I got drunk with and had lunches and dinners with. The heaving social round I used to have, you know?' Michael wouldn't know what a social round was and he knew nothing of Roly's. 'A new friend would be nice, a good friend, a true friend who would accept me for all my...' *Stop there. It can't be him.* 'I'm not a stranger now am I?' 'No, you're a new acquaintance.' Michael's dance had come to an end, he leant back against the wall and reached out to sketch a pattern absently on the door with his finger. 'So... am I your friend?' He looked at Roly again and Roly caught his gaze and held it for a while. 'You do not want a man thirty-five years older than you for a friend,' he said and it came out astringently and he'd meant it only to sound discouraging. He immediately regretted it. Michael reacted as though he'd been mortally wounded. It dawned on Roly, despite what the boy had said, that he could be missing a father and that these oblique nudgings of his were his green way of, of what? Seeking a surrogate, a new foundation to make him feel secure? He didn't know. He had his mates on the street, but no *pater familias* and could be searching for one *in loco,* in the person of himself. But then, why the reference to 'fancying*? I'll be damned, despite my sexual attraction or any chaste affection I have for him, that I'm going to be* that. He apologised and motioned him to go to the livingroom and there to sit down. 'That was ignorant of me. Of course I'll be your friend. What I meant to say was I can't be your father.' There was a long silence. 'If, if there's something you want to talk to me about, something you want to tell me, I'll – ' 'You can touch me ya know.' This was jaw-dropping and Michael saw his shock. 'I don't mean like that ya minter.' 'Mercy. Surely you have your mum for that. You love her don't you and she loves you, I'm sure?' 'I don't mean that either, it's...oh, ya know what I mean.' 'You miss your dad don't you?' 'No,' he shouted vehemently. 'I told you my dad's a twat. 'E made me mum cry and I'll never... I 'aven't got a dad.' The outburst etched his face with anguish. He hated the father he'd had but that only made it seem to Roly that he wanted one the more. He needed a hug too, far more than Roly did, but this was emotional blackmail. Roly couldn't dare to hug him, it could give him an erection and Michael would feel it pressing against himself and then there would be trouble. 'You know somethin'?' His tone changed in a flash, his tempers were chameleon. 'Tell me.' 'I wish I could talk proper like you, will you teach me proper… you know… English?' Another of his disarmers, out of synch with the mood and he said 'English' as though it was a foreign word. 'Ha-ha,' Roly laughed. 'We shall be abecedarians together shall we? Right, say after me, "Hello, how are you?"' ''Ello, 'ow are ya?' 'No, "Hello, how are you?"' 'Hello, 'ow are… 'Hello… 'ow.' 'Hello… how.' 'Hello, how, are.' 'Hello, how, are.' 'Hello, how har – how are – 'ow are – 'ello, how are you – hello – how – are – you – hello, how are you?' 'A herd of heavy elephants.' 'An 'erd of heavy.' 'A herd.' 'A herd of 'eavy, a herd of heavy – elephants, a herd… of heavy… elephants. Yay!' 'Aitch. As in Danny Hodgkins.' 'Danny – ', he began, then, 'P'raps not,' he decided suddenly. 'They'll all call me stuck up if I start talkin' posh.' 'Just what I was called by my council estate contemporaries.' He couldn't wish the same opprobrium on Michael and what was left of his childhood. 'I bet you could teach me about sex though, eh?' He simply couldn't help it, couldn't help slipping in his malapropos insolent asides; he really did have a blatant way of steering a conversation his way. 'Not the sort of sex you want to learn about. I suppose you're trying to tell me how your hormones are making life unbearable. Save your breath, I know all about it. You're dying for it aren't you?' 'Yeah I'm always 'orny. And don't be a divvy, I've 'ad it already, ya know,' he proclaimed with an arrogant look designed to inform Roly and the world not to presume he was chaste. 'Shaggin' rocks man! Phwhoo,' he clarioned. But the eagerness made Roly suspicious; he was far from a boy who still sported the blush of modesty and Roly could imagine him fumbling, groping, touching private parts yes, but he thought back to his clamping of the girl's crotch that night and something told him that had been the gesture of a boy exploring, rather than one who had already reached his destination. *Then again, you may be wrong so don't challenge him.* He didn't want to know either way. 'So, are ya goin' to?' 'What?' 'I mean... if you want.' He heaved his chest. 'S'okay, me mum says everybody needs a hug. She's always goin' on about 'ow Princess Di said you should 'ug somebody. It'll do you good.' Meaning it would do him good? 'Your mum is a wise woman.' 'It'll make it like we're friends.' This was so unstreet, this was childlike and plangent and Roly swallowed in his throat. He felt he was the virgin here, being led on his first step to intimacy. Michael wanted to set a seal, perform a symbolic act, with the warmth of physical contact, or he was seducing Roly in his untutored crass way, or he was asking for a familial embrace, a fatherly gesture. If Roly kept his apology firmly in mind and made it the reason for a hug, it would prevent the dreaded tumescence; but watching the boy's fumbling attempt to suggest this gesture of closeness already had his loins stirring. He couldn't help calculating, Michael being taller than he, that his erection would poke into him round about the top of his leg. Be damned, he'd been a long time not temerarious, so he did it, he stood up, opened his arms as an invitation and the boy went over to him and they clasped awkwardly and it was all very manly and butch and macho and chaste. 'Mates yeah?' Michael said into his ear, making a truce. 'Yes, mates,' Roly sighed back, *as long as you don't call me mate.* He tried his best not to show discomfort or embarrassment. Breaking apart, but still holding his shoulders lightly, 'You're good, you know,' he soothed. 'Be happy.' He held him for a second more. His erection had done what he predicted and feared and had now grown as hard as it got. If Michael noticed it, he refrained from saying anything about being 'pervy' this time. 'And Michael?' 'Yeah?' 'Do me a big favour will you? We're going to be friends so please, please, don't put me in a position where I have to talk to you like a father would. For pity's sake don't ever make me sound like my own father talking to me, I couldn't bear it. We are *mates*, yes, father and son no.' 'As long as you don't kick off at me like me dad did.' Roly let out a loud laugh. 'Oh I'm bound to kick off, dear boy. You're a teenager after all and it's the duty of teenagers to be insufferable and our duty to be grumpy about them. Teenagers like you have to be moody and sulk and grunt and say you're not bothered and generally annoy us. Teenagers are on a different planet, you're aliens. Your music, your culture, your clothes, your lives are anathema to old people like me. And mine are to you. We both have to live with it.' 'So if you kick off at lads, 'ow come ya go large for 'em?' 'Ha!' Roly roared again. Trust a child to point out hypocrisy so slickly. 'Because they tend to be irresistible,' he protested. 'I like looking at a pretty boy, that's all. And as adolescent boys can be a pain in the rectum, it's good that there are people around who are able to redress the scales and give one or two of them a real pain in the rectum when the occasion arises.' 'You talkin' about –?' 'Enough!' he cried. They sat down again and Michael rocked him once more with his inquisitiveness, what to him must have seemed a logical follow up to Roly's mention of pains in the rectum. Roly had said too much. 'Is it good doin' it with a bloke then?' 'It depends what you're doing and if you're both any good at it,' Roly rejoindered, flippantly. 'Are you top or bottom?' 'Michael old darling, I have to say you seem to be unhealthily obsessed with me and a homoerotic life which some people would find morbid. How do you know about top and bottom?' 'I bin on the Puffta website. S'okay, it's for young guys.' 'I know it.' 'Perv!' 'But it's a gay site and you are under the age limit and you're not gay. Are you?' 'No way.' 'And are there no parental controls on your PC?' 'Nah, me mum doesn't know nothin' like that. So what if I 'ave bin on Puffta?' 'So you're telling me you think you *are* –' '– I never said that.' His refuttal was vehement, reminiscent of an alcoholic who denies he has a drink problem. Then he quickly calmed himself, a chameleon change, 'So which one are you?' he inquired gently. He didn't wait for an answer. 'I bet it's murder intit… takin' it up the arse I mean.' Tell him yes, he thought, put him off, even scare him, make him flee from the ogre. 'Is it "murder" for you to eat a burger?' 'Eh?' His brow furrowed in puzzlement. 'There are those of us who are very

grateful –' '– What's burgers got to do with it –?' '– very grateful that there are men who enjoy the exquisite agony of being sodomised. Being a passive man doesn't necessarily mean being a dweeb of course.' 'Speak English will ya.' He did want to know then. 'There are men who enjoy it and there are men who have the pleasure of giving them the pleasure,' he said, in the painstaking way of one inconvenienced at having to explain the obvious. 'Oh yes.' He looked away, he felt rhapsodic. 'The top has the bottom underneath him.' He became furtive, telling a ghost story. 'He bends the other's legs back and he waits, poised, ready to penetrate. He has him at his mercy and that's exactly where he wants to be, lying compliant, waiting for the gorgeous feeling of the penis being pushed into him.' He looked at him, who was exopthalmic now, his mouth wide open too. *Turn a rhapsody into a paeon, that will make you scurry, my boy.* 'Waiting for the pain, the welcome pain, the pain of the martyr being stabbed by an angel, the pain that hurts so much and that he wants so much, he wants to be stabbed for ever so that he can see God.' He paused. 'Oh yes.' He paused again. 'I used to love making my bottom boys squirm and groan and shout my name while I was.. like fury... and some would come while I was doing it and that was –' Perhaps he shouldn't have said that. 'Too much information,' he protested. 'You tryin' to give me a 'ard-on or somethin'?' They stared at each other, one waiting for an answer, the other refusing to give it. Roly studied him, he had given him food for thought, he could see his eye moving from side to side, searching. 'They 'ave to use grease to get their cock in yeah, 'cause it's that tight?' 'So poetically put, Michael. Am I giving proctology lessons now to a straight boy?' He looked puzzled again, the abstruse word... then, displaying his impudent smirk, his dimple flexing, he asked about a particular fetish he must have heard of and Roly sighed an 'Oooh', a deep sigh of annoyance. 'That is some people's predilection, yes.' 'What's a preedy... what?' 'It's their bag, their thing. Personally, I find one or two fingers is sufficient gratification.' Michael began to feel lost; if he knew how, he would have asked him not to obfuscate, so he settled for the familiar common denominator: 'So 'ow many men you shagged then?' he asked. 'Oh Flopsy and Mopsy!' Annoyance became exasperation. 'Two hundred and fifty when I last counted,' he blurted, quick as spit. 'Phwaooor, two 'undred an' fifty?' The eyes stretched again. 'What a slapper! Bet you got AIDS an' everythin'.' 'That's less than ten a year, think of the angst of the barren patches in between, my dear. It was before the plague and then there was only Larry.' He heard Muvvie speak and the sudor welled up and he was jolted by the guilt, the guilt of having the three-times-in-a-night-boy he picked up in Brighton when Larry was away working and the boy in in Wales while Larry was at home watching TV... 'I am HIV negative,' he proclaimed. 'So don't you use no condoms?' 'Ha! The passion killers. No, I don't, they –' '– Yeah, they make ya go soft innit.' '– tend to make one lose the wood,' he patronised. 'Larry and I had no need for them. I'm rather glad I'm celibate in today's sexual climate, there's some consolation in not having the bother of having to avoid being killed by buggery.' Michael fell into something akin to a brown study at these words, but he snapped out of it and asked, 'D'ya think I wanna be a bi-curious?' which sounded portentous, as though he were preparing to embark on a rite of passage; he uttered 'bi-curious' as though he had been influenced by gay website labels. Curious, Roly thought. *Curiouslad.* All sorts of alarms went off in his head. Surely not and he masked his consternation with jocularity: 'Do I want to buy a curious what?' 'Ha ha, you're 'ilarious... not.' 'I think you've latched on to some of the lingo from Puffta and you're showing off. I hope you're not cockteasing,' he said and then immediately tried to rescue himself from his cynicism. 'But I don't like to think you'd do that so that's doing you an injustice, sorry.' He stiffened: 'Hell, I don't know if you're bi-curious Michael, I can't play Doctor Ruth, I'm no guru, it's something you have to find out for yourself. I don't know you well enough, I can't advise you, the destiny of your sexual orientation is not in my gift. And by the way, for your information, when I was functioning properly I preferred to be...' He now leered at him, 'top. 'So if you and me, ya know,' Michael said, 'in bed... you'd do it an' I'd – ' Any tingle induced by giving sex lessons to a pretty young boy was immediately doused; this was beyond tolerance, his persistence had become not only tiresome but sinister. Get thee behind me young Satan. 'Michael, I mean it. Stop. Not with you, not in my bed or yours or any bed. You are doing the fucking now, fucking my head.' 'Givin' you a brain spin.' 'You and I, I ask you,' he said, summoning exasperation. 'I know there are thousands of young men who genuinely desire men much older than themselves and there are unsure young men who think that answers can be found in the affection of men like me, but. Oh for god's sake Michael, you're not of age. The idea of you and I... and if we could, could.' He gave up in despair and held his brow in his hand. 'I don't believe I'm having this conversation,' his voice crescendoed, 'You don't want and I am not your man and we are not, not ever, *never...* GOING TO HAVE SEX,' was his cadenza.

He was still reeling from the word. Curious. A white hot bolt had shot through him the moment he said it. It was time to dismiss him. 'Time you weren't here, young man, time to do some writing and for that I have to be alone. As Jesus said to Satan, bugger off.' Still he stayed and there was another non sequitur: 'What you writin' anyway, a book?' 'Mmm? Yes... well... sort of. I keep a journal, a diary. Every day. Well, most days. And you're in it,' he said ominously. 'You've wrote about me?' He sounded horrified. 'Written. Yes I have. I'm psychoanalysing you and dissecting our interface.' 'Whatever that means. Can I read it sometime, see what you've written about me?' 'You *can* read it but you may not read it.' 'What's that supposed to mean?' 'Oo-oh. When I teach you to speak proper, I'll explain the difference between can and may.' Michael persisted: 'So if I was legal... would you like... go with me, if I was that way I mean, if I let ya?' *If I let you.* 'If you let me? You don't *let* anybody. Look up the meaning of consensual in your dictionary, if you know what a dictionary is and if you have one. You are beyond, young man,' he yelled. Perhaps being flippant was the way to stop him. 'I shall have to report you to the Royal Society for the Protection of Old Queens,' he declared.' No, he had to be serious. 'I can't for my life work out whether this is your process of self-discovery, or if it's simply academic interest.'

He wasn't about to sow any seeds in his immature head by telling him, 'Yes, if I was physically able to I would.' He wanted an end, he didn't trust either him or himself not to complicate matters further.

'Listen to me. Back in the day, when I was hale enough, a boy like you who was unsure, who wanted to try and see, was an exciting challenge and I gladly accepted it. But my stroke hasn't only taken away my sexual cravings, it's changed my attitudes. I can see you don't understand and how can you? I've had enough with straight boys and bisexuals and curious boys regardless of my stroke. They were fun at the time, but I can't make the effort any more, I'm not equipped for it. If you want to test a theory, if you *think* you want sex with a man, with me...' He was treading on eggshells. 'Suppose we did it and you hated it... and hated me? I couldn't bear that. Couldn't bear being responsible for driving you mad. You see what I mean? Once, I wouldn't have cared less, but now... oh, I don't know. Things, life, they've given me a conscience. What I need now is... companionship I suppose, which sounds very boring. If I *were* looking for a partner I would need a boy who was soft, a quiet boy, a pliant boy, a cultured boy. All the stuff that's ever been said and written about the nobility and honour, the purity and beauty of the love of an older man for a younger one. All very well as fine words, but they don't take into account the vast cultural, linguistic and social differences of the age gap; how to cope when the youngster wants to listen to rap or watch a horror DVD? One gets too old for computerised special effects,' he cried. 'And the old bloke wants some peace with Beethoven or wants to watch *On Golden Pond*. Michael, you're a boy, you run with the wind. Your enthusiasm and speed, your excitement, your chutzpah... a thousand years ago that would have inspired me, but my dynamo is worn out now and it exhausts me and makes me gripe. I can't help it, you can't help it.' He'd said enough to squash any equivocation, any tender feelings Michael may be nurturing towards him, but for insurance he added a little levity or, if not levity, then something amusingly grizzly. 'There's also the matter of my pisspot,' he said. 'Most men of my age – and when you are my age, this will pertain to most men of your age – most of them wake up each day but the morning glory they display is unfortunately no longer due to sexual excitement but the bladder. The bladder is full to bursting and they're dying for a pee, not a very sensual state of affairs I'm afraid and I'm no exception and more than just an exception because I can't get to the lavatory in time, so I keep a pisspot next to the bed. There's something fundamentally discouraging about a pisspot, Michael. A pisspot and sex don't sit together in harmony, I doubt if I could make love to you or to anyone next to a pisspot.' Michael didn't laugh or even smile. God's ballocks, Roly thought, as he looked at his expressionless face, he's even thinking seriously about *that.* It really was time to put up the shutters. 'And we stop there,' he said firmly. 'Be gone.'

****

His *Collected John Betjeman* was his absolute treasure, along with the letter the great man had sent him back when; he'd bought the book in his teens and lost it somewhere along the way in one of his many upheavals, moonlight flits, flights, who knew where and he'd never got round to buying a replacement, which was amazing, in view of the reverence in which he held the poet. He creamed what he could find off the net and kept it in a file and that had to suffice. His favourite, *Sun and Fun*, was a frothy decadent piece, so fitting to his own life, or so he liked to think:

And wonder beyond wonder,

210

> *That here where lorries thunder,*
> *The sun should ever percolate to me*

and

> *But I'm dying now and done for,*
> *What on earth was all the fun for?*

resonated so fittingly each time he read it or recited it to himself. Whether on this occasion it was Betjeman's ghost's doing, or some other bludgeoning psychic trope he didn't know, but something had determined that he should sit at the computer eating his shredded wheat that morning as usual but, unusually, that he should open his poetry file. The sun had percolated to him, but it was indeed wonder of wonders when he logged onto chat and was greeted by a pop-up message box, a reply from Curiouslad at last. *'Hey, thanx for gr8 msg tastic I dont get most of it lol Im brickin it cos its my first time Seen as were local do U wanna meet up somewhere? Pse msg me*

The brevity of textspeak, the boy's forte (was he a boy?). He'd also attached a photo, but not the one Roly had asked and hoped for, it was far more unambiguous than a face, it was a picture of a (his?) pair of buttocks, with a pair of hands on them, stretching them apart to expose the *atrium amoris* pointed directly at the viewer and Roly took this to be Curiouslad's idea of bait, a lure to a blind date tryst. The poor boy obviously had no idea what he was laying himself open to but, then he need have no fear of him; in his able-bodied days, he may well have on impulse suggested a meeting and hared over to wherever he was going to be. Of course, the gaping boyhole fired him momentarily; it took him to a place where a fresh and willing boy was waiting for him to ravish him with a passion, but even that was no incentive for any precipitate action any more, such action was beyond his capabilities now. But he would prolong things for sport; he wanted to know why Curioslad was hiding his face and an interchange would keep his desire kindled until either or both of them got bored. He dashed off an immediate response:

Hello again Curious, Wonderful to hear back from you, thank you so much. I'd be delighted to think about meeting up with you and getting to know you. Unfortunately, your camera doesn't appear to know your arse from your face and as I don't suppose you'll be exposing your rear end as a means of identification for when we meet, I would be so glad if you could aim your lens at your public rather than your private asset and show me what the rest of the world can see but I can't – YOUR FACE! Go well & long life, Roly

and waited to see what if anything he did about that.

****

He hadn't written a Journal entry for several days and in the light of Michael's recent mind-blowing suggestiveness, this was remiss in the extreme. He had much to recap and record. Firstly, Curiouslad went entirely out of his head. He heard no more from him, he'd sent no photo and neither did he himself write any more to the boy (was it a boy?). What was preoccupying and exasperating him was Michael's 'fishing'. He continued to be unconvinced that, if he was indeed a virgin and if he wasn't gay but trying to find out if he was, he was sure he wanted his first sexual experience to be with a man, and a much older man. No, he was floundering, the search for self-awareness was struggling with reason and was addling his young brain. The thought that that man could be himself, well it flabbergasted and frightened him. Roly was in danger of mistaking Michael's quest and his fixation about gay sex for flattery, if he fell for that, he was doomed. He harked back to himself at 15, when the thought of sex with an old man of 30 let alone 50 would have made

212

him want to vomit. But, of course, there was no accounting for taste. Why should it surprise him that, in a world where there were young men who found sexual gratification only with much older men, Michael might be one of them? Had he had sex with a girl and not enjoyed it? Did he now want to try man sex, regardless of the cut of the partner just so long as he was older? Or perhaps it had nothing to do with sex at all, perhaps he was looking for the platonic and consolatory and the only way he could ask for it was by probing and testing an old gay man he had found for his responses. He had assumed all old queens were attracted to ephebes; he was wrong, but had happened on one who was and so had seen his opportunity.

No matter if this were or were not the reason, he felt that Michael felt that he'd rejected him that day when they spoke of his father, but then how heartwarming was his idea of a hug! It was a syncretic act following the spat and for Michael a kind of 'blood brother' thing. But had he read more into it? If he had felt Roly's tumescence, which Roly was sure he had, that would have told him and what it told him was to run home and take the only step he could think of to refute rejection and to rekindle hope. Roly was to look back in hindsight with admiration for Michael's desperate determination; he hadn't buckled, had turned rejection to profit, a knockback had been an adjuvant. Bravo. What in fact Michael did after their soul-baring was to dash up to his room and his computer and think hard for once about his next gambit and even about the possible consequences of it. Then he stiffened his sinews; he was going to have his sister take a photo of his face and he would upload it onto his profile.

Roly, meanwhile, remained blithely ignorant of his tactic and for a while, their relationship slid into an affable, almost diurnal routine, with Michael content to be an ordinary kid with an out-of-the-ordinary good heart earning money for tending to a disabled man's everyday needs. Hints of any sexual charge between them went into abeyance, save for Roly's continuing covert lust; there was from Michael no more sardonic teasing, but there was one significant development on his part: it had become his custom to grab Roly and hug him each time he left, to reassure himself, it seemed to Roly, that they were still *mates*. Surely he had registered Roly's penile reactions by now? If so, he said nothing about them. Was he enjoying them? Two weeks went by, two weeks of chores and carrying shopping, carrying patience without agitation, carrying the knowledge that Roly hadn't looked at his tracks. He would know when Roly did look and he was waiting. During this time, an idea for a newspaper feature came to Roly, something very distant from journals and novels and he set to knocking out the piece – about the new laws banning smoking in public – speculatively, intending to send it out to editors in due course.

It was a latish night, a calm one with Freddie Kempe's recital of Beethoven sonatas, soothing and stimulating in turn, flowing through the speakers and a bold bright Venus hanging in the western sky. Perhaps it was the music that put him in the mood, he didn't know, but he had an urge to see naked flesh, to assuage his randiness and he went to the computer to browse. A good hour of chat soon bored him and he moved on to the more effervescent and unequivocal culture of Silverdaddies. After exhausting the faces, pudenda, buttocks and profile texts of a score of men under 30 from San Francisco to Sydney, he went into chat, hoping that a new room with new names would dispel the accidie that seemed to be hanging in a pall over both the rooms on the websites and the one he was sitting in. Great Gatsby and Grammercy! The name Curiouslad stared out at him from the list of names at the side. What was he to do? What, if anything, was he going to do?

The deadlock was broken after a few seconds when, without a beat, he clicked himself out. He had drawn back in terror at the possibility of being recognised and acknowledged by Curiouslad. A message, a call to private chat could have flashed up and he was ill-prepared, composure had left him. It would involve explanations, the solving of riddles, any sort of interchange. He'd come here, basking in Beethoven, seeking solace in erotic stimulation and not to unravel an internet intrigue, not through the inadequate communication of a keypad, in a chatroom, not that way, not now. This brush with danger, for danger it was, plunged him down – and what a plunge – into deep melancholy in no time at all; Muvvie came into the room and sat and berated him with yet another cruel reminder – cruelty he deserved – of the blackest episode of his life.

It was midnight before he knew it and the trauma of Curiouslad combined with the triggering of unwanted memories left him exhausted. He closed the computer and the flat down for the night and went to the refuge of bed.

****

Next morning, he awoke in complete denial of the previous night, wiped and dressed and took his usual breakfast then plunged into his newspaper feature with enough demonic gusto to finish it in half an hour. He read it through, subedited it and emailed the features editor of the *Signal* to introduce himself with the piece and his CV as an attachment. Almost immediately, the voice of AOL announced that he had email and his first thought was, that's what I call an efficient response, most likely an editor's instant rejection. He was wrong. The email was from Silverdaddies. He felt an electric thud but despite it clicked and read, 'Curiouslad has sent you a message' and he shuddered. 'Saw ur name come up in Sdaddies last nite then u ran off. Ill be in tonite if you wanna chat this time. Havent done it b4 but if you wanna so will I xxx,' it went. Kisses now! They gave him the feeling that he was at the centre of a dire conspiracy. Events were taking place outside his purview, someone was making plans for him, manipulating him and he spent the rest of the day in a fair amount of turmoil, unable to decide on the wisdom or otherwise of accepting the invitation to engage his stalker in conversation. He made himself a supper: steamed trout fillet and tomato and onion rice, which he could only just manage to eat, because the foreboding and trepidation he was going through were doing their best to kill his appetite. He took his coffee to the computer, lit a cigarette and logged on to Silverdaddies but Curioslad wasn't there. Whether or not he would have hung on to wait for him to appear was no matter, for the phone rang at that moment, a cruel and unexpected harbinger, replacing the banalities of a sexual hunt with the verities of mortality at a stroke. It was his brother, sounding sombre; as it came to pass, this call was the herald of a train of sorrowful events. He told Roly that their mother had been rushed into hospital and he was there with her. He had spoken to a doctor and the prognosis wasn't good; his mother's kidneys had failed. As he told Michael afterwards, she'd had enough love left in her to tell his brother to ring him. It was the beginning of a sequence over a mere three weeks that carried with it the weight of a Greek Tragedy. I hope, my dears, that you won't think me heartless when I say that it provided a timely relief. It gave him respite; he was feeling mounting coercion over the need to respond to

Michael's aborning sexual predilection, but Michael's flow, so to speak, was interrupted and all attention was diverted from the Roly-and-Michael ménage. The discovery of her death was brutal, the reporting of it cruel, can it ever be anything else? But he thought he knew, as told his journal the next day:

> About 1.30 this morning, while I was writing, a massive shiver passed through me and I thought, yes, perhaps this is the time.

He rang the hospital; the ward sister said she wasn't supposed to give information over the phone but... 'As you're family... afraid to say... passed away in the night... ' were the words he heard.

> I said goodbye and then burst into tears. Didn't think I would, didn't think I could allow myself the indulgence. I rushed as best I could to the hospital and saw the first dead body I'd ever seen in my life and it was my mother's. She lay, opened mouthed, looking as though she'd dropped off as I'd seen her many times before, her skin the colour of the Staffordshire clay she'd spent so much of her life working with and when I touched her arm lightly to say 'Bye mum', it was cold. There was a bible open at Psalm 23 on the bedside table and a flower on it. I'm blubbing quite a bit and my brother just rang me and he said he was 'coping.' 'She's gone now,' he said and we cried together, grief bringing us closer than I've ever known. I went tell Mother's old neighbour and called on two or three more who would want to know. I rang all the friends and acquaintances I could think of and also cousin Paul's sister who was in Nottingham and we had quite a chat. I asked her to pass on the news to

Paul. I must confess to feeling a little echo of a thrill when she was telling me about Paul's son, who is going into the army and to wondering if the son was as radiant as his dad was 40 years ago! I thought about ringing Larry, but didn't get round to it. He'll want to know, mother and he got on well, she liked him a lot. Perhaps I'll call him tomorrow, in the meantime I'm going out to buy a bottle of whisky and fuck if it destroys me.

****

Michael's reaction was lugubriously laconic when he told him. 'Oh,' he said, 'she musta bin very old', the stating of the obvious not said unfeelingly by one for whom close death was not yet commonplace; it was the best expression of logical sympathy at his disposal. And after the funeral, after the befuddled days, days with no hugs and certainly no mention of the quagmire of Curiouslad or Silverdaddies or night stalkers or sexual awakenings, he called in on Roly one morning on his way to school to find him pouring whisky into his coffee and asked why he was doing it and Roly couldn't tell him because he didn't wish or couldn't be bothered to answer such a nonsensical question with the contempt it merited and, in truth, because he didn't know who or what was responsible, if anyone or anything was, for having coffee and whisky for breakfast instead of shredded wheat, so he naturally thought it must be himself; he was upset but not grief-stricken at his mother's death, so it wasn't that. Somewhere, sometime during the drinking of, the making of his way through the dozen or so bottles of Bell's that week, he thought to ring Larry. The number he had for him was unobtainable, he and his man must then have moved on, nor could he locate Larry's mother's number nor those of his sisters. Larry, the last time they had spoken, was working for

218

Coventry council, in the rent department, so he found its website and sent off an email asking whoever read it to pass it on to him, a faint hope.

****

Somewhere, sometime, among the drinking of those dozen or so bottles, among the stupor of them, he logged into the Silverdaddies site again, like a pre-programmed creature, like someone obeying a command unquestioningly. While he was busy clicking on the names of all the under 30- year-olds he could find and perving their profiles, he didn't notice *his*, the one, in fact he didn't notice anything really except the level in the bottle of Scotch next to him; there must be enough to see him through the night and to last him until he could struggle his way to the off-licence next morning. But *his* name, the one name, was there, already there and he was suddenly aware of it, written in red in a 'private chat' box at the top left of the window and he clicked and the box opened up and **Curiouslad >** Hiya was already written and awaiting a response.

He was armed with John Barleycorn, he would take the offensive.

Loveyouth>(For that was his handle) Hello. Are you the same curiouslad who's been tracking me so much?

curiouslad>Yeah

Loveyouth>Your profiles say you live in 2 places, which one is it?

curiouslad>Im in staffs like U. Do u wanna meet up?

This boy (was it a boy?) obviously had no time for a preamble of social niceties. He expected any moment to be asked for his sexual preferences or even the size of his penis. He felt the reference to Staffordshire could be true, he wasn't getting the feel, insofar as one can 'feel' anything

219

through a monitor screen, that this boy (was it a boy?) was an American or a foreigner.

Loveyouth>Are you really a virgin?

curioslad>yea Im looking for my first time looking for a daddy I wud luv for a daddy to take my cherry

This was too bold, too forward, far too keen.

Loveyouth> Why send that pic to me? Why no face?

There was a long pause of no typing.

curiousland>Im not out n bit scared

Loveyouth>I need to see the face of the boy who invites me to swive him.

This situation was surreal, it needed stark language to materialise it. There was another long silence.

curiouslad> if I send u will u meet up?

Loveyouth>If it's a face I like, I'd certainly think about it

Another brief gap in typing.

curiouslad>sent

Before Roly could type an acknowledgement, 'ok', type anything in response, the message box 'User left or was disconnected' showed up with that heartless abruptness that only the internet can deliver. Accustomed to the foibles and manners of chatrooms and their users, he could be sanguine over both voluntary or involuntary disconnections and he waited to see if Curiouslad logged back in, but he didn't and he assumed that he'd got cold feet or that a parent had come in to his room and he heard himself wishing him goodbye and took a drink. He was not yet so fuddled, or perhaps it was another of those jolts of optimistically tinged prescience that strike from time to time: he clicked on his inbox to see if the boy (was it a boy?) had sent him the photo. There was the list of recent messages, there was his name and he clicked again. The box opened and next to the familiar text was the photo. Roly's reaction to the young and attractive face displayed was, unsurprisingly, one of enthusiasm and he took his pleasure for a few moments before scepticism crept in: it was still possible that Curiouslad was playing a game and had put up a photo of some pin-up culled from a website. He could only wait for him to return to the chatroom; if he didn't, then no matter, nothing was gained and nothing lost.

****

It was a wait of two days. For Roly, two days and at least two bottles of whisky; for Michael, two days of growing concern about his charge's mental state. As for Curiouslad, it was anyone's guess what he had spent the time doing. When Roly received the message from him telling him that he would be in chat at seven that evening and hoped to see him in there, he assumed that the boy (was it a boy?) had spent the time gathering his thoughts, feeding his expectancy and, as a hopeful virgin would do, not mulling over the consequences of offering up that virginity to a cyber stranger.

Came the hour and Roly logged in. Sure enough, Curiouslad was waiting and privated Roly as soon as he entered the room. Roly's heart, old and blasé though it was, skipped and he reached for his scotch.

curiouslad>hiya. thought u wunt come after last time

Loveyouth>Why did you run off?

curiouslad>soz guess I was brickin it did u get the pic?

Loveyouth>Yes thankyou

curiouslad>did u like? u still up 4 a meet?

Loveyouth>I like the boy in the photo yes but is it you? What's your name?

curiouslad>Cors its me n my names Jamie

Loveyouth>Have you read my profiles properly?

curiouslad>Yup

221

Loveyouth>So you know I'm a disabled alcholic
curiousland>I no u r Sokay Its kewl

The exchange lasted a good hour, Roly's emotions fought a series of battles: his hankering for a meeting raging against the nagging truth that it would be a disastrous and ill-conceived venture. He didn't refuse a meeting outright, he skirted, he avoided answering, he painted as black a picture of himself as he could, made play of his inadequacies in order to send the boy running scared, impatient and disgusted, but he couldn't douse his persistence.

Curiouslad, Jamie, said he lived just outside Lyme, four miles away and when Roly suggested a meeting in public in the local beauty spot of Black Pool, said he knew it and could get there by bus easily enough. Roly asked him if he could bring a friend with him as a precaution

curiouslad>Y? u want a 3some? lol

The boy had wit.

'I seem to have found an internet shag,' was how he put the planned tryst to Michael and Michael shrugged, outwardly disinterested but thinking, here he is, meaning to go and I'm playing a game and I don't know the rules. 'What if 'e's a queer basher, what if 'e beats you up and robs you and stuff?' He would put obstacles in his way, every obstacle he could think of to show discouragement, that was the way, describe it as a lunatic mission. 'I doubt you'd want to come with me,' Roly countered, ignoring the contingencies. 'Besides, if there are two of us, he may well be scared off and who would blame him? And I could hardly expect you to be here while I perform the necessary with him in the bedroom could I? Think of the screams, my dear, a boy losing his anal virginity can sometimes be an agonising – ' ' – Yeew, please!' Michael screeched. He could see that he couldn't persuade Roly against it: 'I'll see you after...when I come to scrape your bits off the floor' and he scudded, well aware that the sarcasm was redundant but feeling smug nonetheless.

Of course it didn't happen, of course Roly didn't know the reason it didn't happen. What did I really expect? he asked himself. (He had worn his neck cravat especially!) He'd driven to Black Pool and sat behind the wheel of the car smoking, for an hour, more, scanning the carpark, peering into the trees for a sign, a movement, willing a manifestation, as though invoking a spirit, peering for a fair-haired youth in green tracksuit bottoms and a blue teeshirt, carrying a black backpack. This was his first assignation for years and he tingled with all the nervous excitement a boy's imminence could elicit, veering between the expectation of his arrival and the fear he would not arrive, hoping he would and hoping he would not. Oh, the conflict! But no figure appeared; he decided to give up and then decided to wait a few minutes more, fought to go, fought to stay until, eventually, decisionless, he started the car and drove off, drove home; and he laughed, he drove and laughed manically thinking of previous, similarly abortive explorations and how he'd been mortified when they had ended like this one, a no show. Well, he was far too old and cynical for any more of that nonsense. No he wasn't; it was failure, it still hurt. In the flat, he poured himself a very large whisky and soda and drank sarcastically to Curiouslad's well-being. 'Salud, dinero y amor,' he cried to the ceiling.

'Well I reckon 'e's a right twat,' was Michael's verdict. He didn't gloat at the imposture inflicted on Roly, though he did watch with increasing disquiet as he tried to drink failure into oblivion. 'Why d'ya think 'e backed out?' 'He had a better offer I suppose,' Roly said with indifference. *Careful, my bravado is showing.* 'Not a difficult choice for him is it? Look at me.' 'Don't say that.' 'Oh Michael, my sweet pea, you're looking at a man who's chasing moonshine. I was mad to even contemplate it. I'm washed up, a dried up ancient whore, past my sell-by date, don't you see? I'm past it, it's over.' 'Bollocks, you dork. You're not past it.' Roly smiled wanly at him and raided the whisky bottle for another comforter and Michael furrowed his brow as he watched him and in the end could do nothing more than say goodnight – 'Laters' – and on his way home he asked himself, harrowed: 'What have I done?'

****

It was my mother's funeral today; I mark the date for this Journal and say nothing else.

****

I beg your forebearance, my dears, the final curtain had by no means fallen on the Greek Tragedy yet. No, not the failure of Curiouslad Jamie (was he a boy, was his name Jamie?) to appear, not the failure of a sexual encounter to materialise; what happened was far more poignant and it couldn't have been more inopportune. 'Sod's Law,' he said. He'd decided it was time to stop drinking alcohol again. 'Sod's Law.' How easily resolve is sabotaged, what a convenient get-out an ill-timed and disastrous event can provide for the weak-willed. He had first made provision for his safety, knowing that to give up his re-addiction peremptorily, without re-acclimatising his body gradually and under medical supervision, he could and probably would die quite quickly. This likelihood never troubled him while he was in drink, drink removed the fear and made it a logical proposition to carry on fearless. What did trouble him was

224

the economic factor, he was afraid of the day when he had no money left *at all* to pay for his addiction, when he would be dependent and without means, in other words helpless; and that would mean he was approaching the precipice. The idea of having to give up something he cherished because he couldn't afford it, of falling into the pit sober and *aware* that he was wretched – that would be a kind of honourable defeat and that loomed unthinkable and horrific. He had to act, to be sensible this once, responsible – what out of character behaviour was this, what was driving him? – to drag himself to his GP and be referred to the detox clinic where intravenous vitamin B and three daily doses of Valium would not cure him no, but remit him for a time. He waited for a letter from the clinic and made a phone call and a home detox course was arranged. 'You don't want the hassle of struggling around that ward in your wheelchair again do you, think of those heavy fire doors and terrible food?' said the nurse; he had known her before, she was the same one from two years earlier, Vicky; she came with pills, a blood pressure pump and a breathalyser. She was pleasant and plain-speaking, as her training demanded and affable and conversation away from alcohol was banal. He couldn't tell her the truth, addicts did not tell the truth, especially those alcoholics – Muvvie told him this while he sat talking to her – who were thieves and liars and were deliberating over the seduction of a virgin; they did not tell the truth. Or did they? Because when he was at the rehab clinic, Ian shuffled in that morning, his normally pert bright, shiny face so grey, so dully frowning, so unlike him. 'I did it, Roly, I just did it,' he said, with no preamble, just that, not looking at him, sitting down on the chair in the corner by the window, where he always sat. 'When I walked past the house, it was there on the sill so I reached in and took it. I did. I don't know why, I just did. I couldn't stop meself. Jesus.' He was an unmissable young man, sensational, that much was instantly apparent to Roly once he'd arrived, sobered up, seen him, been in the same room as him and could take full note of him, that is. He was blond, pretty in a masculine way, of that ilk; a footballer, sinuous, compact, always shower clean, indeed so very proud of his appearance that one deemed him conscientiously groomed, in the latest designer-labelled sweatshirts and tracksuits. Although personable enough and affable when he wasn't suffering withdrawal, finding much to laugh about each day, he'd never given Roly the impression that he could be serious and had never before chosen to place himself in such a confiding position, alone with Roly as he was then, indeed had never really spoken to him at any length at all, none of the young men there had, in the two or three weeks that Roly was confined with that particular group of addicts, preferring the same camarilla he chose or who had chosen him and staying with them, sticking with them, as they stuck with him, throughout his stay. Perhaps he was put off by Roly's unintentionally aloof aura, his self-isolation, perhaps he thought Roly – by his voice and manner – uninterested and uninteresting, perhaps he saw no common ground between them. But there he was that very morning, alone with him in the smoking-room, on the day, as it happened, before his discharge, confessing to a recent crime. 'I never burgled before, you gotta believe me man.' Roly was intrigued by this: he was indifferent to his committal of a crime yet astonished both at the confession and at being chosen as confessor. He couldn't remember anyone, *anyone,* ever confessing a wrongdoing to him at all. Why him? Was it simply that it was he who happened to be in the room at the time, could it have just as easily been whoever was there? Alcohol, the blatant beast; heroin the euphoric curse of despair, he thought, as 'How big and light and airy,' Vicky the nurse observed of his flat when she came, how pleased he must be with his new car, how she'd changed her car since the last time they'd met, how he must be looking forward to eating again because she remembered how he loved to cook and how sorry she was about his mother's death. No doubt such polite banality would have continued long into the detox course had the phone not rung, on the third day it was, an intrusion he regarded as disrespectful and one that made him jump and he excused himself grumpily to answer it. The voice was a man's, thick Scottish and very slurred. 'Is that Roland Hunter?' Was it, was that who he was? The voice introduced itself as Gordon and after a moment he realised who it was: his successor as Larry's boyfriend, in Coventry, the man he'd spoken with once before, in the early hours of a Christmas morning, when Larry was by then installed in his home, happy with a new love. Larry had rung Roly, who was in the council house with mother, not to gloat, because that was not in his nature, but simply to wish season's greetings. He had told him about Gordon some months before, so there was nothing new to tell; nevertheless, behind the goodwill greetings, Roly heard Larry telling him this was it, there was no going back now for them. 'We have to move on,' he said and Roly thought, you may have somewhere to move on to and someone to go with but not I. The conversation, he remembered, was alcoholically-fuelled but not acrimonious and then Larry had handed the phone to Gordon and all he could remember Gordon having said afterwards was, 'It seems we're both in love with the same person.' All of this coursed through Roly's brain as he listened to Gordon this second time, looking at Vicky the nurse sitting sedately opposite him and this time Gordon didn't speak of a shared love and didn't know that he was in the middle of a detox for heaven's sake; he must ask Gordon to ring back or tell him he would ring him when his nurse had gone, but there was not time. Was he calling to tell him he and Larry had split up, that Larry had gone somewhere, found another someone?   He thought this mischievously. But there was not time, what Gordon said next sent his mind imploding, sent Vicky the nurse spinning out of his vision, sent the voice on the phone into oblivion, sent him and the flat and the village of Jamage and the whole sick sodding arsehole of a world into damnation. 'I have to tell you Larry is dead,' Gordon said and Vicky the nurse saw dumbfounded horror on Roly's face and inferred something of what his caller was telling him and she suggested she leave. Detox was suspended.

****

Youth, effervescence, light, Larry never grew older, there was always light where Larry was, he was dark-skinned and had black hair yet he was radiant and there was light! Light and wraparound love and wonderful warm, cuddling comforting sex. 'He was over fifty like me, but he was always twenty-nine!' Roly cried – his age when they met. A man of incomparable beauty with whom you have spent a large swathe of your life, with whom you have laughed and cried, whom you have told you will never leave and who has told you he would rather die than lose you, who has given his body to you and to whom you have given yours, who has held your heart in his hand and whose heart you've held in yours... And you remember – hell to recall it now – hearing Larry say one night at a quiet gathering of friends, saying it to admonish the fear you expressed of leaving him alone: 'Oh no,' he said, 'I'll go before you Roland.' That was what he'd promised and now he'd kept his promise. But he couldn't be dead, a man like Larry could not be dead, he

228

cannot be dead, he cannot. Better to have loved and lost than never at all? He spits on your words, Tennyson. He hid the dark things from Larry throughout their time together, but he told him when he'd cheated (sometimes) and Larry had forgiven him and otherwise he never lied to him, except for the time in Kensington Gardens. What hurt most: Gordon told him that Larry had died three years previously and Roly calculated it was shortly after the one phone call Larry made to him in his new flat in Bleakridge. Larry phoned him and then died, it was like that. Three years went through his head; three years of the ignorance of death. Gordon told him the story of how Larry had come home from work and gone straight to bed ill, sick with the flu, so ill that a doctor had to be called. The next night, Larry got out of bed and staggered downstairs. He had an asthma attack (Roly had never known him suffer such a thing in his life) and collapsed in the hall. Gordon rushed to hold him and Larry said, 'I love you' and died in his arms. He was cremated. Larry's adorable face and silken body burned and Roly howled: 'They had no right to destroy my Larry's body.' He had just enough presence of mind to ask after Larry's mother and sisters. When Gordon told him that he himself had just been diagnosed with cancer and had himself only months to live, he exerted himself to express sympathy but the words came meaninglessly out of his mouth; the only thing that was vital and meaningful was whisky, his and Larry's favourite drink, and it was vital to go and get a bottle of it as soon as he could.

****

When he told him, Michael uttered another lugubrious, 'Oh' and thought, *these two deaths are nothing to do with me, Roly is hurting and that's bad, but there isn't enough sympathy in my young soul, they were people I didn't know, they were distant and I'm not dead so it doesn't matter;* and

229

then a shocking realisation slammed into him: 'He was the same age as you wasn't 'e?' he asked. 'My mother, whisky, diazepam and no whisky, Larry, whisky. I measure out my life in whisky and death,' Roly murumured. 'It used to be broken threads,' and vinegar laughter poured out of him. He ranted quietly, Michael stood over him anxiously, urging him not to get 'completely munted'. 'I don't like seein' you wrecked,' he said. 'Jeez, it's only 12 o'clock.' 'Oh, don't worry, Michael-angelo, *Michel*angelo. I don't get angry or violent. I don't smash up the furniture or want to hit people. I usually fall asleep. I passed out in the Railway Tavern one night, don't ya know, out like a light I was with a full glass of scotch in my hand and came round half an hour later with it still upright and not a drop spilled, isn't that wonderful and comforting? Once a piss artist... and I know all the rules. You and your cider and ketamine, ha, not in the same league boy,' he scoffed and reached for his glass and raised it in a toast. 'Usquebaugh, the water of life,' he cried. 'In the midst of the water of life we are in death' and he drained the glass in one go. He banged it down and looked at Michael: 'But it won't put out the flames for Larry,' he murmured with black eyes and turned back to the monitor screen, where a young man in Romania was sitting naked on a chair masturbating on his webcam. Michael, following his gaze and bending in to see what he was looking at, let fly a muted cry of outrage. 'If you don't want to watch this, *Michel*angelo, you can go,' Roly snapped. 'I'm not turning it off for you and don't worry, you'll still get paid.' The day before, the day of Larry's death, which wasn't the day but was the day of the news of death, he'd rung Michael to ask his mother to get a bottle of Bell's – make it two – for him from the off-licence and told him to bring it, them, round. He was halfway through the second. He took a gulp from his glass. 'This will put weight on me you know, too many calories. Whoosh, my belly will balloon and you'll hate me,' he carolled. 'I shall be an abomination in your sight. 'Look, I know you've 'ad it rough with yer mother and yer old boyfriend,' Michael said solicitously, 'but whisky won't bring 'em back will it? Anyway, you told me that specialist said you shouldn't drink no more alcohol.' 'Any more alcohol,' he corrected. 'He was educated enough not to use double negatives.' He pointed at the monitor screen. 'I'm going to ask Kleverjo here in Romania to have his orgasm, then I'm going to lie down,' he said. 'Be a good Angelo and leave me alone.' 'Right, I'll come round later to see you're OK.' 'Take a note out of my wallet there and ask your dear Yvette mumsie to get me two bottles for tonight and bring them round.' He didn't much care if he upset Michael right then, or if he'd been upset by having caught him watching the masturbating Romanian. 'I just want to lie down and think of naked boys and see if I can get an erection,' he said as much to himself as to him.

By the evening, when Michael returned with the bottles, he'd collapsed on his bed under the weight of the whisky he'd drunk. Michael peeked at him round the door. 'Are you disgusted with me?' 'I got the whisky,' was the pert and to Roly's ears, pertinent, answer. 'Good boy. I'll drink to you.' 'I'm gonna get 'ome, will you be awright?' 'Who knows, who knows? And who cares?' 'I care,' Michael said and Roly wasn't so sozzled that he couldn't hear what he took to be concern – or was it despair? – in his voice.

****

Michael's greenhorn conscience couldn't take the weight of someone's destruction. He couldn't tell him this but he did tell himself that it would be murder and whatever he was, he wasn't a murderer, but if Roly died... It took him a few days

231

to weigh the balance, the cons of being an angel of death against the pros of being one of mercy and he wasn't entirely convinced that the course of action he knew he had to take was in fact merciful. He did know that he shouldn't just stand back, a passive spectator, watching Roly go under; the more he did nothing, the more sickened he became by the thought that if some cataclysm happened it would be his fault. He had to confess somehow and quickly, face what he was convinced would be terrifying music. After one more evening of watching Roly's eyes grow redder and seeing him and his waitress trolley crashing pathetically and helplessly against the walls, after leaping up from his chair countless times to grab him and stop him from keeling over and having to suffer slings of abuse and insults about his low intelligence and the way he spoke and his heterosexuality, abuse he was intelligent enough to know wasn't meant, he went home determined. 'You will not put me to bed,' Roly had shouted. 'And you will not hold the pot while I pee. Put the washing of urine-soaked trousers down as a new task on the list and if you don't like it, I'll find another lackey. A tout a l'heure, mon petit choux,' was his parting wail as he waved Michael away. He was too alcoholically fugged to notice the tears that were welling in Michael's eyes as he ran out of the room, tears which streamed from his impassioned eyes as he reached home and scurried straight upstairs to his bedroom, like a fugitive seeking sanctuary; his mother mustn't see tears which she could mistake for the result of ill-treatment at Roly's hands and which he wouldn't have the ability to explain away. He merely called 'Hiya' on his way up and heard his mother shout back, 'You awright sugar?, presuming that he was. He flung himself down in his computer chair, crying openly now but resolute and he opened up Silverdaddies. He typed a message and attached a photo of himself and clicked to send. Hugger-mugger, willy-nilly, I-don't-know-what-I'm-doing, he sent it. 'Dont be sick. Im curiouslad and this is the proof,' it said.

Roly's first instinct on seeing another Silverdaddies message in his inbox next morning through the bottom of his first glass of whisky of the day and through his scotch-shrouded eyes was to curse with a raucous laugh. 'Alongside bisexuals, put all adolescent virgins as equal vessels of arse gravy,' he grumbled and drained his glass and got up to trundle his way to the bottle left in the kitchen. 'Frogspawn. Insipid, milk-livered slime,' he muttered further as he poured out the amber. He went back to the computer and clicked on the link, opened the email, read it and spluttered. He spluttered and coughed and started to choke; he thought he was going to pass out. When he came to and composed himself, wiping spattered mucus off the keyboard, he opened the attachment and what he saw sobered him in an instant. He gaped and then incredulity and semi-drunkenness swirled and gurgled and the maelstrom engulfed him.

Michael!

Michael's face, with a bewitching smile on knowing lips, inviting, alluringly defiant. The maelstrom drained away leaving his sodden brain in meltdown; elephants danced on lily pads, rain started falling upwards and he felt like he'd been shot from a cannon into a brick wall. He drank whisky wildly, spilling it down his shirt and guffawed: 'Curiouslad is Michael and vicey versey QED' and didn't give a fig if he caused panic and consternation for the neighbours. He could do nothing else but stare at the picture, awed by the power of a silent inanimate likeness to send him mad. How the hell had he done this? How had he committed this espionage?

'Treason, vile treason!' he shouted at the lady at the nursery window across the way who remained oblivious and, when he was able to compose himself, he asked her what on earth was going on in Michael's young head, but she remained indifferent and went on cooking in her white cook's hat. He swore swore swore that he'd been taken utterly unawares, he'd known nothing. In the woollen haze of lust, worn for the past week, he simply hadn't thought to add two and two, he'd obdurately refused to believe, despite a very minor hint of suspicion, that Curiouslad and Michael were one and the same. He drank some more and as he did, a strange thing happened: the haze of lust grew woollier and he started to snigger, then laugh, then the whole thing became side-splittingly hilarious and soon his laughter was uncontrollable. He was still sober for sure (wasn't he?), by his lights and the haze started to clear as he pieced together the train of events leading to this, Michael's internet self revelation. To begin, his belief that the boy hadn't taken notice of him sitting and moving around alone indoors had been disproved, he'd noticed only too well. There then followed his aleatory assumption: that he, Roly, might be queer and he'd wheedled his way into his sphere via a ruse, the herbs were a ruse. After eliciting from him that he used gay chatrooms, he needed no PhD in maths to find his way in and search for his profile. Having found him, he was at a loss what to do next, other than make his presence and his interest in him known by the constant tracking, which he did anonymously for fear of being identified, as much by Roly as by his own contemporaries, who were in the habit of diving into chatrooms, including gay ones, willy-nilly, for kicks, to take the piss, to be horrified, whatever. He studied the face again, studied and studied it, trying to look at the thing he knew so well as though for the first time, trying his hardest to find something wrong, something he could call ugly, disfiguring even, scrutinising it for some flaw, something merely offputting, something that would tell him he had made a dreadful mistake in ever thinking that it was an attractive face, something to justify kicking the boy out of his home and his life, but he could find nothing. On the contrary, the face pulled him to it with a stronger force, with a spell as of a shaman and despite the sensual allure and promise of it, he feared it may be draining something essential from him, some spiritual lifeforce and he peered into the dark eyes and whispered 'succubus' uncharitably to himself. Succubus the boy might be but he was certainly no pooka. The feeling of being not only manipulated but hypnotically driven, came over him again. He still didn't trust him, he supposed and now he trusted him even less, if only for the reason that the boy couldn't possibly understand the implications and consequences of this photograph, this self portrait. As for himself, he could not, not now, rescue or reassure himself, as he'd so often done, by refusing to accept that it was folly to fall in love with a fantasy photograph, because this was no pouting model in a glossy magazine, no blond hunky fraternity boy in Wisconsin, no sleek and juicy oriental in Manila, no object of unattainable desire. No, he had been smitten by a very real and alive thing and the real thing had been into his home. The rationale didn't pertain. Michael wasn't showing him what he looked like here, he was sending him an invitation, one which he hadn't dared to issue face to face, although he'd made many elliptical overtures in the short time Roly had known him. Familiarity with him had dampened Roly's ardour in as much as, though his lust for him was still firing, he had the fire under control. But what the boy had done now had radicalised all thought and sealed the decree, the photo was a decree and it declared that he was, every inch of him, this old queen's dream. He grew inexorably more and more enamoured both by the photo and by the boy himself as he sat and stared and thought and drank, *because he is offering himself to me.* This was too much, he refused to contemplate what would be, what tempest was churning, what vortex was pulling him down. Lord Henry Wotton transfixed by the picture of Dorian Gray, what a scream! What great romantic tragedy this boy's beauty was planning for him. In the mental chaos a bizzare thing happened: though there was still warm summer evening sunshine outside, with a blazing red patchwork sky, the room went black and he felt lines of cold sweat running down his back, soaking his shirt. It was crazy. He heard a voice. It was Muvvie's, or maybe Denzel's. 'Who? Your cute houseboy? That's him on there?' the voice cried, looking closely at the screen. 'Go-o-o-o-oon,' it sang. 'My backsides! So he *is* a bwatty boy. A bwatty cherry boy. Jeez, they're everywhere around you,' and it jeered. 'And he tracked me.' Roly had to think for a moment. 'He was tracking me for weeks, as soon as he came here. And by email.' 'How come, my man?' 'One of my billets doux, my XXX mails, I sent him one. Oh this is double delight and triple torture,' he wailed. 'What, you wrote to *him?* You wrote him a shag mail?' 'Isn't that what I've just said, dunderbrains? He knew what I was!' 'But you told him anyway.' 'Yes but – oh the cunning, the scheming, the Machiavellian –' 'Just like you then?' 'When he came here! What's going on? What conspiracy is this?' Muvvie/Denzel was now finding the imbroglio hilarious and was creased with uncontrollable laughter. 'He conned me into writing to him,' Roly repeated. 'I thought I was sending a fun email to a young man out of millions out there in cyber ether and I find it's the boy I know, a child. This is hero worship or something unhealthy.' 'Some would say for a guy in your position you're in fields of clover with pots of gold in them, Mister Hunter, Mister Wanger, Mister Wanger-Hunter, so what's your beef?' 'I smell a rat and the rat that I smell is a very smelly rat. He met me and went home and looked me up and received my email and...' 'Show me the XXX.' Roly brought it up. 'Hmm, doesn't seem very XXX to me,' came the dry comment. 'And what's all that about Lovetheboys Cottage? I thought you'd stopped telling porkies.' 'A pun on Dickens you won't understand,' Roly said. 'No sweat. He's sixteen soon and sixteen's legal yes?' 'But the madness of it.' 'Backsides, mister,' the voice barked, 'You sure have changed a lot. That sort of thing would worry you ten years ago would it? Phooeee my arse it would.' Which made Roly's protestations rather pathetic; but he felt duped and toyed with. He was bewildered by what seemed on the surface to be a gargantuan coincidence and one which could well, under different circumstances, have had a fairy story outcome. But this could not be. No, this could not be. 'This cannot be,' he said. 'I must put an end, a polite end, to this Michael. I shall have to, to tell his mother. Don't fret, I'm not going to get him into trouble. He's done nothing wrong, nothing an enthusiastic teenager can be reproved for. No hurt, no damage yet. *Noli me tangere*.' 'Awwww, Mister Hunter. The boy's definitely hung up on you, tracking you like that. And now he's put his pic up there, so he's declared himself. I think he wants you, don't you? You going to make him cry, you bitch? My old pants, a kid of sixteen and you, what d'you say you are, fofty-one? And he's throwing himself at you and... well, I'm lost for words. Which is most unlike me.' Roly went back to the photo, this was still beyond excitement, this attention from a teenage virgin. 'Desirable young virgin boys don't fall out of the sky and into my lap craving to be de-cherried.' But he warmed again to Michael's

Machiavellian tactics and had to acknowledge that he'd followed in his steps. He admired his pluck: his contrived meeting of him, his internet sleuthing, his pursuit of an outlandish dream. If he'd acted with the unscrupulous, selfish and completely unwholesome aim of getting into Roly's bed, he'd shown a devious initiative to be reluctantly admired. He just had to hope that he wasn't, even now, a monstrous homophobe who was going to murder him when he came a'cleaning and an-erranding after all. 'Oh Michael, cover my head with apples, your love is richer than rubies,' he wanted to shout. Or perhaps, 'Poor silly misguided, infatuated boy' would have been more appropriate. Muvvie/Denzel breathed out a 'Sheeeesh, Mr Hunter,' and said, 'You have an invitation to the pearly gates, man' and Roly could see he was a little agog at the idea that some expectancy of sexual happiness may be lying on his horizon. 'It's Sod's Law, if ever I saw it,' he moaned. Perhaps he had found a rarity of great value, a treasure, but under Sod's Law, he had found it just at the time that he really couldn't handle any of it. The boy couldn't be a gold digger, at least, because he'd been here and seen for himself the reduced circumstances in which he lived, so for that he was thankful. 'Man!' Muvvie/Denzel exclaimed again. 'Will you see how you have it made? A kid with those looks! Not that I'm any expert, y'know what I mean? And he's throwing himself at you and you have a problem with it?' 'You know very well I have. This boy somehow unfathomably and unbelievably desires me, no, *thinks* he desires me. But he doesn't know me. He's chasing a chimera.' 'Have it your way, mister, put him off. Go on, what you waiting for? Give yourself some more of that pain you like.' 'What crazy irony. No, there has to be a wind-up in it somewhere, somehow,' he said, reverting to his original dubious stance. 'Backsides and bollocks! That's a lie, mister. Remember all your boys. In Manchester and in *that* city and – and where was it? Whitley Bay. Go for it! Remember Hong Kong and Bangkok, remember Prasong and the boy in the jail.' 'Have mercy, I was twenty-five!' Roly turned back to the photo and again it withered his resolve. The words of what he imagined he would like as his anthem swam into his head: "It is when he thinks he's past love, that is when he finds his last love". But they didn't apply to him, no sir. He didn't see Curiouslad Michael as a free lunch. He saw him as another reminder from Nemesis that he'd been driven mad. It was written. He determined he wasn't going to even pretend to play the game he thought Michael was playing. He'd proved himself to be a subversive, perhaps a good actor. No, he thought, he was overt and honest and kosher. Only by being honest could he be Destiny's torturer. Roly was in disarray. He didn't know what to think. He was between euphoria and despair. If Michael turned up at the gate again he would set the dogs on him.

****

Roly knew this much: confrontation was anathema to him, he couldn't *challenge* and he wouldn't confront Michael over his photo, over the chatroom, over his tracking activities, over anything. Say nothing, carry on regardless, leave it to him, see how long he could continue before the pressure of uncertainty built so high that he caved in. Michael had seized the initiative, who was he to take it away from him? No, Michael must look for some other older man. He, Roly, had a post-stroke condition, he truly couldn't get it up, he'd tried back in his Bleakridge flat with two casual encounters, a nurse from Macclesfield and a builder from Trenton and fear had struck at the vital moment, the moment of penetration and fear of that fear only made it the more impossible to 'perform'. He'd lost the wood. As the nurse and the builder

239

would, he assumed, be only to scathingly willing to confirm. And he had deluded himself into believing that he could try again by meeting up with a slavering virgin in Black Pool. At the back of his mind was also the belief that he no longer had any right to sexual fulfilment; and the idea that he could first take advantage of a virgin teenager who offered himself to him and then go on to enjoy countless days and nights of soft adolescent flesh, of possessing this boy, well, it was too preposterous. The one thing he didn't do to prove that he wasn't totally mad, he didn't run to his Journal to tell it that he'd acquired through his charisma and charm a new young lover and boast to it that all his dreams were answered and that they were madly in love. The day was when he would have done that all too quickly. He had to think of ways to divert him, replace himself as his target, possibly make him jealous so that he would either be forced to play his hand or lose interest in him. He had to hope that such tactics of subtle rebuttal, however, wouldn't spur him to any acts of spiteful retribution against him.

****

He managed to unscrew a light bulb in the hall and dropped it to the floor. It rattled, the filament was damaged. That evening, he rang Michael to ask him to call round, first waiting for fair-haired Mr Peachy Neighbour to come out on his patio and water his backyard garden, as he did every evening. Peachy duly appeared with his hose, displaying his naked pecs again and Roly stood at the sink watching him. He quickly rang Michael and prayed he would be round before Peachy disappeared indoors. His timing was ideal and so was Michael's and he came running past the window and let himself in. Roly tried to imagine what Michael was thinking and as he ran out of his house and across the grass he was thinking that this was the summons, the invitation

240

he'd been so eagerly awaiting, the invitation to a meeting of open hearts between them both and that made him run with a burst of Olympian speed. He ran with anxiety in his bones mixed with enthusiasm and optimism in his head and as he ran, he dismissed or chose not to think at all of any obstacles that could stand in the way of what he had by now conceived as his *qismet*: congregation, if he had known the word, with Roly or 'getting it on' with him, as his own young brain put it to him. Roly had come round to his way of thinking, they were at one in purpose. 'Where are ya?' he called, crashing into the hall. 'Kitchen.' 'What you looking at?' he wanted to know when he came in to Roly focusing, peering, ogling through the window. 'Oh, just enjoying the local scenery,' he said distractedly and he nodded in the direction of the backyard patio. This reception was not at all what Michael was expecting and he followed Roly's gaze and saw what and who he was looking at and heard his muted hummings of delight. 'What? You fancy 'im? You're way off with that one, ya numpty, 'e lives with 'is girl.' 'Oh, I've never let heterosexuality come between me and a boy, flower.' He hoped Michael would hear the note of worldy triumph in his voice. 'Where would we poofters be without our straight brothers to challenge us and be challenged by us and to be conquered by us?' 'E'll most probably come over and total you if 'e sees you. Pervy old sod you are. Where's this bulb you've got?' Michael changed the lightbulb and said he had homework to get back to. Roly gave him money for Yvette to buy two bottles of Bell's for him and asked him to bring them round next day and he was gone, noticeably abruptly, but concealing his disappointment well. And it was double disappointment and overwhelming perplexity: no discussion about Silverdaddies and coming upon Roly ogling a young man. Roly, for his part, thought he'd pricked the desired synapse, shown him there were other young men he could be interested in, but more than that, Michael had come round to him after the earth-shattering episode in Silverdaddies and he'd mentioned nothing about it, or about tracks, XXXmails or photos. He thought his silence must have thrown him into tumult and he was right. He helped himself to a few extra squares of Green & Black's to go with his scotch that evening in smug celebration. As he sat soothed by scotch and chocolate, he recapped on Mister Peachy and as the word 'straight' repeated in his head, bringing Muvvie with it yet again... the quicksand swelled:

Before the cataclysm, there was the – almost – real Roland Hunter and the lifestyle of the local celebrity: success and adulation of ability and talent touched him for a while and he bathed in its watery glory and there were weekend trips to London to see the Australian hairdresser and there was the other Michael, the chorusboy and there were the straight Scouse boys too:

I struck gold this week, slightly tarnished but gold all the same. Pat was first. He appeared from nowhere at the end of my goodbye party. He was perched on the end of the bar, tight jeans, bulging crotch, the works: a blond, denim-clad hunk with seablue eyes. Classic. I asked him abrupty what he was doing at my party and started chatting him up. Was he flattered by attentions from someone on the radio? I persuaded him to go to Tina's Bar with me. I was so drunk I could only take soda water by then, but I eventually found second wind and practically ordered him to go to the club with me. 'I'm not going to any queers' place,' he protested at first, then he gave in and I marched him to the club where I sat him down and spent the rest of the night fawning over him, thinking 'I'm going to have this one.' At closing time I asked, 'Would you like to come home with me and have sex?', just like that and he said no and when I asked him why not, he said, 'I might like it' and that did it; I ordered him to drive us home. In bed, while we were kissing, he suddenly pushed me off: 'I feel like a virgin...It's not like doin' it with a woman,' he said. Two minutes later – you could have knocked me down with a sledge hammer – he pulled me on top of him and we started again. He drove me to get my car in the morning and when I asked him how he was feeling, he smiled with a shrug and said, 'It was all right' and we parted amicably. I saw him working behind the bar at Tina's after that and he smiled and said hello so there was no ill-feeling. I was greatly relieved that his reaction to being seduced was not bellicose if only because in the cold light of day he wasn't as desirable as the surfeit of alcohol and rush of sexual excitement had made him the night before.

The very next Friday was Gerry's night. Wow! It was an acquaintance's leaving party this time. I spotted Gerry, my chum told me he was a student who worked in his shop on Saturdays and to keep my hands off him because he was straight. So, nothing ventured, I went over to him and bought him a drink. He said, 'You're wasting your time with me ya know' and 'Anyway, I live with my parents so I can't stay out all night' and at that, I dug a two-pence piece out of my pocket and pointed to the wall phone. 'All parents want to know is where their son is and if he's all right,' I told him and, without more ado, he took the coin and went to make the phone call! I was practically wetting myself! When I got him home, I pointed to the sofa and said, 'You can sleep there if you don't want to do this' and he said, 'No, it's ok, I'm sleeping with you.' !!!!! Much like Pat, midway through our snogging, he had a change of heart and we both called it a night and turned over and then – I didn't know how long I'd dozed, but I woke up, it was still dark and Gerry had my cock in his mouth!!!!! I asked him the crucial question and he replied, 'I want to feel what it's like', so I went to the bathroom and greased myself with soap and went back and turned him over. Next morning, I drove him home so he could change for work and we had breakfast together at the Pier Head on the way and things seemed fine. I waited for him outside his house then drove him to his shop and he gave me his phone number and I definitely wanted to see him again. More fool me. I rang him a couple of days later and when I said hello, he simply said: 'I don't think I'd better see you again.' And he never did.

This was like reading Proust, it was depressing and it drove him to refuel with more scotch and proceed to his Journal:

...35 years ago the gay community of Trenton was in fear and turmoil and there was an atmosphere of ghetto life. Rumours were rife and police persecution and talk of it were everywhere. Goodlooking young plain clothes officers were sent into the Gazelle and the cottages as bait; parties were raided and drugs planted so that if the queers couldn't be nailed on sex offences, drugs charges would do. The raid on the Saturday night orgy brought the police the human booty they'd been so hungry for as they crashed into the livingroom and found 14 men and boys writhing naked in various stages of sexual congregation on the floor. They disturbed another 12 men – some of them under 21, all of them consenting, but none of them in private – who were paired and tripled off in the bedrooms upstairs. Cannabis and LSD were found, or so it was alleged. The 'scandal' made national headlines, backwater anonymity was replaced by gay notoriety, attracting curious tourists, more persecution, biblical vilification from the puritans and it spawned yet more fervid police activity. Prosecutions and trials followed and five men and three 'underage boys' were sent to prison and borstal. Two of the 'boys', one was 19 and the other 18, hanged themselves.

The Trenton police continued to treat the queers as high-risk criminals and history was cruelly repeated on a smaller scale and much closer to me, a year later, when I was just a few months into my gay career.

Against the backcloth of police persecution, Neville continued to groom me. From taking me 'on town' in Trenton, we had progressed further afield to the fleshpots of Manchester, where I met my first true love, but before that earth-shattering event there was the introduction to David the driving instructor, a significant player in my pages, in the front bar of the Prince William hotel. 'I was comin' over to say 'ello anyway,' said David, shaking my hand and showing his shy smile. 'Always nice to see a fresh face,' he said to Neville, while nodding at me and, I thought, mentally undressing me. I saw a dowdy man of 40 or so, barrel-plump with greasy dark brown hair plastered to his scalp and wearing a shabby blue suit that hung badly on him. He had a brown and white Welsh corgi with him which he took everywhere and he smelled of it. If he'd been younger, rail thin in smart clothes and fragrant, I could still not have imagined a more unattractive man, but there was a diffidence about him and a gentle smiling aspect that invited cordiality. 'Where did Neville find you?' he asked, meaning to be complimentary but sounding solicitous. Any sexual aspirations he had were thwarted when he gave me a lift home and, unlike Neville in the railway alley, showed no restraint and tried to surge. I escaped with a fast 'goodnight' and when our paths crossed again some nights later, David appeared contrite and said the gallant thing. 'I... er... seemed to get the wrong end of the stick the other night,' he said, and this time the smile was one of embarrassment. 'Forget it,' was all I could think to say to him and that was where contact would have ended had David not added, 'I – er- I'm a bit new to all this' and revealed that he was a divorcee of two years' standing. When he also said he was a driving instructor with his own school, I swooped and asked him how much it would cost to take lessons: I was desperate to learn to drive and get my own car now that I was 18. A few weeks later, David was teaching me for next to nothing, which I considered fair amends for his assault on my virtue and we formed quite a friendship from then on. 'You like the chickens then,' David went on after his apology and with terms of engagement established, we could chat on with no ulterior motives. We arranged a day for my first lesson and soon the weekly hour of instruction through the streets of Trenton became a combination of the highway code and boy-spotting, with David constantly having to urge me to keep my eyes on the road and off the pedestrian talent. David, I supposed, liked going about with a youngster, albeit one he couldn't touch and he taught me well; I passed at my first attempt and got a driving licence for practically nothing. I got a few more goodies out of David's driving school and one of them came in the shape of his new pupil, Alan Warburton.

Ah those Friday nights! Alan had his lesson after me and I sat in the back. After a few lessons, David and I asked him out with us and we would have him drive us to whichever pub we were going to (not the Gazelle) and David would drive back. On the third or fourth of these nights, I got into the back seat with Alan and a weekly routine of genteel canoodling began; Alan amazingly acquiesced without protest, though he wouldn't permit any tongues and allowed fondling only through his firmly zipped trousers. I go cold even now, after all these years, every time I think of how that poor boy must have dreaded getting into the back of that car with me every Friday night – 'but he never said no and I never forced him, your worship' I jokingly thought. I spent a good deal of time at Alan's big posh house out in Standon that summer. I took him for drives into the Moorlands, when I'd let him take the wheel while I fondled him some more, but my persistent attempts at seduction yielded no more than those furtive backseat kisses and handfuls of the warm and succulent adolescent genitals, which were indisputably destined for heterosexual copulation in the near future, and a contribution to the population of the planet, no doubt, but I have for ever regretted that he never let me have first go. Another of Neville's acts of philanthropy – or was it damnation in disguise? – was to introduce me to Earl and to lead me unwittingly to the loss of my anal virginity. Abel and Mabel decided to lock the doors of the Gazelle one Saturday night and have a party and I found myself sitting drunk on Earl's lap, bemused and bewildered. Why was I flirting with a man I was not attracted to and who was a few years older than I? 'The chickens have all gone home,' Earl said, with his lascivious laugh. 'Look at your frigging eyes, they're like two bloody great tomatoes!' My head was having difficulty staying on my shoulders. I lolled it, looked up at Earl and heard myself asking: 'Do you want to fuck me tonight?' And I lost my virginity twice that night because, not given to strong language then, it was the first time I can remember using the F word. 'Are you serious?' Earl asked. 'Yes,' I replied. It was the first of the occasions when excess of alcohol and a surge of testosterone made efficient work of washing my powers of discrimination away. I didn't ever want to be 'bitch'; I wanted to be butch – top or active, as the words are now. But any longing I had in that area were dashed by one unsavoury physiological deformity which the midwife had overlooked at my birth; perhaps she had meant to cut more off but she left me with an overtight foreskin which would not retract. It was an impairment but it never made me desire the passive role. Earl leered and leched at this unexpected offer of an arse. 'Roddy's not here tonight is he? Where is he?' 'I dunno. He stayed at home, I think.' 'Well, I won't tell him if you don't.' I was surpassing myself with pushiness. 'Have you got your tin of vaseline in your top pocket as usual? You always go out prepared, I've been told.' Earl went off to negotiate a room for the night with landlady Mabel and soon after he was taking me upstairs to a sparse bedroom where he unromantically and untenderly buggered me. Sideways.

Next morning, I crept out of the back door of the Gazelle, leaving Earl in bed and hurried home to the inevitable parental inquisition into my all-night absence. I had no sensation of an epiphany, but I did have a peculiar and utterly new feeling of soreness in my sphincter, as though I'd been rearranged internally somehow. The loss of my anal virginity underscored the confusion which my brain had registered in its inebriation of the previous night: I liked boys of my own age, so what could possibly have induced me to ask someone older than I was to sodomize me?

Thanks to the 50 pounds raised by my parents and Auntie Vera, I was soon driving myself to David's place for regular Friday nights out in my very own secondhand Mini. It had the luxury of a radio, bought at discount through Alan Warburton's father's electrical business. On the road through Hanbridge Park, I glimpsed David's driving school sign and car in the rearview mirror. With a flash of headlights, David sped past and pulled up in front

249

of me like a police patrol. He hauled his portly figure out and, as he walked back towards my car, I sensed that something was amiss. Looking very pale, but with his insouciant smile, David came up to my window and said simply, 'I'm in trouble.' 'What's the matter?' 'Ooh, I dunno know. I think Lily Law is watching me. They came to see me the other day. Want me to make a statement.' 'Christ! Is it Alan?' 'Noooo,' he said, in a tone which meant that would be unthinkable. 'They were asking about them two, ya know...them evil fucking chickens... Peaches and fucking Melba, whatever they're called. And they wanted to know about 'Andbag Gloria and some boy in Lyme. I dunno,' he added, becoming distrait. 'I'm a bit scared ... You'd better stay away tonight.' I, too, felt a cold fear. Christ! I started to count the number of my offences: Alan, a 17-year-old boy seduced in David's car; then Eric in David's bedroom. All right, I didn't manage to bugger him but he was 18 neverthless and therefore underage. Carl, my first and the town's only gay black boy; another 17-year-old and again in David's bedroom; Peaches and Melba, both 16; Tony in Manchester. *God's Teeth!* Here I was in the middle of a cold sweat panic and yet I was getting aroused counting the boys I'd been with. Shouldn't I be worried about getting arrested and shouldn't I stop myself? Not for the first time, I told myself that I had to find Neville Ladderbanks. Or Handbag Gloria. 'Roddy! How old is Roddy?' I yelled the question to myself. 'I don't know, but he can't be 21, I'm sure, and again, we committed the act in David's bed while David was downstairs!' I'd long lusted after Roddy, but Roddy was Earl's boyfriend. He was out of bounds and not to be surged on. 'Dynamite, that one dear,' was Gloria's terse way of warning me that if anyone so much as looked at Roddy, Earl would kill them. Yet, the night came when I was at David's again and the boy I was kissing was none other than Roddy Bates. We were up the stairs and naked in a blink and I could hardly believe my good fortune: I had the famous and beautiful Roddy in bed with me! 'Are you going to let me fuck you, sugar?' Roddy asked, as he lay on top of me. 'Oh, Roddy,' I said, pleading doubtfully. 'Oh, go on,' he purred. 'Earl won't let me, you know and I want to do it. Go on, let me, I've only got a small one.' So, too proud of my catch to deny him, I yielded and turned over. Then – by Satan – I suddenly remembered Graham! A schoolboy – a 14-year-old schoolboy for Heaven's sake! Having orgams in bed together at the Rose Bowl Hotel. *Oh Jesus, I'll hang!* If the police were to have another witchhunt, this time aimed at the chicken farmers, I, as a 19-year-old practising homosexual and chicken farmer myself, was twice illegal and asking for a double drop.

David went back to his car and drove off, leaving me dazed and contemplating suicide there and then in Hanbridge Park. A week of sweat and stress followed: would the police come to arrest me while I was teaching a class of children, or come for me at home? When nothing happened, I could stand the strain no longer and drove over to David's. The shop door was locked but his car was parked at the the side. I went round to the yard and up to the back door and was about to knock when it was thrown open by none other than Earl. 'Jesus! You better fuck off now,' he hissed through clenched teeth in a gnarled face. 'The cops are 'ere searchin' the place. Scram! Quick!' I fled. The next I heard was that David and Earl were in custody. I rashly tried to get to see David at the police station but the desk sergeant was surly and terse and wouldn't let me, and when I asked if David needed anything, he told me firmly to 'get along' and I went, hoping they were not beating poor David to a pulp at that very moment. David was not a lover or a sex partner but his unselfishness and general easygoing attitude to life had brought him to a police cell and me to distraction. I mulled over the dire situation: I wasn't entirely sure that David actually *did* anything with anybody, underage or not. I realised I'd never seen him pair off with anyone and he'd never talked about so doing. What has David actually done and when and who with, I asked myself? What he and Earl did, or rather what they were charged with doing, was to commit acts of gross indecency with underage males. They were summoned before the city magistrates and I went to watch, against the advice of all the Gazelle regulars. 'You're a bloody fool if you go to that court,' were camp Bill's words of outrage and warning to me in the Gazelle the night before their appearance. 'What the hell do you want to go and advertise yerself for? Do you want to be arrested along with those two idiots? Stay away.' But I had to go, and after I saw David and Earl humiliated and sent down to custody, a third person was brought into the dock, charged separately. It was 16-year-old Gary, known to all as Peaches! *What in the name of Christendom is going on?*

He was remanded on bail. I looked for him outside the court but he'd gone and, without thinking, I drove to his house and knocked on the door. Gary opened it with panic on his face. 'Fuckin' 'ell!,' he blustered, 'you better scram, me Mum's –' And the door was suddenly flung wider by a ferocious looking woman. ''E' doesn't want nothin' to do with the likes of you lot,' she yelled. 'Gettin' 'im into this trouble. You're all filth. ''E's on probation already, yer know. Now sod off!' And with that, Gary's mother slammed the door in my face and watched through the net curtains as I drove away.

I went back to the Gazelle that night to recount the grisly events and the talk was of little else. When I mentioned Gary, Gloria grimaced. 'Ooooooh, you've 'ad trade with 'im, 'aven't you?' Indeed, I'd 'had' Peaches, and Melvyn, aka Melba, too, but Gloria knew this for Gloria knew all things. I could boast of having bedded both boys within the space of a week, and the one had led to the other.

The legal process seemed awfully speedy for proper justice to be done. David and Earl were sentenced to two years in prison. The case made the front page of the Signal and that was a night when I was certainly not looking forward to seeing the paperboy. I arrived home to find my father, indeed, with the paper already in his hand and the 'Driving instructor and underage boys' headline sitting in stark splendour on the front page. *Hell's Bells.* 'This the chap you had driving lessons from isn't it?' he asked. It was useless to deny it. 'Did you know he was involved in all this?' It was folly to admit it. 'Of course not.' His face squashed with distaste and looking to be in pain, my father asked, addressing his question to my mother, as though she were in some way responsible for this family scandal, how a son of his could get mixed up with worthless scum like that, adding that it was a good job he was going away to university and out of trouble. The cloud of heavy embarrassment which descended on the livingroom precluded further conversation, so the television was switched on and I crept up to my room to calm myself by gazing on my pinup of Peter Frampton.

Melvyn and Gary, what a double act. I found myself one afternoon in the little terraced house in Bleakridge where Jim, an electrician lived and 'farmed his chickens'. Jim would go out and about on his jobs and often return either with a chicken he had picked up somewhere, somehow, or, having given a boy his phone number, the promise of one. I met him through Neville and for some reason he took a liking to me, taking me round the county with him occasionally and then eventually showing me that he wasn't parsimonious in sharing the spoils of his hunts. It was Jim who had picked up and nurtured both Melvyn and Gary. Jim's phone rang that afternoon, he had a short conversation and when he rang off, rubbed his hands with relish and said, 'You'll like this, Melba's on 'er way round with 'er mate' and Melvyn, gorgeous, slim, smooth, fresh, golden-haired, 16-year-old, spectacular, untouchable Melvyn arrived half an hour later, with a friend whose name I forgot immediately. While Jim smiled in predatory triumph, I went limp, stunned to be in the same room as such beauty and when, after brief niceties, Jim quickly scooped up the mate and vanished upstairs with him, I was left alone and speechless with Melvyn who initially seemed to be infuriatingly aloof. My powers of seduction, miserably unhoned to say the least, but for the moment totally absent, meant it took an age until I could summon something inane to say. 'You never seem to notice me in the Gazelle,' was all I remember mustering. Of what Melvyn said back I have no memory, but whatever it was I must have taken it to be suggestive, so I edged towards him and laid a hand on his knee. Fortunately, his bottle of testosterone was as ready to pop its cork as mine and in no time he was stripped naked and laying open his box of carnal delights, inviting me to take my pick. Afterwards, not content to lie quietly and soak up the afterglow, he chattered away and smoked a cigarette while I stroked his lithe, adolescent limbs as though in a dream. I thought, perhaps for the first time, how you can sometimes intuit that when you have carnal knowledge of someone who is extra special, it will be the one and only time and as I lay there listening to him, I knew he was never going to let me be intimate with him again. He shocked me with his talk of wanting to be a drag queen. I thought, what a waste. Nevertheless I went along to a local club the following week to see his act, his striptease and that led to my squeeze with Gary, known to all as Peaches, because he was sitting among the small group of Melvyn's fans in the audience. And he was in drag too, alas, very attractive and very boyish turned, that night, into gruesome sham girlish. Why, oh why? I asked myself. I thought he looked glamorously pathetic but for some reason I agreed to give him a lift home when he asked me, or rather a lift to a flat where he was staying, since his mother, understandably put out at giving birth to a boy and finding she now had something trying hard to resemble a girl living in her house, had thrown him out. My car reeked overpoweringly of womens' cosmetics and I felt nauseous, but he asked me in and when he asked me if I wanted to stay the night and I said something like, 'No thanks, I want a boy not a girl and not even a fake girl,' he immediately said he'd 'take the slap off' and I succumbed to the boy beneath the masque. It was a long time before I would admit to anyone that I'd once been to bed with a drag queen.

Roly was to have further to think and say about Melvyn and Gary and their like over the years but they were views he never wrote down. Melvyn and Gary, he would think, were more than junior drag artistes: they were victims of preconditioning, boys following a mindless trend, not making any conscious choice and he asked if that trend wasn't as strong now as it ever was. You see, my dears, he'd wanted them both madly, but he'd wanted *boys,* not girl-boys, then as now. He looked back on the talent they'd had, the talent of male beauty, and he felt sad to imagine that talent draining away day by day until they arrived at complete emasculation, compelled to live a role that was preordained for them: boys who wore mascara and rouge, permed their hair and painted their nails and swapped chitchat about the latest nylons. They were playing an inherited role: the

256

modern-day odalisques, the painted eunuchs, the girl-boys, whose only escape from obscurity and persecution was to be outrageous. Fey and effeminate boys at first, who then adopted complete female personation as a way of life. Some such boys were products of their genes, of course, but he still regretted that the Melvyns and Garys of this world were in helotry to a perverted convention, both adhered to by themselves and imposed upon them by others, which demanded that a young, gay man must have the semblance of a woman in order to seduce and be seduced by the types of butch and preferably straight men they were conditioned to attract and be attracted to. Men who were and are themselves conditioned to believe that sodomy was and is acceptable as long as the young men they were sodomising bore some trace of femininity, which would sanction their act. That way, spearing a boy's bottom was, though still a guilty thing, defensible and boys like Melvyn were the willing sacrifice. These sodomites and sodomised have not learned to be Greek. The Greeks wanted their boys and young men to be just that, boys and young men. The archetypal warrior was the goal of their lust; man strength was their ideal and man beauty not sham female beauty was their craving. The queers of Trenton and elsewhere have botched it.

A plague on this city! Roly said; he said it at the time of the scandal, repeated it often and he said it again now.

I was still Roland known as Pete and I could now count half a dozen sex partners among my town peers, lusting after each one of them on sight and insanely infatuated by the time they had taken their clothes off. The Trenton colloquialism for a relationship or fling, however brief, was "affair" and I had my first one thanks to Neville's taking me on weekend jaunts to Manchester. I knew it was true love this time because I went to bed with Tony more than once, so it had to be the real thing hadn't it? Being mad about Tony probably blinded me to the possibility that he was a bit of a rent boy. But what Tony did on the weekdays between our meetings didn't seem to matter. Besides, I was far less fastidious about having dealings with the sordid seam of life than I was to become. Those weekdays were spent in the knowledge that I would see Tony again at the weekend and jealousy was an emotion I had yet to learn; I really didn't care whether he was a rent boy or not. Tony having extra-curricular fun in Manchester and my having it 30 miles away in Trenton seemed acceptable. We would meet in the Trafford Bar and Tony took us off by bus to somebody's flat or house in Whalley Grange or Miles Platting for an hour of non-penetrative sex. It was great. I was in love. 'I love you,' I'd whisper to Tony. 'Yeah,' he would reply. On the one hand, I had the intoxication of a forbidden love I was forced to hide from the straight and increasingly distanced world around me – which made me feel smug – and on the other, I could shout 'boyfriend' to gay Trenton and feel equally though guiltlessly smug. The ease of establishing and living with this love was such that I wasn't at all surprised by it; odd to think that it didn't seem anything other than completely natural, unspecial. I was young, I was sexually attracted to boys, I had a boyfriend I had sex with every Friday and God was in his heaven and all was right with the world.

So in love was I, that when Tony cajoled me into performing my first act of fellatio, encouraging me with, 'It's clean, pet', it was no big struggle to put my initial aversion to one side and favour him. Yes, this was love. I was stricken when our 'affair' fizzled out, I can't understand how or why it did; all I remember is Tony making it clear one night that he didn't want sex with me again. There was no, 'I've found somebody else', or 'I don't love you any more'. It just was. And I went though the pain of my first lost love sitting in the Trafford one early doors morning, sobbing openly into my beer and whisky to the sound of Aretha Franklin:

'For ever and ever, You'll stay in my heart, Oh how I love you'

and Herb Alpert:

'Say you're in love, in love with this guy, if not I'll just die'

which I played endlessly on the juke box.

Douglas was hanging around at David's place one day that summer. 'Go on,' David said, grinning widely, when I asked who the new dolly boy was, 'he'll do anything Douglas will, if you ask him nicely.' At 17, Douglas, who was a robust road navvie, was a hunk in the making with a body already magnificently-shaped body and rich flaxen hair. It should have been a memorable sexual experience but for my abject failure to satisfy him. The curse of my anatomical abnormality struck again. But he did at least unknowingly set in motion my resolve to get it put right. I rued him for a long time after that day and suffered many a what-might-have-been pang. I had taken him for a drive to the Peak District and lain him down on rough tufted grass and kissed him furiously. We went back to David's and he, stripping naked and jumping onto the bed with no more ado, explained how he could only get an erection even with a girl after a very long period of foreplay and only with a man when he was actually being... He simply loved being bitch. He was unique was Douglas, a council house lad and a navvy with but a rudimentary education, the last sort one would expect to have immaculate locution and not a trace of Trenton dialect! Douglas was completely unselfconscious and unpretentious about that and his sexual openness was quite beyond my own small ken. He turned on his stomach in expectation and I attempted but failed to do what I and he so much wanted. He begged me and the more he asked, the more inept I became, trying to blame his own recalcitrant penis, imploring him to get it hard. 'I told you, I can't, not even with my girlfriend.' I was crestfallen; he simply put his clothes back on and went downstairs. We never tried again, but saw each other on the town; he would be in either male or female company and he always said 'hiya'. He provided perhaps the first impetus to my doing something about the problem that would increasingly burden me: the overtight foreskin I was born with. I had discovered anal penetration but couldn't do it, hence the Douglas debacle among others and I was getting fed up with being sodomized and never finding it pleasurable. It wasn't until I met Murdoch in London two years later that at his prompting I finally took action.

Sufficient to the day was the evil thereof. He'd had enough. He could have chosen much more invigorating latenight reading and writing matter, though for the life of him, he couldn't think what. He poured himself a whisky and soda nightcap.

And woke up in bed, only half an hour passed, tasted dry dirt and remembered he'd brought his drink with him on the trolley – *I'm the original trolley dolly!* – so he sat up and reached for it. 'We have reached an impasse Michael, have we not?' he asked his mirror as he sipped from the glass. Indeed they had and any attempts to resolve it had been shouldered aside by tragedy, not that he, in his heart of hearts, felt entirely sure he would have known how to resolve the impasse if tragedy hadn't struck. Michael's inability and unwillingness to say anything to advance his cause was due to a lack of diplomacy and negotiating skills; Roly on the other hand remained a spectator rather than a participant through lassitude, he had lost all will, all conception of decisive action, although for mitigation he could call on age, failing health, the heap of guilt he carried with him always and, perhaps, the benefit of bitter experience. Tragedy or not, they were now playing a game of cat and mouse: Roly knew that Michael was Curiouslad, Michael must know that he knew and they were chasing these, their respective premises. In his bedroom meanwhile, Michael pondered on how distracted Roly was by the recent deaths and how he, Michael, had had to relegate himself, take second place in the order of priorities, but he nonetheless remained preoccupied with his own future and his mind went crazily thus: 1) Roly isn't interested in me after all; 2) Roly must be waiting for me to ask him if he's seen my pic; 3) Roly is scared of doing anything because of his age; 4) When he gets over his mum and his boyfriend and stops drinking, he'll get back on track with me.

As for Roly and as far as whisky would allow his brain to rationalise, it occurred to him that night and throughout the next day that Michael's impulsive action may have led him to some sort of epiphany which had, like St Paul's, blinded him and made him realise that he was pursuing the wrong end. The more he reasoned like this, the more he was sure that Michael was now wanting to forget about the whole 'curious' thing, which was fine by him. But his own brand of curiosity stepped in. The obstinancy of silence was irking him; a behemoth of quiet lurked somewhere around them and it needed to be dispersed by the noise of clarification, views needed to be aired, opinions voiced. It wasn't as though they were carrying on as though nothing had happened; they were both too well aware that something, something momentous, *had* happened. Nonetheless, he admired Michael's restraint in not giving so much as a tell-tale look or a verbal hint, as far as he could see through the whisky smog that is, but how much was fear holding him back? Who was going to be first to break was anyone's guess. Michael called back that evening and Roly was relieved and grateful to see him clutching the bottles of Bell's he'd ordered in his arms. Michael asked if he had eaten, 'I can get ya some beans on toast or somethin' if you want' and Roly answered, 'Pass me a banana,' distractedly. 'Bananas are rich in potassium you know, very good for the regulation of body fluids, blood pressure and heart rate and the chemical symbol for potassium is K, isn't that amusing?' 'If you're gonna be pissed and nasty, just shurrup,' Michael snapped, sulkily. 'And if you're going to be censorious, you can leave,' Roly retorted. 'Talking of K, have you made up with your girlfriend yet, or found another one?' 'No way and I told you, I don't give!' he snapped and then he softened and smiled in a self-satisfied way and announced proudly that he'd heard that afternoon that he'd won a place in the county swimming team. Roly too calmed himself, toned down his caustic edge and offered his congratulations, he was genuinely pleased and hoped he sounded sincere. 'Well done Captain Webb,' he said, lighting a cigarette. 'You'll have seen his picture on matchboxes I think. It was one of the first things I noticed about you.' 'What was?' 'That I never saw you with a cigarette and matches and I hope I never do. But then again, I don't suppose anyone lights a cigarette with a Captain Webb or a Swan Vestas anymore do they? Michael squeezed his face into a grimace of distaste at the idea of nicotine. 'I was wonderin' if ya wanna come see me in a competition some time?' he asked. 'We're racin' Cheshire schools in three weeks.' 'He was the first man recorded to swim the Channel,' Roly said, distractedly. 'Who was?' *Oo woz?* 'Captain Webb. He was one of the first celebs, became very rich, lost it all and then he drowned. Doing a stunt at Niagra Falls, oddly enough. Yes, a champion swimmer and he drowned! Why do they always die doing what they pioneered? Swimmers dying swimming, joggers dying jogging, bombers dying bombing.' Michael's invitation and its spontaneity had thrown him off balance; he felt inwardly delighted for him but it occurred to him once more that the success of this boy, vicarious success, was the only success left for him to taste. He also thought that the invitation might be Michael's plea for support, a seeking of an endorsement from someone he respected. 'F… oh banjax Captain Webb!' Michael blurted impatiently, 'will ya come?' 'Will your mum go? I'll go with her, I'll take her. We'll ra-ra you on together.' This news of his team selection and the possibility of Roly's going to watch him compete, provided a conversational diversion, enabling them for the moment to avoid commiting to talking about the subject that still lay simmering and festering and unspoken and creating the uneasy space that lay between them. At length, Roly put forward his own offer: 'I want you to come somewhere with me. Not now, tomorrow or some time soon.' 'Where to? And I'm not goin' anywhere in yer car if you've 'ad a drink.' 'I shall stay off the sauce for an hour or two and I want to go to the Manifold Valley.' 'Oh, you're a scenery sucker yeah?' 'D'you know it?' 'We went there on a school trip once, I think it was there. It rained all day.' 'Come, let's go down to the river and see the kingfisher's splendour,' Roly proclaimed in his fustian voice, then in his normal one said, 'It'll be at its best right now, in summer glory and I haven't seen it for years. Staffordshire's finest, second only to the Dove in my opinion, with the Blythe Valley a close third. I can't guarantee any kingfishers but at least we get out of town and on the way back we can stop and buy oatcakes or pikelets for tea to remind us that you're not the only delicacy in the county, my Michael of the Manifold.' Some time, Roly had no idea how much, went by during which he had Michael pour him three more large whiskies. As he sank them, Michael scrutinised him, relieved that they didn't bring on a reprise of the drunken antagonism he'd been subjected to earlier. After a while, he heard Roly mutter something under his breath. 'What you say?' 'Mmm? Oh... I was quoting... a poem I used to know. It just came to me.' 'What poem?' Michael of all people, asking about a poem! '"Let us go then you and I, where the evening is spread against the sky, like a patient etherized upon a table".' 'Oh.' Roly smiled, pityingly. 'You are not belletristical, dear boy,' he said, waving his glass unsteadily at him. 'And like I know what that means.' Frustration was in his voice, making him sound belligerent, but still he had the will to avoid swearing. 'Only that I suspect you have no poetry in your soul, darling, nothing to worry about.'

Tick tock, the minutes dragged on, the intrusive funereal tick of the wantonly purchased mechanical regulator on the wall adding to the shroud of solemn eternity Roly felt they were wrapped in; he, the room, the world, everything was interminable. Michael particularly sensed growing tenterhooks and was resentful that Roly at least had the benefit of his anaesthetising Bell's. He felt, heard, his heart beating, a tattoo it was, thrumming against his breastbone as he continued unable and afraid to speak, a state he'd been in for the previous 48 unbearable hours. He'd become black-faced, sitting with his head hunched into his shoulders, glowering at the floor. The silence grew heavier by the minute, it was drilling them both into the ground. Roly looked over at him and wasn't yet sufficiently drunk to be able to ignore the unspoken thoughts that were pendent between them: stalkers and Curiouslad and Silverdaddies and photos and wild goose chases. At last, he cracked, or, as he liked to think, took the reins. He told Michael to get him a fourth whisky and soda: 'Pour me a drink, heartface, and I'll tell you some lies' and he praised him for 'having mastered the mix just to my taste. But no ice, remember, there's love on the rocks already. Hehe. Then I'll speak to you,' he added and the words sounded detached and rather coldly sinister to Michael's ears. He went to the kitchen with not a little trepidation. 'You took one hell of a gamble, you know, and you mustn't assume it's paid off,' Roly said when he came back and Michael thought he was done for. 'Time to stop dancing around the maypole.' 'Wassup now?' Michael asked, scared by presentiment, unable to tell whether Roly was angry or indifferent or drunk. Roly wasn't drunk, not aware that he was at any rate, but the whisky had foresaken him, the reinforcement and the ammunition he'd hoped it would provide hadn't materialised. He suddenly felt mellow, a wave of uncharacteristic and altruistic sympathy washed over him and it made him uneasy. He could see the boy suffer no longer, he had no wish for more secrecy and pent up emotion to destroy him; he shouldn't be forced to inherit the deceit and dissimulation of the ages. He couldn't bear to have what happened to him mark and damage this boy, as it had him. Michael shouldn't have to resort to the clandestine and the devious to achieve his aims, he'd suffered enough, it was time to end it. He gulped down a large draught of scotch and sat up. 'Let's go back to that first day, I'll call it the Day of the Herbs,' he said. 'How much had you planned? Or did you just jump in blind?' 'I didn't plan nuthin'. Can I get meself a drink as well please?' 'Of course you can, darling and pour me another one too.' Michael took his glass without any show of disapproval and went to the fridge. He came back again and Roly immediately began reciting the litany: the tracks, Curiouslad, the XXX email, Silverdaddies, the profile photo and Michael had no option other than to confess to raiding his computer and finding his details. 'When you were out drivin' on yer own that day. I let meself in. Sorry.' Roly overlooked this; with his own record of plunder he was the last person on the planet to have the right to condemn anyone for snooping, for going where they shouldn't and taking what wasn't theirs. 'You're a creamfaced knave and a doughboy, such audacity,' he said, trying to be jocular. 'I was sneaky once too,' he added, reminiscent though lightly. 'I raided the files at the Spartan club in Pimlico.' Now he was dark. 'One of my celebrity heroes used to go to there and I copied down his home address so I could write to him.' 'What 'appened?' 'Nothing like the result you are hoping for from your pillaging I wager.' Michael deflected this. 'That email you sent,' he said, his black eyes widening and looming larger than ever. 'Wow, it was fierce.' He said he'd been 'gobsmacked' to receive it. 'I never 'ad a pervy mail like that, really freaked me out that did.' Roly shot him a look of disbelief. 'A sixteen-year-old virgin advertising himself on the gay interweb? I'm amazed you haven't been inundated with admiring and what you'd call pervy messages –' '– Oh I've 'ad messages, but nothin' like that –' 'Not everyone has my way with words, you see,' he arrogated. 'In your reply you said you didn't understand it –' 'Yeah, but I got the idea innit?' 'Remember, I didn't know it was you I was writing to.' Michael had blown his own cover on purpose, but still hadn't known what he was exposing. Roly realised how little he knew of the agonies of the uncertain, of the agonies of sexual self-discovery and of what chaos that taking the action he had in order to 'discover' himself had brought about. It had taken a daring and courage which had put the fear of hellfire into him, poor mite. 'Why *did* you knock at my door, Michael?' Roly asked in a very weary voice. This silenced him; confusion and guilt were a shroud. 'I, I sort of… I'd seen ya, right?' he stuttered. 'And I was like, I.' It was painful and tentative; he knew but couldn't express. 'Like I, I'd really like to, to talk to 'im, I mean you.' Something was going on in my head about you was what he meant but couldn't express. 'But I dint know what. I 'ad to get to speak to ya some'ow, it was drivin' me jag and then I thought of the herbs.' *Thee 'erbs.* Roly thought: morphic resonance, the following of the spoor of gay ancestry. 'An' then when ya said ya, ya fancied me, well… ya didn't say that but –' '– You found me in chat.' 'I found ya before,' he revealed. 'Me an' 'Odge went on it one day for a laff… round at my place… ages ago, lookin' for any fagg – queer – anybody on the Trenton profiles to see if we knew 'em. I saw yours then, but

I couldn't say anythin' could I? Not to 'Odge and 'e didn't spot you thank f –. Then I... I raided yer PC to make sure and then I went in chat again but... I was kinda scared on me own. Some o' them, they're right weirdos, spooky people, man! He stopped in his tracks. 'You'd done a very good surveillance job beforehand, I must say. I could never catch you looking at me. I damned your indifference, I was mortified. 'You mean you were pissed off?' 'I didn't think you knew I existed.' 'I saw you 'undreds o' times,' he cried, as though to reassure Roly of his probity. He locked his piercing eyes on him. 'It was kinda more than that,' he said, almost in a whisper. 'Oh I dunno.' 'Don't tell me I was giving you lustful thoughts, please,' Roly commanded. 'Michael Macchiavelli,' he mused. 'So when you asked me at the start if I went into chatrooms you already knew the answer and the next step was to create yourself a profile and track me and when I blathered on about your lack of a photo –' 'I was too scared to put one on at first, 'cause of 'Odge and all them. They could of seen it easy and I'd be fuckin' – I'd be toast. I thought with Silverdaddies bein' American an' all that, nobody round 'ere would know about it.' Roly felt he'd explained himself all he could and he was loath to extract blood. Michael had seen a man, it happened to be him, and had suffered a mania and he couldn't understand what that meant. He'd got it into his head to satisfy his curiosity using the methods that were readily to hand and how could he blame him when he'd done so similar himself in his time? 'That time we chatted, I thought I was like brave, but then I was brickin' it, I was freaked.' 'And you fled.' 'Yeah.' 'But you sent a photo.' 'That? I got that off the amateurqueers site.' *Amachuqueers.* 'I just thought – I mean. Why 'ave you never said anythin' til now?,' he asked quickly. 'Oh yeah, yer mum and stuff. I've bin waitin' an' waitin' tho.' 'I've been waiting too. To see if you'd realise you'd done the wrong thing and give you chance to wipe everything clean, to save you embarrassment. It's too late to tell you to get yourself off there now, but you were very lucky to slip through the age net.' Roly also wheedled the night of the window out of him. 'It wasn't like, like I was spyin' on ya.' Michael pleaded, a plea of shame. Roly could feel no anger, not now, could respond only with persiflage. 'And there was I hoping for a handsome hunky burglar,' he said. 'Aren't ya mad at me?' he asked, fearing Roly's wrath, docked wages or worse, the sack. But Roly gave him none. 'You're a bloody imbecile, it was a very stupid thing to do and it scared me witless. It's a good thing for you I didn't pull my alarm cord and have you surrounded by blues and whites.' 'I –' '– but why? Did you want to see me naked or catch me masturbating or what?' 'I, I 'ad a lager an'… I snook out and walked round. I wanted ta see if you were with anybody kind o' thing. Not spyin', just… I dunno, just wanted to see. And I was outside there with a right stonker, honest. I didn't know what I was doin'. I dint want to scare ya.' 'Pshaw, you young rapscallion! Why on earth did you run off?' 'Dint want you to see it was me innit?' He went quiet. Roly so much wanted to tell him how there wasn't a hope in hell of any future for them, certainly no sexual future, but instead he sat, with a rather helpless doglike gaze fixed on him and he felt suddenly almost tearful. Michael, in this atmosphere of therapy and healing that they'd somehow created, had transformed into a waif figure, he was melting, losing his supremacy and Roly felt impotent. Their chaste hugs had up to then been a palpable symbol of friendship, an affirmation of the bond between them and a tactile token of security. That had now changed; Roly thought of a test. 'Come here and let's have a hug, my frabjous boy' he ordered, gently. They both stood up and

Michael went over to him. Roly touched him as if he were handling gossamer, too afraid to break him. It wasn't that his body was delicate, on the contrary, his flesh was sturdy and secure, but something was telling his hands that they had no right to the kind of touch he couldn't dismiss from his mind, telling his brain it had no permission for that pleasure. He heard Muvvie and felt afraid, afraid that he was stealing again because the boy couldn't possibly be sure he wanted to give of his own free will. Indeed, he had nothing to give, except the widow's mite of his body and Roly hoped he had long ceased exploiting people. Michael would give and give gladly and Roly would take and that wasn't the direction to go, not a step on the road to redemption but one further along to perdition. Michael was in danger of truckling and if he did, he would put Roly in the position of reluctant conqueror. Roly tightened his grip and held him close to protect him and his hardness grew and pressed into the young groin. When he felt the boy's own rigidity pressing into him under his overhanging belly, his hands moved involuntarily down to the boy's rump and he squeezed it; it was solid as a stanchion, not a millimetre of flab. He traced with his hand from the back of his leg, where the steely flesh curved out and round then to the small of his back and he pictured in his mind's eye the Line of Beauty. He turned him around before he could baulk and very slowly his hands glided over the teeshirt and down, down and across the flat midriff, to the waistband of the trackies, down, down until… they reached *there* and, yes, his fingers felt granite. 'Oh Michael,' he sighed and his name came from somewhere deep and the sigh was almost a sob. He had taken the initiative from the boy and the boy had succumbed. But he snatched his hand away as if from fire. Too hot, too much, too *wrong*. He murmured an abject apology and let go of him, turned away and hid his face. 'Roly,' Michael cried in exasperation and turned around. Roly felt unwholesome, even though he hadn't coerced him. 'It's cool 'onest,' he assured him. 'Shit, you got me 'orny now.' He'd interpreted the sexual embrace as a green light and Roly felt doubly sick. Roly turned back and when he only smiled inanely, unable to speak, Michael let out a deep sigh, raising his brows and his whole face looked whimsically quizzical. 'We still gotta wait til February?' he asked in a whisper. Roly felt himself sag. 'I can't… please… not now… it's not… just try and understand will you?' 'Sorry,' he said softly. 'I didn't want to –' 'Please don't ever say sorry to me, Michael,' he told him, gently. 'You're far too fine a creature to have anything to apologise for, especially to me. You're a boy who could well be worth your weight in love but there's not enough room in a heart like mine to hold the love you deserve to receive.' Michael, perplexed, said, 'Yeah, but you wouldn't… do nothin' to hurt me would you?' Roly gathered himself to speak more severely. 'I wouldn't, not intentionally, but you know it's possible to do and say nothing and still hurt someone. That's what scares me. You mustn't let me touch you, those I touch I wreck, I mess up their lives, I pollute them. You mustn't get close to me.' And with that he sent Michael on his way and he left with a sad smile, none the wiser, but then neither was he.

****

It was a day when Michael wasn't revising or busy with swimming practice and Roly managed to go without a morning drink and, what's more, organised himself sufficiently to put together a picnic. He was feeling… not happier, no, but less gloomy. He had no whicker hamper with plates, cutlery and fabric napkins but he packed plastic boxes with food and drinks they'd agreed they would both

271

enjoy. 'Pedestrian stuff,' Roly announced. He wasn't *that* much organised to create anything gourmet.

The Peugeot he drove, courtesy of the Motability scheme, was his sole means of getting about since his stroke and especially, if he had the urge as now, the sole means of reaching the Peak District, the country where his heart was, where he'd first tramped as a lad and which he'd loved ever since. Michael had paid extra attention to his choice of clothes for the excursion, for the occasion and looked very fetching in the brilliant white thin sweatshirt and another pair of those long shorts, khaki-coloured this time. The shorts weren't quite to his taste, the cut not as body hugging as he liked, it didn't show any of the curves or tori that male apparel should, but he grudgingly conceded that he looked very well in them. 'Fetching!' he beamed, looking him up and down, 'but the next pair you buy, make them shorter and tighter will you?' On his head were the ever-present checks. Roly had asked him if he minded pushing him in the wheelchair if necessary, because he may want to go a little way along the riverbank if possible, to feel the valley rather than only look at it through the car window and he didn't trust himself to be able to walk it and Michael simply smiled, 'No problem'.

They approached the valley from the north, joining the concreted former quarry railway track which runs a good length down it. The limestone crags and outcrops on the valley sides were an old familiar and welcome sight, a reminder of the Saturday hikes he and a few fellow schoolboys and teachers regularly took over 30 years before. There was space to park near the footbridge over the river, the river which had all but done its disappearing act, as is its habit in hot dry weather; there would be no more flowing water to be seen until further downstream, where it emerges from the underground limestone caverns, forced up by harder rock.

The gorge was warm and airlessly dry. There were surprisingly few people to be seen by the bridge or at the adjacent tearoom tables and for a while only the faint rippling of the remnants of the river interrupted a silence that was numinous. A single huge cumulus, broad and high, blanked out the sun for a second and rendered the place claustrophobic, then it drifted slowly away to smother another region and lighter white cirrhus and cumulus, cushions you felt you could sink into, gradually slipped into its place and allowed a white hot sun to peek intermittently through them as they inched their way across its face. Alders and ash still lined the valley and their heavy laden branches overhung the river deferentially; aspen and white poplars mounted the steep sides majestically, with leaves shimmering and trembling all the way up to the top ridges. All were at their greenest glossiest summer best.

Phil 'Pedro' Bell and the other regular hiking schoolmasters came out of the trees with five or six schoolboys at that moment. He saw himself in his red anorak and big boots, the Dunn & Co deerstalker perched on his head and the duffel bag over his shoulder. 'We walked for miles all day,' he said in a dreamy voice, addressed to the valley sides. 'And we talked of seas and ships and sealing wax and we listened and learned.' 'What you goin' on about?' Michael asked and without waiting for an answer, took the wheelchair out and assembled it and pushed him along to the bridge where, with the help of his stick and his arm, Roly got out to stand and peer over the arid riverbed below. Not water, but happy 30-year-old memories washed over him and helped him to forget embarrassment and awkwardness for the moment. Looking at the few tourists and walkers, he was heartened to see the the Peak District could still be sparsely peopled, not quite as it could be then, but by no means crowded. His embarrassment was caused by the ablebodied ramblers, one of which he once was, looking at him, old wreck that he was, being pushed and helped by a hale youth. Despite the human activity, the valley retained its quiet; there was more noise from the trickling of water over stones and a frog holding a conversation with itself somewhere out of sight than from humans. There was no sign of kingfishers but a pair of fluffy brown ducks paddled silently in tiny puddles, dipping their beaks in unison and the sight of them evoked the ceramic ducks of his childhood and he chortled to himself. The tranquillity was affecting. Roly heard *Ombra mai fu* humming in his head as the aura of Arcady touched him: he was here in a gorgeous valley with a gorgeous boy, both sublimities within his grasp. He had known this kind of fulfilment before in his life, but only ever too briefly and then he'd thrown it all away; where there was peace and harmony and well-being as such a place as this afforded, he had brought always only tumult and unhappiness.

They stood side by side on the bridge, he still peering wistfully down on the riverbed; it reminded him, Muvvie reminded him – 'Like some piece of dirty driftwood,' he murmured. He turned his face probingly to Michael's profile. 'I was taken by the flood, swept out on an effluent tide and I couldn't swim against it.' He looked back down. 'I don't think I was ever intentionally malicious, but that's the universal plea isn't it, by people who do a lot of wrong like I have. I just wanted to escape my inferior birth, my inadequacy.' The sombre tone disconcerted Michael. 'What you talkin' about now? You sure you 'aven't 'ad a drink before we came out?' 'I just wanted to break out of the mould, to enrich my life with the fine things I already had a taste for... including boys, of course… but instead I fouled up. Beautiful boys, drink and money weren't my downfall, the misuse of them was, but they were always paramount.'

He looked up from the river and addressed the hills around them again. 'Don't you think "boy" is the most beautiful word in the language?' All the nature was heady stuff, it was making him skittish now. 'Errmm, I dunno. What d'ya mean?' Roly closed his eyes. 'I use the word broadly.' He opened them and looked straight ahead again. 'By boy, I mean one who is old enough to –.' *Don't say old enough to know what his penis is for.* 'Young men then, how's that?' Oh his leitmotif: young men. In shorts, young men on bicycles, young men with gross tattoos across their pecs and down their arms, those stripped to the waist digging the road, or those playing football on Sunday mornings in Holland Park. 'As a boy myself it didn't take me very long at all to reach' – he broke off and glanced sideways at him – 'my Christopher Marlowe stage' and gave a hearty laugh. 'What the motherfuck *are* you talking about?' 'How many times Michael? That barbarian tone again, it gives me the hives! And here in Arcadia! ' 'I thought we were in the Manifold,' he ribbed. 'It is possible you know. Style, Michael, style. And tone and light and shadow and inflection. Cultivate yourself, don't just be a beautiful boy, be a *stylish* boy.' Michael received the reprimand in silence, which Roly hoped indicated he was thinking about acting on it rather than rebelling against it or ignoring it. Oh really, what do I think I could do with this boy? he asked himself, what if I *did* deflower him? He would be chaste for – how long does penetration take, five seconds and then what? Once plucked he was sure to fly off – it's not *me* he wants, it's *it* – or even worse, what if he turned out to be a monogamous boy and stayed and clung to me? 'Me, his First,' he muttered aloud.

He sat back down in his wheelchair. 'Let's walk for a while along that way.' As Michael pushed, Roly pondered. And then what, would they live together for ever? Could he see himself sitting him down of an evening to share *Gurreliede* or *Manon* with him? Could he take him out to dinner? Could he discuss Georgian architecture or global warming with him or the ideas of Adam Smith and Tom Payne? 'Who was Christopher Marlowe anyway?' Michael asked after they had gone a little way.

'When they deliberate, the love is slight;
Whoever loved that loved not at first sight?' Roly intoned.

'Or in the modern case, "whoever loved that loved not first on the website?", I suppose. Christopher Marlowe. He was a screaming Elizabethan poet playwright. He said that anyone who didn't enjoy tobacco and boys was a fool and I agree with him wholeheartedly.' 'He was a perv like you then.' 'I certainly believed there was nothing worth doing and nowhere worth going unless I could have a cigarette, a drink and there were boys to look at.' 'Roly. Give us a break will ya? Michael asked, sounding long-suffering. 'Ow much further d'ya wanna go anyway?' 'Are you tired?' 'No, but I'm 'ungry.' 'So get me down to the grass bank there, boy and we'll eat.' Michael negotiated the slight slope down to the water's edge, helped Roly to squat on the grass and they rummaged in the bag and produced the food and began to tuck in. *Boys and masters, under a tree, on a rock, in a meadow, my anorak and deerstalker, tinned pilchards – Would you care for a pilchard sir?' – Earl Grey tea with lemon and always Sir's favourite, Garibaldi biscuits.*

'Here with a loaf of bread beneath the bough,
A flask of wine, a book of verse – and Thou
Beside me singing in the wilderness –
And wilderness is paradise enow.'

'You and yer poetry.' 'A disparaging tone, a squashed up grimace on a boy's face, what eroticism!' Two ducks swam by. 'Do you have flying ducks on the wall at home, Michelangelo, I didn't notice when I was there?' he asked. 'Flyin' ducks?' Michael asked, taken aback. 'Oh, ya mean them china things? Duh, no.'

You know what he meant, don't you my dears? The Wanger household had the one set of three flying up the walls of the parlours and livingrooms in the three different homes that Roly lived in as a boy. Their pottery beaks painted bright glossy yellow and their feathers in various hues of garish blue. They were either hideous or tasteful, chic or vulgar, he didn't know. Nobody questioned it; they were simply there and, what's more, they were manufactured locally, so it was provincially patriotic to buy them and show them off. But when he moved out of Trenton and into new loftier social circles, he found that flying ducks were *aves non grata, so* he went with the flow and poured scorn on them and would never admit to having liked them let alone lived with them. It was more than his life and reputation were worth to let people know he'd ever been associated with such things, much as he'd never own up to once having lived in a house with an outside toilet. Until flying ducks became fashionable, collectable kitsch, then he could feel comfortable with them, but it was a narrow escape before that. 'It was all a matter of taste,' he mused. 'And I, despite my claims to the contrary, never had any. I always had to leave that for others to decide for me and go with whatever was the acceptable flow of the time.' There was more, such as his having to pretend he liked and understood the bits of Wagner that were unhummable, just because he had contemporaries and colleagues who said Wagner was brilliant. But on the other hand, he was at the premiere of

Berg's *Wozzeck*' at Covent Garden and *Wozzeck* was a far more atonal work than anything Wagner wrote and yet he loved it. He genuinely loved it, yes, but he wasn't bold enough to vaunt an avant garde, or minority, or noncomformist view, so he kept quiet and by keeping quiet, wrapped himself in an ever winding spiral of aesthetic and cultural angst. He had tried turning to his Auntie Vera. Auntie Vera, who lived a spinster life with her mother, his grandmother, in their largish council house, the aunt who of all the family had a conspicuous elegance, with an expensive wardrobe of smart dresses, coats and hats and an elegance which was antimony, deliciously at odds with her working class status in Trenton; she was an ordinary worker in a pottery factory after all, who got covered in clay dust every day. But whenever Roly pictured her, it was nothing like seeing his mother, who did exactly the same job; where there was nothing surprising about his mother's position in the industrial set-up, Auntie Vera didn't belong there in his eyes, she was out of time and out of place. His mother walked to work every morning and walked home every night; Auntie Vera was driven to her job every day by the managing director of the factory and driven home each night. She was a big figure in the chapel choir, had friends who were businessmen and professionals and one who was the Lord Mayor of the city and maybe he subconciously tried to emulate her, but got it wrong when emulation turned to delusions of grandeur and (never to be admitted for years) snobbery. There were the likes of Alan Warburton, who lived in a mansion of a home with his company-owning father and their two cars, one of which was a silver Volvo, like the one The Saint had on the television; and James Malton, who lived on the other side of the lane from his grandparents' house, the private, money side, whose own grandmother lived in opulence in a nearby house which had once employed servants (the pantry was still there, not long out of use) and into which he was introduced; and the Cameron brothers, sons of the doctor whose surgery and mansion, for another mansion it was, was directly behind the council house, who were schoolfriends and sometime playmates who invited him for tea. Why as a boy was he exposed to these people? Mixing with them, he saw only now, sowed the seeds of discontent which flowered into blooms of envy and snobbery which grew into lies. Or were those seeds already sown *in naturo,* was he born with them? 'Flying ducks, Rolf Harris, Covent Garden premières, Auntie Annie, well-to-do friends,' he muttered again. He turned sharply to Michael in a sort of confrontation and asked him, 'How did I *instinctively* know about fish knives, eh? How come I didn't have to be *told*?' He posed the query so forcefully, it made Michael jump and they looked at each other in astonishment. 'Have you ever skinnydipped?' Roly then asked, quite calmly. 'I'd like to see you swim naked in this river,' he whispered. Michael looked horrified. 'What, now?' 'I want you remove that profile before they find you out and I don't want anyone else to see you. Tell the men who message you to go hang.' Michael could only stare at him more, mystified, wondering and half hoping if Roly was jealous. They finished off their picnic, tidied up and Michael bungled him back into the wheelchair and trundled him back to the road. 'We have nothing in common you know,' Roly said at last. 'What's in common? Like yeah, no, I know I'm not clever like you, but if it means groanin' on about flyin' ducks and fish knives, I think I'm better off bein' a durbrain. Like I said, you know words an' stuff and I wanna speak nice, but –' It was Roly's turn to cut him off for once. 'Speaking "nice" in Trenton is a blight,' he said. 'Yeah. Anyway, you wanna do me and I want you to, so that's in common for a start innit?' Michael grinned. *Do me. I can't escape his coarseness even in the Manifold Valley.* 'Come on, let's get back and get those oatcakes.' On the drive home, he asked him if he was busy next day. 'I've got nothin' on,' he answered, suggestively. 'I want you to come on another journey with me' and Michael asked where to and he said, 'Harworthy.' 'Where's that?' 'Not far, just beyond innocence.' 'What you goin' there for?' 'I want to find a demon.' Michael felt fretful, sure that Roly really had flipped, while Roly only gazed on him with a doleful smile. 'I have to try and find something I lost. It's a mistake, always a mistake to go back they say, to look for something you once had and is no longer there but you think it is, you remember it and it still is. I know I won't find it but please say you'll come.'

****

The drive across the plain, in warm sunshine, leaving the fortress folly of Mow Cop standing on its hill astride the county border, its brown brickwork looking fresh and resplendent against a blue sky populated with white summer cumulus furballs, passing by the great wide telescope dish tilted and glinting in the sunlight while it listened to the sounds of the black universe – he thought of the previous day's impulse. By some convolution of logic, he was now thinking he really could tackle 30 years of searching for remorse by offering himself up to Harworthy as a sort of sacrifice in the hope of manumission from the slavery of his wrongs. He was going to face demons and look at the house in a kind of spirit of penitent commemoration or remembrance or dedication or whatever one was supposed to do. He didn't know. Michael assumed they were on their way to meet an old friend of Roly's and Roly didn't disenchant him.

280

He was surprised, after the years, how easy the village and the lane were to find. He'd made this journey once before, about 15 years after the Fall, but that was at a time when he experienced far fewer intense sensations of sackcloth and ashes. He stopped the car at the top of the lane and looked down the still unadopted, potholed roadway, peering through the luscious beech, birch and sycamores that lined it on both sides and unable to see the house through them. They must have grown and thickened even more, he thought. But he could discern the whereabouts of the drive opening and so locate its position. He lit a cigarette and sat with Muvvie and his memories, looking about him for anyone who might come by and recognise him, such a small chance, but the waves of persecution rolling over him just then made him believe it was possible. They sat for a while, Roly looked into the distance and smoked on. 'What now?' Michael asked at length. 'Is this a stakeout or what?' Before he could answer, Roly saw a figure emerge suddenly from where Harworthy must be. He couldn't make out its sex at the distance. Could it be Smollet or his wife walking home? Surely they were both long gone. It wouldn't be one of Muvvie's family – if they still lived there – no, they'd be driving. He couldn't risk it, couldn't wait to find out if he would recognise him or her or he or she, him. The figure continued up the lane towards them and Roly saw it was a man, youngish. It was Sergeant Lewis of the Merseyside constabulary. He stubbed out his cigarette, switched on the engine, engaged gear and sped off. He went for about a mile then saw a small lay-by on the main road and pulled over. He was shaking.

'You all right?' Michael asked. 'Who was the geezer? Somebody you didn't want to see you right?' 'Was it a he?' Roly turned and looked him in the eyes; he saw that something behind them again and couldn't speak. How could this baby carry or even share his burden? He looked past him and saw that Lewis had followed them; he was standing in the field by the car. He lit another cigarette. 'He got very angry with me in the end,' he murmured in a preoccupied way as he stared into the field. 'Who did?' 'He found my Journal in the chest of drawers – yet again it had landed me in trouble! – and he waved it menacingly in my face over the desk. I used to write everything down. Well, everything to do with sex. Sergeant almighty self-righteous Lewis, guardian of Merseyside morals, was ranting by now because, although I admitted taking the money, he was sure there were sex offences to condemn me with hidden in those pages. That Journal was his ordinance. "And if I find out that any of those lads you mention in this diary of yours are underage, I'll have you for that as well." I remember he didn't use the word paedophile to me.' Paedophile was a word Michael recognised and he perked up. 'Roly, what's all this about? They didn't try to lay pedo stuff on you did they? Did they beat you up?' 'You don't know the dark ages, my darling, you weren't there. An 18-year-old was jail bait, regardless of his consent and willing participation and in the eyes of the police if you slept with an 18-year-old you were nothing less than a filthy sick child molester. Lewis banged the desk with his fist once I remember, frustrated that I wasn't confessing anything. As for paedophilia, that wasn't in fashion yet. I was lucky, it wasn't yet the age of the great unwashed plebian army of single pram pushing smoking mothers and their cavalry of shaven headed earringed boyfriends, they who could be relied on to get it wrong. There is nothing so ludicrous as the British public in one of its fits of moral outrage, as the man said. Anyway, I wasn't on trial for paedophilia but for murder.' 'Murder?' Michael seemed to jump back in his seat and squeeze himself against the door as though trying to move as far away as possible. He sat and stared, open-mouthed, with his lips moving, but unable to form and utter any words. Eventually, he said, or rather croaked, 'You're scaggin' me,' and when Roly looked icily back at him without response, he said again, 'Murder? You tellin' me you killed somebody here?' Still Roly said nothing, simply continued staring at him. Michael's lips were moving soundlessly again. 'At a house down the lane back there. Harworthy,' Roly whispered. 'What, you lived there?' 'She made the mistake of trusting me enough to go to the bank for her every week. A hundred pounds every week, which she kept in her handbag on the floor next to her. And when she'd gone to bed and I wanted to go to a club for drink and boys...' 'What? What you saying, man? Fuck.' 'She forgave me, she said she forgave me. It was her grandson. It was Sam. Nemesis' 'Wh-who's Sam? Who... what? Roly, 'ave you gone – wha-what's goin on?' If only Muvvie had been my mother, Roly said to himself. If only. Muvvie was in the car with him now. Roly turned returned to his earlier subject and spoke as though in his sleep. 'Yes, the marching army of ignorant anger. They found a convenient label they didn't understand, thrown to them by the tabloid press to incite them and started calling child abusers paedophiles. Fwah! In their frenzy they didn't take the trouble to work out that paedophiles are lovers of children, not abusers of them. What were they to know? Did they know Greek? *Pais*, boy, *philos*, lover or friend... Do you know what, what was the laughable pinnacle of their campaign? A mob vandalised a house some years ago when they saw a brass sign on the wall which said 'paediatrician'! A little learning, eh? I always worshipped, adored.' He stressed the verbs. 'I didn't *abuse.* Lewis had me completely wrong. And I've never so much as touched or thought of touching a child, I'm as appalled by the idea as the next man. 'Anyway, the problem wasn't my sexuality. Or maybe it was; everything was mixed up together, it was a mess. Like I said on the bridge yesterday, I wanted to break out of the mould, but... I've always fouled up, Michael.' Michael's body had untensed, the tautness of his face had slackened, he sat again normally in his seat. 'Don't you ever get me like that again,' he said. 'Fuck, Roly.' 'Oh Michael,' he sighed, smiling now. 'Do you know I've been committing suicide for 30 years? No, of course you don't, you couldn't possibly. And you'll never understand, so it's no use my trying.' He let out another long sigh, doused his cigarette and started the engine. 'I shouldn't have asked you to come with me. Should never have thought I could unload on you.' Michael had nothing to say in response to the apology, instead he furrowed his brow for a moment, completely lost in a sea of misunderstanding and bewilderment. 'I got the sack for my crime,' Roly said, pensive again. 'That was no surprise, of course. I was sacked even before I was put on trial and pleaded guilty – against my barrister's advice, I hasten to add. Now, if that had happened to me today... today, when a prominent figure in the media (which I by no means was) is found using crack, he's sacked first and gets his own talk show a few weeks later! Dear god, what would I have become, what would I have averted, if I'd taken that barrister's advice? Does pleading not guilty in the dock make you not guilty in conscience?' Again a sigh. 'What did you do after?' Michael asked in a timid voice, almost afraid to speak, it seemed, not wishing to intrude. 'Where did you live?' Roly snapped to again. 'What did I do?' he asked flatly. He took a deep breath. 'It wasn't the last time I'd be homeless,' he said ruefully. 'I ended up being a nomad for one reason or another, a reluctant Romany, all my own fault. Usually.'

284

'What did I do? I left in disgrace and went back to London to try and get a life back. I stayed with Murdoch, the man I'd lived with in Chiswick before I came here –' '– Your boyfriend yeah? Roly laughed at the question, his laughter, though bitter, seeming to steer their conversation away from murder and trials at last, much to the boy's relief. 'No, a good friend, too good for me.' *Murdoch was adamant I was his lover; I never disillusioned him – I was scared if I did that I'd lose succour; I was a kept man!* 'I told him what had happened and –' ''E didn't want to know?' 'No, he wasn't like that – he didn't kick me when I was down. I went to see Chris one evening too, he was a lawyer, I'd shared a flat with him too – ' '– Was 'e yer boyfriend?' 'Michael, d'you want to know what happened or not?' 'Awright, keep yer nipples on.' 'He just said, "I hear you've had an unfortunate time." Then I had to swallow my pride and come back here to my parents, the worthless prodigal. I remember I stopped over in Leicester, where two old friends of mine had moved to. They just said what a silly boy I'd been. Good grief.'

He slouched in the car seat again and slid back into a reverie of disintegrated time and saw the boy in the Leicester disco that night, the boy he looked at and who smiled at him, the boy he took back to his friends' house where, in bed, he asked him if he could do it, to which the boy answered, 'Yes, but slowly please'. And afterwards as they lay touching and holding and whispering in the dark, the boy asked him, as though he knew the inside of his soul and knew the answer already, 'Have you ever done anything bad in your life?' And, there, in the blackness of a room that was redolent with sexual tension, there with a pretty boy in his arms, he confessed: 'I pinched a pen from an office I worked in once,' he said.

'Roly?' The intrusion jolted him, he sat up sharply. 'What? Oh. Oh,' he said, the pretty boy gone from the Leicester bedroom. 'I was remembering a boy.' He spoke in awe, awed by the vision. 'What was his name?' 'I don't know, he asked an unbelievable question.' And he told him the story. 'Wasn't that an amazing thing? 'P'raps your mates told him.' 'No-ooo, never.' 'Maybe 'e was psychic.' The levity was welcome – to both of them for a second – but then Roly looked out of the car window, seeing nothing and Michael saw that he saw nothing. 'I wonder if that was the first time Muvvie spoke to me?' 'Eh? Muvvie? 'Who was he?' *Oo woz 'e?* 'What? Oh,nothing. Nobody. Nobody you want to know. May you never. Let's go... let's go home, Michelangelo. They drove back to Jamage not speaking; Michael didn't know what the hell the journey had been about, only that it had been aborted and Roly, he was too full of the memories he'd gone insanely to expunge to say anything and he'd found that Michael was not the redeeming angel he was desperate to find. He dropped Michael off at his house. 'You be awright?' the boy asked him and Roly was taken aback at the note of concern in the question; it sounded real. 'Tell you what. Bring yourself round tonight with a can of Fanta, or a beer or cider if you want, I don't mind. Come round will you? I have things to tell you which you must know. Please.' 'I'll be round after me tea, after you've had your *supper,'* he said, turning on a smile which Roly felt was an attempt to reach out with some kind of affection and which was in danger of bringing up a sob from his chest. Roly went home and searched his brain and his cupboards for much needed relief in good food. He was glad Michael had found the monkfish and other things he'd dared, *nolens volens* in his indigence, to splash out on and he lifted it from the freezer and pulled down his wok and could now look forward to a small and satisfying banquet. Mix the ginger, garlic, chilli sauce and marinate the fish, heat the groundnut oil to smoking, soften the onion, mangetout and babycorn, add the fish, beansprouts and spring onions and stir them for five minutes. Drizzle with toasted sesame oil and toss and have it with jasmine rice. He licked his lips and rather slavered at the thought of it. Michael came round at eight in his baseball cap and not wearing tracksuit bottoms but a pair of what Roly thought were black Chinos, snug, figure-hugging Chinos. *A fashion innovation or tantalising gesture?* 'Very nice,' he said, admiring them as they sat down together. 'I 'ope this isn't gonna be more 'eavy stuff,' Michael said. 'You doin' Alan Sugar on me and firin' me?' he joked, but seriously. 'No no no,' Roly assured him. 'I can't do that, you're indispensable now. That means I can't do without you.' 'Oh, can't ya?' With a firm 'Listen to me', Roly wasted no time and launched into what he'd been preparing to say all evening while he cooked and ate his stir-fry. He strove hard to keep the moral philosophy he knew was necessary simple and to the minimum. He remembered he wasn't drinking alcohol, he didn't have that crutch, but he pressed on, beginning with an exposition of his life of elaboration and invention, 'Not as it happens to hide any great wrong, but to hide being gay and that required one grandfather of a lie,' he told him, 'lots of them.' The straight world then required one to be a liar, subterfuge and deceit were the oil on the cogs. Gay people had to learn to dissimulate as soon as the closet door was opened by them or for them. He admitted that his troubles came from having carried dissimulation too far, he never lost the habit, in that he was victor ludorum. Then he learned resentment. What he was and where he was, coincidental with being gay, meant he entered a world where, he could see through no fault of his own, it was going to be impossible for him to be honest and before he knew it, like Macbeth, he was too far steeped in blood to go back. The lies multiplied, without his doing anything, and the money problems and seemed to follow so naturally, just to make a deeper morass to plunge himself into. And there he soon was, in a totally vicious circle of lies and sex, sex and lies, debt and drink, drink and debt and begging, borrowing and... and all of the crimes, committed for a purpose, the purpose being to live a life he thought he should have. 'I'm telling you, incorruptible angel that you are, Michael angel, Michele angelo, Michelangelo, I was born bad and grew worse and I warn you not to look up to me for anything. I could say they were attacks of kleptomania, or blame my genes, which is the fashionable thing to do now, but no, I just think I'm a plain old rotten sod.' *Now see if you're a redeeming angel.* 'If you despise me, Michael, I will understand, but please don't ever say it to me direct,' he said to finish and then fell quiet. How much of a struggle it was for Michael to listen to the longest flow of words he had yet heard him come out with, without interjecting once, or how much his rhetoric had entranced the boy into passive listening, he could only imagine, but sure enough, Michael had sat and listened, sipping his can of soft drink and watching him speak without once diverting his black questioning eyes. A heartbeat passed and then Roly jumped, or rather struggled, to his feet. 'What you doin'?' Michael asked in alarm and jumped up too. Roly, leaning on his stick, shuffled towards him. Without asking him and finding no resistance from him – he stood on the spot and didn't protest – he slowly removed the baseball cap from the boy's head and ran his fingers through the lush hair on top and at the back of it. 'Thank you for growing your hair,' he curred, for Michael had been leaving it to grow ever since the day Roly had said how much he disliked shorn heads and it now covered the tops of his small ears. 'Yeah, no sweat.' Michael sounded suspicious and raised a hand to touch his hair. 'But I'm not turning emo for ya though,' he jokingly warned. 'What on earth is an emo?' 'Ya know, hair down to here,' he gestured, 'over the eyes like f – like vampires or somethin'.' 'Oh, right,' he muttered, mystified. 'And don't be a numpty... my hair,' he poo-pooed, smiling. 'I've no idea what a numpty is, I'm just trying to find out if your beauty can forgive me.' He took hold of him round his waist and hung on to him as though life depended on it, certainly he thought their friendship did. He knew exactly what he was doing and knew he had absolutely nothing to lose. 'I grow old,' he chanted. 'I have caught an everlasting cold. Shall I dare to eat a peach?' He laughed manically and Michael drew away and looked at him with that quizzical frown which Roly had noticed he was now accustomed to adopting when he thought he was going doolally. 'Don't get spooky again.' Michael said this to reassure himself as much as Roly. Roly clasped him to him, too hard, and breathed the words in his ear: 'Now then, if you were wearing just a pair of tight white briefs... ' 'Briefs?' He recoiled, wide-eyed, horrified. 'Ello? I don't think so. Me in a pair of nut grips... NOT,' he added. 'No way.' 'I'd stroke you all over and feel your curves and your... prominence and I'd rip them off and then...' Roly went on lasciviously. 'We got a gig, yay!' 'Michael, you are incorrigible,' he said, releasing his hold and they stood face to face, their eyes locked on each other, frozen in a moment; Roly felt they were a hundred miles apart. 'That chat,' Michael said, as though he'd just heard of it and in an effort to snuff out the dark feeling that had seized him momentarily. 'Have you been in there again?' 'No, I just think about it sometimes,' he said airily. 'I mean, why's everybody into tight white tight briefs for f – for banjax sake? They all talk about 'em, like it's some kinda – I don't know. Nut grips, they are. I'm a boxers boy me.' And while he was on the subject: 'And what's fetish an' nipple play? And what's that one, frottage? (He rhymed it with cottage). I don't know nothin' that's my trouble.' He may have managed to find his way into Caffmos, Gaydar and Silverdaddies without any difficulty but he had as yet gleaned only desultory know-how. 'Oh Michael,' Roly sighed and he held him to him again, now pressing his cheek against his and addressing his thoughts over his shoulder: *do what you can, I won't mark you out of ten, but please don't see yourself as sacrificial. I am not the Minotaur and you are not a vestal youth.* Michael looked out of the window, rabbit-like. 'If anybody goes past…,' he said. Roly brushed his cheek swiftly with his lips, held him at arm's length and stared at him. 'You gotta show me what to do ya know,' Michael said, now in his bossy petulant way, 'when we… ya know… shag I mean.' Roly winced; he might just as well have said 'when you teach me how to play Scrabble'. 'Shag' and 'business' sounded cold words to Roly. 'Forgive him for he knows not what he says.' He threw his head back and laughed and laughed again. 'February the fifth next year and even then I don't –' Rationality hit him with its club. – *don't think for a moment it's going to happen.* 'Today was out of order,' he said, softly now, regretfully, 'I never want to violate you.' 'Don't know wotcha mean – violate?' 'I have no right to use you, let's forget it happened.' 'What? You mean –?' 'It's hard to believe, I know, but it seems I've developed a killjoy streak in my decrepit old age.' 'I dunno what that means, you an' yer big words. 'Ave you gone off me now then?' 'No,' he emphasised. 'On the contrary, I'm *on* you more than ever.' What was the use of trying to explain the future, the chaos he could foresee? Michael was a tyro who simply couldn't see beyond his hormones and, as though telepathically responding to this thought, Michael became agitated and started his dance to silent music but it was a feisty polka this time. 'What's stoppin' us now?' he asked. Roly was aghast. 'Oh no, nothing in desperation, Michael, no unthinking frenzy, I'm beyond all that. There would be regret and that would be disaster.' The promise of something that should be wonderful, especially for the boy, was evaporating rapidly in the air between them. 'Hey,' Roly said after a moment. 'Come here.' Michael moved without hesitation and Roly took hold of him again at arm's length. 'Please try and understand me,' he pleaded. 'This, this seduction, this sparring, it's so much how it's not supposed to be.' 'I'm not desperate, ya know, well I am sort of, but I'm kinda –' '– eager. It's the hormones.' He sighed, 'Are we still mates?' 'Michael, you're my best mate, I mean it, let me tell you.' The screw turned. It turned Roly's indecision suddenly. All his old liabilities were cast aside, the potholed path was covered over and in a subliminal blitzkrieg he sent himself to perdition without informing himself. He wanted desperately to kiss him, to give way totally, lose all willpower, all self-denial and bloody well kiss him. With a passion. But a kiss would illude him so, lead him on, damage him, them. *If I kiss him, it will take him to the edge and I might abandon him there. I want him to change his mind and stop.* They stood motionless, their eyes centimetres apart, locked and vulnerable, Michael waiting for Roly, Roly for him. 'So are ya gonna kiss me or not?' Michael asked finally. 'Michael, please don't.' 'So you were lyin'. Ya don't fancy me then.' 'I have not lied to you but think about it. You don't really want me to kiss you – *me* – to kiss *you.*' 'If ya fancied me ya would.' Roly had to temporise. 'I *do fancy* you, which is exactly why I don't want – I don't want you… to want me… to kiss you. Have you thought what happens to us if I do and you find you don't like it? You'll hate me. You'll change, your view of me will change. And for the worse. I advise against it. Even if you like it, we'll change. It will change us both. Either way, I'm not worth the risk.' 'For fuck's sake Roly, stop soundin' like a, like you're always tryin' to figure things out, like a scientist.' 'It's merely dialectics, dear boy. Studying cause and effect. Best you should master causality while you're young, it may avert some tragedy later on. Have you never heard about the butterfly flapping its wings in Kyoto and causing a tornado in Oklahoma?' 'I dunno know what the fuck you're talkin' about.' His frustration was mounting. 'Queen Victoria was a carrier of haemophilia you know, she passed it on to every royal household in Europe and the son of the tsar of Russia had it and Rasputin was brought in to cure him and the bolsheviks didn't like his power and that was the cause of the Russian revolution and – and oh wouldn't if be a different world if things didn't *happen* and cause other things to happen?' 'Why don't you just shut up and snog me?' The question brought everything to a halt, it somehow blanked everything about them, then after a sempiternal inertia, 'I'll kiss you,' Roly said, 'but that's all for now. Understand? Can you handle that? That's all until it's time, if it ever will be time.' 'Oh yeah, please, man. A snog.' His face had the look of an expectant puppy, expecting but unsure if the treat being dangled before him was his. 'I don't want to give you false hope,' Roly told him. 'This isn't at all what I thought it would come to and my... my strength...' he fumbled for words. Never having been a man, no matter how intense his feelings, who could easily use soft and tender tones, he spoke as soothingly as he could: 'Since there's no help,' he whispered, 'let's kiss and part' and before he knew it he'd stepped out of the fying pan of reason into the fire of folly and closed his mouth over Michael's. Long sweet, warm and moist it was and he thought of veteran lips blending with unschooled ones as he felt the tingle of old shockwaves renewing themselves, felt the boy's electricity as the glossa probed him deep; intense arousal laced with a determining thought, to so overpower and brutalise him as to make it repellent. But he was thwarted, because the response of Michael's body was perfervid, the kiss flourished and Roly was overcome by a calenture he thought long dead: he tasted – oh, let's say it was the taste of Aromas de Montserrat sipped in the heat of the siesta hour in Salamanca's Plaza Mayor or finest Barbados nutmeg sprinkled on an apple charlotte, shall we, my dears? – and he felt a gigantic release, a trapdoor was flung wide, he floated weightless, beyond gravity, unbound and he felt an ineffable tingle, the triumph which only the taste of forbidden fruit can provide. At first Michael's body, the body that was so youthfully robust, had tensed, only to go limp and crumple as the kiss went on. Roly ran his hand through his hair as his passion increased and Michael clung to his shoulder. Roly heard him murmur, low and yes, aching a tad, then he heard his own little voice and saw Muvvie and felt the icy pang; it wasn't only guilt, but something censorious, something that told him this was utterly wrong and it warned him, perhaps for the first time in his life, that he should be responsible and 'do the decent thing'. After a few seconds Michael pulled away, his eyes were that now familiar exophthalmic once more. Brazen astonishment – and he took it to mean, half hoped really, that the boy regretted the kiss instantly, found it sickening, rebarbative. 'What's the matter?' he asked. 'Don't like it?' But Michael was awestruck, struck dumb too, the hackles at the back of his neck rigid (he'd known this sensation before, when he'd kissed a girl, but this was different, so different). Then he puffed out his cheeks and let out a blast of air through pursed lips and spoke. 'Fuck,' he gasped, 'tongues! I couldn't breathe. I didn't want to neither!' The cataglotism had rocked him, literally taken his breath away and Roly knew then that although he may have kissed, *being kissed* was a completely new experience for him. He hates it, he thought. But no, a split second passed, Michael licked his lips, took breath and banged his face awkwardly against his. Michael wanted more, wanted to know more, for with these kisses, Michael realised that he knew very little, very little indeed about wanting and even less about being wanted. Up to then, he'd thought that kissing and erections and sex and even love – that they were all about what you want, but now he realised that wasn't the case, he realised there were two sides to this thing: wanting and being wanted, giving and being given and this kissing, this pressing of Roly's mouth on his, was telling him he liked being given. It had awoken something that had been sleeping, or had created something entirely new, in his brain and as he felt Roly's hand grip the small of his back tighter than before and the other hand cup the back of his head and felt his face squirm into his, he tried to give back, tried by pushing back into him. Each of them now felt the hardened groin of the other rub against him and it was then that Roly finished it. He pushed the boy gently away and it was his turn to sag. 'Oh dear,' he said, aloud but to himself. 'That was probably another mistake, mine not yours.' He let out a deep sigh. 'What *are* we doing? Do we know?' Michael brushed this aside: 'It was good tho' wa'n't it? Ya know, you've got thin lips but you're well brilliant at it,' he said and beamed a great wide satisfied gleeful smile. Roly stroked his cheek. 'Michael, we must stop ourselves. I'll see you tomorrow yes?' 'Ooooooh banjax!' he cried; he was light-headed, riotous.

'Now I gotta go an' 'ave a wank, look!' he declared as he looked down at himself. 'Oh fuck! Oh, what's so wrong with sayin' fuck anyway?' He was abandoned, the kissing, being kissed, being kissed by a *man,* had given him a mania, he was here, he was there, nowhere, everywhere and he jigged a very disorientated jig. Roly tried to quieten him. 'Better go now,' he announced with affectionate resignation. 'Yeah, better had,' said Michael, accepting fate.

When he'd gone, Roly breathed gratitude; he was grateful to the gods that he seemed not to have done any harm and a calmness washed over him. He was sure Michael didn't understand why he hadn't whisked him off to bed there and then but he dismissed that midstream as it were. He was relieved to see his acceptance, or at least his show of it. Michael would now go home and lie on his bed and instead of masturbating, would have, he dared to half hope, gigantic second thoughts. He would reassess and come to the conclusion that what he thought he wanted was a falsehood. This rethinking, this reversion to the status quo would mean the rejection of the homosexual thoughts and leanings he thought he was developing, it would be the end of curiosity about men and it would also facilitate Roly's much-needed get-out, he would no longer find himself pressured into besmirching the boy. They hugged goodbye in the hall and Roly chained the door after him and leant against it, feeling neither honourable nor martyred, but rather base and craven. *I'm doing nothing but making him and me confused. Michael, what phantoms you've roused, what putrid flesh you've dug up. You're craving to be given, given what you think only I can give you, but if I did give you what you want, I would paradoxically be taking from you and I hope I have long ceased to be a taker. Taking has been my downfall and if I take from you it would be yet more self interest, making me yet more irredeemable.* He dragged himself to the sofa and sat semi-comatose but shaking a little, too drained even to make the effort to go to the kitchen and pour himself a whisky, which he desperately needed. He tried to make sense of everything, of this sea of conflicting emotion they had both drifted into and were floundering in. He didn't know how long it was before he was disturbed by a noise, a tinny jingle jangle and for a moment he wondered if the sturm und drang of the day had brought on his tinnitus to an extreme level. It could easily happen. Then he realised it was his mobile phone lying beside him. He picked it up puzzling over who may be ringing him on a phone which was hardly ever in use and saw a text message waiting. *'Will cum tomoz 4 another snog LOL I meant wot I sed It ws gud I WILL WAIT FOR YOU 4 ever.'* Roly slammed the machine down next to him and he laughed, oh how he laughed. How long is 'ever' for someone like Michael?

****

Into every life, it seemed to him, three drops of rain must fall at once. Two had fallen over the past weeks, two huge drops, a flood in fact. In the Manifold Valley, he'd seen his fondly-remembered Spanish master, 'Pedro' Bell, emerge from the bushes and didn't know at the time that what he'd seen was a ghost. Some months before, he'd come upon the FriendsReunited website and had looked in from time to time, looking what the boys whose names he remembered from Trenton Grammar school had written about themselves, curious to see what they were doing 35 years on and, reading their posted reports of the successes and fulfilment of their lives, grudgingly comparing them with the failures of his own. Quipp was there: his profile said that he'd had a book published, damn him. Stephen and Martin, his cherubs

296

from Katie Beans field were married fathers with happy families and successful careers in Gloucester and Norwich and Alistair Witcombe seemed to be likewise situated in Northampton. He posted his own semi-mendacious profile and some time later, he couldn't remember when, but it was certainly after his trip to the Manifold with Michael, he received a message from Leslie Dalloway, who he remembered clearly, an innocuous white blond stripling, he sometimes tagged on to the group of regular Peak District hikers with Pedro and the other teachers, a boy for whom he never had feelings however. Leslie's message said 'Hi, remember me' and went on to tell how he'd been a teacher in the locality all his life. And then the line that ended the final act of the three-act Greek Tragedy that Roly had been a part of for the past few harrowing weeks, so cruelly lapidary: 'Alas Pedro is no longer with us.'

The legacy some of his schoolmasters bequeathed, the imprint they left, was one of hatred, in some cases fear; 'Pedro' had left behind only respect, even love, in the post-High School world. Philip 'Pedro' Bell was posh, from Middlesex, friendly and the boys had warmed to his mild manner readily; he taught them Spanish and opened the beauty of the Peak District to their eyes, taking pleasure in using his weekend free time to impart his love of nature and his wisdom on their long walks; a man who in his retirement had become a leading light in the Trenton Samaritans and whom Roly once rang in one of his bouts of alcoholic melancholy. Now Pedro was dead and, as with his ma and Larry, it was a third party he learned it from. He rang the Samaritans and a kindly man who had known and worked with Pedro there told him the sad story and Roly thanked him and put the phone down and poured himself a whisky and toasted, if that was the word, his third loss in almost as many weeks and felt utterly bereft. His last scions had gone; last parent, last lover, last teacher. Soon, he thought, it would be the last of Roland Hunter.

****

He awoke the next morning and when the fug had cleared from his head and eyes he saw and felt with more than usual clarity how awful it was to be 51. He thought of Horace and his dire ode of passing years and began to recite it to himself, *'Eheu fugaces, Posthume... labuntur anni.'* He thought, I'm an accumulation of years but the years have built nothing. 'I'm deconstructed,' he said, dolefully addressing the mirror on the wall opposite the bed, 'a little man in the end, my littleness attended by so many intimations of greatness.' He thought of Michael and of Youth and he felt... futile, *old*. 'A wonder that I can have any ancestors,' he thought again. 'I could be everyone else's ancestor,' he muttered. 'Where have I heard that before?' (On other mornings, he didn't suffer this mental ritual, on other mornings he would merely look in the mirror and announce: 'I want to forget my existence'). He sat up unenthusiastically, straining with a deep moan and uttering a phrase he had come across somewhere: 'Put on the day like a pair of trousers and wear them til night' and swung himself out of bed. Over his coffee and cigarettes and his shredded wheat, doubt began to creep over him. Yes, kissing Michael – Grand Guignol of the biggest magnitude, a gigantic grotesque mistake, *mea culpa* and now he had to think of a way to stop floundering and leap out of the sea and no, he mustn't entertain any more sexual aspirations or visions of him, must certainly scorn and dismiss any faint possibility that they might go to bed together, must never even touch him again, not even in one of his *matey* hugs. That meant that when he came to tell the boy that there was no future for

298

them, Michael could quite justifiably accuse Roly of breach of promise, such was the surreptitious power he held over him; he was using what had become his infatuation as a way of sanctifying Roly and Roly couldn't, wouldn't tolerate that. He was treating him like some Don Quixote while he was Dulcinea, he was subverting and refuting Roly's role of foolishly dilapidated knight, not because Roly was putting him on the pedestal of virtue and making him angelic, he was that already, but by making *his* Dulcinea idolise *him*. But he, Roly, wasn't riding out to tilt at the windmill devils in cornfields, he was charging at the ones inside him. His immorality meant nothing to Michael, Michael could look beyond it and dismiss it and that made him feel pathetic, Michael was trying to create a marble idol of him out of the morass of cheap and filthy rubble he stood in.

He had no plan, but he must think of one quick, last-ditch offensive. He wouldn't have a shave today, he'd stop shaving altogether. As it was already, he shaved only every three days. He'd make his physical appearance as unappealing as he could, grow his hair to infinity and not shampoo it, so that every time he moved his head there'd be a snowstorm of seborreah flakes around him, neglect to change his briefs, wear the same clothes for days and not go to the loo but sit instead in his own pee. Extreme problems needed extreme solutions, extreme enough to drive the boy away. He thought back to Michael's text message, he'd have to say something about it, thank him for it, at least acknowledge receipt of it.

For the rest of the day, a day Michael had warned him he would be absent for as he'd be in Lyme practising for the forthcoming swimming competition, he attempted a Journal entry, read and tampered with his manuscript, played Sudoku, visited Gaydar and Caffmos, but each time he saw names he thought he felt like chatting with, he either decided against going in or went in and quickly changed his mind and left without a word. He wasn't inclined to perv any profiles either, he could summon no enthusiasm, indeed overall he felt peculiarly enervated and once or twice found his eyelids drooping and had to bolt himself upright to stop himself nodding off. For lunch he had a rice salad which he ate with half a slice of baked ham, ate a pear and afterwards gave up at the computer and put on his CD of, accidentally appropriately he thought, Michelangeli's Chopin recital from Turin in 1963 and flopped on his sofa to listen to it for a while. Siesta finally claimed him at some point and he fell asleep, an unusual occurrence for him and he awoke with no idea of time an hour later, disorientated and to a momentary deathly hush. Then his clock struck the half hour, but Michelangeli had finished playing and he knew he must have slept for an hour or so. He felt a pang of hunger and it took him a moment to remember that he'd eaten recently, so he stirred himself and trundled to the kitchen to satisfy his appetite with a mug of coffee. He drank it, had a cigarette and thought of supper; he'd already decided to make duxelles which he would have with a fillet of sea bass and a roasted halved tomato.

He heard the key turn in the lock as he was clearing away, heard his footfall and his shouted merriness, 'Hiya' and Michael appeared, wearing his white flimsy sweatshirt again, this time over dark blue trackies which had a broad white stripe running the length of the leg, his face still flush red and his hair (when he removed his cap) still water fresh and he looked to Roly overall particularly appealing yet again. He immediately remembered the text message but, not knowing what to say about it, avoided mention of it and asked instead about his swimming practice, at which the boy mentioned a time of some minutes point something which Roly took to mean it had gone well. 'Yeah, we're gonna hammer Cheshire next week,' Michael crowed. Conversation, stilted so far as if between strangers, came to a momentary halt and Roly, feeling he could steer clear from that text message no longer, thanked him for it in a throwaway manner and Michael, not wishing, Roly supposed, to appear 'cheesy' and a 'wuss', said a polite and airy 'S'okay, no probs' and there followed another slightly tense and embarrassing pause which Roly broke with 'Michael?' in a drawn out thoughtful tenor. They intrigued each other; there was something in the air. Then Michael heard him ask something about chatrooms. 'He wants to know about chatrooms!' *What did he mean by these days, hadn't it always been so?* Michael of course knew nothing of the pre-internet era. 'People in 'em… they don't 'ang about gettin' down, you mean,' he said, 'so?' 'It's a generation thing, I suppose,' Roly observed. 'For people like me it takes a lot of getting used to, for your generation it's the way it's always been, it's nothing revolutionary and you don't know any other. To people as old as I am, it can be exciting but sometimes it's too instant, too crude, there's no courtship ritual.' 'I'm not with ya.'

'Thenadays –' Roly went on. 'Thenadays?' 'As opposed to nowadays, Hollis the handsome. Thenadays, in my day you see, we had no internet ghetto, bars and clubs were where we met. And in a bar or club you wouldn't dream of going up to a new face, at least I wouldn't, to ask how big his penis was and whether he had a hairy chest before you asked him if he wanted to go to bed with you. Top and bottom, butch and bitch, hairy and smooth, well-endowed – these things were discovered in private, sometimes, granted, with disastrous results. We had no click buttons on a computer you see, no click and fuck. The internet has taken away surprises, pleasant and unpleasant, removed mystery and anticipation. It has emboldened people, they can be outrageous behind a computer screen without fear of embarrassment, but it has also removed the sacredness, something almost holy and it has removed intimacy. Do you understand what I'm saying?' 'Yeah, right, but we aren't on chat are we?' No he didn't understand at all, why should he? 'Er, no that's true,' Roly conceded and for an instant ended his line of argument. Then he resumed: 'You've seen those profiles, every detail of what people are looking for and what they think they have to offer has to be listed, like an inventory. It's like stripping off in public, naked advertising, everybody must match up and it's all purely physical: big cock, cut or uncut, hairy chest, bears, twinks, cute, straight-acting, tv, cd – all labels and not what people *are.'* 'I know what you're like though and you know what I am, so.' It was useless to expostulate with him, he was too ingenuous and it disarmed him, making him so charming. 'Oh bloody hell,' he said, frustrated now, he wasn't saying what he'd earlier planned briefly to say, he'd lost his thread. 'Listen,' he said, summoning some authority. 'Many young men who are into older men, the daddy lovers, God help us... their daddy must be hairy, they all seem to be fixated with body hair for some reason. Do you crave body hair, Michael? Does old men's hair provide a security, a comfort you need? I don't have much myself.' What was he doing? Was this his way of trying to 'put Michael off' him, the tactic he'd outlined to himself yesterday? If when the boy saw his naked body and his enthusiasm was dampened by such an insignificant flaw as lack of hair, he would probably be relieved. Roly was only confusing himself, body hair wasn't what he wanted to discuss at all. 'Heaven and earth!' This was part of the burden of responsibility Michael had manoeuvred him into carrying. He needn't have wasted his breath, Michael showed nothing but a matter-of-fact response to any of what he'd just said. 'I 'adn't really thought about it to be honest,' looking at him as though the lights had gone out.

****

'The business', Michael had called it – making love or, in his case, having sex; the business. He had never, as far as he could recall, referred to 'making love', he said 'shag' more often than not, such an unfeeling word. It repeated in his head and disconcerted him. Michael didn't picture the path that led towards his first conjugation as a rose-strewn one trodden to the sound of flutes, he saw only the fulfilment of some purely solipsistic purpose. He was merely desperate to lose his cherry and by calculation or fluke he had found in him the man to take it, or so he thought. He was his agent of ritual, nothing more. 'If there was ever the chance it would be me, it would have to be because you *want me*,' he said to him at the time, continuing to be contentious. ' 'Course I want you to do it,' Michael said. 'Whaddya think I'm waitin' for?' 'You're waiting for somebody, anybody.' 'Whaddya mean by that, d'ya think I'm dissin' you or somethin'? I could've 'ad a million shags by now. You wanna see the messages I been gettin', specially after I went on that Silverdaddies.' 'What did you call it?' 'Like what?' 'You called it "the business", making it sound like a deal, when it should be something… blessed and precious.' 'Sheesh, behave will ya? That's me innit? I 'aven't got the words like you.' 'If you don't see it the way I do, Michael, it won't work. I promise you, I won't be able to do it. There must be feeling, meaning. I shall be taking something very precious from you, but you must want to give it and give it to *me*. I'm not a sex machine, something you can wind up and kick start.' 'Whatever.' Perhaps indifference was his protection; it enabled him to hide any commitment. 'Don't be cheesy, 'course it means somethin'. It's you I want. To do it I mean.' This grated on his worn ears, irked; the sound of a boy trying too hard to convince himself. 'You not gonna wimp out on me are ya?' he asked, but Roly kept quiet.

The day of the inter-county swimming contest came and it would be the day when it was useless to gainsay Michael's allure any longer, the day he'd be finally, if he'd not been before, in its thrall. Ever the slave of turpitude, he allowed himself to be persuaded and he caved in; he knew he was on the brink of committing a wicked mistake but his yielding, come the hour, would be awash with whisky and soda and that would mitigate him. He and Yvette drove to the Northwich pool where the contest was being held and from their seats in the gallery they cheered their Olympian loudly, Roly inwardly slavering over the sight of Michael's powerful taut body cutting through the water like some speeding boat and when he came first in the crawl and second in the relay and raised his fist and smiled broadly in triumph, Roly felt his joy in his soul and celebrated as though victory was his own. As Michael stepped up to the platform to receive his medals, Yvette looked down with pride and he with admiration and lust and as they applauded, Roly felt a gentle nudge in his ribs and heard Yvette whisper something in his ears which was astonishing in its ambiguity and suggestion. 'Roly, 'e told me 'e wanted to do it for you,' she said. They drove home and when Roly left them at their door, Michael leaned into the car and asked, 'You up for tonight yeah?' and Roly, without thinking anything of it, said, 'I'll be in.'
For supper, he poached a chicken breast in stock flavoured with a shallot, a bay leaf and a sprig of thyme for 10 minutes

and left it to infuse in the liquor for another 30. He had it with oven chips, marrowfat peas and redcurrant jelly, the latter made by a lady in Crewe and sold at the farm shop round the corner. Michael turned up two hours later and when he took off his treasured cap, revealed hair that looked specially groomed for the occasion. He had superdressed in immaculate white pants and a navy blue top and looked trig. He was still on level nine after his swimming triumphs and when their talk moved tentatively close to the *intime* and he begged, 'Why can't I just sleep with ya?', his exuberance put him in the position where to deny him would have been a monstrous act by even his own louche values. 'I don't care if nothin' 'appens, honest, we can 'old each other or turn over and go to sleep or… I just want to.. I mean it'd be so cool just to be, ya know, with you… in the same –' and Roly cut him short and shook his head in long-suffering disbelief. 'You have no idea what you're suggesting, my sweet swimmer. What, you lying aching and me not doing anything? You'll never be able contain your urges, you'll go mad.'

He illustrated his argument and attempted to put Michael off the idea by pointedly and graphically recounting nights when he'd found himself in bed with various straight boys he'd befriended and intended to seduce, boys from the Middlesex Post, boys who had found themselves at the 'wrong' disco, boys at parties; he described the agony of being next to someone, desperate to make love when that someone was not, his body creaking with frustration, not daring to make a move, or if he did dare and reached out to touch, hoping that the boy was asleep or pretending sleep, or if he was awake, hoping that he thought his move an involuntary reflex. 'I don't think so, Michael, do you?' he posited. 'They were insufferable nights and I wouldn't wish the same for you.' 'It won't be like that for you and me though will it? I mean, if you touch me... I'm not gonna pretend to be asleep or tell you to gerroff am I? And are you gonna push *me* away? I want to Roly, just sittin' 'ere talkin' about it gives me the –' 'We're talking about sleeping together, Michael, not sex. And remember the pisspot,' he reminded him, hoping the lavatorial aspect of sharing a bed with an old man would mean repugnance getting the better of his libido. But Michael had a ready counter to that as to all his attempted vetos. 'That's cool,' he said. 'Leave the pisspot in the toilet and when you want a piss, I'll take you,' and after some debate and toing and froing and the gradual dissolution of his resistance in the face of eager pleading and cajoling Roly, before he knew it, had capitulated. So on the night of the poached chicken and Michael's immaculate white pants, Roly went to bed first and nestled under the duvet and waited. He shouted to Michael to turn everything off and shut down the flat, then watched him come in. 'Don't strip naked,' he ordered and averted his gaze as he undressed, 'leave your boxers on' and he did as he was told before hurling himself down on the bed next to him, making huggling snuggling movements and noises as he settled. Roly switched off the bedside lamp and they lay on their backs for what seemed to both like hours, Roly remembering the times he'd talked about and Michael petrifying with apprehension of the unfamiliar, Roly trapped in a black cavern, waiting for either release or death, Michael wondering what lay within the cavern's mouth. He felt Michael's tension and suspense, how unbearable it must be for him, until at last he heard his breathing pass into the regular sibilance of a sleeper. To be sure the boy was sleeping he spoke. 'So hold me,' he whispered, expecting no reaction but was then startled when Michael turned to face him and reached out and dropped a warm hand onto his thigh, obliging him to do the boy the kindness at least of offering him the opportunity for some relief. 'Not like that, hold me,' he said. 'What you mean?' He stayed quiet. 'You mean, hold your –?' 'Yes.' 'You mean it?' 'Yes,' he rasped. 'Get on with it.' He felt the tentative grasp. 'Now,' he said, 'if you want to masturbate you can.'

He awoke to Michael still fast asleep, lying on his side facing him, he watched and he marvelled. His face was a mere breath away and he wanted desperately to move his own a solitary inch and kiss his mouth – *He wants to be my boy* – but he let him be, left him to curr. After some moments he was aware of his bursting bladder and sat up carefully to swing himself to the side of the bed and empty himself into the pisspot, then he lay back down to watch over his tranquil Adonis. How long he didn't know but, suddenly, the eyes in the sleeping face shot open, two huge black orbs of startled disorientation. Recognition and memory dawned gradually and it was a good few seconds until Michael was fully aware of where he was and who Roly was and then, without a word he shuffled his body into Roly's and threw his arms around his shoulders. Now Roly was the startled one, not least because he could feel the boy's morning erection pressing into him. Michael buried his face deep into the crook of his neck and clung on and Roly heard a long baritone murmur ooze from him. He put one arm around the boy's back and they lay like that, rigid, neither speaking. Then, Michael threw his head back and fixed Roly with his stare again, questingly now and his mouth opened and a question came, softly. 'Do I belong to you now?' he asked. Roly stared back at him hard. '*Belong* to me? Wha..? I... *belong* to me? Do you want to belong to me?' Michael gave no answer but swiftly thrust his head back deep into Roly's neck again and at length let out a low muffled 'Yes' and squeezed and clung again. 'I wanna be your boy.' Roly was propelled by an irresistible force and lifted the boy's face and kissed him and when he felt his response made the kiss impassioned. He couldn't help himself; he rolled on top of him, his mouth stuck to his, his tongue deep. He could feel the boy's body accepting. He pressed his cheek to his. 'I want you again,' he said in a raw whisper, kneading his flesh. 'Like last night again?' Michael asked. 'Yes. I want to be inside you again like I was last night. I want to fill your sweet cavum pueris.' 'Did I shock you by giving you so much?' he asked. 'Did you know I'm a bottomless well, that the more you drink from me the more I can give you to drink? I never run dry. Now I'm really yer bitch,' he said through clenched teeth. 'You futtered me, you swived me as befits a lovely young hunk.' 'You liked it didn't you?' 'Liked it? 'Course I liked it. It was... I never... never imagined...' 'Imagined?' 'Like it was like that, so... ooooh... so... immense.' 'You're my boy, that's what you are and your epagoge is finally over, you have passed through experience into knowledge.' 'So I'm your fuckboy now?' 'Far more than that.' 'Hmm,' he said and stopped to ponder. 'I squealed when you were... banjaxin' me,' he giggled under his breath. 'I heard that,' Roly said, squeezing his neck and making him chortle more. 'And you didn't squeal, you moaned in rapture. And you've had sex with a murderer.'

At which point he did wake up; Michael was lying on his right side facing away from him. His full bladder really did need emptying – *Must micturate before it's too late* – and he aimed into the real pisspot and when he finished he stood up and gazed down on the sleeping Michael and swore mutely at his antic hypnopompic illusions while he wondered just how bewildered the boy was and he went out of the room. He was at the computer when he heard Michael stir and get dressed. 'Morning,' he said when he went into him. 'Yo,' said Michael, squinting. 'Did you sleep well?' 'Great. Thanks for.' 'For what? What thanks?' 'For... ya know... lettin' me stay.' He made no move to mention the brush with carnality they'd had and Roly also thought it best not to comment for fear of embarrassing, or worse, shaming the boy. 'It was lovely having you here.' 'Was it?' He sounded surprised and performed one of his softshoe shuffles and touched the wall with his finger to draw an invisible doodle. His eyes were pensive and his lips and dimple moved faintly to indicate the kind of apprehensive inquiry Roly had seen before. 'Can we, can we do it again?' he asked warily. Roly leaned back in the swivel chair. 'Let's put the canary down the mine,' he said equivocally. 'What's that supposed to mean?' Roly smiled. Michael took his finger from the wall and let his arm fall straight beside his body, as the other one was, he ceased his shuffle and stood momentarily like a young cadet at sloppy attention. 'K,' he said, compliantly. 'I better go.' 'Yes.' 'Laters.' 'A tout à l'heure, marvellous Michael and don't fret pet,' he spread his face into an uncharacteristic and supercilious beaming smile and held him with widened eyes. 'All things shall be well and all manner of things shall be well,' he sang. Michael, not understanding, leant forward and Roly, understanding both what he'd said and Michael's movement, reached out to him and they hugged. 'Mates?' Michael asked. 'Mates.' Michael pulled away and looked hard at him. 'You're cool, ya know.' 'Cool,' Roly echoed, hollow-voiced. 'A gas, fab, groovy, swinging.' 'No. I mean, I mean... ya know... you don't need Levitra at all for...' 'Oh don't I? That was nothing,' he said, with a mock glowering look. 'A rod of iron will be required for more...' He grabbed the arms of his chair to help hoist himself to his feet, '...penetrating affairs,' he said, sotto voce. Michael looked blank in return for a moment then spun round and called 'See ya later' from the hall and Roly called back and looked out at the summer morning and gazed lazily up at the strands of cirrus floating across their cerulean backdrop above the nursery and housetops. He felt oddly buoyed by the night's adventure and the figment played in his mind of doing what the boy wanted on his birthday after all. 'Muvvie could hardly ruin that for me could she?' he asked. 'Not while I was in the throes of esctasy, ruling the universe, with god kissing my feet.' Then he shuddered and he wished, mightily wished, that he hadn't been such a recreant and could have made that hug just now a goodbye hug.

****

The picture of a Michael triumphant, victor ludorum, with his team made it to the back page of the local freesheet, Michael called to present Roly with a copy and he stayed to share Roly's bed for another night, at his own fervent request. 'I'm not into one night stands,' he quipped as he stroked Roly's head in supplication and Roly acceded to what he felt was his better judgement, whatever that was and mitigated himself: allowing the boy into his bed again was his tribute to the boy's success. 'Mum wants to know what yer doin' for Christmas.' That time already! 'Don't *you* want to know what I'm doing?' he asked. 'Okay you know what I mean and I know what you're doin' – nothin, yeah? – but she said – ' Roly, anticipating an invitation, cut him off firmly saying that he was grateful for Yvette's kind thought, but. 'But what?' 'My loathing of Commercialmas is well-known, my dear and I've spent years nurturing it. I hope you and your family all have a wonderful time with lots of presents. I shan't be giving any and I don't expect to get any and I mean that. If you or Yvette even think about buying anything for me I shall roast

310

you over an open fire, baste you with hot Béarnaise sauce and feed you to next door's cat.'

Which is how he came to be, on Christmas Day, sitting in an armchair in Yvette's parents' house in the nearby village of Halmerend, digesting a turkey dinner prepared by caring, if, in his opinion, amateur hands and watching *Shrek* on the television. He drank soft drinks, refusing all offers of alcohol all afternoon. When his hosts suggested he take a glass of the supermarket Shiraz that was on offer at table, he thanked them and said, as gracefully as he could, 'One is too many and ten isn't enough.' An aphorism he felt fell on stony ground, indeed Grandad gave him a look to invoke the devil when he came out with it, but one which he nevertheless adhered to with fortitude.

****

Michael's birthday was a month away and by many almost daily furtive hints and sly comments he was making it clear that he was counting down the days. He eventually assembled the hints into a formula and an evening came when he announced that he had a plan. Nothing had been mutually decided nor even discussed, he'd decided their objective was a mutual given, that no consultation was required and assumed that Roly's wish for fulfillment was as great as his. Roly, on the other hand, had the now familiar feeling that he'd been manoeuvred once more into a trap. Michael delivered his strategy pat, he was like a sergeant major reading out the drill, brooking no objections, eschewing all causality. He cast Roly as lord of the manor, offerering him *ius primae noctis*, but not a virgin under duress, rather a willing one. On the eve of his birthday, Michael said, he would 'tell me mum I'm stoppin' over again'. They would watch DVDs, drink Fanta and eat chocolate, 'all cosy like on the sofa'; he might even, if it was okay with Roly,

311

bring a couple of cans of lager to drink: 'Only two though, I don't wanna get munted and useless.' They were to wait until Roly's new wall clock struck midnight, 'then nobody can't say I'm not legal and you can't get done as a pedo, as if I'm gonna tell anybody anyway' and they would then go to bed 'and do the business yeah.' 'You make it sound like you're taking your driving test,' Roly said. Michael thought about that for a moment and then perked up: 'Yeah, that's right. I'm still a learner and you're my instructor. D'ya think I'll pass?' And he gave Roly one of the slyest smiles he'd yet seen him give, a smile of a hundred recondite meanings. Roly chose not to take issue with his idea save to caution him. 'Just don't cook your rabbit before it's caught,' he said. 'What's that supposed to mean?' he asked and he genuinely didn't know.

****

Birthday Eve duly arrived and passed into Birthday Day, Deflowering Day and the day that followed was shrouded in the blackest melancholy. He found he could do time travel when, by means of some cerebral machine, he went back over the five years prior to the event, years of sanguinity, of resigned acceptance of his physical inadequacy. Then his whirlwind, his teenage hurricane had swooped – a boy who hadn't even reached his sexual peak yet! (The experts would have it that one like him still had a year or so to go to attain that), a boy who attained legal age but who was still a sexual and emotional toddler. Yet it took but a snap of his fingers to snare Roly and Roly knew the trap was there and still he walked into it, imagining as he walked, that lust was strong enough to overcome physical dysfunction.

And on Birthday Eve, Michael arrived, delectable and fragrant and eager for midnight. He brought lager and drank it and asked tantalising questions and Roly put his mouth in his ear and whispered, 'We will coddle and futter. I'll enter the cavum pueris amoris and futter you in silk and sugar, mio Michelangelo maschio. It'll be supernal.' 'I don't know what you're talkin' about mister man,' said the boy. 'Is it some kind of special language that I gotta learn?' And they kissed for forever and Roly whispered more and when their lips parted, his mind's eye saw sculptures of Priapus with enormous, ithyphallic genitalia standing in gardens and fields, guaranteeing an abundant crop for the people. He saw the epigrams showing Priapus using sodomy as a threat towards transgressors of the boundaries he protected: *I warn you, my lad, you will be sodomised; you, my girl, I shall futter; for the thief who is bearded, a third punishment remains. If I seize you, you shall be so stretched that you will think your anus never had any wrinkles.* They didn't sit intently watching or listening to the clock, though Roly was aware of the augury of its tick, not even when midnight was just a minute or so away and when it came, the chime took them both by surprise, Roly the more so, because it was a chime that told him this was beyond all imagining what he'd bought the clock for. He kissed the Birthday Boy, who heard something about 'the morning of your manhood' and with no further ado, told him to stand up and take off everything but his boxers and he did as he was bid and stood there, a kouros. A statue before me, Roly thought, not a body, no human body is so perfect; it's a figure, sculpted with chisels of wildest imagination, pure fantasy and he stood and moved around the boy to caress him from behind, to cajole the body. 'How are you feeling?' and his reply was a groan of content, deep and long. 'Oh, yes. This is it, the time yes,' he said and his slight body tremor stopped and the man who had asked the question felt him go limp and pressed him to him and ran his hands all over his torso and murmured, 'My prince, my kouros.' 'Kouros,' the boy repeated' 'Ssshh, it's a compliment,' said the man. 'You're my statue from the ancient world, deliciously and desirably draped. Is this all for me?' he asked, still gliding his hands over this, his own, living statue and the boy breathed, 'Yes.' 'And I can do what I want with you?' The boy reached behind and squeezed and giggled and the squeeze and the giggle were bravado to hide his nervousness, because now that he stood in the vulnerability of near nakedness, youth's arrogant mandate had evaporated and he cried out in a pained voice, 'I don't know what to do.' There was nothing the man wanted less than he should feel frightened and he whispered, 'You will know' and placed his hand on the front of the boxers.

'Michael?' 'Yes?' 'Is it what you want?' 'Yes it is... I mean, I think so.' 'You think so?' 'I mean... yes, I want it... It's kind of what I've been thinking about... I mean, it's what you do intit?' 'Yes, what queers do, some of them, some of the time. But don't you want to yourself?' At first he didn't understand, then he saw: 'What, me? Me do it you mean?' 'Yes.' 'No way... I mean... no, I want to... I want you to... I want to take it.' 'Go and put on the briefs, I want you spatchcocked,' he murmured.

In the bedroom, in Priapus' field, Michael lay, no kouros now, but very much a vibrant thing, on his back on *his* bed with the white briefs, the 'tighty whities', fighting to contain the obtruding flesh. 'Your massif central,' Roly called it. His right arm lay straight along his body and his left was curled up behind him so that his head rested on his hand. He looked expectant, a little apprehensive, but there was a subtle half-smile on his face. His legs were stretched out long and straight and Roly looked at the white triangle of fabric nestling prominently between them. He lay down next to him and touched the now familiar granite and whispered, 'Almost a sin to remove it and spoil the picture.' He stroked with gentle fingers. 'Michael, I have to ask you again.' 'What?' 'Are you absolutely sure you want to do this?' Michael let out a deep sigh, moved both arms and rested his hands on the back of Roly's shoulders and looked straight at him. 'Roly, I gotta tell *you* again,' he said with slight exasperation, 'I want to do it, I really do.' Roly smiled and looked down again and addressed the white triangle, 'A beautifully wrapped gift,' he said, 'all for me' and Michael made a soft sound of agreement and stood and Roly peeled the briefs away from his body and as he stretched them, the flesh sprang up and leapt out at him panther-like and he had to say something and 'The wand of youth,' was what he said, as though thinking aloud and he gave a deep salacious giggle which Michael misconstrued. 'What's so funny?' he asked fearfully, alarmed. 'Nothing funny,' said Roly reassuringly, looking up at him. 'Nothing funny at all.' He looked back down and reached out his hand to caress and savour the textures and felt the rock hard core in its warm, silken flesh, the glorious length of young rigid muscle wrapped in its skin of lust. 'Foolish men like me live for this … we worship it and we destroy ourselves for it.'

****

The success of the long-awaited night, oh my dears, was qualified and that is putting it kindly. Naked, (the first time Roly had *seen* him naked), Michael positively glowed, he was peach-curved and sleek, rampant but receptive. He coped well with Roly's flawed mobility, his clumsiness, his hobbling around, his struggle to position himself, to manoeuvre and he made no allusion whatsoever to the bedside pisspot. The boy who was confidently feral in the

315

world was transformed by the intimacy of the bedroom into a creature of obedience, craving domination, relishing it. 'Oh Jesus!' he cried and Roly lifted his head from between the hairless legs and said 'Penilinctus. It's not in the dictionary but it's what's giving you your paroxysms' and he had hardly time to taste the sweet flesh further and riffle through the lush pubescence (soft and warm, like nutria) with his fingers before Michael climaxed (quick, but so what?) with a loud 'Wow' and Roly drank. Then, rested, recovered, rejuvenated, the boy's body writhed anew to Roly's practised anilinctus. 'If ever Hebe smiled on a boy, she smiled on you,' he told him. But… well, perhaps he was less adroit than he'd always liked to think, perhaps the stroke had been more debilitating than he dreaded, perhaps he no longer had the technique he fondly imagined he once did. He'd been conservative, perhaps not adventurous enough, only ever the missionary position; adventure came with lithe long-limbed Mark in… in *that* city for a while, the boy who introduced him to riding, the same once or twice with Larry, but he'd never been hampered like this before, not ever, and perhaps he'd watched too many porn films – thinking he could be the athlete stud, thinking it was what Michael would expect, demand. He told him to get on all fours again and he licked and fingered some more and the boy's body writhed again. Success was imminent. His serene body belied impatience while Roly used the spray behind him, hiding, explaining the curse of premature ejaculation and that made the boy snigger for a moment. 'Old men need all the 'elp they can get,' he joked. Some said it was good to laugh during sex; he wasn't so sure. 'I was hoping you'd want me to last out a bit.' When he asked, 'Are you ready?' and heard the murmured 'Yes', he'd expected uncertainty, perhaps anxiety, but heard and sensed determined compliance and empathised with the boy's awed anticipation, the exquisite pain that was seconds away and he felt pandered. He pressed his head against the atrium.

And he failed him, oh how he failed. Flaccidity, the inability to penetrate, the sighs, sorries, moans, tut tuts, 'never minds', 'don't matters' – uttered by both of them in varied mollifying tones, but all sounding harsh, full of bitterness and regret and shame, shame for him. In short, my dears, Roly could do nothing but offer amends by whipping him over onto his back and treating him to another wordless helping of oral pleasure, feeling abject the while. When they lay back, unable to find any more excuses, Michael's solicitude tore into him: 'S'okay, it 'appened to me. Me an' Tracy tried an' she laughed in me face. You think about it too much an' you can't do it, yeah?' *Oh please, out-of-the-mouths-of-babes-and-sucklings percipience from a suckling, a fledgling, isn't to be borne*. He was either being kind or the last pleasure had smothered his annoyance and frustration. Roly broke a golden rule, he'd given up smoking in bed a long time ago, but he needed nicotine and told the boy to fetch his cigarettes. 'Maybe you're right. You need a dick pill.' Michael was jovial when he came back in. 'That'll do it for ya next time.' 'After that you think there'll be a next time?' He lay back down on the bed and propped his head on his arm, locking his eyes onto Roly's and what hurt, what stung was that there was no sign of disappointment on his face: at which, he jumped up in his turn and, although he felt a complete bedraggled fool, a wet dishcloth, standing unsteadily at the foot of the bed in his flaccid nakedness, he harangued him: '... told you I was pathetic... men out there forming queues for you... hundreds of them waiting with their stiff greased cocks in their hands only too eager to pork a just legal lilywhite like you...' There was no excuse for the vitriol, caused as it was by having a succulent submitting 16-year-old body lying on his bed, aching to be ravished and he powerless. The only thing he could do was to use his belittlement to belittle him, to be thoroughly caddish. He thought Michael reddened at his eruption and more's the pity that this boy, of all boys, had to be the recipient of venom. The two back in Bleakridge he could dismiss, because, to be honest, handsome as they were, they hadn't come anywhere near to his ideal. He was a dead man now and felt the more mortified because of the maturity of Michael's response. 'Chill Roly mate, it's okay' – soothing words for him, probably the most heartfelt consolation he could muster and given sincerely. 'Oh Michael,' he was wailing by now and suffused, surely he wasn't as angry with him as he was with himself? *What a bastard I am.* 'You know... you know you're the... the key... my key to the Paradise gate. How can I handle that, how can I?' He collapsed into the corner chair. 'This can't be, it cannot. I DON'T DESERVE YOU. I have no right to you, I have no right to happiness, don't you see?' Michael collapsed too, back onto the pillow, breathing out deep exasperation. 'What the fuck,' he sighed. 'What is it you done so wrong Roly? What's with all this guilt stuff? I don't give a toss what you done.' For a split second he wanted to cry out and remind him, "I killed an old lady twenty-five years ago! I'm a murderer, hasn't that sunk into your woollen brain!?" Instead, 'Oh Michael, the things I've done, the earth would quake to look on them and if I told you about them it would harrow up your soul. I haven't the heart to tell you, I thought I had but no,' was all he could manage. Michael sat back up. 'Ang on a minute,' he said, 'somethin's not right. Are you sayin' you're such a rotten person you don't deserve to have sex any more?' That was straight through the heart. 'Why's that suddenly got to ya, stoppin' ya? It never did before did it? Two 'undred and fifty you said you've shagged, so what's wrong with me? I mean, it's not like you're rapin' me or somethin'. I wanna do this, you're not makin' me, right? I wanna do it. Why can't you get that?' He had no conception, of being in the same room as a murderer, of penile dysfunction, of its underlying medical causes and certainly not the emotional ones: 'You've seen what's happened,' Roly said weakly. 'It's me intit?' came the response. You don't like me in bed. I'm no good 'cos I don't know what to do.' He was sounding almost tearful. How could such a peerless being imagine he could be anything other than desired, in bed or out of it? Useless to ask, useless to explain, what a pathetic first night adventure for the poor boy, a dream could not be in more tatters, he must get over it and go from him. 'Of course I fancy you,' he hissed through clenched teeth. 'Yeah, you get an 'ard on but that's just you gettin' yourself off on a boy intit? Closin' yer eyes and... I could be anybody... 'Odge, d'ya fancy him instead? Do ya?' The knife was turned and it went on cutting; the first wound wasn't always the deepest. 'Michael, you are so wrong.' 'So tell me you still fancy me.' 'I can tell you that a thousand times, yes, I want you, I want your body, but I can't have it the way we both want can I? Look at what's just happened, or hasn't.' Michael slapped his thigh, his eyes alight. 'I'm gonna get that Levitra off 'im, just you wait,' he announced shrilly and threw himself back with petulant force, a boy who had not got his way and was angry with the injustice of the world. They remained silent for what seemed an age, a palpitating panting silence, until Michael's quiet treble piped softly, 'Are you comin' back 'ere or stayin' there all night?'

Somehow they went to sleep friends, Roly not believing that Michael, or his raging and thwarted hormones, could forgive him. He was upset, yes and disappointed beyond measure, of that he had no doubt and he was so so wretched. He wrapped his arms around him by way of placating him, fearing it was doing nothing at all. After a while, he felt his body trembling, he thought he was crying. He was about to say something comforting when the murmured query came, floating, almost disembodied, out of the pillows: 'What's it taste like?' 'What?' 'What's it taste like? Is it like milk?' The trembling Roly felt was sniggering and he, too, now laughed. 'There's a Caribbean dish,' he replied, giggling into his neck and squeezing him for dear life, 'and it's called… ha ha… it's called jerk… ha ha… jerk chicken. It tasted like chicken,' and they both exploded. 'But I suppose you… arehahahaha… you are… hehehe… jizz chicken.' Like a cobra striking, lightning quick, Michael swung himself round to face him and eased him by the shoulders onto his back. 'I 'aven't dun it to you 'ave I? Shall I 'ave a go? Jus' don't laugh. I 'ope I can get it in me mouth that's all.' Roly stared at him wide-eyed, disbelieving, so unexpected was the offer. His doing that would be subjection, as though he was the one at fault, he was the one making amends. *It's wrong, he owes me nothing.* Yet if he told him not to do it, would he feel even more undesired? Before he could decide or speak, Michael lowered his willing head: 'I can't swallow like you,' he said, before his mouth touched and covered. So he made sure to give him warning and pull him off in time and yes, it was a novice's effort, but no less relief for that. In the morning, what could he do about his waking erection but empty his bursting bladder and return to bed and give Michael a special oral birthday present? And Michael, on his back, sighed dreamingly emptied at the ceiling. He dressed without washing, refused food or drink and made to go swiftly. It seemed he couldn't wait to get away from the scene of the débâcle but then again, Roly thought... that selfless act. *What am I to think?* As he left, he confounded Roly further with a hug and a brushed kiss on his lips: 'I'm gonna get that Levitra for ya,' he whispered and Roly wanted to cry.

When he'd gone, the flat was eerily quiet, a vacuum. The morning after he met Larry was as vivid as the view from his window. He walked along the Fulham Road and the day sang in the new Easter sunshine while the flagstones danced and leapt up to meet his feet walking above them; he was free and impregnable, floating past shop windows of mannequins and jewellery and cuts of meat and travel posters and telling them all that he was in love. How crazily different it was now. He had the carnal knowledge of Michael to boast of, but he felt no victory, only emptiness. He felt no increase of happiness, no fulfilment of the spirit. Knowing Michael and his body hadn't enriched him and there was no salvation.

****

He had once hoped – it seemed an ancient hope now – that the previous hug, the one on the morning after they'd shared a chaste bed together, might have been a farewell. But Michael was his carer as well as his aspiring lover and this meant his continuing with his domestic duties and chores. He came and jaunty as ever he was, the complete contrast to Roly's glowering curmudgeon and he went about as though nothing had gone amiss and omitted any reference, whether through reticence or coyness or remorse, to their new-found status as sexual familiars. Roly, too, feared to broach, to confront, even attempt to work out the bones of their new relationship. He was at a loss to know where they were and what they were: friends, mates, master and servant, lovers, thwarted lovers? Perhaps Michael now

321

wanted to erase the whole sorry episode from his thoughts. Silence and denial would preserve their sanity, or at least keep disturbing feelings and doubts and uncertainties suppressed. He did notice, however, that the boy was wearing a black jacket with a hood and dark bottoms and he thought the stark figure he cut may be widow's weeds, mourning for impotence. He sat in the computer room and let Michael get on, but after a while the boy's apparently oblivious or indifferent behaviour got the better of him. 'I ruined your birthday and your initiation and I didn't think you'd ever want to see me again,' he shouted, more blurted, to him in the kitchen. Michael heard him, dropped what he was doing and came to the door. 'Look, I know you got problems, but I bet we can... I mean, what I mean is, I'm sure you're gonna be able to with the Levitra stuff.' His understanding tone threw Roly off balance yet again. 'Give me a bit o' time yeah?' *He can wait?* 'I told you I'll get some. 'Odge knows 'is dad's uses it an' 'e's gonna pinch some.' From 15 to 16, a few days older and an age wiser, what overnight maturescence had come to him with only a single taste of the flesh and that a flawed one? 'You know it's my fault and not yours don't you Michael? I'm as bewildered as you. I'm fantatical for you and helpless. I'm the dampener not you, I want you to understand that.' He smiled, but he was so serious. 'We 'ad sex didn't we? Okay it wasn't a full shag, but. All I know is, I wanna lose it and I'm gonna lose it with you. Sorted.' His calm clear vision inflated Roly's resentment, inflamed the bitterness over the injustice of what his stroke had caused to both of them and the self-abuse that caused the stroke and he was close to boiling over. 'I bin thinkin',' Michael said. 'And?' 'When you couldn't –. 'Is it 'cause I've never taken it? Am I too tight for ya? So, 'ow can I, ya know... 'ow do I make it so you can go in easy?' Oh this innocence, this naivety gone mad. 'And don't be a mother and tell me to get a cucumber!' 'I'm sorry Michael,' Roly spluttered weakly and then, composing himself, 'Too tight! That's not the problem, you twerp, it's *my* problem and it's psychological. I have to not want too hard to do it, but. Oh this is crazy,' he moaned. 'Oh for other times,' he sighed. 'Ou sont les neiges d'antan and all that, what d'ya say my little filament? If only we could have been where we are now before I went and had a stroke. Dashed inconvenient eh what?' 'Like I care about yer stroke. You can get... you know... I've seen it haven't I? Ya just need a bit more help.' He went up to him, grabbed him and growled playfully. 'Wait 'til I get that Levitra... phwoar... we'll be doin' it all night, just see.'

On a Sunday evening, early, after days of regretful, remorseful analysis and after he'd had a good feast, had pushed the boat out for it – peppered rib of beef and a pudding of lemon curd, blueberries and crushed lavender leaves, port cream and shortbread biscuits – he had a sudden mad urge to go to church. He was a murderer and he wanted to go to church, the church of his (relative) sinless youth, but he wouldn't go to confess, not to the minister anyway, Methodist ministers were not versed and the Methodist church didn't pursue, the ritual of confession and absolution. If he were to confess, it would be to the old faces he'd possibly see, faces from the days back when who would now be old like him, and he'd pull them to one side, they'd be delighted to see him, or pretend to be, after all the years; 'There's something I have to tell you,' he'd say and he'd sit them down and confess to them. So he mustn't turn up drunk and morbid, they'd frown on that, oh they'd sympathise with him, but that would be all they'd do, they wouldn't understand; no, if he was going to confess to his one-time coevals in religion, he must be sober, clear-headed, know exactly what he was saying and doing so that they'd know and not dismiss him politely as a sad drunken, hopeless case for whom there really was no help, save from Jesus, Jesus would save, so it was out of their hands and in the Saviour's. Pass the buck to a higher authority. (He wouldn't mention to them that an angel saviour had already found him and was trying his damnedest with him). Would there be anyone he still knew and who knew him there? And could a gap of 30-odd years be bridged? Did friendships, albeit false and fragile friendships, survive the intervening vicissitudes? Liz Butcher might be there; she didn't like him, she'd worked in the solicitor's office which had handled the business of Muvvie and Sam and the letters and so she'd known all along that he was a thief and a murderer; she'd remember him and would be 'nice' and pseudo-friendly, but she'd be anxious to get away from him, nervous, she was a timid woman, always was, big on Christian theory but short on the practice; love the sinner, hate the sin was a nice idea, an ideal, but not a philosophy for living, not in the prim and proper and prudish spinster Butcher house, where charity began at home and stayed there, secluded. They were good women, the Butcher sisters, no doubt of that, but only if you were good too; they could forgive anything except sin.

No, he thought not, he thought he wouldn't go to church.

****

Shropshire dry-cured bacon and pork and garlic sausages from the speciality shop in Lyme, more things from Morrisons and when they got home, Michael cleared out the big cupboard and tidied and Roly cooked the bacon and sausages with beans and fried potatoes – to hell with cholesterol levels. Michael had been eating three or four

324

times a week with him by now, always insisting on paying half for the ingredients and very complimentary about the food and Roly was delighted that there was a little of the foodie in him, a rare attribute, he supposed, for a teenager; sitting at table together added conviviality to the already sensual dimension of their friendship (he would still not call it relationship) and Michael was useful, in view of the deleterious effect of Roly's strokes on his taste buds, for giving him an honest answer about what and how much he could taste to reassure him that he still had the art. 'I can't fuck but I can still cook.' 'Stop that.'

While they were waiting for the Levitra to materialise, the drug of his fond hopes, what he saw as the cure-all for Roly's ills, Michael had been dropping hints, great galumphing hints: 'D'ya wanna try shaggin' me again this weekend anyway?' 'Such finesse!' Roly continued to dampen his eagerness with spurious excuses and urgings for patience, still half hoping that he would give up the idea altogether, become bored with waiting and perhaps go hunting behind his back for another internet candidate. But he scotched this half-hope when he showed Roly the messages he'd been receiving nearly every day from the dozens of would-be's, admirers and the downright scurrilous old – and young – men in the gay network and vilified them all. His forswearing all others before Roly mystifyingly did not diminish.

****

Michael did well enough in his mock exams and his results meant that he could, if he wished, go on to the city academy and take higher level subjects. Roly thought because he'd volunteered no news himself about his results, his academic successes or failures not figuring large in his life just then, virginity and sex, the loss of the former, the fulfilment of the latter, were the things prevalent in his thoughts. Roly heard

325

about them when his mother rang him in the week, asking him if he was happy with her son's work and when he told her his work and care were excellent, she said maybe he would never be a rocket scientist, but if he was doing that well and enjoying it, perhaps that was all she could hope for. As a reward for his results, he cooked the aubergine casserole Michael had so enjoyed before ('That's an aubergine, I know that now,' he'd said in the greengrocer's. 'And I like 'em.') and after they had eaten they cosied up on the sofa together once more. From the beginning, they had fought over music, sparred rather and in that crucial area of his cultural life he'd soon concluded that they would never see eye to eye. Michael brought round his Ipod and plugged it into the hi-fi and, being a man of all music, Roly was prepared to give his favourites a hearing, but there was very little he could enjoy of Q Project, Fat Daddy and Cyantific. On the other hand, try as he might, he couldn't induce him to appreciate any opera or Chopin and Mozart seemed to pass entirely through his receptors unnoticed, to his great dismay. That evening and further 'intermediate' ones were spent kissing and hugging (there was always the bonding hug at home time; he thought that meant as much to the boy as sex in a way), but he was adamant that they went no further and to Michael's credit he managed to contain his hormonal rushes and to Roly's he was careful not to lead him to the point of phallic agony or, if he thought the floodgate was about to burst, he would send him home to relief from Master Palm.

He asked him one evening, as he stroked his hair and with Cyantific pounding through his speakers on suffrance: 'Aren't you bored with waiting?' To which Michael's answer was a warm smile, which he took to mean he wasn't yet. He couldn't refrain from occasionally alluding to *that* night. 'The problem didn't exist with my lover John,' he told him one evening, 'because we never had full intercourse, not to mention the fact that I was a long way from a stroke and it didn't with Larry because, well because I was too egotistical I suppose. I had the best looking man in London on my arm and that was all the insurance against penile dysfunction that I needed.' 'Aren't I the best lookin' in Trenton then?' 'Of course you are, Michael milksop, but please remember I'm a shadow of my former self. You've unfortunately ensnared me past my sell by date –' '– Bollocks.' 'Bollocks aren't germane to the problem, an unreliable penis is.' Michael cuffed him playfully.

After saying that he'd never wished to talk to anyone about years of love which were now dead and may never have happened, he opened up to him. 'I think, I *think* I want to feel love for you Michael, but I'm scared.' 'I dunno what you gotta be scared of.' 'You don't scare me. I scare me. You see, when Larry and I made love, had sex, when we… I can only remember once asking him if he enjoyed being passive.' 'And what did 'e say?' 'As I remember he told me he was fine after the first few thrusts, or something like that.' 'You're scared I won't like it aren't ya? That's what's givin' ya the droop.' 'I think that's a little of it, but I'm more frightened that I won't care if you do or don't. Looking back, I see what a lousy lover I've been – how we deceive ourselves! More preoccupied with my own self-gratification than giving pleasure to my passive partner. Though I have to take comfort in assuming that when Larry and others were in passive mode, I was giving them what pleased them, don't I? Whenever I was rogering Larry, all I could feel and think in the height of passion was how good he was *for me*. Too busy getting my own stimulation, d'you see? In short, a selfish and inconsiderate lover, not a caring one at all.' 'With this big end' – he grabbed Roly's privates – "ow can you be rotten in bed?' Michael reasoned, as ever, from base point and Roly laughed with him to keep him in the frame. 'You're being your usual coochee self. What I mean is, I never took the time to ask myself if I was respecting him.' 'If you and 'im 'ad sex an' if you both wanted it, that's respect.' 'It's what I hope to achieve with you and that's what I'm scared of, that I won't feel it. To say that I want to feel that you're special goes nowhere near what I'm trying to say and is the worst kind of dreary cheap cliché.' 'Whatever.' He was quickly uninterested in metaphysical speculation, Roly feared, but he had to persist. 'That's not enough for me. I'm frightened. I have no problem enjoying you physically, the physical joy I feel with you isn't in question. Every time you touch me I feel like a Titan. But that comes back to respect doesn't it? When I, when I'm inside you, if I ever will be –' '– Stop sayin' that. You will.' '– I know I'll be feeling *here,*' he thumped himself hard. 'Ha!' he bellowed. 'Michael the magnifico, you will be a sensation. Having sex with a pretty 16-year-old boy can't be anything else but sensational. Oh the bliss, to lie with a youth, a virgin! But when I do will I respect you? If I don't and if I don't even bother to ask the question, I'll be insulting you. If I don't convey to you that having sex with you is the way for me to make you happy, that will be failure. I'm talking more than orgasms, d'you see? An orgasm is not the ultimate goal, which sounds an illogical thing to say and quite daft.' Something went ping in his head. 'Yes, that's it,' he cried. 'My word of the moment. Quiddity. The quiddity of our sex with each other must be respect.' Michael looked through him, as if he weren't there. 'Roly, you talk like your on weed or somethin' sometimes. But if you're sayin' nice things about me, respect to you as well. Now shurrup and listen to the sounds will ya and let's 'ave another snog.'

****

When Michael called the risi e bisi that Roly had prepared for them 'fuckin' brilliant', Roly thanked him for the compliment but had to reprimand him yet again. 'Keep it for sexual references,' he told him, 'because in the depiction of penile penetration, it has no equal and no-one, to my knowledge, has ever coined an alternative. So, if it was always so useful why was it ever considered obscene? Was it the Victorians sticking their prurient oar in again? How long before it could be used on the news for instance? "The Foreign Secretary described today's bomb attack in Jerusalem, which killed at least 50 people, as a fucking tragedy." Frequent use and overuse, even increasing use, hasn't really made it lose, for many, its demonic and not-quite-the-thing-to-say-in-polite-society status. Fornicate. You can't really say, 'I'd love to fornicate you' and sound as though you really want to can you? Anyway, isn't fornicate an intransitive verb? I'd like to coddle you, do you fancy a roger? I want to awl you, swive you, cornhole you. Shaft, spear, lance, spike, skewer, prick are all rather violent. Can I impale you? May I shaft you? Lech you? We had a really good ravish. Ravage, stick. Pork is charmless. Brown-me-pigot, Elizabethan again. Puncture, scuttle, drill, screw, riddle him, tunnel him, cleave his rectum, breach his butt. How about, I want to sodomise you or I'd like to pink you? Pinking hell. Anally corrupt, colonically corrupt, enter the chocolate tunnel, bifurcate the buttocks, take deliveries to the rear entrance. No, only fuck has the succinctness, the total absence of ambiguity and I'm sure better scholars than I have tried and failed to find a substitute.' He hauled back his thoughts. 'Your hair is absolutely the loveliest I've ever known,' he said, as he wove

329

his fingers through it. Michael looked up at him with a deadpan face and thought for a moment. 'It's Elvive,' he intoned, mimicking the TV advert of the day. 'Cause I'm worth it. Micronucleic pro-bionic enzyme toners give it its full body shine. Wanna you like to see my bathroom cabinet? I've got a year's supply of hypoderm fast vanish wrinkle cream in there.' 'Michael, I believe you're getting camp.' 'I'm straight actin' me not a fem!' he protested. 'Where are you goin'?' He was going to the kitchen and after a few minutes, Michael called out, 'Are you awright?' and went in to find him standing motionless over the sink gazing out of the window with the kettle in his hand. 'You makin' another brew?' 'Michael my charming charboy, I have a dilemma.' 'Whassup?' 'You see this kettle? I've put too much water in it.' 'So pour some out.' 'I'm having a conservation moment. I wanted just enough water to make a cup of coffee.' 'Hello, okay?' he said in the sarcastic way of highlighting someone's stupidity. 'So pour some away.' 'Ha, but there's the dilemma. If I'm trying to save the nation's energy resources, as we are constantly exhorted to do and save money in the process, what's best do you think? Do I pour the excess water away, which means it will take less electricty to boil the kettle but will waste some water, or should I boil the overfilled kettle, which means I waste electricity but have water left over to reboil next time? I'm asking for your calculated opinion here, so think carefully. Does it cost more to waste electricity or water?' Michael wasn't amused by the polemics, sighed audibly, took the kettle from his hand and set it on its stand and switched it on. 'Shall I ring Offsted or someone?' Roly asked him. 'Or the Society of Yoghurt Lid Lickers or whoever it is and ask them?' 'No, they're closed. Jus' naff off and sit down an' I'll bring you a soddin' coffee.' As Roly went out, he glanced at the digital clock on the microwave, even though he heard that faint voice in his head telling him not to. Yes, it was showing 21.11!

He went back to the sofa and the drum n' bass cacophony and drifted into another reverie. He looked out at another dark grey sky hanging over the Trenton urban blotch and felt its oppressiveness. He wondered why cigarettes came in packets of 20s and not 21s or 23s. No. No use thinking of the 'why-nots', that was a negative. What are the whys and wherefores? Why are there 15 players in a rugby team? There is enough space on a pitch for a few more. If the pitch were smaller, there wouldn't be, of course. So, why is a rugby pitch the size it is? Or a cricket field? Did the size of the field determine the number of players on it, or vice versa? Did anyone know the answer to that? When they played Shrove Tuesday football in Ashbourne they used the whole town as their field. Would he have a right, as a customer, to ask Morrison's to be obliged to sell him three and a half bananas and 17 ginger biscuits, or was there a consumer law which said bananas have to be sold whole in their skins and ginger nuts only in 330 gram packets? He stopped himself. If he didn't, he'd feel melancholia quickly setting in and start thinking of executions: what Anne Boleyn was feeling the moment before she had her head sliced off and the Taliban and those awful television pictures of that poor woman being shot in the back of the head by a brute with a rifle in a crowded football stadium. Think, instead, of something pleasant and sexy. Pictures of naked twinks on internet porn sites, or meeting his 'Chinese doll' in the Sombrero and the two halcyon years that followed. Yes, my dears, they really *were* halcyon. Weren't they? 'But good times came to an end,' he reminded himself, 'and the memory of them is sorrowful.' All his memories a jeremiad now...

Michael brought him his coffee and Roly told him to turn off the jungle rhythms. 'They were the days when I was earning a lorryload of money working for Esso, with lunches at Wheeler's, an Alfa Romeo to drive – ' 'You 'ad an Alfa?' He omitted to tell him it was only a humble contract hire Alfasud. '– and days of meeting my new friends in Kensington, one of whom, Alistair, who could be biting, would later remind me, when I was in one of my down-and-out-periods and asking him to lend me money, that I was a 'flash cunt when we first met you' and days of chatting up a drop dead gorgeous boy on that Southampton train.' 'Oh yeah, you told me about 'im, said I reminded you of 'im or somethin'.' 'Did I? I don't remember that.' He gestured the boy on the train away with his arm.

'A boy on a train, a body on the common,' he said, distractedly. 'Eh?' 'I was a rotten lover and a rotten son, Michael. All that selfishness, all that disrespect.' His voice, his face, the room all went black as he remembered. 'If you give bad out, you get bad back...'

It served me right. I was scratching around yet again. I won a freelance contract with the jazz radio station in London and in the shabby safety of my Earls Court hotel room, I reflected sorrowfully on that night's cruising, while I sponged the swelling on my forehead. The cute 'student nurse' who had smiled invitingly at me in the bar turned out to be rent and, when I'd refused to enter into commercial negotiations as we stood on the pavement outside, delivered the head blow the resulting abrasion of which I was now massaging.

The hunky, pigtailed youth who had beckoned to me at closing-time the night before had – on telling me to wait for him in the minicab office doorway while he went 'to score some' with the Afro girl on the corner - vanished, then appeared half an hour later three streets away where I, in the company of the handsome young American who had picked me up in the interim, was waiting to hail a taxi. Pigtail asked me the very question I wanted an answer to from him. 'Where did you get to? 'I've got a geezer round the corner. 'E's givin' me 60 quid for a blow job, then we'll go to your place for a shag, innit. 'Ang on there for a mo.'

I did get a little further with the American. Half a mile further. To the Nags Head in the Fulham Road which, in the still semi-restricted days, had a licence extension until one a.m. The two of us sat down with two beers whereupon - was I really that surprised? - he quickly made it plain that if I had any plans for a sexual liaison in due course, there would be a fee. I put 30 pounds on the table before excusing myself to go for a pee thinking, though I couldn't really afford it, the boy was cute and, at last and at least, I was going to get sex. That hope rapidly evanesced when I came back from the basement loo to find an empty seat and he nowhere to be seen. He'd left behind the 6 bottles of Grolsch I'd bought to take back to the hotel with us.

So I stood over the sink holding a towel to my eye wondering what on earth had become of gay life in the city, what mercenary plague had come down in the 10 years I'd been away. Was it the jacket and tie, my added years, the additional girth, perhaps the slightly greyer hair, that was now turning me from averagely successful seducer about the street into a rentboys' mark? Oh, dear. Perhaps the panthers I'd feasted so long with had decided it was time they feasted on me. I had to accept that I've reached the point where pleasures of the flesh don't come free any more.

In the Rodeo again, the garage music thrummed, tee-shirted and half-naked bodies thrashed about, silver light cut savage streaks through the haze of smoke and sweat and Billy sat on his bar stool, twitching in rhythm, sipping Bacardi and watching out for a punter. The drag act came on and told the old joke about his 'husband', the tin bath, the light switch and the basin of water. Time was getting on and Billy had no money for another drink, let alone that week's rent for his bedsit. Then he spotted one. Dark suit, greasy combed-down hair, gone to beer-belly fat but, gold bracelet round his wrist, what looked like a Swatch on the other, patent leather shoes and a piece of folding as a tip for the waiter who brought him his drink. White wine and soda or mineral water? 'Let's go,' he said to himself as he bared his teeth, widened his mouth and pushed his tongue slowly over his lips while he smiled at the man who had now seen him. Five minutes later, Billy was sitting next to the punter, having the inside of his thigh firmly gripped. He hardly had time to take air before the clammy mouth engulfed his own with a swamp of saliva and hot air. 'Rent money,' he reminded himself to counter his revulsion.

The man walking his dog on the damp and mist-coated south London Common next morning stumbled over the naked body slumped behind the London plane and could have not the slightest notion – as indeed Billy would not – that the boy's final attempt at earning money to pay his way through the next fraught day would end thus in a crumpled mess of two broken legs, a ruptured kidney, pearl-white front teeth shattered, the Arlani wrapjacket, like the throat, cut into blood-soaked shreds. 'Jesus!' was the only word he could find as he staggered away from the dead thing, wide-eyed and off balance. He raised the alarm, the police came and surrounded the tree and Billy's body with yellow tape and a murder with a suspected gay motive was reported later in the evening media.

'That's what I meant when I wrote my entry about, what was it, the loss of the rose-remembered days? But I'm rambling again, you won't know what the hell I'm talking about.' 'You've 'ad a right pervy life innit? he said. 'You see how little you know me. I've even been cottaging in my time.' 'Is that queers doin' it in toilets? Is it true that's what they did in them days?' 'In *those* days. Try and speak proper like what I teach you.' In those days it was...

Visits to the Gazelle for a half pint of Ind Coope, a 100-yard walk down the road to the bar of the William Hotel "to see who's in" and the nights ending, inevitably, standing shivering and furtive, nursing a mental hard-on, frustrated and alone, in the entry outside Foundry Square cottage, watching the silhouetted figures who stood still and those who 'clicked' and slinked off into the the smog-laden darkness together for an hour or a night of open-air or terraced-house passion, while I lingered on in the forlorn hope of getting or giving whatever urine-flavoured sexual thrill I was looking for before the last bus home. We were were criminals looking for love, or rather, because we were looking for love and sex, we were branded criminals. I consider cottaging a loathesome and sordid pursuit, but it was what one did. There was nothing else. There were people who wouldn't be seen dead in a gay pub, but who were only too willing to risk police action and society opprobrium for what Neville Ladderbanks called "a bit of dick" on the street.

'What was 'is name, that sex geezer? Casanova, that's it. I bet you were 'im in another life.' He folded himself into Roly's midriff with a boyish leching chuckle. 'And by the way,' he went on, 'it's pants.' Roly thought he meant his storytelling. 'That bit about turnin' 'eads in the street. That is so naan. I don't turn no 'eads.' 'I saw you in the street and you turned mine.' 'That's 'cause you're a desperate old man and spooky,' he taunted. 'Well Casanova is pants too. Six virgins in all and they didn't exactly take much seducing.' Roly stopped his chortling by grabbing his head and kissing him. Hard. 'Perhaps I'll settle for a pornographic autobiography after all,' he told him, hoping he wouldn't have to.

****

He'd been sitting again in a catatonic, or perhaps it was a cataplectic, state; 15 minutes of it had gone by. Michael had texted him his good news: 'got Levitra 4 U YAY n I can stopover agin 2nite if U want Gonna be big n hard no probs LOL Cant w8 C U @9xxxxx' Texts sealed with loving kisses, now. Loving? He must get out of this. He was sweating, hot and cold, shaking, he was palpitating, clear thought wasn't possible through these abstractions and near hallucinations.

****

He was back home from hospital. His last entry, the one he could barely type, ended when he was just about to ask himself the question: was he going to let this boy manipulate

336

him any longer? He had to think of the best way to stop his trying to be his saviour without appearing ungracious. The deadline had come again and he was a doomed man. He had no wish to take anyone else, especially Michael, down to Hades with him. He would be coming again that evening and he couldn't stop him. He spent the rest of the day in a haze, in a quandary of suggestions and alternatives. By bedtime, his brain was exhausted with auto suggestions, computations and possibilities about the boy who had stormed into his world and shifted from innocent curiosity to scheming ambition so stealthily and who had become fixated, oh not by him, not at all, but by his need for man sex. He was no longer master of his fate; his routine was being invaded and disrupted, he was indignant and felt violated. They had a failed attempt behind them but despite that, the boy hadn't given up on him and run to find another, oh no, instead he'd become more affectionate, calmer and then began to speak of things like love. 'Why are you talking about love?' he asked the boy. 'You don't need to waste time with love. Love lasts for minutes. Infatuation should be your aim. You can infatuate for life.' In distraction, he wondered what was wrong with him: here was Michael, unsullied Michael, willing to get into his bed without any coaxing or coercion and give himself to him – HIM! This was a free lunch, he'd been offered them in the past and had taken them, but now he had no appetite; it was all so unbelievably, intemperately, outrageously wrong.

He slept surprisingly easy and well and in the morning awoke to a decision. Whether it was a right decision, even a justifiable one, he didn't know and didn't care. It was, at the very least, the only one he was capable of formulating and he gave not the slightest thought for the trouble it would cause. He looked at his alarm clock, expecting a dreaded 11 minutes past something, but was spared at least that dismay. Michael would be here sooner than he knew, but there was yet plenty of time to organise himself. He had to wash, dress, eat something, write a note, gather what emergency chattels he could, dig the wheelchair out of the closet and order a brisk taxi. He'd decided to turn tail, to desert, to give up. He couldn't, simply could not, deal with Michael any more. He was more or less ready and picked up the phone to ring the taxi company that knew him when – catastrophe! – a breathless Michael burst through the door. 'Where are ya?' 'Michael, what are you doing here?' He just managed to close the bedroom door on the suitcase evidence of his departure and thanked the gods he hadn't yet put his coat on. Jesus, the wheelchair! He saw it. 'What's that thing doin' out? You're not thinkin' of runnin' away are ya?' he panted. 'I, I was going to trundle myself down to the shop for a Radio Times,' he whimpered. 'I get that for you tonight, dick'ead. Wait a mo, it's Monday, it's not out today.' 'Senior moment,' he smiled and the wisp of a suspicious frown crept across boy's brow. 'I said, what are you doing?' 'Ran from school innit. I got dead 'orny thinkin' about it. Look,' he dug in his pocket and produced a pill. 'Danny did the business. His dad's. Whoo!' he whooped and danced a crazy half whirl on tiptoe. 'Stonker night up ma love tunnel baby!' He let rip a manic laugh and grabbed Roly and slapped his hand on his groin. 'Take it an hour before I come round,' he commanded. 'I'll be 'ere at nine, okay?' Roly didn't respond. Michael planted a swift kiss on his mouth and with that, turned and made for the door. 'Laters,' and was gone, leaving him spinning in the backdraught.

He had seen and suspected nothing, so Roly hoped. He paused for a moment to gather his thoughts and convince himself of that, then rang for a taxi. He didn't ask for Jaffer or any of the drivers he knew because he knew, when *they* saw what he was doing and where he was going, that they wouldn't take him. A car arrived and the driver wasn't familiar. He helped Roly to install himself and folded his wheelchair into the boot. 'The Railway please,' he instructed and they set off for the pub a mile or so away in Turnhurst where he was once a regular and which he knew he could get into without too much difficulty. He hadn't been inside the Railway Tavern for a few years; it had long changed management and acquired a new clientele, which was good because he would know no-one and as hap would have it no-one would recognise him. The taxi driver saw him inside and he paid him handsomely. Behind the bar was a barman he didn't know and there were two flat-capped elderly men sitting at separate iron-legged tables drinking pints of ale. He ordered a J20 and the barman brought it to him at his table in a corner. Two or three hours of drinking J20s passed by. The barman proved to be attentive and friendly but not, he was pleased to see, inquisitive as to the reason why a disabled man was spending the day drinking fruit juice alone in his pub. The loo was on the level which Roly could walk to with his stick and this gave him as much peace of mind as he could reasonably expect in the circumstances. He exchanged pleasantries with the few drinkers who passed in and out and the time passed quickly enough. He was thankful that none of the many regulars who were familiar to him from his boozing days and who could easily have interefered with his plans had they seen him, came in.

Late winter dusk was now gathering outside and he wondered if Michael had popped into the flat on his way home from school. He tried to guess his reaction at finding him gone: had he panicked, flown into a white hot fury, given up in disgust and gone home, or had he persevered, roused the neighbours and started a manhunt? Had he called the police? What would they say? He imagined a search party being organised and wondered where they would start searching. Questions and frenetic speculations swirled through his brain: he took no sadistic pleasure at the thought of the chaos he may have left behind him; his own state of distraction simply made him indifferent to it and, in fact, he leaned back in his seat and conjured a wry smile at the weirdness of it all.

Eventually, he asked the barman to call him another taxi and soon the second Asian taxidriver of the day was being morosely helpful, reassembling the wheelchair on the pavement at the bottom of Pittsbank, where he'd asked to be taken. He wasn't at all sure he was doing the right thing. 'Will you be all right mate?' the driver asked in a concerned voice, handing him the plastic carrier bag containing the bottle he'd commandeered him to stop and buy for him at Bargain Booze on the way. 'Where are you going to now?' 'Katie Beans Field, my man,' he said crisply, taking the carrier and hooking it over one handle of the wheelchair and handing him his last 20-pound note. 'Where's that mate?' he asked, taking the money. 'I've never 'eard of it.' 'Where it always was,' Roly told him, beaming. 'Thanks for your help. Salam alekum or shukurun or Inshala or whatever it is.' 'OK, mate. Be careful.'

The doubtful taxidriver drove off and he sat stationary and helpless, watching him disappear into the misty gloom. There were no pedestrians about and cars and lorries passed him by unaware or unconcerned. It took him a very long time and effort for which he was ill-equipped to push and navigate the chair up the slight incline of pavement at the bottom of Pittsbank, before turning off down the track of broken granite chippings which runs down and then up to where the loopline used to run. Forward motion, pushing the wheels, was severely hampered by the large chippingse; the wheels sank into them with his weight. He had to push, wriggle and haul the chair from side to side, a straining, onerous task made the more so as he was sitting in it; then reverse a little when he hit a particularly obdurate and immovable piece of stone. This was the same loopline, even more unrecognisable now that it had metamorphosed into an urban green walkway, part of a continuous level artery that meanders through the entire city of Trenton from north to south, the same loopline over which he walked home that night, so long ago, after dipping his pristine toes into the gay waters under the lamp post with Neville Ladderbanks. That lamp post, if it was still there, was half a mile away down where the line ran. *It's all come round, if that was Alpha is this Omega?*

By now he was sorely out of breath, already physically drained and emotionally wrecked. He was fighting back tears of physical strain as he applied the brakes to the chair and leant back. As he did, because he was stopped pointing upwards on the path, he almost tipped himself backwards. *I am no expert at being a cripple.* If he could struggle as far as the former railway track, it would be rough but at least level. Progress was almost nil, more painful and painfully slower. The more he pushed the wheels, barely a fraction of a revolution at a time, the more the muscles in his arms, shoulders and neck burned. Acid started to scorch through his veins and his heart began to drum. At times, there was no motion forward at all; the angles and perspectives of the landscape around him didn't noticeably change and nothing, no tree, no bush, no clump of grass, moved its position relatively to him. *This isn't even one step forward and two back.* The backs of his hands and his knuckles were showing blue with cold and his breath was vaporising in rapid bursts. That novel came into his head, there was a resonance of it in the air, the one where the hero found himself stranded in a Scottish bog in the middle of the night, struggling against the increasing hostility of nature to fight his way out and get home. He was going home, too, in a way. It took what he thought was at least another 30 minutes to reach the level of where the track once ran, but it was much longer than that because it was by now quite dark and that was the last thing he remembered before waking from a fitful doze with no idea where he was, how he got there, how long it took or what time it was. He was so glad he hadn't put on his wristwatch, nor mastered setting the timer on his mobile phone, which was turned off anyway, because that meant he couldn't see what he knew would inevitably be 11 minutes past the hour on it. He'd won that battle at least! His neck had stiffened intolerably, practically locked now and he had immense difficulty turning his head. He was aware that he couldn't feel his legs or feet and that he was shivering in the clear raw chill of the February evening. February the whatever-it-was, after Michael's birthday, after he failed to take his cherry. He looked around, panic stricken, trying to work out how he'd been abandoned here on this hillock, the same hillock on which he felt so abandoned and helpless 36 years ago.

Below him, the grassy slope ran down to a dark pool with a brook running silently out of it. Behind him, white poplar and silver birch trees towered and swayed imperiously against the gathering navy blue backdrop of sky. *Ah yes, I remember them from my old bedroom window.* He saw no-one and nothing moved except occasional cars' headlights rushing soundlessly up and down the hill of the now distant Pittsbank, which he had fleeting glimpses of through the alleys and entries between the back of the row of houses that lined it; and the lights in those houses flickered, one by one, into life and then were masked as the inhabitants inside drew their curtains and blinds and the houses gradually wrapped them in the warmth and comfort of soft living-room light against the increasingly hostile night outside. This wasn't the Katie Beans Field Roland Wanger knew as a tortured teenager that sweltering summer, where he lay fantasising about Stephen and Martin. But if he wheeled himself up to the brow of that hill in front of him, he could look over it and see the back of *that* council house, the one of awful memory and look at his old bedroom window. What would he feel if he did, he wondered?

I got home from the Concourse coffee lounge, or it could have been from a day's hiking, or from cycling – I can't recall now, five years later – to strife in the council house. I went into the back room to play the piano and was very quickly brought to a stop once again by another of my mother's protests. 'Ooh, Roland please stop banging' and 'Take your foot off the loud pedal, will you?' The 'loud' pedal, I ask you! 'I don't understand why you ever had the idea I should have piano lessons in the first place,' I protested in my turn. 'Well it wasn't so you'd bang, bang, bang on it all the time,' she yelled back. I loved my piano too much to vent my anger by slamming the lid down so, as I'd done so many times before, I closed it in dudgeon. I could only feel contempt for my mother's lack of musical knowledge as I stomped upstairs. I was made to feel I was taking my life in my hands whenever I made a move to play my piano in that uncultured house and my request of, 'Can I play the piano for a while?' was invariably met with grudging and glowering permission. I was grateful to my parents for planting, watering and nurturing my musical acorn, but now they seemed to stifle my every attempt at musicality with their philistinism. I could understand their dislike of pop music – in that they were normal parents – and I understood, though I didn't comply with, their requests to keep the Dansette player low in my bedroom when I was listening to my Kinks or Alan Price or Cilla Black records, but having to ask permission to play the Mozart and Grieg, Schubert and Chopin I thought they would appreciate was beyond the pale. It made their reason for having me learn the instrument in the first place all the more perplexing. I took revenge on them by buying copies of Bartok sheet music, to the consternation of the lady assistant in the music shop and subjecting them to much piercing atonality. I'd never heard of Bartok and didn't know what I'd bought, didn't like it one bit, except for the name of 'Micromegas', but played it to annoy and show off. 'Your trouble is you can't hear the genius of the music,' was my accusation when they complained. Neither, if I was honest, could I.

No, I wasn't going to be a concert pianist, but I had quite a few decent records and I did genuinely like opera from very early on (one more thing Quipp sneered at). 'Aesthetes and poofs are supposed to like opera, you feeble-minded ninny,' I told him. Perhaps I would be an actor? I did strut and fret, after all. I showed off with a local amateur group, though my talent went unheeded at school, where I failed the audition for *The Mikado* and was demoted to the prompt corner for *The Caine Mutiny* production (getting my revenge later when I wrote and performed sketches for the sixth form revue and received 'rave' reviews in the school mag.

The piano problem, by the way, would eventually be solved, brutally and in a cowardly way, behind my back, when I got home on my first college vac (when would I stop calling it home now that London was my home?) and it provided the first confrontation of my homecoming as soon as I'd stepped through the door. 'Where's my piano?' 'We sold it,' my mother explained and, seeing my look of dismay, turned an accusing glare on my father. 'I told you,' she said, righteously. 'Well, it's not as if you're here to play it any more are you, son?' My father said fatuously, trying to soften the blow. Could people – your own parents – really be as hurtful as this? It was as though they were saying, 'You don't belong here any more; there's nothing left of you here now, we've made sure of that; it's your fault, you shouldn't have turned your back on us.' I'd been robbed, robbed of whatever small gift I had for making music. 'And you didn't think of telling me you were going to do it?' 'And you might as well know, we've sold your Dinky cars as well.' This was too much to take; I came as near as I ever dared to firing a four-letter expletive at them. My cherished and pristine Dinky cars – so precious that I would never let my friends play with them without the vigilance of my eagle eye, my consolation for having parents too poor to own a real car, as so many other boys' and girls' parents did – gone! In that council house of strife, I hardly dared ask, 'How much for?' about the piano and the Dinkys, as my mother showed faint sign of remorse. I knew that the sale must have been my father's idea, against her better judgement and overriding her wish not to upset her son. 'Now, don't try and say you need those any more, will you? Ten pounds, if you must know,' my mother added, rallying and rubbing in the salt. I heard a voice in my head say something about selling off the family silver. Had these people never heard of an investment? I bet those cars would be worth thousands in years to come and, of course, I've been proved right. The philistines! The boors! Had my parents had any pennies with which to cut me off without, this is surely what it would feel like.

A plague on this place!

And the night I had several people, including Neville and Roddy, round for what was practically an orgy; that was a kind of revenge too. Wasn't I naughty? My parents were away on holiday and thank god for the blanket of heavy fog next morning which hid Roddy, Neville and the others from the neighbours' curious and probably outraged noses when I let them surreptitiously out the front door. There was the afternoon in the school holidays when I took Jeff Barrett home for a romp on my bed after we'd been to see *Camelot.* And who was the chicken I took home once? Earl lent him to me for the day. Either that or the boy lent himself to me and we had to take care we weren't seen walking together in public by any of Earl's friends who would put two and two together and tell him and...

...he knew the house would still be there, all 50-and-more years of it. Even if it had been knocked down and something else put in its place, it would still be there, a dread spirit. But there were no marlpit, no brickworks, no mechanical diggers, no shouting workmen, no *A Rebours* and, worst of all, still no Martyn and Stephen, though he could plainly see their angel faces. He was not 18 any more and no virgin, either. Much good had it done him.

Denzel will be looking for me. What am I saying? Michael will be looking for me. Or will he? Will anyone? He sprang out of lugubrious reveries and regained a vague sense of his present. *Will I be found here, rigid and frozen?* He looked down at a clump of grass. He couldn't kick it now in frustrated temper, so he scowled at it instead. He couldn't set out to find Neville Ladderbanks either, not any more, to help him on this journey. *A journey to where? What happens next?*

While he was asking himself this question, his hand went involuntarily to his pocket and he pulled out his mobile phone and turned it on. Then he reached round behind him to unhook the carrier bag. From the bag he took the bottle of Bells, his favourite blended, unscrewed the top, put the neck to his lips, reminded himself that he had never enjoyed it neat and took a massive gulp of the dark gold liquid, which immediately stung his gums and, as his throat contracted with a swallow, burned and forced him to retch and rasp. The oral discomfort was eased immediately as he felt the warmth of the alcohol coursing through him. He took another gulp in a defiantly triumphant gesture that stuck a finger up to all the medical advice and warnings he'd been given. *Drink and be damned.* And another, before laying the bottle carefully down. He was curious to find out what if any enterprise Michael had shown and searched for his home number in the mobile. He pressed it and put it to his ear. A young voice he recognised shouted hello. Michael's.

'Holy fuck! Roly!' he yelped, full of panic, hysteria. 'What's happened? Where are you?' 'Oh dear, Michael, what I've tried to instil into you about cussing with panache has gone out the window I see. Why waste my breath? So you're in the flat? Darling, I hate goodbyes.' He was trying to be clever but knew he sounded callously cavalier. 'What the blue fuck's goin' on? Your car's here and... I didn't know... Roly, I'm goin' crazy 'ere.' 'So you do love me then?' 'I've called the police and 'ospitals and everybody. Why was your phone switched off? Roly, please, where are you? Where did you go? What's goin' on?' 'So there's a manhunt? I'm amazed.' 'Roly! What –?' 'I know, I know.' 'Where are you?' 'It doesn't matter where I am. I'm looking for something, I suppose, trying to find where it went wrong and see if it can be put right, but I don't think it can somehow.' 'Roly, please, for fuck's sake tell me where you are. I'm goin' mad 'ere. I wanna get somebody to drive around. Where are you? We'll come an' get you or somethin'. Tell me where you are. Oh, what the fuck do I do?' He tried to explain over Michael's babble that he was fine. 'And wait for me there til I get back. If I ever do,' he said. 'Don't try to find me, you won't. Stay there and wait for me. I don't know how long. Make yourself at home. Mi casa es tu casa,' he laughed wildly. 'Or if you want to go away, please do, I won't blame you. I'm all right.' 'I'm goin' nowhere,' Michael cried. 'I want you to come back here and I'm gonna come and find you or... please Roly –' 'My journal,' he said, enunciating it clearly and closing the call. In his madness, he had given him a cryptic clue and he asked himself whether by wanting him to play Sam Spade and work out where to find him and come and rescue him, he was seeking a lifeline or was setting him a cruel and perverted test of loyalty. Or was the task impossible, his self destruction inevitable? He would have to give up and go home. He would finally realise that he didn't want ever to see him again, that he'd been playing a sadistic game. Perhaps he would think he was taking revenge on him for his tracking games and engineering and his resentment had finally bubbled to the surface and overflowed and he despised him for having one over on him.

He picked up the bottle at his side and took a second massive gulp. Seconds later his phone rang and he saw his own number calling on the screen this time and he let it ring, imagining a frantic Michael at the other end. He wasn't calling him out of love but concern perhaps. He took a third massive gulp from the bottle and stared at the gadget and it seemed alive with urgency, flashing its light and ringing its hideous tinny tone, but he didn't answer it. He could do nothing. He looked up at the sky, which by now was a black and increasingly oppressive canopy and he felt that the stars that were stuck on it were jigging and laughing at him. Their pinpoints were brittle and he could feel their iciness from where he sat. The phone's carillon grew dimmer to his ears, either the batteries were going or it was somehow telling him that its patience was wearing thin and it was starting to give up trying to rouse him to an answer. He took another drink from the bottle. Looking up again, he noticed that a thousand pinpricks of light had now multiplied into a billion, or maybe a trillion. How was he going to count them? Behind him over the hill, he heard a voice. He heard no words, only the sound of words and the tone was a derisory, raucous one. Someone was making fun of him. The voice seemed to get nearer and louder and he took yet another drink from his bottle. The voice was now very close, its derision intensifying and he began to feel very threatened. What will they do? Overturn him in his wheelchair and leave him floundering and freezing, or maybe use some brute force to send him hurtling and helpless down the bank? Then the canopy fell on him and everything, everything went black.

****

He was in a bed, not his bed, he thought it was a hospital bed; shadows of various uniformed people were scurrying noisily around him, they were rummaging through some things near him, the few belongings that had been salvaged, he thought; they're trying to establish who this drunken disabled vagrant is. Half awake half asleep, half sober half sozzled mangled memories and sensations bombarded his sodden brain and from this neurological wreckage emerged, of all things…

…Virgins boys, Adam, Gerry, Pat… who else was there? Then came Harry and Murdoch… He moaned to the scurrying shadows, 'Everything connects… the butterfly flaps its wings in Kyoto and starts a tornado in Oklahoma'. He heard in the far distance, 'He's coming round.' Then someone shouting, 'Roland, Roland, can you hear me?' *They know my name! They've found my wallet and credit cards! Why are all these nurses and doctors shimmering like desert mirages?*

It was Sunday lunchtime in the Peg o'Wassail in Belgravia, the only time it was a gay haunt and the drinkers were packed like sardines in a can as they were every week, over-scented men heaving and struggling gamely to maintain their dignity and poise in the appalling crush. Signs on the walls and above the doors warned patrons not to take their drinks outside because the management of the Peg o'Wassail lived in fear of offending the affluent residents of the well-appointed mews houses around it and discouraged al fresco gatherings on the pavement. There was no room for

350

shoulder pads and the clientele complained about having to try to enjoy a drink squeezed cheek by jowl in the morass, after waiting an age to be served. But still they came, it was one of the places to be seen and so gay men put up with it, week on week.

The gay community did a lot of 'putting up with' back then, perhaps they still do. The main thing was putting up with inflated prices at pubs and clubs throughout the land and especially in London, usually after having to talk one's way past bouncers and door personnel crouched like spiders in a web in some cramped booth behind a grill, who were always dubious about giving out entrance tickets and reluctant to let anyone into their premises at all unless the customer could first somehow prove that he was not a heterosexual troublemaker or an undercover policeman. Gay men and exploitation went hand in hand.

Murdoch Harrington and a good friend of his were sweating, trying to drink their gin and tonics and have a conversation, while fighting off the bumps and buffets of the other 200 or so customers in the bar. One young man squeezed past him with an 'excuse me' and Murdoch, rather taken with him, launched his one and only chat-up line. 'Oh, I say,' he said to the young man. 'Haven't I seen you playing tennis at my club?' Murdoch always boasted about the effectiveness of this quaint ploy, while Mel and others never failed to scoff at it. 'You'd be surprised how well it works,' Murdoch would counter. The young man took the inquiry literally and said, politely, that he had not played tennis since he was at school and never at a club. After an apology for the mistake and a brief exchange of pleasantries and, when the young man indicated he would not be averse to playing tennis again, Murdoch produced a visiting card from his pocket and handed it over with an invitation to ring him some time.

That young man was Roland. Did he see in Murdoch a touch of class and have an eye to a main chance? He must confess and admit he supposes he did. And he soon became friendly with Murdoch, under his aegis and he gradually became Roly, which Murdoch called him and, as with Neville Ladderbanks, found himself cajoled again into living with another name.

For reasons of irrelevance to my tale, my dears, it isn't necessary to explain how at this time, Roly was homeless, having been asked to leave the flat he was living in after he bounced a rent cheque. What a stroke of good fortune it was then, bumping into a stranger at Sunday lunchtime in the Peg o'Wassail in Belgravia and that stranger was Murdoch and he had the glad eye for him. And so he became Murdoch's flatmate but, because Murdoch was under the impression that flatmate was synonymous with lover, he found himself for the next two or so years somewhat at his mercy. He had become a whore.

What a mess, why was it all so sordid? He was not his boyfriend. Murdoch certainly never was a lover in his eyes, the idea was preposterous. But for some reason they stayed together in Murdoch's smartish flat in Chiswick, in a block with a communal swimming pool. Murdoch had a few 'gentlemen callers' who would arrive on occasions to keep him happy for the night – they were all much younger men and most of them were bisexual, one or two married. But Murdoch was in love with Roly and though he couldn't reciprocate, Roly needed Murdoch and his security. He believes to this day that he can say in all honesty that he never conned Murdoch, never made him false promises. He ducked and dived, he took advantage but he did not, surprisingly, steal from him, there was no taking of pound notes from the bedside drawer this time and in return for this self-constraint, he had to put up with a life of continual evasion; he was compromised, having to endure nights on the sofa in front of the TV and the unwanted attentions of Murdoch's 'wandering palms', cringing in silence and thinking up a thousand reasons and excuses to avoid his solicitations for sex. Why did Murdoch put up with it? Why didn't he throw him out? Because Murdoch was a gentleman; he knew that Roly had not sought him out, rather the reverse and he knew that Roly wouldn't admit even to himself to manipulating him, flirting with his affections, using him and his money to his advantage and he gave him the benefit of the doubt and accepted that, unintentionally or not, that is what he was doing.

Murdoch, the aristocrat *manqué* (his ancestry of Scottish lairds had long since petered out and the family estate passed to other hands), the public school only son of a colonel, his *Daily Express* midshires Tory Englishness, for whom life had never been the same since the abolition of capital punishment and the decimalisation of the pound, whose gentleman's status was now more cerebral now than material, had impeccable manners, ate bacon and eggs religiously for breakfast, drank dry sherry before dinner, played Bridge with some smart people in Harley Street, counted his stocks and shares and bored for England about socialism taking away what little private wealth he had and had one asset of particular benefit to Roly - his silver Ford Capri, the talent magnet, which he let Roly use and which Roly did to his sexual advantage on many an occasion.

So, why did Roly screw up? (This was before Muvvie). The world would say he was a snob and he will now admit that he was, but he didn't know it then, or refused to see it; he couldn't draw the line between culture and refinement and snobbery. He couldn't, he supposed, handle it; he was inept. And he could not, would not, believe that of himself, would he? And what, it must be asked, had all this got to do with his foreskin problem?

It was Murdoch who gave him the final push towards the surgeon's knife, after his earlier failure and humiliation with Douglas the navvy. He was by now 21 and had not yet penetrated anyone. Murdoch had an ulterior motive, of course, he was desperate for Roly to screw him, so he sent him to his GP who in turn sent him to St Stephen's Hospital to have the offending tissue cut off. Roly, semi-comatose and brimming with alcohol, surrounded by ethereal voices and fragmented kaleidoscopic images of uniformed people, confused and frightened, thought it a good idea to own up that he *was* a little bit kept in Chiswick. 'Oh no, I didn't have sex with Murdoch for money,' he told himself, 'but there was no rent to pay, there was dining out every week with Murdoch paying the bill, the use of the Capri – and finally there was the money Roly persuaded out of him for his escape.

'I was in work, I was earning money.' He explained one day in a fit of self-defence, confessed it rather hectoringly as though he was being accused. 'But I spent it all on boys and booze and was always overdrawn. I was hopeless and Murdoch was the first in a line of gullible or kindly "patrons", people I preyed on to bail me out at every turn, but all the help in the world could never prevent my having to be one step ahead of the landlord, the bank manager, various publicans – always good for cheques – and the corner shop. I have been, overall, an unaccountable man.'

He repaid Murdoch's kindness and concern in the way he was learning to repay almost everyone else's – by thinking only of himself. He celebrated his new-found circumcision, waving goodbye to his virgin spigot not with Murdoch, but with the Bristol boy. Murdoch had to wait his turn, over a year in fact, when they were driving to Spain in the Capri; they broke down in the middle of a crowded Saturday market place in a backwater called Evreux and they had to put up in a bar-hotel while they waited for a local garage to fix the car. It took them three days and on the second night of incarceration, Roly inexplicably snapped, there was a rush of blood to his brain and his manhood and he jumped on Murdoch, flipped him on his stomach and unceremoniously porked his capacious prats, straining his utmost the while to imagine and pretend that they were the more pert and peachy ones of some lithe and supple youth.

Roly eventually freed himself from the chains of Murdoch's infatuation courtesy of an extraordinary young *deus ex machina* called Stuart, a handsome youth who came to work in the advertising department of the Post and immediately caught Roly's eye through the glass partition between them and the newsroom. 'Who's the new chicken in sales?' he asked whoever was listening. 'Oh not again for chrissake,' his colleagues groaned in a voice. After a few days, with nothing more than a 'good morning' between them, it was Stuart who took Roly by storm when he invited him to share a sandwich and a can of Coke with him on a park bench one lunchtime and asked him if he'd like to see *The Poseidon Adventure* at the local cinema that evening. 'Can I ask you something?' he asked, boldy. 'And, please, you won't say anything will you? But do you want to go to your place after the film and take me to bed?' Yes, just like that, out of nowhere and Roly was incredulous: 'This doesn't happen to me!' But it did and they had sex in the spare bedroom at Upper Addison Gardens while Murdoch slept longsufferingly

in the next bed, but a few weeks later, Roly learned that, while he was away at his block release college course, Stuart had climbed in with Murdoch, too. Murdoch told him all about it and although Roly had lost interest in the boy by then and claimed no proprietorial rights, he could feign the most awful hurt and pump the emotional blackmail into Murdoch as heavily as he might. What a bastard Murdoch was and how guilty he must be made to feel. The opportunity for feigned outrage that Murdoch's 'cheating' gave him coincided with his landing the job away from London and so the stalemate was broken and Roly asked for and received Murdoch's 'loan' and headed north for his downfall.
  Sic biscuitus disintegrat

After Harworthy and refuge in the Trenton council house, Roly headed back to London. Harry had replaced him in Chiswick, but when Murdoch met a toyboy and set up home with him in Pinner, Harry and Roly took a flat together in Clapham. Harry was a blistering Cambridge graduate, dusky-skinned with a deep silky, cultured voice that was seductive. Murdoch knew all about Roly's debacle and Roly feared he may have disclosed it to Harry; he wanted desperately to appear to Harry as unsullied, with nothing to hide, in the vain hope that Harry and he could become romantically entwined; if Harry did know, he never mentioned it. Know or not, there was no romantic entwining with Harry, but it was a flatshare blissfully free of stress or pressure of any sexual nature, unlike the one with Murdoch and his wandering palms. Neither was there any kleptomania, only the constantly recurring and accreting memories of it. Nevertheless, he was crazy about Harry, but Harry soon became involved with an air steward, which precluded any intended overtures he had in mind. He was acutely lonely in

Clapham but, one night, arriving home after yet another fruitless search for sex while drinking to excess in the Sombrero, he had inspiration, he would mount a crusade, as Harry and his air steward were making love in the next room, he sat and dreamt of lavishing a noble and Platonic love upon Harry to cocoon him from the world's ills. Though the notion had evanesced by morning, there came ills that did crash down on Harry without warning when he fell prey to a mysterious ailment and it was this misfortune that did, in the end and in a small way, launch that very crusade while at the same time bringing Roly a euphoric encounter with Adam, the Whitley Bay virgin.

'Welcome to the cottage!' Roly thought the booming voice of the gargantuan camp figure standing in, filling, the doorway of the quaint stone gatehouse could be heard all over Northumberland. This was 'Lydia', a friend of Harry's and his erstwhile adolescent lover, Freddy. Poor Harry: all his gorgeous lush hair had fallen out in handfuls and he had a breakdown. Roly didn't notice, Harry's wig was a good one and must have cost him dear; he had to take prolonged sick leave and went to his family home in Whitley Bay. After a while, his parents went abroad and he invited Roly to go and keep him company. One day, Harry invited Freddy for dinner and Freddy reciprocated by taking them on a trip up to Lindisfarne. On the way they called for Lydia. Welcome to the cottage! 'Frederica!' he bellowed again into the sharp coastal wind that flapped the longest woollen scarf imaginable that trailed about his 16-stone frame. 'My flower, how divine to see you and all that. I know you're fine and won't ask. And Harry – long time, long time, dearie, and who's this delicious creature you've brought?' Lydia squeezed into the car and they set off for Lindisfarne, timing it for when the tide was out. From the off, Lydia was effusing about the new and '*devastating*' stablelad who has just come to work on the estate to which his 'cottage' was the gatehouse. 'It's the only word for him, my dear. As soon as I saw him, I thought of you and I know you'll lose all reason and be committed to the Home for Deranged Poofters as soon as you meet him, but it'll be worth it. He's coming for supper tonight and I'm dreaming of sodding him in the hay loft with his riding boots on. It'll be very biblical because his name is Adam. He'll kill me, I know, and I shall die exquisitely in flagrante. He's olive all over, legs up to there and all 5 feet 10 of him is enticingly illegal. He's 18.' And Lydia continued singing his fulsome praises about Adam all the way to Holy Island, hands flapping with every effusion. 'With plenty of meat on him, but not hefty. More a *Vulcan* boy than *Him.* I've seen him with his shirt off. Oh, the body! His eyes belong in a bedroom and his bottom – well, it's *aching*, I just know it.' Looking out on the passing landscape, he recited, 'There's a boy across the river with a bottom like a peach; Alas, I cannot swim' in a wistful tone and then burst into hearty laughter.

Freddy thought it sounded very promising and Lydia said, 'As a box of Turkish Delight, sweetheart. He moved here two weeks ago and he's from ungodly Ashington, dare you think it, so he's a *butch* boy, isn't he?' At which Harry chimed in with a lampoon about the notorious town: 'He'll be known for his leeks then' and Lydia, whooping raucously, riposted: 'He can leak over me any time he likes! And I can't understand a word he says, by the way, which is such an advantage in bed, don't you think?' 'Yeah but is he a friend of Dorothy's?' Freddy wanted to know. Lydia's huge frame shook with bellowing laughter once more. 'If he isn't there's no god,' he said. 'Carpe diem, darling and carpe puerum! I've got nothing to throw to this godforsaken wind except my caution. A straight boy who plays is every bit as good as a genuine nancy. Anyone care for a Freebourg and Treyer? It's so hard to tell with these modern boys, anyway and sodomy is hip this year. Life would be far more difficult if they weren't all so all wised-up. God bless androgyny.'

On Holy Island, the sun glared with no warmth through stark air and the sea wind was relentless. The four trippers explored Lutyens' fort and Roly gazed down on the neglected overgrowth of Gertrude Jekyll's garden and absorbed its feral melancholy. He bought a souvenir bottle of mead at the monastery shop and tried to strike up a friendly conversation with an islander on her doorstep, but all she had to say, in a voice laced with unwelcome was: 'You'd better get moving, tide'll be in soon.' They paused on the causeway and stood, faces to the wind, blasted and damp, watching North Sea billows rolling with stealthy power towards them and threatening to engulf them any minute; they created a surreal sensation and it was one he'd never forget – it seemed he was standing *beneath* the level of the water. He looked up at Bambrugh Castle in the near distance, perched on its crag like a giant black rook ominously silhouetted against the grey sky, then at the inexorable sea again and then back at the island and Roman Polanski's *Cul-de-sac* sprang to mind; he felt his mortality acutely at that moment, a tiny thing trapped by titanic elements.

Back at the gatehouse, Lydia made gin and tonics and everyone mucked in peeling potatoes and battering cod for supper. There was a knock on the door at about 6 o'clock, Lydia threw up his hands and shrieked,

'Pudding's arrived!' and flounced out while a blanket of lascivious expectancy fell over the room. 'The poor creature doesn't know what he's in for,' said Harry, in the way he had of feigning disapproving prudishness. As soon as he spoke, there was a movement, a sensation and Roly felt a sudden compulsion to turn and look towards the door where a figure had appeared. Harry and Freddy must have felt the same force, because they too turned their eyes. To Roly, it seemed he was having some kind of vision, he swore the room was suddenly bathed in an inspiring light; he studied the boy who stood there and how he envied his talent, the talent to make people happy to see you. Recounting the moment many times over the years to many friends, 'I kid you not,' he'd sat. 'The intake of breath when we saw him was enough to suck in the window panes. He was *gooooorgeous*.' Fair hair, naturally streaked with grey-blond slivers and cascading from the top of his head almost to his shoulders. Lots of it. Lydia introduced him, beaming from ear to ear and Roly simply could not unstick his gaze from the olive skin and the tall wide, strapping frame. He was a boy of the land, handsome and hearty, a working boy, rugged but graceful, wearing bright yellow C & A flared trousers and a magenta fleece sweater. For once, Roly was glad to see the absence of the ubiquitous teenage badge of the day, the earring, and hoped he had not succumbed to the other one, a tattoo. He looked into his eyes, blue-grey siren's eyes, luring him, full of nascent sexuality and he thought, if he isn't family yet, he surely wants to be, or am I dreaming? He sighed inwardly and his customary negative thoughts of inadequacy suffused him – Oh what's the point? The sun will freeze over first. But yet...

is this a virgin boy, with no cumbersome heterosexual habits that need to be seduced out of him?

Adam was soon at his ease, answering questions and sharing his knowledge of horses, smiling all the while. 'Ah've bin ridin' since I could walk. Ah luv horses, ah do. Ah wish ah could have been a jockey - but look at me size, man,' and his melodic burr, pitched between boy's treble and man's tenor and with a gruffness to it and his accent, with its questioning lilt at the end of every sentence, washed over Roly, invigorating him nearly as much as his face and body, this was an aural orgasm. He smiled at him and Adam smiled back and, after the fish and chips and plenty of wine, he and Adam were walking together, he didn't know how, in the twilight among the beech trees outside, Adam talking about life in a mining town and telling how lucky he was to get his stable job. 'Ah wud've died if Ah had to go down a pit, man.' The scenario was all too Victorian and resonated with Lydia's early eulogy: here the labouring boy and the master out to swive him. Roly felt ridiculously squirearchical, but then realised that this was how he'd been trying to feel since his teens and tried to act the part. He mentioned Lydia and asked if he liked him. 'Oh aye, e's canny. But a bit overbearing, like. They all call him Widow Twankey here,' his laugh was innocent and chiming. After a while, Roly was losing inhibitions, asked: 'You have to be up very early of a morning, I suppose?' 'Aye, ah've got to be at work by five.' 'I'm staying in Whitley Bay for the week.' 'Oh aye? Nice beach there.' 'Why don't you give me a ring and come down? Have you got a day off this week? You can stay the night.' The boy needed no time to think. 'Ah'd like that. Are you shooer? Ah've got a day off on Wednesday so Ah could come Tuesday night.' Smiling at him, he could hardly believe his own ears: 'D'you have a healthy hard-on in the morning?', he blurted out, astonishing himself with his peremptory lechery and blushing at his gaucheness. He tried to cover it: 'It's getting quite dark,' he said, not waiting for a response. 'Shall we get back?' 'Ah suppose Ah do,' Adam said; did Roly imagine the lubricious curl of his lip. 'What?' 'Wake up hard.' 'Oh, I – ' 'Man, it's the best alarm clock.' Adam was was now grinning broadly at Roly's discomfiture. 'Be nice to wake up to someone else's one day.' Roly felt his scalp tingle. Adam was laughing now and teasing. 'Is that your way of saying you'd like to stay the night?' His eyebrows shot up in an arc and his face beamed. Roly looked around, averting his eyes, trying not to feel embarrassed. Adam mistook his silence. 'Ooh, Ah'm sorry. Ah thought... you a friend of Widow Twankey an' all... Ah thought –' Roly turned back and smiled diffidently at him. 'Adam, are you...are you talking about ...? With me?' 'Ah don't see any other goodlookin' man here at the moment. Ah'm sorry, ah thought you were that way divven't I?... Ah hope you're not, well –' 'I'm not anything except delighted and, of course, I, well, I think you're fabulous and, yes, if you're sure about it ...' Adam jumped what seemed like six feet in the air. 'Oh, man,' he yelled with delight and punched the air, then he brought himself to a stop. He looked at Roly and then down, sheepishly. 'Ah have na ... I mean... I haven't dun anything yet... I've never been, ya know...' This was the first-timer's fear of putting off an admirer. 'I mean, d'ya still want to –?' 'That's what makes you so desirable, apart from the little matter of your stunning beauty,' Roly reassured him, now reaching for his face and stroking it. 'Why you choose me, I can't imagine.' ''Cos you're bloody canny, that's why! And if you like me and I like you, there's nah problem, right?' 'No. No problem at all.' 'How did ya know about me, anyhow? Ah've said nothing to Widow – to Lydia – to Billy.' Roly laughed inside at the jejune logic: if this man finds me attractive, he must know I'm gay. How did he find me out? 'It's in your eyes, Adam,' Roly said, intuiting his question, 'and don't worry, you're not going to lose your job, nothing awful's going to happen.' 'It's just... well...if you knew what Ashin'ton was like. Ah never thought I'd find anyone...not heah.' Roly could only hope at that moment that the boy knew what he was saying and that he wanted a kiss right there. He leaned towards him, put his arm around him and tasted his country mouth. 'The unexpected can be so delightful, can't it?' he said gently. He moved his hand to between the boy's legs and gripped the healthy hardness firmly. Adam responded with a strong embrace and his novice's mouth rippled in keen exploration, devouring Roly's tongue. He moaned quietly. Their lips parted, and the seducer and the seduced – which was which? – both opened their eyes. 'Ah cannot believe this, Ah cannot.' 'You're not alone,' Roly replied, 'but let's believe it.' Roly was marooned; Adam's eyes were questing pools and he thought they must be mirroring his own. 'Come on, the sooner we get back...' Adam threw himself at him and kissed him back quite ferociously. Roly smoothly pushed him away. 'Look what you're doin' to us!' Adam cried and looked down at his eminence. 'That's you!' he beamed. Roly held him again and guided his hand and Adam grasped. 'Oh, man,' he sighed, 'can't we do anything now?' Damn, they had to break apart and soon the three travellers were tooting and waving their goodbyes to Lydia, Adam and the gatehouse. *Keep your hands of him, Lydia, he's mine.* Adam had Harry's phone number in his pocket and all Roly could do was wait and hope. 'Is he going to ring you, dear?' Harry asked as they drove along Morpeth High Street and the phone ringing back in Whitley Bay next morning answered the question; Roly quite snatched it from Harry and fair bristled at the sound of Adam's voice. If Roly still wanted him to come, he was ready to get on the coach now. 'Poor innocent wretch,' Harry goaded again on their way to meet him at the coach station and back home, Roly helped him prepare beef fillet with ratatouille and they drank a refined Margaux which he'ad found in a wine shop overlooking the bay on a previous walk round the town and after supper they sat in the evening garden, Roly utterly content with the tingling expectation he was feeling as he gazed longingly at Adam through the balmy night, with a million stars stuck like pinpoint snowdrops on a thick black drape spread over them. The resort fairground was a jingle-jangle in the distance, not nearly intrusive enough to disturb the *Siegrfied Idyll* drifting through the french windows and across the tailored lawn.

The next Roly knew was that Adam had washed and dried himself almost before the water drained from the sink; he came to him in the bedroom smelling sweet and toothpaste fresh, his hair damp and the skin of his moorland face dappled and ruddy. Roly took hold of him and slowly peeled off the towel round his waist to unveil an incomparable form, his curves were from a Caravaggio canvass and the pristine pubescent triangle at the top of his legs was black and mysterious. He'd expected, imagined, he didn't know why, that it would be sparoid, but to his surprise his fingers found it delightfully soft, lush, velvety. There was no excess to him, no ugliness, nothing at all offended the eye, everything delighted it and he could only stare in awe. As he gently skimmed his lips over the skin of his neck, he was in adoration of a god. Adam arched his neck back and gently gasped. Roly smoothed his hands in soft circles all over the sturdy frame then pulled him tightly into him and kissed him deeply. He kneaded the mounds of flesh and thought of anilinctus. He studied his power, wanting to dominate it but at the same time wanting a strong physical response. He was neither delicate nor frangible, there were guts and gusto in his soul, he was going to make love powerfully. He thought of passive boys, those who were pacific, who enjoyed penis-domination because it emphasised their vulnerability; they enjoyed being so because their masochism not only enabled them to wallow in the pain but also thwarted their natural male aggression. Adam was of the other ilk, *actively* passive, his body and spirit inviting invasion but saying, 'make sure you can match my masculinity, which I am not surrendering. You may dominate my body sexually but my spirit is not submitting to your soul. I'm making decisions as well as you.' Adam had a fire and he was going to burn him with it but Roly walked into it voluntarily. The boy's hair was prickling, his brain churning and and the blood in his boyhood pulsing, his breathing was shallow, he was straining in every fibre and nearly passing out with the yen for a man's naked body on top of his. Roly imagined he was impatient to be taken and stood over his prostrate dreaming body. 'I don't suppose you've ever seen an erect penis, have you, apart from your own, I mean?' 'No.' 'So pull my knickers down and see one.' 'Knickers?' The poor boy was alarmed. 'Ah hope you're not a wench in disguise!' he cried, but when he did as he was bid, 'No, I can see you're not!' he exclaimed and Roly sidled onto the bed beside him and that night, they were in a country of great solace, one with rolling hills and deep, lush forests and warm breezes and flowing, endless rivers and it was lovelier than any singing of it and more vivid than any painting of it. Their eyes were closed but their souls saw the beauty and heard the singing, their two bodies sang together and they whispered goodnight and Adam turned over to unwilling sleep, drifting deliriously towards Somnus who, in his dreamy post-passion, appeared to him as Roly.

There was a strange mix of flavours when they woke next morning, there was certainly a feel of mutual after-sex satisfaction but Roly also felt some apprehension, something star-crossed. 'Adam?' 'Yes?' 'You ok?' He didn't answer, Roly persisted, 'Adam?' and he heard him mutter something barely audible. He sat up and pulled him to him by the shoulders, his head drooped but Roly lifted it and his face was stricken. 'O-oh,' Roly moaned and held him close. 'What happens now?' he asked; he looked helpless, lost, questing. 'Ah'm sorry, Ah canna help it, Ah cannot.' 'O-oh,' Roly soothed once more and stroked his hair. 'Ah've got to go and you're gannin' away too.' It dawned on Roly that of course he had no concept of a one night-stand. 'Ah've never been so happy,' he whimpered. 'And you are going to be happier. That's impossible for you to understand right now, I know, but you will. Come and see me in London, any time.' 'Ah'd like that. Thankyou, anyway.' 'Oh, for what?' 'For bein' a canny teacher!' he beamed now. 'No regrets?' 'Only that you're gannin away and I got to as well. What we going to do?' 'You knew we'd have to, but there'll be someone.' 'Ha-way, thar's no chance of that happenin'.' 'That's where you're wrong, just you be ready for him.' They made love in the cool early morning and after a cosy breakfast Harry walked with them to the bus. With a 'Ring me and come and stay with me in London if you want to', Roly thought how some morning-after goodbyes, the getting off the short ride on the merry-go-round of brief encounters, are awkward, others can tear at the heartstrings and he was in no doubt which one this was. He truly did want to see Adam again at that moment and truly wished the boy felt likewise.

I have shaken my head with sorrow every time I recall our phone calls; somehow a long distance telephone line was too fragile to sustain the enthusiasm and then there was no more. Fervent, hungry phone calls, 'Can't-wait-to-see-you-again' calls, then, 'Not-next-week, I'm- at-the-BBC-all-week' calls, or 'I've-got-so-much-work-on' calls. Until interest waned and the unthinkable happened – unthinkable of and to Adam, that is. 'What it is, I've met somebody,' he revealed and he sounded very regretful and reticent about it. Or was that my imagination?

That was bad juju, providential revenge: there was a blind date, a week or so before he'd gone to Whitley Bay, one of those PO Box number arrangements, before the days of the internet and chat rooms and email and mobile phones. He'd arranged to meet the boy he'd exchanged letters with outside Shepherd's Bush tube, but when he drove up to the station and spotted him waiting, he drove off. He left one boy stranded and another boy stranded him in turn and that was just deserts. He didn't know even now if it was cold feet at the tube, but he did think of the hypocrisy of those who were easily judgemental about those who stand people up; he was one of them.

****

One of the blurred uniformed shadows was rousing him, shouting, he heard the word 'detox'. He opened his eyes and felt ghastly. He knew it wasn't a hangover because, being an alcoholic, he never suffered from them. He was sweating, the warmth of the hospital ward alone couldn't produce this amount of perspiration. He wiped his brow. The fall of dry skin, like someone shaking a salt cellar over his head, told him that his intake of drink had also aggravated his seborroeah and he was flaking badly. The middle-aged nurse with candyfloss hair spilling over her spectacles was explaining that it would be a good idea for him to ring the alcohol abuse centre when he got home, advice he could only half comprehend. She wrote what she said was a telephone number on a piece of paper, placed it on the bedside cabinet and went away. Roly shut his eyes tight again and grimaced and tried to imagine Michael naked in bed with him, but his thoughts meandered elsewhere.

After what seemed both a moment and a lifespan, he was again disturbed, woken, shaken by another bellowing voice. What the blue fuck d'ya think you're doin? it yelled and it was a voice more desperate than angry. 'Michael!' another voice, a woman's, it chastised. He must have been masturbating and one of the uniformed shadows had caught him, the bed was awash with semen and she was livid. His delirium, if it was a delirium he was in, had lifted, or not. He shot up or thought he did. In fact, he was already sitting up, on a crane high above Manchester Town Hall. He stepped onto a balloon which was passing by and started eating crabmeat and pickled onions; the balloon was slippery but he was balancing effortlessly on it and managed to return the tennis ball that Rod Laver hurled down at him over the net on the

Centre Court at Wimbledon, then the shouting crashed into his eardrums again and he realised it was...

... Michael's voice, a yell of exasperation and outrage which echoed round the hospital lounge room as he stormed in with what looked like a doctor close behind and a female nurse, but a nurse in a vibrant lime green sweater and a flimsy long summery dress, her neck, throat and hands swathed in flashing golden jewellery. Michael's jet eyes blazed and his voice was hoarse with rage. The three towered over him in his wheelchair where he'd been sitting quite serenely thinking his mind had gone. 'Roly?' 'Michael, profane one, yet another inappropriate "fuck",' he said, addressing the floor. 'Go and sit on the naughty step right now.' He looked up, lethargically and disdainfully, at him and then at the doctor and, when he glanced back at him briefly and spotted the resemblance, the same nose and the black hair, he realised the woman wasn't a nurse at all. He held out his hand to her: 'Hello Yvette. I should call you Sphinx for coming to see me after I've been away for so long.' She smiled a puzzled smile, Roly didn't think she recognized his parody, but her face was inviting, smiling, warmly concerned. She squatted down on her hunkers to be at his level and put her face close to his. 'You okay sugar?' 'Quite an adventure,' he said. 'Ow ya feelin'?' He took in the same familiar Trenton accent, the same dropped aitches and gs as Michael's. 'Roly, 'ow are ya feelin'?' Michael echoed as if to confirm this. He waved a slow hand at him. 'It was the clock, darling. Oh, can I call him that Yvette?' She chuckled. 'Would you believe it, the time was 11.11,' he lied, 'and and you nearly sabotaged my flight by coming in unexpectedly. When was it, how long ago? I'm fazed. I'm too dazed to ask why you're all here, but thank you for coming.' 'Come on, you bin discharged, you crazy wazzock. We're takin' you 'ome right now and man, you better –' '– Leave 'im alone Michael. Not now,' Yvette interposed and she sounded as though she just might have an inkling of what Roly was going through. 'Roly,' was all Michael could manage to say as he stood over him, his face etched with ghastly furrows of bewilderment, which disfigured him for a moment and then what Roly presumed might be a faint glimmer of relief flickered in his eyes. He studied that face as though seeing it for the first time and Michael peered into his, fixing him with a baffled inquiry which was benign rather than hostile. They were eyes that wanted to know him and his truth. The strain of his past 12 hours gradually drained away and he summoned a smile which banished the ravage and restored his soft radiance.

'Yes, your youth and beauty are more than a match for stress and adversity aren't they? You're triumphant once more,' Roly told him and Michael's bemused look swept over him again. Roly lifted his stick and waved it at him, 'You see? I warned you!' hoping his hostility showed his disapproval of Michael's ever having come into his disabled ambit in the first place and entwining his sexual tentacles around it. 'Can't you leave your young brusqueness at home for once?' he asked, harshly. He could think of nothing more mean than to try and offload his feelings of guilt about the mess on *him* and he did so regardless. 'Why did you bring this on? Why didn't you just stay at home with your watering can? I've told you, I'm a horrible person.' 'The stick suits you, man,' Michael beamed sardonically and for an instant he seemed to Roly not a jot perturbed and there was no antipathy in his voice. 'Michael the angel,' Roly said under his breath. 'Michelangelo.' 'This is very good of you Yvette,' he said meekly, ' but really you shouldn't have bothered, you know.' 'It was Michael not me,' she said. 'If it wasn't for. Well, never mind, leave it for later. Come on.'

She, Michael and the doctor who wasn't a doctor, he realised, but a strapping porter, waiting for no further words of apology, excuse or explanation, wrestled for the wheelchair together and pushed Roly unceremoniously out of the room and along corridors. He was bungled like airport baggage into a taxi and driven home in awkward silence, where they unloaded him with equal efficiency and deposited him on the livingroom sofa.

'I'll put the kettle on,' Yvette announced. 'Ah yes, the panacea,' Roly called. 'No whisky left I suppose.' Michael was standing over him looking down at him, grimly. 'Worst fuckin' day and night of my life,' he said with a hissed tone of reprimand. 'I've told you, it was the clock,' he lied again, 'it was showing 11 minutes past. One of my jinxes.' 'You're ravin'.' 'You'll have to put me down.' 'For fuck's sake, man, right yeah?' He was goading Roly to be rational, he supposed. 'I was thinking. The last time I was in hospital...'

I can't swear to this day whether I was hit or not, though that was my story for ever afterwards. Whether the thump on the back of my head was a blow or whether it was what I felt when I hit the pavement, I'll never know. I was found in Gower Street and I told UCH that I'd been mugged and I don't suppose they believed me for a moment. My wallet was gone and the nurses had to put stitches in the back of my skull. I was kept in for the night and the one consolation was watching the very attractive young man in the next bed to me, who had been injured when he was pushed onto a glass table at a nightclub, getting dressed next morning with his back to me and giving me a view of his tight round peach bottom. Very tasty it was too. When I was discharged, I stood in the street outside, a little rough but trying very hard to look as bedraggled and pathetic as possible and so elicit some sympathy from god knows where or who. I hailed a taxi and when the driver said I looked like I'd had a bad time I lied that I had. Brazen wasn't it? He tutted sympathy and when he unloaded me in Marylebone, he became the only London cab driver I've ever known to refuse to accept payment! Bless his heart for falling for my cozening.

Yvette came back in with a mug. 'Ere ya go sugar, drink this.' 'I've put you to an awful lot of trouble,' Roly told her, taking the drink. He was contrite, he swore. They weren't, after all, her advances that had driven him away. 'Don't matter about that,' she said, making herself comfortable on the sofa beside him and putting a hand on his leg to comfort. 'I know about, about you and this one,' nodding up at her son. "E may think I'm daft –' 'I never said that!' Michael interjected with protest. 'But... well he told me last night but I knew somethin' was goin' on. I'm his mum for god's sake.' 'And a very savvy one,' Roly smiled at her conspiratorially. 'So you know I'm an old queer and I've been trying to get into your very young and illegal son's knickers do you?' 'Fuck off Roly, legal now.' Michael chimed in. 'Er, a bit the other way round from what I can see intit?' Yvette smiled. This took Roly aback; indeed she wasn't daft. He realised she knew why he'd run off! He looked up at Michael. 'Oh Michael what have you been saying? Have you blown our cover?'

The story of the night's events unravelled. Michael had indeed cracked Roly's cryptic clue about his Journal, in that he'd shown more nous than he had credited him with. He'd gone to his computer and reexamined the first few pages and conjectured or as it happened, deduced correctly, where he was. He ran hell for leather home and demanded of his mother where Katie Beans field was and, drawing a blank from her had, doubtless in his one-breath manner of narration, told her all he could of them and chatrooms and tracking and seduction and his birthday and sex and... What a coming out! Katie Beans field had turned about, after all the years of posing as a symbol of secret and frustrated desires, and assumed the role of instrument, the fount of liberation. It was hilarious. And they rang the police to ask them, told them they thought a disabled man was in peril and persuaded them to go and have a look and they did and all was finally – well, if not well – at least over. He wasn't charged for being drunk in charge of a wheelchair and that is how he was to be found *in delirium tremens* but safe in a hospital bed.

He sank back with a heavy sigh. 'Hey ho, round and round the room we go, speaking of Michelangelo.' (He pronounced it the anglicised way for the benefit of the audience.) Yvette gave out a burst of girlish laughter, 'You're funny,' she said. He looked at Michael, he was black and scowling. 'You look as though you'd like to spit at at me Michael. I know, I know, I've caused you bother and I'm very very sorry, truly I am but don't take it amiss if I say that it would have been better for everyone if you'd left me there to go to sod.' Yvette tut-tutted and made murmuring sympathy sounds. Michael's stoney expression stayed put. "E's still pissed mum,' he said with disgust, looking at him. 'All right, I'm a bastard,' Roly cried, spreading his arms in admission. 'I bring havoc to everyone who gets involved with me. I don't do it on purpose, it's the way it is and I can do nothing about it. Both do yourself a favour and keep away from me. I'm fatal distraction, that's what I am.' His outburst was met with complete, dead silence. Roly thought his two visitors were either stunned into it by what they must have seen as his lack of feeling or they were forgiving – Yvette at least – and put his behaviour down to shock and mania. 'I think you better go lie down and get some rest,' Yvette whispered at length, confidingly, patting his knee again. 'In a darkened room, you're right love. There'll be questions and recriminations to follow no doubt but, for now, I'm overwhelmed and unable and unwilling to provide anyone with any satisfactory explanation for my behaviour. I just hope you can both... not forgive me, I don't deserve that, oh no I don't... but... *dismiss* me. And now,' he said as he made to raise himself up, 'you must at least pardon my manners but I vant to be left alone and whether you're interested or not, that's exactly what Greta Garbo is said to have said.' Yvette, not getting the pathetic attempt at humour, said 'You'll feel better' and urged, 'Go on.' I'll see to things and we'll let ourselves out, lock the door, don't worry.' And like a child being sent back upstairs for throwing his egg at nanny, Roly was assisted up by her and out as far as the bedroom door. He turned to her. 'Thank you Yvette,' he said and he hoped she registered his effort at sincerity. 'Ssh, go on,' was her final kindness. 'I think you're a good woman,' he told her and went into the bedroom and closed the door, probably leaving her in no doubt at all that he was in need of psychiatric help. 'Gone to sod. Like all of us,' he thought aloud. 'I was dreaming about him, he was naked and lying under me and it was driving me insane. I had to escape. Your son.' He didn't know if she heard him, she was never to say.

Snatches of their conversation drifted into him as they prepared to leave. 'Stroke, funny things, don't know what they're sayin', you don't remember yer other nan, went just the same, will 'e be like this for good, 'as 'e flipped?' The latter in a voice of deep concern from Michael. He didn't know how long it was, but he awoke in his clothes still feeling disorientated but managing to shuffle into the livingroom to find Michael sitting on the sofa, looking forlorn. He felt immediately deflated at the sight of him. 'Why, Michael,' he spoke listlessly, 'why are you here?' He saw the question frightened the boy and sat down beside him to, he hoped, put him at ease. 'What I mean is: why are you bothering with me at all?' 'Oh yeah, right, you're a wankin' prat mank bastard.' 'You forgot cunt,' he said and like so many people whom he never understood why were, Michael looked shocked by the word. 'It's odd you know,' he mused. 'Just what it is that has earned the word cunt the reputation of the last taboo expletive, don't you think? Navvies, drunks, cutthroats, myrmidons all seem to hold it in reverence, hide it behind cockeny rhyming slang – Berkeley Hunt and Granny Grunt – use it only in the most extreme of *in extremis*; it's idiotically and hypocritically regarded even among the most inveterate of four-letter exponents as a repugnant word, the worst thing you can call anyone.' Michael recovered equilibrium and scowled at the pedantry. 'Why did I make you run away?' was what he mustered and the childlike way he asked it made Roly pause as a sensation of burning water in his eyes came to him. He couldn't answer him and Michael went on with unexpected calm: 'We were never off the phone. Police, the social, 'ospitals, even yer doctor when I found 'is number in yer address book, anyone we could think of. It's like it's my fault,' he wailed. 'I drove you away.' Roly was staggered. *Heavens to Murgatroyd, this is worse than I thought, blaming himself.* 'Oh no, no,' he soothed. 'I found that thing on the PC, what you wanted me to didn't ya? When you said on the mobile about your Journal an' you gave me that clue like that film and I worked it out you'd got yerself to that Katie Beans place, but I didn't know where the fuckspick that was, so I rang the police woman back and she said wait and we were 'oldin' on for ages and then she found it, where it used to be and they came round for us, blue lights the lot and took us there and I was well scared, you looked all frozen and blue and dead. 'Ow the fuck d'yever get yerself up that 'ill? And we got you to the 'ospital and they put you in a bed and said you were OK and they were keepin' you in, so they bought us back 'ome.'

It was a tour de force one breath effort once more; the momentous events called for it and he didn't shirk. 'But.' A worried glower shadowed his face and he fell silent. 'But what?' 'I've done somethin'.' Silence again and Roly gave him his head, didn't prompt him. 'I – what I read. I snuck back 'ere an took yer backup disc with me an'... stayed up all night readin' it... all about what you've wrote... I mean about me an' you an'... all of it. I shouldn't of done that innit?' 'Oh dear,' Roly groaned. 'All of it?' 'Yeah right.' 'Well, no privacy with you around then.' 'I didn't think. I mean, I wasn't spyin'. I thought it was like a book ya know. I didn't know it was real like.'

Roly couldn't put his arm around him to forgive him because in his reflected opinion the boy had done nothing wrong. 'It's all right,' was all he could say, feebly and he hoped that was all he needed to hear, because he didn't have anything else except, 'I've scared you. And your mother. I didn't care. I'm a shit.' 'And in that 'ospital room. You looked pathetic, I just wanted to... You were all like, people when they're pissed and wrecked.' 'And I wasn't even acting.' 'I defo wanted an 'ug then.' At this, he managed a smile, a timid one. 'I should have given you one, I wasn't thinking.' 'I'm a right wuss now.' Emotion was embarrassing him. 'And with mum there.' 'Mum? She's well cool about it. She's tastic.' *And not at all fazed by unorthodox parings, a depraved and ageing homosexual who has his voracious and depraved designs on her dear darling son.* 'She's very like you,' Roly mused. 'She's cool.' 'Cool. Ah yes, that,' he echoed distractedly. He felt this was neither the time nor place for strong opinions; that we ought not to feel we should be grateful to other people for accepting our sexuality. Leave that for more philosophical, less fraught times Nevertheless he still longed (a long held wish) for the day when it would be heterosexuals who had to do the defending, to make an "admission", to "admit" they were straight, a wish for the end of the era of apologies and excuses. 'You didn't want to, you weren't gonna top yerself were ya?' He didn't wait for a reply to his question, which he felt was too dangerous, would elicit an answer he didn't want to, couldn't bear to hear. 'Can I get meself a drink? You want anythin'? Cuppa tea, coffee?' he asked quickly. 'May I.' 'Eh? Oh yeah, right,' he said, the correction registering and he went to fetch a coffee. 'That Denzel,' he said, handing Roly a mug and two digestive biscuits when he came back. 'Is 'e, like, anyone ya know or did ya make 'im up? And all that about livin' on your own and slaggin' Trenton off and your mother and the vandals round yer place in Bleakridge?' 'Some fact, some fiction,' he told him. 'And it's no matter. I'm just grateful my literary efforts held your attention and you took it all in. It speaks well for sales forecasts.

'How calm you are now,' he said. 'After all that's happened, all I've done. It's the confidence and heedlessness of youth, I suppose. You chase me, get to meet me, flout all the precautions, I run off, you rescue me and I react like an ingrate. I hurl your kindness back in your face and treat you like dog dirt. How can you put up with that?' Michael looked at him with the same tentative and inquiring eyes as he had the first time that day on his doorstep, but there was a touch of longing in his smiling eyes which Roly had never seen before. Any anxiousness he may still have had about the great sexual adventure, he hid well. He was either indestructible or incredibly stupid. He'd taken the poker by the red hot smouldering end and hadn't flinched, determination had lain long beneath uncertainty and now it showed itself again, it was written in his now changing features, but it didn't harden them or make him ugly. He was quite unbelievable. Roly suddenly couldn't bear it. 'Oh, Michael,' he said, 'this is madness. Why don't you just go and tell yourself this never happened, that you never met me? I really am not worth the hassle, you know. Can't I make you understand?' 'Don't be a muppet,' he laughed and his laughter said he would never be deterred, no matter what this man did or said, never take no for an answer. 'You've read the journal, you now know that I'm a total cunt.' Roly resorted to the vulgar of vulgars again, using all deterrents at his disposal. Surely this, combined with the abysmal character reference the Journal had provided Michael with, surely this was enough to make him put an end to his pursuit of him? 'Can't you see I'll destroy you if you persist with this?' Roly was shouting in frustration now. 'Disruption confounds me, I'm not geared for surprises any more and I certainly can't handle a doting faun... with the face and body of a... and the heart of a... of an altruistic paragon. You're not too good to be true but you're too true for your own good and certainly mine! Why the hell didn't I make it clear to you at the start that there could be no awakening for you, Michael? Not with me. Why did I let you inveigle me? You've wasted your time, I've wasted your time. I should have turned you away but instead what I did was kiss you in this room and – ' 'Chill will ya? You're not such a tosser as you like to make out ya know.' He hadn't absorbed what he'd read in the

Journal, not taken in what Roly thought of as his corruption. He'd learned nothing about me, he thought. Either that, or he was blinded by love. *Don't flatter yourself, Hunter.*

'For fuck's sake Roly, what's the matter with you? Even if you were as bad as ya make out, even a wicked person's allowed to 'ave a shag aren't they?' He waited for Roly's answer, but he couldn't give him one. 'What's a waste of time anyway?' He wasn't having it, he was indomitable. 'Anyway.' Roly waited, bated. 'I've still got that Levitra pill, so you're still gonna prick my bubble butt, I'm gonna make you do it.' Just then, the doorbell rang and Roly told him to go and answer it. It was Yvette. 'Ow you feelin' now sugar?' she asked Roly as she walked in. 'Yvette, what can I say?' Roly said plaintively. 'Oh, bugger off and stop sayin' sorry, you'll wear the disc out. Come on you,' she said to Michael. 'This one's got 'is swimming today,' she said to Roly. 'Oh no! Today? Oh Michael I'm sorry.' 'Sorry sorry on a lorry,' he chanted. 'I'll tell y'about it later.' He bent over Roly and gave him a hug, yes, right in front of mother; 16 and liberated and uninhibited and whispering 'Levitra' in his ear and giggling. 'No runnin' off,' Michael admonished from the hall. 'I'm lockin' the door, okay?'

They left Roly to his thoughts and his reflection that he wasn't sorry about what he'd done, it was one in the eye for Muvvie, ha ha, and his all-round apologies were, he had to face it, a show of courtesy to both the boy and his mother, not remorse. He could only reach the stultifyingly bleak conclusion that Michael's desire to be buggered was still his main preoccupation, that his animal urge still overrode any discernment he had in his choice of the sort of man he wanted to do it. Or why, after all that had happened (and the one thing that didn't when it was supposed to) IS HE STILL HOPING IT WILL BE ME?

****

Roly was numbed by all the mulling when Michael got back from another swimming competition. 'You'll never guess what me mum said on the way.' (He had come second, by the way, in the crawl and relay, the thing he neglected to tell Roly until after his one breath). She said, I 'ope Roly doesn't make ya sleep on the sofa after you've 'ad sex, and I was like Muuuum, shurrup! She was well out of order. She knew about us ya know, before ya ran off. I could tell she was nosin', the way she asked if it was a good night when I got in after, after –' '– after I didn't pop your cherry.' 'Will ya stop that, it's gonna happen, I've told ya. 'An' all she wanted was, like, as long as you know what ya doin' and I said Roly never tried anythin' ya know an' she was like, I'm sure 'e didn't, 'e's a nice man. Burra I know she can't ask me about it like if I was a girl, can she? 'Cause I don't think women think about that for men, it's just wankin' and kissin' innit, they don't think about, ya know, up the arse do they? Anway, yeah? She's cool about everythin' an' you an' me, I'm yer partner now yeah?' Roly felt ice at the word. Partners. He couldn't come tonight because Yvette was taking him and his sister to his grandparents; he thanked the gods because he didn't know how he would cope.

He left after his bulletin with a hug (the Michael hug was now a hug and a kiss of course) and Roly was poleaxed. What brainwashing had he performed on this boy, what rose-tinted glasses had he given him? Partner? PARTNER??? He wasn't going to dare flatter himself by thinking that Michael had fallen in love with him, but this was the biggest helping of infatuation he had seen so far. How the hell did he get out of this now? And when Michael came again, when he came next time armed with Levitra and expecting to be deflowered, what next? It was time to let him down again, intentionally now, time to drive him away by exhausting his patience and increasing his frustration until he gave up altogether. Why the hell couldn't Yvette be disgusted by her son, first by his being gay and, maybe having come to terms with that, by him then being besotted with the idea of surrendering his virginity to a man 35 years older than he? That was what any sane, loving mother would do wasn't it? How had he managed to come into contact with a blatantly liberal, not to say devil-may-care, parent who couldn't give a tinker's cuss about an elderly penis penetrating her boy's anus? He couldn't share his misgivings with her. He could see her being grateful for not having a son who would be responsible for an unwanted pregnancy, she would be just be that kind of mother. Hell's teeth: Prometheus had shown how to make fire and now he, Roly, was bound.

****

Hell's teeth.

It was Saturday morning and I was upstairs in my room when I heard the doorknocker, then my mother's voice calling: 'Here's somebody for you.' 'Who is it?' 'Well, if you come down you'll find out won't you? It's Robert Scobie.' 'Hell's teeth and buckets of blood! Robert Scobie! What's he doing here?' I muttered angrily under my breath and panicked. How was I going to hide my fib, about the radiogram, this time, and this time from Robert Scobie, schoolmate and son of Dougal, who was managing director of the factory where Auntie Vera worked? Robert lived in a big, smart house in Park Road and had never come to call for me before. Ever. 'Are you coming down?' 'Yes!' and to my further horror I heard my mother invite Robert in. I bolted downstairs and there he was, six feet and 11

381

stones of him, standing in the living room. In *our* council house living room. 'Hiya,' he said. 'Coming down for a game?'

Football in the park, yes and quick, anything to get him out of here. 'OK, yeah, let's go,' I said immediately, and bungled him out of the door. On the way to the park, besides devising the best scheme to murder my mother for being crazy enough to invite Robert Scobie inside the house, I said apropos of nothing and to divert any awkward questions, 'The radiogram's up at Alcock's being repaired at the moment.' This was to hide my previous mendacious claim to him that we possessed such a luxury and to explain its absence. But Robert was either completely indifferent to my prevarication or ignored it and he hadn't called on me to test my veracity, only to get me to the park to play football.

He could see those two boys (himself one of them) as they walked to the park that morning; Roland not yet aware of the signifcance of this second deceiving of a schoolfriend (this one about a phantom radiogram, following the first about his father's phantom car) not aware that both lies – born of envy, keeping-up-with-the-Jones's or keeping-up-with-my-schoolfriends-who-don't live-in-council-houses type of lies, harmless and childish enough in themselves, merely to show his contemporaries that he was every bit as good as they were and had everything they had – were the beginnings of congenital mendacity; he knew only that he'd lied in order to preserve the social status he *though*t he had a right to.

He probably felt justified in fibbing to Robert Scobie because Robert had a fleeting 'thing' about him; they had spent an evening in his house shortly before that Saturday morning visit, when they romped wildly from room to room groping each other's private parts. Roly enjoyed it more than Robert did, but when they mentioned the romp in the park that day, it was Robert who suggested they might do it again some time, though they never did. He recalled that in his adolescence he had wondered how much longer he could reconcile playing cricket, football and tennis with being an aesthete, let alone with being queer. He condoned those orthodox teenage pursuits by telling himself it wasn't *de rigueur* to be epicene. 'I'm not a nancy boy,' he reminded himself.' Life as a New Queer Boy, however, was not flourishing. To date, it had been restricted to lusting after the boys at school, posters of Cat Stevens, Brian Jones, Scott Walker and Gene Pitney sellotaped to his bedroom walls, body builders in a health magazine he sheepishly and surreptitiously managed to buy one daring day in W H Smith and the male underwear models in his mother's catalogue. But the time came when he had to put away childish things, when posters and pictures weren't enough; he was now 19 and a virgin and had to get his hands on a boy's body, not in schoolday gropes, but with a boy who wanted it as much as he did. What he wanted was sex, real sex, before he exploded.

****

'That was immense,' was Michael's verdict on Roly's savoury mince and Roly was delighted and grateful as ever for the accolade. 'Ace cook you are, Mister Roly Delia. Respect,' he said and insisted on clearing away and washing up the dishes himself. When he'd done, he went to sit next to Roly and they listened to music which, as Roly had cooked the meal and because of the treat that was lying in store for him later, Michael graciously let him choose and Roly hoped

383

it wouldn't spoil the mood. Michael settled with as polite a grunt as was to be expected for his choice of Dusty Springfield and there they were, man and boy in cosy togetherness, progressing from kissing and holding to moderate petting, managing, through who knew what willpower, to restrain themselves from stripping one another naked and having sex there and then. It was a hard fight and Roly finally had to tell him enough for a while and Michael complied by lying back with his legs stretched across him, still at fondling if not kissable distance, so Roly kept his hands busy stroking his shins. 'You still fancy me?' Michael asked. 'What have I told you about that word and what a silly question to ask a fully accredited boy addict like me.' 'Me pecs are comin' on.' 'Good, I like pecs I can handle. Not muscle Mary pecs, beefcake pecs, but *boy's* pecs, not quite fully developed, but toned enough to provide a cleavage of breast bone inviting my eager hands to cup them,' he beamed sardonically. Michael sat up with a questioning look on his face. 'What you goin' on about now?' 'There are those who regard this development of boyhood to manhood, with its big hands and feet out of proportion, as ungainly and unappealing, but I'm not one of them. Yours will be a magnificent swimmer's chest, your nipples sitting proudly surrounded by inviting amber areolas.' 'I got a good arse.' 'Yes you have. It's like a firm round, tight peach and it sits on solid legs. You're a pageant of pulchritude, that's what you are. What an ugly word pulchritude is, don't you think?' 'What does it mean?' 'It means beauty. Weird that, isn't it? An ugly word for beauty.' He went quiet and then in a dreamy vague voice said, 'When I saw you in the street... No, whenever I see a tasty youth in the street like you, do you know what happens?' 'Ya come in yer pants.' 'Haha. Maybe I *do* get aroused if I'm in the mood, but more likely these days I get a reminder of my mortality. Youth reminding me of death. I see a boy and I'm jealous – no, more than jealous, I've always been jealous of other people's beauty. No, I'm resentful, angry. I resent that I'm going to die and the boy is going to live on, but then I feel sad for him, sad as I rejoice in his beauty, because I know one day the big black car with the empty coffin will call to collect his corpse too.

"Golden lads and lasses must

Like chimney sweepers come to dust".'

'Eew, that' sick,' Michael said and clammed up. 'Are you scared of dyin'?' he asked at length. 'Are you scared of my dying? What will you do when I'm dead?' 'Shurrup. You're not gonna die.' 'I'm not? Then I'll be the first person who doesn't.' 'Stop it will ya?' 'When we know it's here, when we're lying semi-comatose, do you think we care? Are we happy about it at last, or resigned or indifferent? What did condemned people feel the moment before the axe fell, or heard the hangman pull the bolt or the captain of the shooting squad shout "Fire!"? Was any one of them in that last instant of despair, all hope gone, bothered? Darling –'
'– stop callin' me that.' 'Why?' 'It's crappy.' 'It is? Then I must go on saying it.' 'It's gay, I mean it's cheesy.' 'What I say is, there are plenty of far better people than I who have died, so if it's good enough for them...' Michael's lips broke into a half-amused, half-nervous smirk, Roly quickly dropped his false smile. 'Who am I fooling? I'm not *afraid* of death, I'm obsessed by it, more now than I ever was. Sometimes the realisation that one day I really am going to die is too terrifying to bear. I suppose the knack is to reach the point where life becomes so intolerable that the thought of leaving it is a comfort rather than a fear. I sound like Hamlet. And your question comes from a young ignorant mouth. Dying isn't something that youth can conceive of, to you it's a

remote intellectual concept. To me, it's a safety exit. You don't need one because you're young enough to run off in another direction. You have no years on the clock, so for you death is simply something that happens to other older people.' 'Me other grandad died last year. 'E was cool. 'E bought me my PC.' 'The day my first driving licence arrived in the post, I opened it up and saw the expiry date, two thousand and 25 it was and I was horrified to think I'd be 75 in the year 2025, but of course in 1967 that year was never going to arrive, 75 wasn't conceivable. Please, carry on growing up but don't grow old and die,' he told him. 'D'ya believe in god an' all that 'eaven stuff?' 'Which god?' 'There's only one ya dwork.' 'You mean there's only one that most people don't believe in. The Christian God who doesn't have a Christian name, but what about Allah, what about Buddah and Zoroaster and Ganesh? They all come a close second in terms of followers.' 'Oh, bollocks, I've started you off now.' 'Do I believe in God, a god? Well, I'd say I'm with Pascal. He, sensible man that he was, said that if you're going to bet on the existence of God, you should bet that he does exist rather than he doesn't, because you get better odds on the possible outcome of the former than the latter. I believe in a mathematical equation which explains the universe. If there was a choice and I could take it, I'd go for the Greek variation. It's much more poetic than a garden with a snake and an apple tree and it has ribs in it like the Bible version.' 'You're so weird.' 'Because they're weird stories, mythological Michael! And as for heaven, heaven is the concept of a dimension the human mind enters after death to restore all the rights that were wronged, mete out justice where it failed, exact peaceful revenge where necessary and make full retribution where required, in other words to reverse and redress all the imbalance and impurity that pertained in its previous mortal sphere.' Michael lapsed into darkened thought for a moment and then brightened. 'So you better shag me while you're still 'ere,' he cried and burst out laughing. 'Yes, take you and corrupt you.' 'Was that Denzel bloke in your book, was 'e a real person?' 'Are you worried that he was? Denzel had to go, that's all.' 'Because you 'ad 'im?' 'God's ballocks, no-ooo! Whatever d'you think I am? Denzel is fiction, dear boy, pure fiction and fantasy.' 'But he's in yer journal.' 'Yes he is and what better place for fiction than that! My record of fact and fiction, lapsed memories and half truths woven with an elusive thread into a diaphanous tapestry. ''Ere we go, Mister Brainiac again,' Michael sighed, mockingly. 'It's pathetic, really. I thought up a character for a book I kidded myself I could write, but it was the desperation of fantasy. I was desperate for his desirable face and his one-point-eight metre honed body, clothed in stone-washed, sprayed-on Levis, framed in the doorway which I could possess. You know, you've read it.' 'I'm not a fantasy though am I? I'm real, look! What d'ya want, fantasy or real?' 'Ha!' Roly roared. 'You. You are already my Adonais, Hyacinthus, Narcissus, Antinous and Sebastiane in the split second I've known you. I'm trying very hard to believe in you.' 'I just don't get you sometimes.' 'Believe that you're here, that I'm sitting here holding glory's head. Believe that you're an angel. Do you think you are? Do you think you've been sent? To rescue me? Michael the angel. Michele... angelo. Michelangelo. You see, you're a reincarnation. I think you *are* an angel or at least you are magical, supernatural.' Or his David come to life. That was it; he was stealing again, stealing divinity this time. What did one do with a stolen divinity? He didn't have the right to *ius prima nocte* with a boy, let alone a god.

****

A building site had sprung up which he could see out of the window at the back. He had a view of part of the end eaves of the roof of the house they were putting up and could see workmen in their jeans and white helmets climbing up and down, sawing and hammering and knocking off to have a smoke or saunter to the Co-op shop to get their pies and drinks. He saw one particularly fine specimen arrive in his Range Rover and get out to put his flourescent jacket and his helmet on. But distance and eyesight failed and infuriated him because, although he could make out a fine head of blond hair he couldn't discern whether it was that of a trim fit 40-year-old or a hunky, tight-jeaned youngster. He wished he would come nearer.

Michael had been at swimming practice all day, preparing for the forthcoming match. 'What did ya think when I sent you that text message?' he asked when he called next. 'I thought it was yet another nail in the coffin of my conscience, another reminder that I still need to learn penance. But I managed to put that aside. A boy who drops into your life and asks you to bugger him concentrates the mind wonderfully.' 'If I 'adn't met you,' Michael reflected, 'an' if we weren't 'ere and if I didn't know you'd sent me that triple X an' that I got you in that chatroom...' If what? His Socratic deductions deserted him for the moment. 'You would know where my fiction ends and real life starts. Is that what you're trying to say? Well, I hardly know that myself, so perhaps you can help me. First there was my Journal, then my novel, then I mixed the two together. I created a boy called Denzel and instead of being what he would be to a million other writers, he became part of my everyday life and I let him usurp me. Now he's gone, you will move in and out of the story from now – if I continue with it – and one minute you're in the fiction and another you're here. Where the hell are we?' 'F – sod all that, I'll show you I'm real.' Michael sat down on the bed (he was making no sexual move, it was 8.30 in the morning and he was on his way to school and Roly happened to be still under the duvet) and Roly felt the tingle again. How he once relished adventure at inappropriate times, but now... 'Where did it go, that yestergo?' Yesterdreams, yesterfools, yesterme, yesteryou...' Suddenly, Michael was on top of him and Roly was kissing him and his warm, soft morning lips tasted of those Aromas again. 'Michael the miraculous mandarin.' Michael jumped up with the usual 'Laters' and added a *'Dahling'* with an effeminate pose which looked crass and he was gone, leaving Roly smiling sardonically at the Wildean pain, the pain of being parted from a dear one for a short time, rather than the pain of parting forever, which was easy. He got up, wiped and dressed, had coffees, cigarettes and shredded wheat and set to writing more of his words, wondering what the words were for and what he was going to do with them, if anything. At some point, the doorbell rang and he felt the customary annoyance at an unscheduled intrusion, choosing at first to ignore it and then deciding to answer it.

He heard her shout as he approached the door, 'Hiya.' It was Yvette and when he opened it, 'You busy?' she asked, with a wide smile and her head cocked to one side. Her hair cascaded over the lower ear, her gold necklace and rings spangled and she looked fresh in an ankle-length, spun cotton, light pink thin dress. He held open the door for her and she followed him in. What was this, a visit of maternal concern? He had a momentary black thought: had Michael's unprecedented morning visit heralded some shift, some reversal in the emotional current? Had mother suddenly reneged on her initial blessing of his and Michael's union? Had Michael himself overnight finally had second thoughts and, unable to tell him when he called earlier and sat on the bed, sent his herald with the bad news, the kiss of the Godfather? Had he had another and better offer through chatrooms? Did Roly hope that this or some of it was the case? He invited mother herald to sit down and she, still smiling, opened her mouth to speak and he wasn't sitting comfortably. 'Er, I'm not bein' funny but...' He felt more uncomfortable. 'I don't really know where to.' She had looked calm on arrival but in truth she was flummoxed; he thought she was trembling. This was indeed bad news. 'Oh god, you're gonna kill me.' She took hold of the small shoulder bag she had strapped around her and dug into it. She seemed to take hold of herself a little. 'Ya know Mikey's... told me all about it don't ya? I mean 'e's mad about ya an'... well.' Roly recognised the beginning of a Hollis torrrent; Michael's habit was genetic. It had begun at a crawl, any moment the dam would burst. She let drop her hands as if to drain her tension through them. "E's told me about yer problem, ya know, an' I know you 'aven't, that you 'aven't yet, an' 'e said, 'e said about Danny's dad's... stuff...' – the torrent was gaining momentum – 'e uses, an' Danny was gonna pinch some for a laugh 'cos Mikey told 'im to get some so they could, well ya know what lads do, an' I told 'im not to do that an'... anyway.' She rummaged in the bag again and produced a handful of blue lozenge shaped pills. 'I 'ad a word with me dad an' told 'im I'd met a guy an'... me an' me dad 'ave always, ya know, been 'onest like an' I told 'im the guy's gorra problem, so me dad give me these an' I got 'em for you, 'cos of what Mikey... told...me... about... about.' She clammed, the torrent was stemmed and the silence was thundering. Roly looked at her, at her eyes, which were at that moment stuck wide in a Stan Laurel what-happens-now? bland gaze of bewilderment and fright. 'Yvette,' he said, emphasising the name slowly. 'You're a saint. What a kind thought. Would you like a coffee?' He had taken her aback. 'Oh!' she piped, a bird sound. 'So... you don't mind? I mean, I 'aven't... I thought you'd think I was...' 'I don't think anything at all.' He smiled as sweetly as he could. 'Thank you.' He held out his hand. 'They'll be a great help I'm sure.' And she leant over to deposit the Levitra in his palm. By Jupiter, he thought, your 16-year-old son has lost all reason over me and it's making me lose mine. You know nothing about me, you accept me and with your ignorant laissez-faire you practically *invite* me to have sex with him. Now what's more you bring me the pharmaceutical means to make sure I accomplish the deed. You have no idea how contaminated he will be. 'Come here, give us a kiss,' he said and she jumped up. 'You're a good lass, lass,' he said, as she bent over him. Any tinge of prudish embarrasment she may have had, the tension – it drained away and Roly could hear her relief and she regained her confident poise and tone. 'You stay where you are,' she said, 'and I'll make us a coffee.' 'I feel very stupid,' he told her as she sipped and he smoked. 'It's a wonder how Michael has come out to you and I can only marvel at both of you, how you've responded to him and especially to me. The idea of your young son and me. Well, look at me.' 'You're awright, you're only a bit... aren't ya?' 'My age and Michael's age,' he corrected her solemnly. 'Don't tell me you weren't shocked.' 'Nothin' that one does shocks me anymore, shug.' *Shug, Trenton short for sugar.* 'I can't help comparing it with the traumatic time I had in the last century with my parents and oh, lordy, I sound like a war veteran don't I, or a suffragette, so I'll shut up. It was bad enough for my parents with me and other boys, and they were boys like I was, but Michael and an old man?' 'You're as young as ya feel,' she said fatuously. Why hadn't she said something like, 'My son would never have turned queer if there weren't any of you homosexuals around to start with'? 'It's pathetic 'ow some people get worked up about it' she went on. 'Did you see about that poor barman got beaten to death in London, an' they said it was just 'cause 'e was gay. Shockin'. 'E was just walkin' 'ome wasn't 'e, poor creature?' Roly wanted to bring up his running away, but then he thought, do I really want to confide in this woman, kindly soul though she so patently is, so they finished their coffees and talked about what a good job Michael was doing for him and his swimming successes and she said again what a good lad really he was and then it was time for her to go.

Michael came for supper and Roly made stir-fry mango chicken with rice and his own concoction of cucumber relish, 'Better than the takeaway,' he said and followed it with some bought fruit crumble and créme fraiche (which he thought Michael might baulk at but he didn't). One of their 'cuddling up' sessions on the sofa came next, accompanied by the DVD Michael had brought with him, some daft American supposed comedy, full of groomed and glittering teenagers with perfect teeth. Roly found it very unfunny and there wasn't even a cute redeeming boy in it; he was bored after the first few minutes and though he continued to watch for Michael's benefit, he didn't see what he was watching. He tried to make conversation, but Michael was engrossed and giggling at what was on the screen. When he made mention of the day's events and what he called Yvette's engineering of them and her well-meant intervention, Michael said, 'Me mum's cool like that.' 'Yes, she is,' Roly agreed. They both fell quiet for a moment, then the same telepathic signal struck them simultaneously; Roly looked away from the television and turned to look at Michael at exactly the moment he did the same and they fixed each other with the same intense silent stare, like two friends who haven't seen each other for many years and who aren't sure of who the other is. Roly felt a sudden surge, an electrical impulse such as starts up a machine. Then he had an irrational thought and he made an instant decision – to suspend of his own accord, without consultation, their mutually agreed moratorium regarding heavy petting. Without really knowing why, he made a frantic grab for Michael's neck and pulled his head towards him. He saw a flash of the night in the chamber of the restaurant in France with Murdoch, the night of his reckless pounce. He thought, I'm pouncing now like I did then, but my object is far more desirable and lowered his gaze to Michael's full waiting lips and kissed them hungrily. He drew away, leaving Michael surprised and panting and then he ordered him, quite brusqely, to take his bottoms and shorts down and stand before him. Michael did as he was told and stood there, fully aroused. Neither spoke and Roly, after taking in what he saw slap bang in front of his eyes, took hold of Michael's thighs, pulled him by them to him and moved his head forward.

Later, in bed before sleep, Roly questioned his actions. Michael had asked if he could stay the night again and before Roly said no, he considered how best to make a refusal sound absolute, to make it sound final so that Michael would infer that intimacy between them had come to an end thenceforth. But his valour failed him; he dithered as though he were weighing pros and cons, then resorted to refusing him in gentle and gracious terms, convincing him that it was best that he go home to mother after all and promising him he could stay the next night. He had never been one to perform sexual, or indeed any other kind of selfless acts.

Michael too lay awake. He was naked and he hugged himself tightly and touched himself erotically and tried to imagine they were Roly's arms that were wrapped around him and his hands carressing him.

****

Roly was getting out of the car and saw that the nearby building site had acquired a new hunk, the young man tramping by him slowly in his brown ankle boots on his way back, presumably, to the site from the shop: close-cropped head, all rough and animal and butch but in a gentle kind of way. He was eating a pie. He noticed Roly briefly. Roly saw him through the window later at work up on the roof of the nearly completed house. He had also caught a snatch, the merest of glances, of the new dustman and postman. The dustman was a magnificent negro hunk who wore a sleeveless teeshirt and showed great ebony muscles and the postie was a boy, by the look of it at a distance, who walked with a young jaunty gait at any rate and was younger than his predecessor. Tall and slender in a baseball cap. He wished for a close-up of both of them some day.

****

'You're capable of such… overpowering affection, you can be very endearing, Michael… and that caressing tone of yours could make any man feel virtuous, any man but me that is' and with that the deed was done. He had the Levitra, his ordnance and ordinance, he was fully armed and he'd run out of alternatives and excuses not to go into battle. For that is how he felt, going into battle, or rather going to the scaffold after his inevitable traitorous defeat and he turned his thoughts to something gastronomic, to something that would befit a last supper: he picked confit of lamb and potato

394

torte, so they'd driven to the town and Michael helped him into the butcher's where he bought a shoulder of lamb. 'You'll be amazed,' he assured him, when Michael expressed his horror at the amount of time involved – 'Two days to cook a piece of meat!' – it was too complex for him. 'Really it's not,' said Roly, 'just lengthy and you won't ever before have tasted such succulent meat, I promise you.' He called on Michael's firm hands to seal the joint, wine and garlic head in foil and put it in the hot oven and six hours later he stripped the meat from the bone with two forks. Next day they sliced potatoes and chopped garlic and scattered rosemary and parsley and layered everything in the pan for second baking and the next day Roly instructed him on the slicing and wrapping of meat and potato wedges and, after a third bake, the meal was ready, but for the steaming of sliced carrots and spinach. He allowed Michael to fetch two cans of lager to drink and they sat down to eat. The way Michael attacked his plate and the number of 'Mmms' of satisfaction which peppered his chewing had Roly wondering whose last meal it was and which of them was feeling condemned. When they finished and Michael had cleared the supper things away and washed them and they settled on the easy sofa, Michael with his second can of lager and Roly with coffee and cigarette, Roly decided to have a last stab at being a wet blanket, cancelling or at best postponing the inevitable. He took hold of Michael's hand: 'Stop playing Pollyanna. Why don't you just accept that I'm a curmudgeonly fractious captious old bastard and have done with me. Why don't you? I'm no good for you and you are too good for me.' Michael made a moue of displeasure and boredom and pursed his ample lips. 'Oh, please, not the – whaddya call it? – melancholy again,' he moaned. 'Melancholy, it sounds like a load of veg or somethin',' he chortled. Roly wasn't to be distracted: 'Sin is a miserable thing and so is poverty,' he went on. 'Look at me, clear the mist that's shrouding your eyes for once and look. I have nothing because of my ruined health, which I ruined myself, the little things that once upon a time when I was fit and able-bodied would annoy me are now cataclysmic disasters and they make me rage and rant. It can't be any fun for you. Don't be a doormat, a masochist, a martyr, don't lie down for me.' 'But you 'ave got somethin', like I said. Me! And who needs money? Sex doesn't cost nothin' unless your doin' a rent boy and I'm not a rent boy am I?' 'Oh the simple solutions of the simple mind,' Roly said and he stretched his face into a still life of a pained grimace. No, Michael wasn't a vendible commodity. 'How little I value you, please forgive me. I have no money because I can't sell my work and I have to constantly reassure myself that it isn't because it's not worth selling, or delude myself rather. I have no income and I don't deserve any because when I had one I pissed it down the toilet. I don't expect you to understand. I don't assume I have the right to be wealthy, I assume I'd be richer than I am had I not wasted so much. Comfortable at least is what I should be by now, perhaps. I have no pension, no capital, no savings, no financial future. I know such things are meaningless to you. The knowledge that I've never had the house that I wanted, nor the right quality hi-fi, nor the hand crafted furniture, the works of art and antiques, the Aga and the aluminium coated stainless steel cooking utensils – this never used to bother me because I could excuse and reassure myself by telling myself that there was plenty of time to acquire fine things. Now that time has gone, Michael. Now I have nothing and I never will have before I die and that's what terrifies me. I've lived the majority of my years beyond my means and I've known debt. Now, it's not that I'm living beyond my means, rather that I have no means beyond which to live. I sit here day after day blanking out the worry of how it's going to take infinity paying off my credit cards, while I feel guilty that I can't send pennies to help the victims of the Iranian earthquake. I'm filled with deep resentment that the 14-year-old boy I saw in an amateur show 15 years ago has now won an 18 million pounds record contract while I have to claim housing benefit –' 'You talkin' about Robbie Williams?' 'The same.' 'And I can't rave at the injustice of it all because it's all my idiotic sodding fault! I hate idiots and losers, I'm an idiot and a loser, ergo I hate myself.' He stopped abruptly, taking in what he'd said and allowing Michael time to do the same. 'But at least I have the consolation of my friend Dr Johnson,' he sighed with disinterest. 'Who's he when he's at home?' *'Ooz 'e when 'eeez at 'ome?* 'Oh, just a clever and undervalued man, like me. He said if you make a beast of yourself it takes away some of the pain of being a man.' Michael turned his gaze on him, bedraggled and bewildered and pitying and he seemed to be looking on him for a moment as something alien, malformed and lost. 'I'm sorry Michael, it's not your fault and I mustn't encourage false hopes and impossible dreams, which I've had too many of and don't want you to inherit from me. I've lived the life of one for whom cheating has been a law of the universe, but I refuse to cheat you.' This last suddenly evoked the chimera of Peter Lindrop towering above him like a dark phantom. Peter was a friend of Larry's whom he had commandeered and nurtured because – if he was honest – because he was a prosperous city broker and a fertile source he could call on to finance his extravagances and haul him out of predicaments. He was one of the dozens of people he had never repaid back. 'I still owe so many so much,' he murmured.

Was it charm or impudence or my ability as a conman that enabled me to manipulate Peter, whom I hardly knew and only through Larry, into taking me to a branch of his bank in Piccadilly and draw out 15 hundred pounds on his Access card? Money he was giving to me to pay the rent arrears, but which, even as soon as I had it in my hand, I knew was destined to be very quickly dissipated on the whisky I was sure to buy with it.

'You can't pay him back.' It was Muvvie who spoke, in a strange faraway censorious voice, 'but if only you can find out where he lives now, somewhere in Yorkshire isn't it? But what will you do if he's no longer alive? And when you've done that you should do the same with Joan, Barry, Helen, Monica and Teddy in Wales and at least two landlords in London and two banks and Meals on Wheels in Trenton and everyone else you've borrowed or begged from, ripped off or plain defrauded in your blatantly profligate life. Maybe Teddy has harboured you no ill will, maybe he hasn't been execrating your name all these years. You'd like to think that wouldn't you? Because you remember that night he told you that your cheque had bounced, when he wasn't at all angry. In fact, he looked as though he couldn't be bothered at all. He let you get away with murder, let you take advantage, which you did with so many. You were plausible and had a silver tongue, you old dog, but you can exonerate yourself because it's not your fault that people are so gullible. You can blame others for your own unhappiness, which is a solace to you, a solace which is the final deceit of the desperate. And Audrey, dear Audrey. What a coincidental story she told you! How her husband walked out on her one Christmas morning never to return. That's exactly what you did, shortly after she told you. With her 300 quid!'

Such were the turgid recollections that sprung from his well of inferiority, pretence and dishonesty. He had always had to fight dragons in the presence of good people, fight to stave off the inadequacy they made him feel and here and now in Michael was a good person. He had never subscribed to the adage that said you are as good as the next man, because he wasn't, all the men and women next to him were far better than he and he hated them for it, that was the root of the misanthropy he directed towards people *en masse* and the envy he felt seething towards many of them singly. He had only ever faked being worthy and he had no intention of attempting to fake with Michael, not emotionally, because he was trying so hard to 'reform', to renew himself and not physically, because that was impossible.

'Tell ya what,' Michael said. 'Take the pill and make me 'appy and I'll make you 'appy. And remember, I'm wearin' them whities for ya.' 'D'you reckon it's time?' Roly asked. 'Sooner ya take it, the sooner we.' Peering closely into those deep infinite eyes, Roly discerned... a kind of hope, he supposed it was... and he felt despair, despair for himself and for the forlornness of that hope. He reached out to run a finger down his nose. 'Yeah, what?' 'This.' 'Me nose?' 'Yes, it really is il piccolo sexy muso di Michele,' he cooed. 'It makes your profile completely un-Greek, it looks as though it wants to fly off the way it turns up so delightfully at the end.' He kissed it. 'Roly,' he murmured, thrown by this foolish diversion of a nose, 'I really want you big time, you know what I'm sayin'?' *Yanowomsayin.* 'And what is it you want?' 'I wanna do things right an' be a good f – a good sh – I mean be good for you – an' make you feel good and not make a dork of meself.' 'Like I did you mean.' 'Behave, I don't mean that. Just remember to tell me what to do, everythin', like ya did before.' 'Do you like being told what to do?' 'I like it when you tell me we're gonna have sex yeah. Shall I go an' 'ave me shower now?' 'Yes and make sure that sugar button of yours is clean.' 'You bet.' 'And don't forget the tighty whities.' 'Oh I won't forget the nut grips. Tell me what we're gonna do first.' 'You know what we're going to do.' 'Yeah but I wanna 'ear you tell me.' And Roly took him in his arms and whispered kiss and stroke and suck and squeeze and lick and nipples and boyhole lubriciously to him and Michael moaned and wriggled. 'We're going to do everything we want to do,' he said, 'and then I'm going to –' '– take me cherry? Dah, stop it you cherry-picker you.' 'Me, a cherry-picker?' Roly pretended to bristle. 'Do you know what a cherry-picker is? It's a hydraulically raised platform which carries workmen up to fix street lamps.' Michael dug his ribs playfully. 'You did cherry boys you perv. You took lads' cherries, you were a cherry-picker and you still are. You're a cherry-picker,' he said it again and laughed raucously. Roly thought, he's like a child with new toys. 'Sometimes I didn't even know I was doing it,' he said, 'because they didn't tell me it was their first time, or couldn't when they were foreign. But I loved it, even finding out afterwards I loved it. No, I'm no cherry-picker, I'm more your faunolept.' 'And what's a fornowotsit when it's at 'ome?' 'A faunolept,' he said, 'and I quote, "is an artist and a madman, a creature of infinite melancholy with a bubble of hot poison in his loins and a super-voluptuous flame permanently aglow in his subtle spine". No matter what his physical condition, he told himself. 'Cherry-picker, cherry-picker,' Michael chanted. ''Ow you gonna pick mine?' 'By debauching you. On your back, young man, with your legs hooked around my waist and me deep inside you where it's hot and tight and I'll be kissing you all the time.' 'Ooh Roly,' he moaned and pressed his face into his neck. 'You like the sound of that?' 'Yeeeessss.' 'But what if you can't take it?'

'Whadd'ya mean?' 'If it hurts you too much, promise you'll tell me?' Michael nestled deeper into him. 'You can 'urt me all you like.' 'And you'll take it like a man, hmm?' 'Like fuckin' superman.' They both giggled at that and when they stopped, they held each other in silence. 'Roly?' 'Yes?' 'I lied to you, ya know.' 'You did?' 'About 'er... that girl you saw me with that time.' 'Oh? What I saw wasn't a lie.' 'Yeah but... I never did anythin'. I mean, I 'aven't yet... done anythin' with anybody.' 'Yes well, that's all about to change isn't it?' he said, smiling at him. 'And now I'm going to brush my teeth and I shall lie down and wait for you, my Michelangelo, my David.'

After his toilet, he went into the bedroom and undressed and lay on the bed naked, looking at his now Levitra-ed penis standing at as near a respectable perpendicular as the ravages of time would allow. He heard Michael go into the bathroom and turn on the shower, he listened to the spray and wondered if he was taking a necessary precaution against a possible premature ejaculation. If he is, he thought, it is no matter; the boy is an ephebos and as such can be quick to repeat. He waited, exquisite suspense.

Sompont, the Thai boy, suddenly came to him through the kaleidoscope memory. He would tell Michael about Sompont and the most exciting sex he'd ever had and he would see if Michael could equal him.

I was with the Irish boy from the night before; I didn't want sex with him again. I was wondering what to do when Sompont solved my quandary for me. "I want you!" he shouted suddenly, pointing at me. With that, I took a very rude leave of the Irish boy, grabbed Sompont by the arm and walked him out of the club and all his friends round the table cheered and clapped us offstage. When I got him home to Clapham and in bed, Sompont said, 'I want fuck you' and I said, 'No, I want to fuck you', and Sompont said, 'OK then'. And it was incredible. We started with me fucking him face down, then he turned on his side, taking me with him; then he manoeuvred himself on top of me and spun round on my cock to face me. All in an unbroken movement, without me slipping out and I pumped up into him and watched his cock waving madly up and down in time to the thrusts and I pulled his torso down to make his face meet mine and I kissed him while I fucked him. We had a repeat performance a few nights later in Sompont's bedsit in Earls Court, and – small planet huh? – I ran into him in a nightclub in Bangkok when I was there the following year, but he was not available again, because he had a young European wrapped around him and I was with my own Thai squeeze of the night.

He called out: 'I want my eye candy, my totty,' and heard Michael laugh. 'Nearly there, 'ang on,' Michael called back and a moment later he walked into the bedroom. With the white briefs gripping his loins and the torus formed by his satyriasis thrusting arrogantly forward, he stood hands on hips: 'Is this right then? I feel like a ponce,' he wailed. Roly saw his true kouros, his telamon, vivental now and draped skimpily as statues of exquisite boys should be, in white linen that covered hardly anything and suggested everything. In that moment he was he headed the litany of boys: Stephen and Martin, Jack, Larry, Adam, Prasong, Jason, the sum of all them and the palingenesis of a thousand years and Roly felt he was in the presence of majesty, or at prayer in an act of devotion, worshipping youth, exalting the *youngness* now before him. 'Oh you beauty,' he growled and hoisted himself to his feet and held him as tight as he could and breathed the word, 'Majesty,' as he caressed his face and brushed it with his own. He stood at his front then turned him, using both hands simultaneously to catch the wholeness of him, planing them across and up and down the surfaces of his flesh, smoothing, touching, squeezing and he turned him sideways and raised his arm behind his head and held his shoulders and biceps between his hands as if carrying them, gauging their breadth and the mass of muscle and sinew. 'Please don't melt,' he whispered, in a voice that was distant and he drew his finger slowly and lightly across the line of his mouth, traced it along the curve of a pectoral and along that of the solid mound of flesh that arced from the small of his back to the top of his leg. 'Now the lines of beauty are mine.' His voice was hoarse now, despairing, 'I'd hate them to disappear' ... the boy listened behind closed eyes and hoped he understood, he heard and felt but couldn't speak because he was floating away, above them, leaving them standing there... then a mouth was forced on his and he was kissed by lips and a writhing tongue. He was turned around again and stroked, the finger now running along the cotton edges of the briefs... Roly sat back down in front of him and pulled the briefs over his thighs and he knew what he would see and it sprang up, cantilevered... and the boy looked down at himself and giggled... and Roly took hold of it, it was peremptory and engorged, like a dormant piston on his palm, he closed tender fingers around it, rock hard it was but wrapped in warm thin muslin. 'Warm, silky, smooth,' were Roly's words as he stroked on... 'Here's the old cherry-picker come for his naughty nymph'... and he stood and held his body to his again and it seemed to sink and droop and hang on to keep from drowning ... He ran his fingers roughly through his hair ... 'I want your treasure, naughty nymph'... 'I want you,' Michael begged at last. 'I want you, Roly' and Roly sat again and looked up at him, his hands around his waist... 'D'you know what boys are made of?'... 'Whad'ya mean?... 'They're made of fruit, ripe juicy fruit'... his hands stroked... 'This is a peach and these, these are your plums'... 'And that's a banana I suppose,' he sniggered... and Roly took him in his mouth while he cupped the bag of plums and felt how ripe they were, how near the boy was to the edge ... 'Oh, Roly, I don't wanna ruin it again,' Michael cried, straining to contain himself...'Do you want me inside you, Michael?'...'Yeah'... Roly slid across the bed leaving him standing there again...'Turn sideways... now turn again and let me look at your sweet peach'... He had him posing, a piece of sculpture in a gallery... 'Come here, lie next to me'... He lay next to him and Roly was quickly on top of him, smothering him in kisses... 'Now up you go on your hands and knees,' and Michael obeyed and Roly got behind him, gently pushed his head down into the pillow and tickled with his tongue then probed into the delicate tissue and Michael shot his head up in spasms ... Roly licked for an age, tasting musk, then put him on his back, spread his legs and lay between them and pushed him into the pillow with kisses... Michael was stronger than he and Roly felt the counter resistance until it faded to submission and they kissed on and their breath and saliva mingled... He moved his mouth to his ear and heard 'Aah' and Michael's body tightened... moved his face down over his chest, skimming and stopping to lick, which brought moans... brushed his stomach and licked and tasted his way to rigid flesh... he wanted him to realise that, any minute, fantasy would be no more and Michael did realise it and it sent him over, his resistance gave, his muscles lost hold and he felt it... 'Again!'

he shouted... 'The little death,' Roly hisssed as Michael passed out into that delicious darkness to wake immediately, helpless, something draining from him and he writhed and his arms flailed and he clutched Roly's shoulders and a low sound came out of his mouth, 'Nnn... I couldn't'... Roly brought his face up close and stroked his cheek to quieten him... 'All right,' he whispered, 'just shine on, my angel boy' and Michael lay back, pulled Roly on to him, held him, smoothed his back and waited... Roly's body wrapped his and he felt how warm and unbothered it was now. It wasn't long before Roly heard, 'You wanna do it?'... 'What?'... 'Inside me'... 'Do you want me to?'... 'Yeah'... 'Only if you want it, Michael, only if it makes you happy'... 'I want you to and I wanna be happy'... Roly grabbed the spray and then the lube... 'Are you ready?'... 'Yeah, ready'... and Michael felt his legs lifted and bent over his shoulders... Roly was poised above him and Michael was at his mercy, his eyes closed, waiting... a strong virile youth stretched out naked on a perfumed silken couch, waiting to receive pleasure and to give it back... Roly ran his gaze over the recumbent body... he could do absolutely anything he wished... he slid inside him... burned him... 'Relax and don't fight it ... if it hurts too much, I'll stop'... 'No, don't... it's... bigger than... it won't... it's too... Agh! Oh fuck!... Don't stop!'... and he was filled... an alien, slippery, hard pain incised him and he was bewildered because it was excruciating and wonderful... He gasped at the pain of the pleasure, the pleasure of the pain... The First Pain... pain should make him cry but he felt only joy... the agony of wanting was over... 'Tell me you like it'... 'Oh yes'... 'I want to hear you say it'... 'I do... I love it... I love you fuckin' me, Roly'... and Roly reminded himself that this wasn't just a virgin, this was Michael.

After all was over, there came the inevitable ingenuous question of the boy, wanting reassurance, while Roly smiled in the darkness to hear it. 'Oh Michael, Michael. You're a Palladian villa, Haddon Hall, Durham Cathedral, the Brunelleschi Dome, Mozart's music,' he clarioned and Michael laughed triumphantly. 'And you'll be happy to know that your beauty is as great as it was before. Are you feeling as gorgeous as you look, my disvirginated diabolo?' 'Tastic and brill,' he said and Roly told him to go and 'wash that sweet quinny'.

'Tell me what it felt like.' 'Awesome,' Michael answered. 'Ha!' 'The way you did it, it felt like I was...' 'Filled,' said Roly, 'and do you want to be filled again?' 'Yes please.' And Roly told the story of Sompont. 'Let's see if you can bounce higher than he did,' he said and there was kissing and stroking and caressing and Michael's acrobatic manoeuvres and pushing and pulling and thrusts and the thrusting was fiercer than before making Michael breath out loud. 'Now turn yourself round on me'... Michael lifted his legs and balanced carefully and faced him, sitting astride him... Roly hung on to his waist, Michael was riding... 'Lean back'... Michael supported himself on his arms and Roly watched himself sliding in and out of him and saw Michael's penis swinging up and down to the rhythm like a flagpole in the wind... then he pulled his torso down upon himself and they kissed... he pushed him back and wriggled on top of him to pinion him once more to the mattress and though it hurt much more, he didn't want Roly to stop... Roly kissed his mouth again and then his teeth were gnawing into the soft skin of his neck, clamping it... he lifted his face... 'Soon,' he gasped... more thrusts, more burning, more pain, more ecstasy... 'You come too... come while I ram you... let me hear you'… 'Minute… keep on,' he cried… Then a frenzy took hold and he let fly another 'Aaah', this time keening. 'Oh do it… rrrrrrr… your big… ooooh… fuuuuck meeee!' he wailed… He was a noisy boy… Orgasmic oblivion gave way to consciousness and it was over again and they lay back once more.

This time, after the interval of recovery, Michael raised himself and was the one to lean across and plant a kiss and Roly marked the show of tenderness, affection. 'Hey, Roly,' he called. 'Mmm?' 'It was immense. Awesome and wicked and immense. Thank you,' and he kissed his mouth again and it made Roly wonder about the effects the discovery of sex had had on him: it could be that it was smoothing his crude edges, turning his coarseness into politeness and sensitising him. 'You're wicked all right – I love you, man.' There was sincerity, but Roly heard the blind and doomed youthful optimism and it seared into him. 'I love you too, Michael, I really do.' He hoped not for the first time that he didn't lie, but it didn't make him happy to say it. 'Aww, Roly,' Michael murmured again. 'Mates?' 'Yes, mates.' 'Promise you'll never run away from me again.' In that instant, Roly forgave him his dysphemia, his linguistic GBH, his ubiquitous 'fucks', his paltry learning, his rude manners, but he couldn't forgive him for loving him. He turned him around so that he could enfold him from behind and Michael fell asleep almost immediately with his back pressed into Roly and Roly lay awake clutching him, sending his unspoken gratitude to him through warm hands until he too slept.

In the morning, Roly awoke first and kissed his hair; when Michael stirred and groaned, he wanted him again, he found him even more desirable, how was it possible? He went to carry out the customary and obligatory emptying of his morning bladder and when he came back, Michael was sitting up, a grimace of fatigue on his face; this was no shining morning schoolboy's face any more. He greeted him, 'Tell ya what,' he said. 'Ya sure know when ya bin fucked innit? Feels like I've got a fuckin' great stick still rammed up me. You an' your big end.' 'Oh dear,' said Roly, getting back in beside him. 'Where are the soft and tender words, the expressions of endearment, you Visigoth, you hooligan?' He told him to turn over onto his stomach. 'Poor plucked boy', he murmured, smoothing a hand across his rear. 'Are you sorry now?' 'What you mean, about doin' it?' 'Well?' 'Give it large!' he roared. Roly stroked on. 'Michael?' 'Yeah?' 'Did it hurt?' 'A bit at first, but then it was great.' 'Not being buggered, you lummox.' 'What then?' 'When you fell from heaven.' He lifted himself on one elbow and looked down at his back. 'You know I've had sex with quite a few boys don't you?' 'Yeah, yeah, 'undreds,' he acknowledged, sounding a tad weary. 'Well I just want to say that there has been nary a peach like yours, ever.' 'As if I know what that means,' he said and when Roly explained, 'Is it the best you ever shagged though?' he sneered. ''Ow do I rate on the bubble butt scale?' 'Don't be so sniffy at being admired,' Roly reprimanded. 'Accept a compliment gracefully.' 'Hey, no probs,' he said and flipped himself over onto his back, exposing his towering morning glory; a tyro, a virgin only hours ago, unversed in the rituals of ephebophilia, but now a graduate. And he seemed to recant, with his characteristic crassness, bravado being ever the tool of his sensitivity. 'Are you gonna spend all day lookin' at it or can I go get a drink o' pop first?' Roly gestured to let him get up and he stood with his back to him. He slapped both hands loudly on his two buttocks. 'If ya gonna fuck it for fuck's sake fuck it,' he sang and then he moved and he and his buttocks bounced out of the room. 'But I need a drink,' he called. Something very silly leapt into Roly's head, a melody that leapt from its own obscurity and he began to sing it: 'I'll buy you one more frozen orange juice on this fantastic day-ee.'

****

Michael got up, put on his boxers and a teeshirt and said he would go and make a coffee. 'I wanna,' he called, to quieten Roly's protests about being cossetted. 'I'm 16 friggin' years of friggin' age now and I'm domesticated. 'Ow's that for a big word for ya, Mister Dictionary Brainiac?' 'A 16-year-old, domesticated – I wonder what the opposite of a virgin is? You're now a domesticated stoned cherry, that's what you are.' 'And you are weird.' As Roly hated both eating and drinking in bed he got up too, wrapping his dressing-gown around himself. 'Don't move,' he said, when Michael brought the coffee into the livingroom. 'You're a man boy now, but please stay a boy man for a time. Keep your neoteny safe.' 'Neoteny,' Michael repeated, deadpan and shook his head. 'It means keeping the characteristics of your youth although you're an adult,' Roly explained. 'I hope you never succumb to the alchemy of corruption and decay we call growing old.' Michael nodded his head, calculating. 'Act like a grown-up kid ya mean?' 'Exactly right!,' Roly laughed. 'Like I said, brainiac.' He shook his head again. 'Roly?' 'Yes, Michael the Miraculous?' He didn't speak for a moment, then said, hesitatingly, 'I just wanna know... if I didn't do it good, ya'd tell me yeah?' 'You're fishing again. I have nothing bad to tell you my flower.' 'Was I as good as that one who... ya know, when I was ridin' ya an' you were rammin' up into me?' That was Michael all over, never one to use a euphemism when cacophemy would do. Roly sat back. 'The sex act transforms people,' he said. 'Sense of being, identity if you like, is sublimated. When we were making love, you were all there

409

was in the world and I hope you were feeling the same, but in a way it wasn't you and it wasn't me. When two people are engrossed in passion the passion transforms them.' Michael's brow darkened and he looked pensive. 'We were in a different dimension, one outside humanity.' He looked at Michael and saw perplexity and incomprehension in his face. 'Oh all right,' he said to mollify him. 'If you want a physical assessment and insist on a comparison, yes, you "rode" me every bit as well as the Thai boy if not better.' Michael smiled broadly at that, that much he understood. 'I'd describe you as mercurial in sex.' He had been no palfrey mount, it was true. 'Supple, feline and quiescent, but then ravenous and that is a talent. No simply lying back for you, you use passivity with power, you like to be controlled but that in itself is paradoxically controlling and that's a delicious combination and usually takes practice, but you have the quality inherently.' Michael, taking all this as unqualified praise, beamed again. 'Passive but not helplessly submissive sums up your sexual behaviour, which is a sublime combination. In simple terms, everything was tickety-boo, Michael.' Michael moved over to stand in front of him and bent down to put his arms around his neck and pressed his head pressing against his. 'It's gonna get better every time,' he whispered. 'It's important yeah? I mean it's great and… it means something, don't it? Oh, I 'aven't got your fuckin' words,' he sighed in exasperation, standing upright again. 'Yes, I know it's important to you.' He put his hands tight on his arms. 'And what about the boy? Was he pleased? Did his man do well?' 'Oh, you were rockin', the business, the man!' He flopped down beside him and Roly felt his warm breath as he reached round to touch his lips with his. He said, so quietly Roly could hardly hear him, trying to find conviction, 'Don't laugh but I think I'm in love.' But Roly did hear and the words were like a stab of angina. e held back a sarcastic, 'Who with?' and instead counted the dozens of times he himself had uttered those very words after a single night of sex and the dozen hearts he broke when he regretted what he'd said and changed his mind, when he thought it was what he wanted but then discovered that it wasn't or that it was but that it wasn't meant to be. 'Them boys you 'ad before –' 'I hope you're not looking for any more comparisons,' Roly warned. 'Look at the very weird courtship we've had and come through somehow and now that we've consummated –' '– Does that mean we've shagged?' 'I don't say it wasn't heavenly, but neither can I say we've done the right thing. After all, I did do my utmost to put you off, didn't I? I ran away, remember. But you've been unstoppable, you set yourself a target and you reached it and I have to admire you for that.' *Yes, you devil, you demon, you defeated me.*

Roly didn't think he wanted to hear about implications and consequences at this juncture, he was far too carefree and irresponsibly caught up in some kind of new happiness, so he changed tack: 'What are you doing today? If you want to come for supper again tonight, you'll have to come shopping with me first, but I'm not sure you'll want to when you hear what I've got to say.' 'Supper and afters,' he said, in a suggestive tone. 'Afters indeed. Please don't make out you're insatiable, I can't handle insatiable any more. Go and get dressed and go an see your ma.' 'Oh, so you want rid of me now you've 'ad me arse.' 'And don't be crude, I still have much sanding down of those clodhopping corners of yours to do if we're to go much further.' Michael did as he was told and went to put his clothes on. 'What d'ya mean,' he asked with a puzzled frown when he came back, '"after what you've got to say"?' 'Stick around my flowerpot, my morning dewdrop, you read my journal didn't you and I've told you…

remember Harworthy and the rest? The worst is yet to come. There's enough sin in me for a hundred confessionals.' He stood up, leaving Michael mystified. 'I want to get ready and go for a drive. Alone. D'you mind?' 'Whatever. Ya want some space from me?' 'I don't want you stuck here with a cripple, bored and trapped.' He tch-tched in sardonic sympathy. 'I 'ope you're not gonna try runnin' away again.' Roly ignored this. 'We're all brought down by our own foibles you know. I hope, I really hope you won't be and you won't be brought down by me. The heartaches and the thousand natural shocks and all that.' Michael must have understood little and Roly didn't want him to hang around to find out; he gave him his assurance that he wasn't planning another escape and hugged him au revoir and the hug included an enthusiastic long kiss. When Roly looked down to see the outline of what he'd just felt poking against Michael's pants, he couldn't help himself and pointed to it: 'I'm glad to see I can arouse you as much as the girl by the wall.' That was cheap, it was the small-minded resentment he wouldn't forgive him for causing and wouldn't forget. 'Girls ain't got what you got 'ave they?' Michael said with a salacious grin. 'Laters,' he said and hugged Roly again and scampered out.

That night, after meatloaf, champ and vegetables, strawberries in raspberry purée, Fanta, Doctor Pepper and coffee and one of Michael's less dire DVDs, they were conjugal again; Roly carried him with him to the empyrean and on the journey Michael kept him safe from Muvvie, which for the time being was Paradise enough. Afterwards, they spoke in whispers: the whispers of entwined and naked lovers, when the enfolding blackness becomes a warm and enchanting world devoid of all danger and beyond mortal time. Each whisper blew sweet breath on the other's face. 'I hope you know how much I want you.' 'I'm glad you still want me after last night.' 'Of course I do.' 'I was scared you wouldn't. Scared I'd blow it.' 'Last night was wondrous and this morning was awesome and tomorrow night will be sensational and the next night and the next and for ever... you and me, yes?' *We may well have become lovers.* 'Oh yes,' he said and held on tightly. 'Please.' His voice changed from merely soft to mellifluous. 'I want you to f – I want your hard c – no, I want your... I want you inside me any time you want to put it there.' 'You liked it that much?' 'I fuckin' – I mean it was totally...' 'What? What do you love? *It* or me doing it?' 'Oh no, it's gotta be you.'

****

No, Roly didn't go to his keypad to proclaim to the Journal that he had a new lover, didn't claim a victory he didn't deserve, didn't cry: 'I'm not nor ever have been a good person, yet I've been showered with prizes.' Neither could he imagine that Michael ran home to his mother on delirious winged heels to report that he was in love, but then... *knowing him as I now do, he might do it, for the hell of it.*

Oh dear, how his cynicism had matured with age; it wasn't like the days of yore when he'd enjoyed a fantastic, truly memorable squeeze and fallen in love at the drop of a pair of briefs and told everyone about it. Not that Michael was a pick-up, there had been no urgency of the one-night stand about him. (He chose not to think about those other days of yore, at the disco, where beauty was often in the eye of the beerholder and next morning the pick-up wasn't quite the sensation he'd appeared to be the night before.). But these weren't the days of either yore, this was now and there was gloomy moony, sad Sibelius Number 5 playing on the hi-fi, a Houseman-ensanguined evening sky, lulled and dumbfound streets outside and Roly and his thoughts of a boy. He can

413

see a boy who is besotted, who has lost all reason over him, who is confounded and who confounds him. What Roly did do was take stock, make an assessment, an inventory, he had to count the profit he'd made from the conquest of the new territory, the territory of Michael, and balance it against the cost of the damage incurred in the war, for damage had been done he felt sure, to himself and not, he earnestly hoped, to Michael. His rediscovery of sex had been, in the final analysis, intrinsically dissatisfying, not through any malfunction, certainly not through any lack of ecstasy and certainly not through making the most beautiful love imaginable with the most beautiful boy imaginable, but because of the inescapable knowledge that he'd felt *Michael's* exaltation, had experienced *Michael's* orgasms, he'dd celebrated because Michael had celebrated, triumphed at his triumph. And why? Because of his now cemented, fixed and fixated conviction that he *had no right.* He was a thief again, Michael had inveigled him, in a reversal of the scenario of Fagin and the Artful Dodger, to steal. And what made this all the more abhorrent, *he had been a willing victim.* Roly's conquest, his victory, was a false sexual one, its components of ecstasy and elation were impostors and he'd experienced them vicariously, as he did Michael's swimming triumphs: he'd celebrated Michael's celebration. He was a vastly changed man to the one who'd won Jack and Larry and the virgins and the straight boys of his young days and with change, the corruption had festered and increased until it had taken over entirely. The taste of ambrosia and nectar was now tainted, innocence, long since tortured by him, was now murdered, the music was discord, all sense and senses nullified. I cannot be happy any more, he thought; not even when all the pleasures of the flesh that any man could dream of are presented to me on a golden plate and covered in rubies.

As for Michael, as he stretched out lazily and dreamily on his bed, he thought of Roly's words, he was now the man boy, he had matriculated in the college of sex and his epagoge was complete. He too was changed, but it was too early to tell whether for the better or worse but what, still neophyte that he was, did that matter? He pictured Roly's face, felt the warm security of his body, heard his voice, revelled in his words which, though he understood but little of them most of the time, always sounded because of their authority so important and full of *meaning* and portent. When Roly spoke to him it was as if he were explaining his life to him, making him see things he knew nothing of but had to experience. He could care for him and he could swim, those were his skills, but Roly would teach him the skill of life.

****

I do not mean to convey, my dears, that this preoccupation of Roly and Michael with sex was obsessional. Sex, delirously pleasant though it was for them both in its newness and intensity, was by no means a quotidien event, nor were they to be found in nightly embrace. It was true that a kind of semi-cohabitation had now been established; though not living together, they were together at all times and this of course meant that sex was always there too. It was a constant, in the sense that its presence was integral, permeating the air of the flat, hanging between them like a comforting vapour and over them like a protecting baldaquin. But Roly was old-established *lache* and wasn't an impulsive or hasty man, his cup had at various times in his 'thenadays' overflowed, never to surfeit alas but amply enough, and now it was replenished; Michael was no longer the overeager

415

imago and although he too had been sated (though not nearly yet enough) and his awareness of his transformation was contagious and the new butterfly in him wanted the pecks on cheeks, snatched kisses, touchings, huggings and all the paraphernalia of sexual gambolling at every opportunity, he was content with his lot and could bide his time and also stand and wait too.

The boy was enthralled by the novelty of togethered bliss while Roly still clung to its delusory and ephemeral promise. Michael was his – *No, better not think of him as my catamite* – he was his doxey, his dove. They slept together regularly but didn't make love each time; Roly was more than willing and happy to drift away holding Michael the Morpheus close to him, his Levitra-less semi-erection pressing into his back and his hand gripping his slumbering herm-like one, for sometimes he was too weary for sex, an unthinkable state now that he had almost 24 hour access to an adorable adolescent body, certainly unthinkable just five years ago. And this was good and fine, because Michael had surprised him somewhat by turning out not to be himself a rampant 'every night' boy. He hadn't lied when he told Roly weeks before that sex for him came second to the orgasmic effect of emotional fulfilment (he hadn't been able to express it like that). If he should want physical relief, Roly told him, he wasn't to be afraid or ashamed to obtain it for himself while he held him, or Roly might fellate him, but there were times when he simply didn't have the want or he divined that Roly couldn't provide and he accepted with equanimity. There was no anxiety over the loss of interest on either's part, no fear of a falling away of desire and whether they'd made love or not, Roly had the ineffable joy of waking up each time next to the feel and scent of youth. This is an idyll, he thought, and I should be grateful but as in all idylls, there are monsters beyond their borders.

'The feel and scent of youth,' he murmured to himself at his keypad. Yes, making love with youth was so utterly different from making it with a full adult. An adolescent is more succulent and has a far sweeter taste than a man; he has a unique odour which isn't affected or infected, flavoured or tainted by labour or alcohol or tobacco or the wear and tear of maturity; youth's skin, not yet bearing the creases of responsibility and care, has a smoothness and softness of its own; there is a pristine suppleness in the sinews and a new strength of recently moulded bones before the erosion of adulthood begins. Blindfold a person and lay a naked youth and a naked man next to him and see if he doesn't instantly distinguish the one from the other with a single touch.
****

Sometimes, Michael and he lie entwined – just like with the inquisitive boy in Leicester an age ago but, unlike him, Michael asked no intrusive questions – and there is no need for words or requests at all; a cuddle leads to a kiss and in legato movement he is taking Roly inside him again almost before they realise it. Each time he needs Roly to move him, position him, instruct him, not because he is an inept or ignorant lover but because he wants to be Roly's boy and a good boy and do as he is told.

Love by night and sometimes in the waking dawn was their routine (but by no means a chore); love in the afternoon, when Roly, feeling a sudden erotic surge, would interrupt Michael playing his rowdy Xbox games and lead him unprotesting to the bedroom, was an occasional treat, highly decadent. 'Come with me young man and prepare for your debriefing.'

Another time Roly waits while Michael takes a shower and then walks to the bedroom and stands behind the door. 'Can I come in?' 'Yes come in and enjoy the privilege of being made love to by me' and he walks in with his freshened face, the thong around his glistening body, looking like a mouthwatering white confection. The heavy load in the thongs points at Roly and he sits on the edge of the bed and takes Michael by the thighs and bends forward to kiss and lick it. 'Is this all for me?' 'You and nobody else.' 'Come and lie down.' He lies next to him and asks, 'What are you gonna do?' 'I'm going to pleasure you and you me,' he says and moves to lie on top of him, his face close. 'Do you want me to?' 'You don't 'ave to ask me ya know, jus' tell me you're gonna do it.' 'Do you want me to?' 'Do you want to?' 'Yes, but do you want it?' 'I want what you want, anythin' you want.'

Roly sometimes shows remorse for using his body as a mere facility, an object, for sex without the show of affection but Michael has none of it and tells him, 'Hang me upside down from the ceilin' if you want and do it like that.' 'But I don't want you to be a toy I switch on and play with at will.' 'Roly,' he grunts in a chiding tone, shaking his head. 'Any way with you is awesome.'

'I'm not your father. I don't want a son,' he tells him.

418

'As long as ya don't sound like 'im when you tell me what to do, that's pukka.'

One time, Michael said: 'Somebody asked me, right, when I told 'em about all the food you make me, "D'you live to eat or eat to live"?' He fell quiet, as though he were asking the question there and then and was waiting for an answer. 'So what does that mean then?' he asked at length. 'What do you mean, "What does that mean"? It means what it says, my dear neanderthal one. It means without me you eat to live but with me you live to eat.'

Sex and food, good sex, good food: an orgy for two, an orgy of both for both, two things at the orgy for two people. Another time, he tells him to stand at the foot of the bed. 'Let's go vulgar, give me a sleaze show' and he lies back and watches him beat and pant and he slavers over young virility and marvels wide-eyed at the jet force. 'Oh, I love the fountain spurt,' he cries. 'A boygasm!' – and he laughs wildly.

Another time, he says, 'Take me in your hand, look at it, study it and get to know it. Worship it, don't be afraid of it, caress it, handle it tenderly, gently, then more harshly and vigorously. Lick up and down and tease with your tongue.'

Another time, Michael takes Roly unawares when he cosies up to him and whispers, 'There was one of them safe sex sites...', and there is a gentle mischief and cunning in his voice. 'There were some pictures of different positions...' 'Yes,' Roly queries, 'what are you plotting now?' 'D'ya want to 'ave me over the table?' I've never done it,' Roly tells him. So the pupil teaches the teacher.

Another time, Michael is supple and agile, a master of manoeuvres. 'Where have you learned this?' Roly asks him. He climbs on top of Roly on the sofa, his back to him. 'Point it,' he orders and tucks his bended legs behind him, 'Yeah, got it' and in one slow smooth move slides himself down onto Roly's waiting Early English Gothic Perpendicular and calls out in his nympholepsy: 'Tastic!'

****

At the risk of being accused of using hyperbole, I'm reluctant to say Michael is eugenic, but I really can't find anything amiss, his face and body are flawless; but if his smooth silken skin, his toned muscles, his budding pecs, his prominent nipples on their large amber areolae, his soft thick pubic bush, his wholesome plums, his perfect penis and his divine firm butt are defective, then I must be suffering from Panglossian optimism.

****

On the other hand the boy certainly was no pinchbeck; he satisfied his delectation, met all his finical criteria, so wasn't the perception of him in reality as rewarding as it was in fantasy? Wasn't he an absolute to him if not to others? Perhaps others carped at the natural flaws the progression from boyhood to manhood threw up, found the development of maturity unappealing, with the transient dimensions, the unfinished and disproportionate growths, the ungainly protrusions, the at times awkward bodily coordination. But Roly perceived none of this, or if he did, paid no heed. Maybe the boy's eyebrows were too heavy and his nose too snub and the dimple on his chin and the lusciousness of his mouth too intrusive for some tastes; perhaps his ears were too small and his feet too big, perhaps all this was so, but Roly's doting blinded him. Perfection, he said, at any rate

420

wasn't a universal constant; it existed only as a subjective interpretation of itself. Roly *perceived* perfection and that was enough.

****

It came to him, the conclusion, one day and it hit him like a juggernaut. 'He is the one who has come to me,' he said. It was when he was looking up a Wikipedia reference to Hermes because he had for the moment forgotten who was the messenger of the gods – he needed help with a crossword clue – and it was in that very reference that he saw the word. Later, he couldn't remember which occurred first: finding the word or realising what Michael meant, why he had come. He went from the word on Wikipedia to the dictionary where he read, 'an angel or spirit sent to escort newly-deceased souls to the afterlife'. The word was 'psychopomp', Michael was his psychopomp, not his saviour, his angel of redemption, but his 'psychopomp'. Later still, 'It doesn't scare me that you've come, Michael,' he whispered to him, it was during one of their nights of langorous caresses. 'I don't understand. Why should you be scared?' Michael asked, deeply puzzled and when Roly couldn't give him an answer, he laid his furrowed brow back on the pillow to receive more kisses and when the kisses were finished, took a long time to fall asleep and all the while Roly thinking, 'I have lost my reason.'

****

The night came when Michael had to say, 'I hope tomorrow never comes.' Roly for the moment had completely forgotten that it was the day he was leaving for Barmouth for his two weeks Hollis annual family holiday. His mother and sister and he spent it in his grandparents' caravan every August. Michael had been obdurate when he first told Roly it was imminent: 'I'm sixteen now, I don't 'ave to go any more. It's a

421

tastic 'oliday... not. It's just so naan.' 'It's your family's big yearly thing,' Roly told him. 'You mustn't disappoint your ma and your grandparents.' 'I will one day, I won't be goin' to Barmouth when I'm 30 innit? I'm not goin'. This is my holiday with you and it's gonna last for ever.' 'You're not exclusively mine, you know. I don't own you. You must go.' 'Why can't you own me?' he asked, almost seriously. 'Why don't you adopt me and then nobody can take me nowhere without your permission? I wanna be owned by you. Anyway, why you so mad keen to get rid of me for two weeks? You got another virgin cherry waitin' to be popped off chat, eh? So you're tired of me. What's up, don't I please you no more?' 'Please me? That's hardly the word for what you do. Perfection doesn't please, it... it... perfectifies.' *Though perhaps not in my case.* 'Ya know I'm crazy about ya doncha, yanowamsayin'?' *That's right, go on, tell me you love me and pile on the guilt.* Roly gave out a loud long sigh. 'There's much to be said for infatuation, I suppose. You bring Marlowe to mind again.' 'That the geezer ya told me about, got stabbed in the eye?' He recited it once more for him,

Where they deliberate, the love is slight:
Whoever loved that loved not at first sight?

and held his face in his hands and looked deep into his eyes. 'Let's keep it slight, shall we? For now? That way I won't feel so bad when I throw it all away, as I surely will. Anyway, love shouldn't be your aim. Love lasts for two minutes, whereas infatuation can stretch to a liftetime if you spread it around enough. 'Oh, Michael, Michael.' He heaved another deep tired sigh, his heart seemed to die inside him a little and he shook his head sadly. 'I look into your eyes and I see such –' He spoke low and haltingly, searching for the words. 'I see *goodness.* You are *good* and I'm not being sentimental, cheesy to you.' And he saw too the reflection of something else. He saw all his mistakes and sorrows and he saw Michael trying to take those on himself and redeem them and wasting his life in the attempt. He gripped his shoulders tightly. 'I won't allow you to go to sod on my account, to destroy yourself. I won't take your future away.' Michael smiled wanly and seeming to ignore the warning, dug a hand into his pocket and pulled out a piece of paper. 'I found this on the net,' he said. 'I printed it out, I s'pose it's kinda... ya know... like swearin' yer love or somethin.' He handed it to Roly and Roly read:

'I will not fail you, my friend. I will continue on the path we share and I know you will be there to help me, as you always were and when we meet again at the journey's end and we laugh together once more, I will have a thousand things to tell you.'

'I was gonna leave it for you,' Michael said quietly. Give you somethin' to like remind you. Of me.' 'Everyman,' Roly said with a sorrowful smile. 'You see it before?' 'Yes... yes, it's lovely and...' Roly was somewhat rocked and rather touched, he felt those inconvenient burning drops of water on his eyes and his vision blurred. 'The idea of a memento is lovely,' he said, pulling himself together. Not, he thought, a memento mori, I hope. 'Thank you, my dear,' he said, turning away. 'I don't get you sometimes. right,' Michael said, a touch of brittleness in his voice. 'What d'ya mean by "throw it away"?' 'Oh,' said Roly, turning back as if just awakened. 'Nothing... that I was just a boy, that's all.' Michael looked hard at him with questioning disappointment. 'What do you want to do Michael? What does life hold for you? You must have things you want to do,' Roly said. 'You haven't told me anything about your dreams.' Quick as light, 'Win Olympic gold an' wave it at you in the crowd,' he said. *Love me, that's right, go on, pile on the guilt.* 'Awww Michael, you darling, soft as fluff.' He must never have his wings clipped, he had to fly. There were years of people and places ahead of him, so he must go to Wales for two weeks and he must go to the world for years and there would be many separations on his itinerary and perhaps he would never come back. On this, his first separation from something however misguidedly he held dear, he looked unutterably forlorn. Roly couldn't allow himself to be a gluepot in which he became stuck so he put the knife in, to try and immunise him: like the nurse injecting the crying infant, 'This needle will hurt you now child, but it will prevent the greater pain you could well feel in thirty years if I didn't prick you with it.' 'Michael?' he asked, holding his head tightly against him. 'Yeah?' 'Do you think you're in love with me?' 'Yeah, I am. For ever.' That *ever* again. He snatched his head away, there was a horror in his face. 'Why are you askin' that now?' 'Because you're going away, sillybilly.' Roly smiled comfortably and hypocritically. 'An' you love me yeah.' He said it as an incontrovertible truth. 'Oh yes. I love you more than you'll ever know. Ever.' *Ever.* 'I love you *cap-a-pie,* from the blackest hair at the top of the crown of your princely head right down to the tip of your little toenail.' There was no facetiousness, no insouciance, no indifference any more, but terrorised concern, a need for reassurance. He had now committed himself and was facing the cost. 'An' you'll be 'ere when I get 'ome won't ya an' I'm gonna text you every day and can you ring me mobile at least once or twice?' 'Oh, yes Roland Hunter will be here and he'll ring you.' Roly kissed him, hugged him and had to push his recalcitrant body out of the door. He waved him off as he left, he was dragging his feet like the unwilling schoolboy with the shining morning face, but this boy was going to pack his bag for a holiday he wasn't looking forward to.

Roly would forgive you in advance for what you are thinking, my dears. For thinking he had had his oats, he had had his way with the boy, he had got his rocks off, he had overcome all odds and barriers, both endogenous and exogenous and got what he wanted and you see him close his front door on a victorious chapter, fully satisfied with himself.

Roly was thinking too, in fact as soon as he closed the door he descended into the deepest agonising: what did the future hold? Michael's seaside break was providing the respite during which he would have to lift his head out of the sands of sensuality and sex in which he had been lately so deeply immersed and face reality's hobgoblins. Was Michael now hoping to – to what? – to live together, travel together, get civil partnershipped together? And did he himself envisage growing old with this boy, being tended by him and supported by him, having his bum wiped by him when he reached the ga-ga days?

The difference of age between them wasn't a matter of concern, would that it had been; as far as he could remember, this had never occurred to him, never cropped up as a consideration to be cautiously weighed or to be taken as any kind of hindrance to their prolonged union, if there were to be one. Michael had never displayed the least concern about it, never even mentioned its existence during any of their conversations; so as far as the counting of years or years' difference went, if Michael was content, he was too. The pairing of a younger and a much older – it was more common than the world, even the gay world, liked to think, not that he paid any heed in this respect to what the world thought. No, any let or hindrance there may be lay in the physical, or rather the pathological plane.

Uncertainty prevailed in another, crucial, quarter, which Roly knew only too well. Their relationship, he felt, hadn't yet reached the level where what was 'devoutly to be wished' lay and he wasn't sure that there was time or indeed the inclination on either his or Michael's part for such aspiration to evolve into the final bliss. He had to concede that, passionate and all-embracing though their interaction so far had been, it had also been friable, superficial and somehow intangible. There had been no sensation of *love speaking to love*, which he had long held to be the plimsoll line, the mean of dedication and commitment, the test of faithfulness and of partners' willingness to persevere through adversity as well as fortune. That's what he felt, at any rate, for Michael's part, he couldn't say but he suspected not. He felt reluctantly and instinctively that Michael was simply far too much of a greenhorn, far too young and naïve to be able to chart the path he had so impetuously set his feet on over a year ago and which now stretched before him into the distance towards – he supposed this was what the boy saw – the rainbow. He believed Michael's view was that of what he *thought* was love speaking to love and here he was being arrogant in thinking that Michael was as yet ill-equipped to comprehend love.

You cannot be sure that these were the things Roly was thinking, my dears; Roly couldn't be sure either that this was what Michael was thinking, wasn't sure if Michael was thinking across the same stratum as he was at all.

What Roly did conclude was that at this juncture there were no conclusions, no solutions, no ends neatly tied, the threads still hung, tattered and no matters were settled, either favourably or unfavourably to each or to both. Biggest unknown of all was Michael's life; he stood on the

426

threshold of one while he, Roly, was approaching the exit; Michael didn't yet have redemption and salvation to seek but he did. Michael was confined, safely, by his short-term requirements and his appetite was sated by the sexual gratification he had found in Roly. Michael had achieved his dearest wish, perhaps all the wishes he was aware he had, which was, bluntly and succinctly put, to find fulfilment and the happiness he had sought by being buggered and he, Roly, had buggered him. *I have done duty at last; I have prosyletized and evangelised!*

In the meantime, 'the canary was down the mine' again, as it was once before, long long ago at the beginning of their rites, and it would remain caged there until it was set free either by the completion of the Journal or by his death; clearly neither of these was accomplished yet. Could they bear the amaranthine separation of two weeks? Would their relationship, if relationship there was, survive it? Or would Michael meet a fine figure of an older man walking along the beach one day, with his trousers rolled and his hair parted behind, eating a peach and would he, like the mermaid, sing to him?

Maybe. Perhaps. And why did Roly hope this might happen? Perhaps because Michael shouldn't have been such a good teacher, both teaching him novelty and helping him to relearn what once had been new. But there was no completion. 'You may have taught me to love you, Michelangelo,' he said aloud, 'but you have not succeeded in making me love myself.' Perhaps he shouldn't have shown Roly how to be rejuvenated, perhaps he should have let a sleeping dog lie. The dog had learned new tricks but the leopard hadn't changed his spots.

****

Roly must spend the next two weeks telling Denzel, telling Muvvie, all about finding his redemption in Michael's love and beauty and about trying to feel as wholesome as his reprehensible past would permit him. But he will lie, because Michael's forebearance and his refusal to judge his sins, though laudable and comforting, don't make him a saviour. He smiles wrily at the irony: that he need never have let the boy know of his dark side in the first place yet, despite this, Michael is still wrong to believe in him. Roly's lame brain-damaged body will go on pushing itself and his ridiculous hostess trolley around the flat and walking what little distance it can outdoors with a stick. He will continue to keep the Journal and, for the moment, he is the guardian of a voluptuous 16-year-old body and soul. The well-to-do Over 50 Breakfast Club members who have money and means and private villas in Biarritz and Tuscany tell him he too is rich. He wishes he could believe them.

He has finished his book and it is a most peculiar sensation. He simply sits at the computer, looking at the first of the 96 thousand words he has somehow strung together, with emotions horribly mixed; he is tired and bored with the words, he despises them, he wishes he had never created them and he feels as empty and helpless as a newborn. He has no idea what to do about them, about his goddammed *book,* or about himself.

Floccinaucinihilipilification!

The Journal is the one thing left that was ongoing. He has taken up a mirror to his life and seen the lifelong quest, that was the simple and prosaic sum of it all. Life with Michael may be gratifying, sexually at least, but it provides no guide to the future, no clue as to whether or not he is foretasting a loving relationship and he certainly doubts that the gift of Michael's beauty and the vicarious enjoyment his achievements bring, or Michael's fixation with him, can be alchemized. Perhaps he has to go on for ever trying to alchemize his crimes into his art; that is why, whether he is any good at it or not and because it is the only hope he has left for ever again earning some income, he has to continue to write. He already has afflictions, the disease of writing would be no great extra yoke. He seeks justification, consolation, by turning to those artists and writers, great ones, whose criminality augmented rather than diminished their credentials; Genet and Caravaggio come to mind, one a thief the other a murderer, idols both in his eyes. (He never regarded iconic Oscar as a criminal.) And Wagner, whom he didn't much admire, but who was a genius in art and in life a thief, did *he* die redeemed? He thought not. Did the other two? Was he any better than they, or was he worse? Could he emulate the creators of *Our Lady of the Flowers* and *The Beheading of Saint John the Baptist* and be, if not respected exactly, at least glamourised, perhaps admired, for what he achieved artistically? He may be capable of getting away with much, but can he get away with art?

****

So, 'if only', the little voice whispers – of all the times! And he smashes the wooden spoon into the saucepan and thick globules of soup fly out and spatter the kitchen tiles and he slumps…

****

He had a vision of Michael standing on the other side of the road with his friend Danny 'Odge, watching the coffin being brought out of his flat and put into the hearse. 'Your old queer mate's a goner then, Mikey,' Danny observes. Yes.' 'With all you did for 'im, I 'ope 'e left you 'is money.' 'He didn't have any. He gave me something better,' Michael says. 'What's better'n'money?' 'He left me his book.' 'A book?' 'He

429

wanted me to get it pub... to print out for him.' 'A book?' 'Yes. Like his life story only it wasn't, it was more than that. I'll show it you one day.' 'A book? What's it called?' 'Yeah, a f – I mean a book. It's called *Banjaxed*.' 'Why you talkin' like that, Mikey?' 'Like what?' 'Stuck up.' And Michael smiles. 'It's not posh, Danny,' he says. 'I'm just talking properly that's all.'

****

If. If only. Roly, Roland, Wanger, Wanger-Hunter, Hunter thought, 'If only there had been no Michael.'

END